ON
FIXX

a novel by

Jason Squire Fluck

Fredonia, NY

Published in 2014 in the United States by
Quercus Publishing
Fredonia, NY 14063

www.quercuspublishing.com

www.jonfixxthenovel.com

Cover design by László Zakariás

Printed in the United States

First Edition

ISBN: 978-0-9864456-0-6

Specially dedicated to Miriam, Zion,
and the Little-One-On-The-Way.
You make it all worth it.

Contents

1
October–Early November
Los Angeles

Don't judge me.

I needed to hear her voice like I needed water.

I avoided calling those first days after the breakup, but eventually the pull was too great. I needed contact. My mobile was private. She couldn't be sure it was me. I felt a cheap thrill when she answered the phone, her irritation a balm to my wounded soul.

"Hello."

Silence.

"Hello!"

This was my fourth night in a row.

"Look, Jon, I've had it." Damn! How could she be so sure it was me? I never spoke. "I'm sick of these calls! You're obviously not dealing well with our decision."

Our decision?

"It's 3 a.m.! You're behaving like a juvenile." Pause, silence, maybe a regretful moment, I hoped. "Look, I'm sorry it didn't work out between us, but that's reality. You need to move on. I have. Goodbye, Jon."

Click.

I stared at my PDA, a picture of the woman who'd just hung up staring back, her ice-blue eyes mocking me. There was no way I was going to let her off that easy. She'd turned my life upside down, turned me into a sleepless wreck. Since the breakup, I'd been unable to do any work, so forgive me if I felt entitled to a few late night phone calls. If I can't sleep, why should she?

After that night, Sara found a way to block calls from my mobile, so I was robbed of the convenience of calling her at will from my newly acquired, post-break-up shoebox of an apartment. Not one to easily accept defeat, feeling there was a deeper psychological goal to be won here, I started making phone calls from the pay phone at a local minimart a block from my apartment building. No slouch herself, Sara quickly caught on, placing a block on that pay phone as well. So began my nocturnal jaunts in ever widening geographical circles from my apartment, looking for new pay phones from which to harass my still loved ex-lover. Within a few weeks, I was beginning to tire of the game, feeling the emptiness and futility of what I was doing, no longer sure of the why or wherefore. At first, I just craved the cadence of her voice in my ear, but later on I enjoyed her fully expressed anger. To my chagrin, though, my nightly excursions came to an abrupt halt in a manner that I never could have anticipated.

My last call was made one night at the beginning of November. I open here because I consider it to be the true beginning of the story I'm about to tell, even though much of the action started well before. On this fateful night, I hit my emotional rock bottom, the despair sucking the last bits of hope from my soul, leaving me with the shell of a body but no feelings to fill it. I felt my life was over, that I would never recover from this breakup, that I had become a walking, loveless zombie of a man. Little did I know, or recognize, once I hit bottom, I couldn't fall any lower. I'd reached my emotional ground zero, which meant there was only one way for me to go. I didn't have the slightest idea of what a wild ride was in store for me because I was too wrapped up in my own misery.

As the light slowly faded from the day, an overwhelming feeling of claustrophobia gripped me, manifesting itself in shortened breath and a rising panic. This was new. I tried to ignore it. The panic warped my sense of time, making five minutes feel like fifty. I sat frozen in my only chair, counting the seconds, wanting them to move faster. Unable to shake the feeling, I took action. I jumped up, grabbed my car keys, and left my tiny apartment. By the time I climbed into my car, I felt a little better, the feeling of claustrophobia receding. Not sure where I was going, I stuck the key in the ignition of my '82 Buick, backed out of my space, and jumped onto Moorpark. As soon as I put some distance between my apartment and me, the feelings of claustrophobia disappeared altogether. I found myself on the 101, heading south. Though just past midnight, the freeway was filled with cars, bright headlights bouncing off the side mirrors, overloading my senses. I floored the gas pedal to keep up with the nighttime flow, joining the defining bloodline all members of the Los Angeles community shared—the freeway. My Regal reacted instantly, jumping forward. I cleared Hollywood in minutes, drove past the set of L.A. high-rises that passed for downtown, then merged onto the 10, heading east toward Las Vegas. A large sign off to my right told me I had two hundred and seventy miles to go. Five hours, probably less at this time of night. I figured, why not?

As the miles slid by, the sprawl of Los Angeles began to thin out. Night settled in around me, a sense of peace. I was escaping, driving away from my life, hoping the farther I traveled from Los Angeles—from Sara—the better I would feel, hoping for just a little while I could forget about her. After two hours on the freeway, I spotted a sign for a Howard Johnson's Rest Stop and ubiquitous Starbucks. A sense of vague familiarity washed over me. Automatically, without thinking, my hands steered the Regal toward the exit ramp, through the extended parking lot, past the gas pumps, up to the front entrance. I put the car in park, listening to the quiet hum of the Regal's well-tuned engine. Through the glass doors of the entrance, I could partially see the interior, the Starbucks sign just inside pointing directly back, the restaurant off to the right. An arrow for the restrooms hung below the Starbucks sign. Suddenly, I realized I'd been here before. With her. On our first trip to Vegas together. I closed my eyes, trying to push her image out of my mind, but with little success. The realization there was no escape from my mind—Sara was implanted there like a microchip, her face, her memories—made me feel helpless. Even now, without knowing it, without realizing what I was doing, I'd followed her here. I dropped my head in defeat, and then opened my eyes, my vision centering on the restroom sign. Knowing the pull was too great, I gave in to the urge. I turned the car off, climbed out, pocketed my keys, and walked through the doors of the Howard Johnson's back into my past.

I found myself standing in the lobby, the restaurant to my right, staring down the hallway at the door leading into the women's restroom. I looked around to see if anyone was watching, noticing as I did so a large family sitting in the back corner devouring what I could only assume to be their late night dinner. Even in my heightened state of agitation, I couldn't help but stare. The father must have weighed at least four hundred pounds, his jowls jiggling as he stuffed a fork filled with pancakes, dripping syrup and butter, into his mouth. No slouch herself, the wife out-weighed her husband by fifty-plus, though she wasn't eating anything. I wondered how she could be that big and not be eating constantly. Their son weighed somewhere in the mid-two's, though I was sure he couldn't be more than twelve years old. Plates of pancakes and French toast before him on the table, he was holding a fork in each hand, his right descending for another helping of French toast while his left was on the way up with a large serving of pancakes. He ate with a fever as if this might be his last time. While the father and son stuffed their faces, the mother stared off into space. Suddenly, the son looked up from his plate, locking eyes with me, his look voracious and feral, as if when he finished his pancakes and French toast, I'd be next. I shuddered, then blinked. When I looked again, the boy's eyes were glazed over and dull, his gaze quickly returning to his plate.

Shaking my head to clear it, I turned away from the family and focused on the task at hand. I stepped toward the restrooms, glancing around to make sure no one was watching. With a quick look over my shoulder, I stepped through the door. Once inside, I listened for the rustling of feet and clothing, but heard only the hum of the exhaust fan in the ceiling. The restroom was extra clean and looked odd to me, like something was missing, when suddenly I remembered urinals were not necessary in the women's restroom. I passed the first three stalls, pushing the door open to the fourth, the big one set up at the end of the row for handicapped people. It had more room than the others, Sara's choice. I stepped inside, bolting the door behind me. The toilet paper roll was almost empty. I was glad I didn't have to go to the bathroom. I sat in the only place I could, lifted my feet off the ground so no one could see my masculine boots, and then willed my memory to bring my past into the present, even if only for a few moments.

Back on that first trip to Las Vegas, we'd been together a few months, a time in our relationship where faults were overlooked, fights dissipated like the wind, and our kisses carried a passion charged with a storm-like intensity. Sara had checked the restroom to make sure it was empty, then pulled me inside and dragged me to the back stall. At first, I was self-conscious of where I was, but Sara seemed completely unconcerned. We fumbled our pants down low enough for easy access. Out of necessity, taking into consideration the logistics of the small space, Sara turned around, offering herself up to me. As the memory gained traction, it took over my entire body. I could almost feel her touch on my skin. I squeezed my eyes shut, wanting to hang on to the memory as long as I could. She'd been so excited that night. I could feel her hands reaching behind, grabbing hold of my waist, her body pressed against mine, her—

"—Excuse me. What are you doing?"

My eyelids shot open. A muscular, black security guard was standing on the tips of his toes staring over the stall door at me. A large red keloid scar, running the breadth of his forehead, made him look even more imposing and threatening than he already was. I glanced down at myself, sitting on the toilet, my knees pulled up to my chest, tears streaming down my cheeks. I appeared utterly ridiculous, I realized a little too late.

"Could you open this door? Please."

I stepped off the toilet seat lid and planted my feet on the ground, opening the door but unable to move past the large, muscular obstruction before me.

"Now, could you get the hell out of here." He took a step back giving me just enough room to pass.

Without a word, I quickly sidestepped the guard and double timed my way out of the restroom, the giant on my heels. With my head down, I ran directly into the oversized mother who'd been staring into space, standing directly before me, a look of disgust on her face. I bounced back a foot, apologizing as I did so.

"Pervert!"

My head dropped another two inches in shame and, without looking back, I ran straight out the front exit. Moving toward my car, I noticed a line of pay phones off to one side of the parking lot. I barely missed a step, as I turned in mid-stride away from my car toward the phones. I was crying again. By the time I picked up the receiver, I was a teary, blubbering idiot. I heard a voice in the distance getting closer and louder.

Don't do it! Do you hear me?

Quickly I turned, first one way, then the other. I couldn't

see anyone. The parking lot was empty. Then I realized it was the Voice in my head who visited me from time to time, the Voice of Reason that stopped me—or at least tried to—from doing the most idiotic things in life. This was the Voice that warned me away from dangerous situations, when to keep my mouth shut in social situations, what women to stay away from—enough said. My Voice was often wrong, so I paid no mind. I grabbed the phone.

You moron, do not make that phone call!

Shut up, damn it!

Idiot, that's what you are. She's finished with you and nothing you do is going to change that fact. At least save us some respect. You know she's getting it on long and hard with the French guy you saw—

I slammed my head against the side of the phone booth as hard as I could. I had been avoiding this for weeks, but knew sooner or later I would have to deal with these thoughts. At the moment though, it was more than I could bear. I figured a good whack to the head would silence my Voice. I felt a lump forming on my forehead, blood rushing to the bruised area.

What, you think a little pain is going to shut me up? You're wrong, Jon. I'm just here to help you get through this, but at the moment, you seem to want to do everything except forget about her. She's over, gone, caput. Do I need to spell—

I slammed my forehead against the side of the phone booth again. It didn't hurt as much this time, so I did it again, but I got carried away and before I knew it was banging my head over and over against the metal siding, the pent-up anger and frustration and hurt flowing out of my body. I stopped when I felt blood dripping down my forehead. I stood still a moment. Silence. Nothing. My Voice was gone. I glanced around the parking lot. The large family was staring at me.

"What? Haven't you ever seen a person mutilate himself in the name of love before?" I yelled at them. I turned my back on them and grabbed the phone receiver.

This is what you call love? True love flows in both directions, Jon. Sara doesn't love you any longer. She loves the new guy. You see what I'm saying? Don't you have any pride? Doesn't that make you want to—

I slammed my head so hard against the phone booth that—

I was gone a couple of minutes at most, I think. Next thing I knew, the black security guard was standing over me with the marathon eaters flanking him on either side, all of them staring at me with a look of frightened fascination.

"You okay, my man?" the guard said, his voice not unfriendly.

"I think so," I muttered as he helped me up. Vertical, my head did a one-eighty. I lost balance, but the guard held my shoulders and kept me upright. I felt like a doll with his gigantic bear-sized paws holding me. My head was ringing.

"You got a good lump."

My fingers skimmed the top of my forehead, a large lump formed above my right eye.

The son pointed at me. "Mommy, what's wrong with him?"

The mother leaned over to her son. "He's a pervert."

The guard turned around. "All right, folks, let's get along. There's nothing more to see." With some indignant glares and a few grunts, the family backed off and headed for their car. The guard turned to me. "She must have done a number on you."

I nodded, so happy to have a sympathetic ear. "Yeah, she did."

"My name's Donovan."

"Jon. Jon Fixx."

"Nice to meet you, Jon Fixx." He guided me over to a bench and helped me sit.

"Thanks."

"No problem." Donovan looked over my face. "Listen,

man, any woman makes you do this to yourself ain't worth it. If she was worth it, you'd still be with her. Know what I'm saying?"

"Sorry for causing a ruckus." I took a deep breath, looking off into the distance.

"What are you talking about? Working night shift out here can get real slow. Watching you bang your head against the phone booth was better than going to the movies." He laughed with a deep, hearty guffaw, but I didn't feel like he was laughing at me, rather that he was laughing with me, sharing in my pain. Across the parking lot, I watched the marathon eaters climb into a Volkswagen Beetle. I could have sworn I heard the car groan as the father settled into the driver's seat. Donovan followed my gaze.

"Be glad you're not them. They stop here once a month on the way to Vegas. They never talk when they come in, just order the same food, eat, and leave." He paused, still staring at them. I thought he was going to say more about them, but he turned back to me. "Here." He placed some quarters in my hand. "I know that look. You got the fix. Once you get the urge, you gotta take the hit, whether it's good for you or not." I stared at him. "Make the call." He laid a crooked smile on me.

I noticed his left front tooth was chipped. The scar on his forehead seemed to be glowing. I bet this guy could mix it up. Maybe I could hire him to take out the new guy.

"I have to get back inside, make sure everything's going fine in there." He turned for the restaurant doors. Over his shoulder, he looked back at me. "Next time you're heading to Vegas, make sure to stop in. I work the nights." He waved to me before he stepped inside the restaurant. "Good luck to you, Jon Fixx."

I waved back and watched him disappear inside the double doors. I felt like I'd made a friend. I stared after him a moment longer, then turned to the phone. I picked up the receiver and dropped all four quarters into the coin slot.

I dialed a number I'd dialed a hundred times before. The phone rang, and rang, and rang—

"Allo." A very tired, just awakened male voice answered with a French accent. His name was Michel. I knew that much. Stupid name! I held the receiver in my hand, frozen. This was new. Sometimes my Voice could be so irritating in its accuracy. I said nothing. Again, "Allo." He drew out the "o" in a patronizing manner.

A rumbling started in my chest, slowly rising up through my lungs into my throat, gaining force as it moved through my vocal chords, forcing my mouth open into a scream of terrifying proportions, loud and incoherent, primal. I directed the noise into the receiver with all the energy I could muster, and after several seconds of this, the scream dissipated into a garble, then to silence. I was completely spent, drained. I placed the receiver back to my ear.

"*Connard.*" Click. Asshole. I looked it up when I got home.

And that was that.

Broken. I felt broken. I was broken. I slowly hung the phone back on its hook. I leaned against the booth, trying to gain some semblance of order in my head but realized there was no order to gain. My head was empty, as was my soul. A French guy was sleeping at my lover's—ex-lover's—house. And if he was sleeping at her house, then of course they must be—

See, what did I tell you? You should have listened—

Just shut up.

Okay.

I was tired, defeated.

I turned my back on the booth, lowering myself down to a crouch, my head falling into my hands. I felt numb. I knew it was over. I leaned against the booth for an indeterminate amount of time. When I finally gathered the energy to stand, I had trouble getting vertical. Both my legs had fallen asleep. Head hanging low, I stumbled over to my car in an aimless stupor. I drove the two interminable hours home, pulling up to the ugly, pink building that housed my one-room cave, feeling far worse than I felt when I'd left, which I didn't think possible. Even through my depression haze, though, I noticed a not-so-nondescript black Lincoln Town Car parked in front of the building. The windows were tinted, so I couldn't see inside. Pulling into the underground parking lot, I glanced in my rearview mirror for another look at the Lincoln. It creeped me out, as if the car were watching me. I passed through the security gate to the external set of stairs and climbed up to my first-floor apartment. In the hallway, twenty feet away, a man wearing a black suit exuding forceful nonchalance was leaning against my doorframe.

He was taller than me, with large shoulders and lean, angular features. I knew immediately I had never met him before, but he had official written all over his face. It was 6:00 a.m. This guy was not good news. But I was not in a frame of mind to do anything other than walk right into the gaping jaws of fate. I closed the distance between us in seconds.

"You're Jon Fixx."

"Since I was born," I answered. But he wasn't asking. I waited.

He pulled out his wallet. I could see a shoulder holster holding a .357 tucked under his jacket. At this point, I didn't care if he arrested me or shot me. Over the last few months, as my life fell apart, I'd done a good job at pissing off some very powerful interests so I figured this guy was sent by one of them to clear the air.

"I'm Ted Williams. FBI." He flashed his badge at me proving he was, in fact, an FBI agent. My instincts were right. Official. But why the FBI was paying me a visit, I had no clue. Keeping my cool, I squinted at the badge, indicating confusion with my look.

"Isn't he dead?"

Williams stared at me, a grim look on his face. He didn't find me amusing.

On a roll, I said, "Where's your bat and glove?"

"Do you know why I'm here?"

"You didn't see any good trannies on Santa Monica Boulevard? Thought you might have better options in the Valley?" I figured whatever this guy was planning on doing to me, it was preordained, so what I said, or didn't say, would not affect the outcome in any way. He was going to do what he was going to do, regardless. I was feeling reckless. Something inside my soul had unlatched earlier in the night when I heard the new guy's voice on Sara's phone.

My response to Ted Williams' question earned me a punch in the solar plexus. I doubled over for a second, realizing maybe I did care about what happened to me. The punch hurt. I was in more trouble than I thought. I took a deep breath, steeled my solar plexus, and leaned upright. "Wrong answer?"

"Open your door."

I complied. He followed me into the apartment, turning on the overhead light by the front door. He took a quick once-over of the place, taking in the messy apartment, the empty pizza boxes and clothes strewn all about. His eyes settled on the dartboard hanging on the wall near the front door. I'd put a picture of Sara up on the board. At the moment, every dart was sticking somewhere in her face.

"Michel said you were strange."

Michel! That got my attention. Standing in the middle of my room, I stared at him.

"That's right, Jon. I'm here because of the phone calls. And the late night stakeout-stalker sessions."

Oh yeah, the stakeouts. Forgot to mention those. I'd been parking outside Sara's house at night so I could see for myself what was really going on with her. The first few nights I was there nothing happened. Then one night, a man I had to assume was Michel pulled up in a Jaguar with Sara in the passenger seat. Over the next few weeks, I saw Michel go to the building on Tuesday, Wednesday, and Saturday nights. He usually showed up around 7:30 p.m. and left about midnight. I had to grudgingly admit he was a good-looking guy. Blond hair, probably blue eyes, though I never got close enough to find out. He was fit, I could tell. I knew enough to know that the general public would not consider my behavior healthy, so I never did more than observe, though the thought of confronting Sara and Michel crossed my mind many times.

"How do you know Michelle?" I asked, doing my best to stand tall, appear confident.

"It's Michel." He pronounced it mee-shel, accent on the second syllable.

"I prefer my way."

Williams ignored my comment. "Michel is my cousin."

"But he's French."

"They have cousins in France." He stared at me, his eyes narrowing slightly. "Jon, it stops today. Leave Sara and Michel alone. No more phone calls. No more drive-bys. No more parking outside her building. You understand?"

I felt completely betrayed. Sara and I had shared our most intimate secrets, dreams, desires, everything together. Only weeks before we were lovers. Now, I was her stalker.

"If I don't?"

"I was hoping you would say that." Williams smiled wide, sadistically. He slowly took his suit jacket off, his arms reaching out behind his back, the jacket easily sliding off his shoulders.

"Do you practice that move in front of a mirror?"

His smile disappeared. I noticed his button-down shirt was a size too small, intentionally, I figured, to show off his bulging biceps. He circled around behind me. "On your knees, Jon."

"Thanks, but no, that's not my thing. Not that there's anything wrong with it, if that's what you're into."

I felt a solid impact against my shoulder blades, my knees buckling involuntarily, dropping me to the ground.

Williams stepped behind and leaned over to be extra menacing. He threatened me with all types of terrible images about arrest and jail, anal sex, and an inmate named Bubba. This guy had a way with words. After a few minutes of this, I relaxed a bit. He was not here on official business. He was doing a favor for his cousin. Therefore, I was probably not in much danger. Then I turned this thought on its head, thinking that maybe I was in more danger specifically because this guy was not on official business. He didn't have to check in with anyone, so he could do whatever his personal moral code would allow him to because there was no official oversight. But the FBI was the least dangerous of the many different government protection agencies as far as I knew. The CIA and the NSA—those guys meant business. The FBI consisted of Boy Scouts compared to the other organizations.

"Stand up," Williams demanded.

I complied, my initial fear now replaced by a slow burning anger. Hearing Michel's voice on the phone had sent me over the edge. My relationship with Sara was over. I understood that much. Williams circled around to my front. He took a step toward my dartboard, pulling a dart out of the wall.

"You're not going to torture me with that, are you?"

"Shut up." He turned around, regarding me. "Michel told me you'd be a piece of cake, wave the badge and the gun around a bit and that would be that. But you're not scared, are you, Jon?"

I shrugged. Williams crossed behind me. The dart whizzed past my ear and struck the bullseye on the dartboard. Williams leaned into my ear.

"You should be. Let me show you why."

He proceeded to illustrate several different ways in which he could immobilize and then kill me by breaking or slicing my neck, piercing my heart, crushing my brain or, my favorite, shoving a key into my temple. As he moved me through these variations of near death, he usually stopped the moment before the final blow would have finished me off. I remained limp throughout the exercise of intimidation, figuring my relaxed compliance and lack of fear would be the best way to upset him. Standing before me, car keys in his right hand, he had a hint of satisfaction on his face. This was his Achilles' heel, as far as I could tell. His arrogance and cocksureness would get him into a situation one day that would be more than his capabilities could afford. Williams looked at me. I stared back at him. He wanted a response.

"Are you going to show me dance moves next?" I asked.

Williams scowled. He pulled his gun out.

"Do I need to show you how this works?"

I shook my head. I felt empty inside. I'd had enough. I wanted Williams to leave so I gave him what he wanted. "I'll leave Sara alone."

And I meant it. Even if Williams hadn't shown up with his unorthodox and illegal display of government power gone astray, I knew I would not be contacting Sara any more. Beyond that, I had no idea what my future looked like. My mind felt fuzzy and unclear, not like I'd come to a crossroads but rather that I'd hit a brick wall head first, and no matter how far I looked to the left or to the right, the wall stretched as far as the eye could see. I would have to sit in this spot until I found the tools to take the wall apart a brick at a time. Williams peered at my face to see if he could find any hints of irony or deception, but I gave him back only the truth. He put his gun away, grabbed his jacket, and threw it back on in one move, then stepped to the door. He turned around.

"A piece of advice, Jon Fixx. Be careful who you associate with. You could find yourself in a world of trouble if you spend time hanging out with the wrong people."

And then he was gone. What the hell did that mean? Standing in the middle of my apartment room, I stared at the closed door, the image of Ted Williams in the doorway still visible in my mind.

Now what? No more Sara. It was over.

In retrospect, our breakup could not have come at a more inopportune time in my life. Over the last several months, my professional status had drawn me into the service of some unusually powerful clients, clients whom it was extremely unwise to disappoint. But my mental and emotional faculties had been so compromised during this same period that my decision-making skills had diminished below any healthy, rational level. The attorney general of California was threatening to sue me, or worse. I was mixed up with a Mafioso boss and his family, which I didn't yet fully understand the ramifications of. Now, to make matters worse, I'd bothered my ex-girlfriend so much that I had just received an unexpected visit from an employee of the Federal Bureau of Investigation waving around a .357 magnum Colt and doing his best Dirty Harry imitation. My biggest problem, however, was that without Sara, I felt like a complete and total loser, and if I wanted to avoid making my situation even worse than it already was, I had to figure out how to stop feeling that way.

Maybe understanding how it had come to pass would be the first step. With the feel of Williams' hand still fresh on my shoulder, I sat down on the floor of my dingy apartment, staring back in time, searching for some clarity. The Sara cold front had been moving in on me since early summer, having a solid, negative impact on my work. Throughout the summer and into the fall, I tried to convince myself, not very successfully, that I'd run into a good case of writer's block. Then one fateful day while I was in the middle of working on a project that was beginning to feel like it could have life or death consequences, Sara came home from work and turned my life inside out. She threw her keys in the basket on the bookshelf, closed the door with purpose and, standing legs akimbo in the entryway as if she were facing off in a Wild West gun battle, locked her eyes on my face. Backlit by the light peeking through the open space between the door and the frame, she looked beautiful, blond hair cascading down over her shoulders, her trim waist highlighted by the tight blouse she'd worn to work that day. It was almost dark in the room, the light from the hallway blinding me a bit so I couldn't see her eyes. She stood there for several moments, silent. I glanced back at the computer screen where I'd been diligently working, though the screen was blank. Everything I typed was immediately erased. This inability to write anything worth saving was creating an ever-present panic deep in my gut. Sara's voice interrupted my mental dithering.

"Jon, I'm not in love with you. You need to move out."

She may as well have said, "Sure was nice weather today." No emotion. Flat. I responded in kind, because when you're in shock, that's what happens. You go into autopilot.

"Why?" Meaning, "Why should I move out?" I tried to ignore the first part.

"I've fallen in love with someone else."

Three things wrong with this answer. First, I didn't ask her if she had fallen in love with someone else, I asked, "Why should I move out?" Second, I didn't ask her if she'd fallen in love with someone else! Third, during my most recent visit to New York, I had decided to pop the Big Question, and this significant a change in our relationship status would severely hamper my sought-after outcome.

After that, things unfolded very quickly because that's how Sara liked it. Make a decision, then act without hesitation. She had those words taped above her computer at work. She wanted it over. She'd moved on. She was finished with our relationship. That first night, I went overboard. I cried. I begged. I pleaded. I followed her around the condo all night, peppering her with questions about who the new guy was. She was ice. Not a word out of her. After a time, the tears stopped, the threats started. I intimated that when

I discovered this guy's name, I would hunt him down and break his legs. I would make him pay for destroying our beautiful relationship.

She was brushing her teeth for bed when I reached the threatening stage of my process. Her movements purposeful, she picked up a water glass resting on the bathroom counter and quickly and efficiently rinsed out her mouth. Setting the glass down with finality, she said, "Jon, you will do nothing of the sort. You and I are over. If it had not been Michel—" Michel, French! "—he would have been someone else. Our relationship ended a long time ago. I'm doing this because I know you. If I don't make it final, you will drag it out. I think you are a wonderful person. Someday, you may even realize that. I need someone else. Not you."

I spent the night on the sofa chair by the front window staring out at the L.A. skyline. She slept in our bed—her bed. In the morning, we didn't speak. She left for work. I packed up and moved out. Luci, my best friend in the world, helped me move. I found the small aforementioned studio apartment later that day. It was dark and dingy, just like a cave, and I took it against Luci's advice. He wanted me to stay with him and Izzy, his girlfriend, but I didn't want to subject them to my misery, so I politely declined his offer. I bought a TV, futon, and plastic silverware, settling in for the miserable weeks and months to come. Within days, the glow from my computer screen was the only light in my life. The sparse, unkempt, cramped apartment became a metaphor for what I was feeling inside. My better half was gone. Pizza boxes stacked up. Luci stopped in every so often to check on me, to give me a pep talk, but having known me for many years, he didn't expect much.

Several weeks into my self-imposed exile, I heard Luci's knock on the door.

"It's unlocked."

Luci stepped inside. At six feet, lean and fit, straight brown hair to his shoulders, he looked imposing in the doorframe. He was wearing a white gi and sandals. There was a little comfort in the sight of something familiar, unchanged. He was carrying a picnic basket. He gave me a once-over. My arm was cocked, ready to throw a dart at Sara's picture. I'd already gotten direct hits in each of her eyes and nose. I was now aiming for her ears. He looked from me to the cardboard frame, taking it all in.

"Well, this is something new."

I lowered my arm. Luci closed the door behind him, realizing that the only light in the room came from the small light fixture I'd attached above the kitchen aimed at the dartboard. He shook his head slowly from side to side, toeing the stack of pizza boxes near the door. "This is a little out there, even for you, Jon."

"People hang pictures of their loved ones on the wall all the time."

"Then spotlight the picture and throw darts at it?"

I shrugged.

"I guess you're nowhere near letting this go?" Luci asked, knowing the answer.

I looked at Sara's picture and shook my head.

"Listen, Jon, I know you love Sara, but sometimes things don't work out because other better things are on the horizon. You understand?"

I stared at him, completely unwilling to consider any future that was not a mirror image of my past, even though I knew there was truth in his words.

"OK, fine. But so I don't have to worry about you, would you answer your damn cell phone when I call? Izzy's worried about you, too. She asks about you at least three times a day."

"Sorry about that. I've been avoiding the phone. I'd rather not take a chance on answering."

"San Francisco? The Nickels?"

I nodded glumly.

Luci took in the information silently. After a moment, he

asked, "How's the writing coming along?"

I pointed to the computer screen sitting on the plastic outdoor chair I'd been using as my writing table while seated cross-legged yoga style on the floor. The screen was empty.

"That doesn't look promising."

I smiled for the first time in a long time. "I agree."

Eyeing the pizza boxes, Luci said, "Pizza is dead food. You need to eat something healthy. The pizza will only keep you depressed." He motioned to the picnic basket on the floor. "Izzy figured you could use some home-cooked food. There's pesto pasta in here, a spinach salad with tofu, and a chocolate on chocolate cake. You need it more than I thought."

With sincerity, I said, "Tell Izzy thanks."

"You need anything?"

I stared at the floor. "No, I'll be okay. Thanks for coming over."

"Call if you do."

"I will."

Luci stepped into the hallway, closing the door, the light in the room leaving with him. I glanced back at my computer screen, realizing I hadn't done any decent work since before August. By that time, I had finished all my interviews and research for "The Coffee Shop Lovers," the novella for Scott Michaels and Anna Jensen, my November wedding couple. In August, I had been working on the first draft of their story while attempting to complete a final draft of "The Internet Love Affair" for Candy Nickels and Edward Bronfman, due mid-August for an end-of-August wedding.

In the eight years I'd been doing this, I'd never missed a wedding deadline, but by the beginning of August I was in danger of doing just that. I'd written several drafts for Candy and Edward, but they seemed flat and uninteresting, not remotely representative of my normal product. I had ambitiously intended to finish all my projects by the end of August so I could spend the final four months of the year working on my forever-unfinished first novel, a labor of love I'd started just before entering college and was still trying to complete. The biggest obstacle for reaching this goal was the overwhelmingly negative impact my degraded relationship with Sara had on my writing. By August, everything I wrote had a dark slant to it, not a characteristic conducive to love stories. How was I supposed to write love stories for other people while my own romantic world was falling apart? The due date for "The Internet Love Affair" came and went and I was nowhere near having a finished product for them. If I had given them what I had at the time, they would have asked for their money back. But the problem was not just my personal crisis of love interfering with my ability to write. The couple themselves also posed a problem for me. If I had liked Candy, or Edward, the whole situation might have turned out differently. Maybe I would have been inspired in some way to get the story done. But as fate would have it, I didn't like either one of them. They were self-involved, spoiled, shallow, and boring. Third-generation wealthy, their trust funds provided what the grandparents, and then parents, had worked hard for. They enjoyed all the money without the benefit of having to put in any of the hard labor. Candy said the words "me" and "I" more than any client I'd ever interviewed. Edward was just an arrogant prick. With my relationship drama in full swing, I didn't have a chance in hell of finishing their story.

Several days before the wedding, Candy's father, the current attorney general of California, called with veiled legal threats about missing deadlines and financial repercussions and the like. I hate bullies, and I hate being bullied even more. I decided I liked the father even less than the daughter. Looking back, I should have returned their money immediately after hanging up the phone and begged personal mental illness. I should have asked for more time, though Candy's father had made it clear that was not an option. So I just sent them what I had, which was definitely a mistake. The phone calls started coming the day before the wedding, and they have not let up since. Now, anytime my PDA buzzed, if I didn't recognize the number, I didn't answer it. The messages they left were disturbing enough. I didn't need to hear them live. Nickels Sr., Edward, Candy, and even her younger brother Nick Jr. were all calling. In a strange twist, Nick Jr.'s messages were more vicious than the others. I hoped eventually they would tire of harassing me, but they were relentless. After two months, moving into November, the calls were still coming.

When I first stumbled onto the idea of writing short Hollywood-framed love stories for couples about to become newlyweds, I never imagined one day I'd be ceaselessly harassed and threatened by my clients. Over the years, one of the side benefits of the job had been honing my skills of perception while interviewing the couple and their family and friends. I often discovered closely guarded secrets kept by one, or both, of the newlyweds-to-be that, if revealed, would shatter the delicate bonds of trust needed to keep the couple's happiness intact. Generally, my clients wanted me to write what they wanted to believe to be their history together, not actually what was their history together. Over time, one of the harder parts of my job was realizing early on what each half of the couple actually wanted to be written, and not written. Regardless of my clients' wishes, however, I considered it my job to know fact from fiction. Finding out about the petty fights, the side flings no one knew about, the breakups that happened before they finally settled in, the ubiquitous ex was the ground neither member of the couple wanted to cover or discuss, but which family and friends were more than happy to gossip about *ad nauseam.* Usually, the happy, positive, loving information came from the couple, while the juicy, racy information was provided from those close to the couple. Once I had the truth,

I would then write the story I knew the couple wanted their friends and family to read, and often it was not the complete truth.

But writing anything other than the complete truth for Candy and Edward became next to impossible. I grew to hate the assignment far more than any project I'd ever taken on, wanting nothing more than to be done with them. As August wound down, I was on a crash course for failure, but I was so wrapped up in my own romantic demise I was unable to see the bigger picture.

I looked down at my computer, opening up the Nickels folder, clicking on the final draft I had sent to them. I began to read, stopping myself only moments into it, realizing I had been incredibly foolish—and mean—for turning over to them a story that had no filter. I'd given them a truthful, unedited version of who they were or, at least, how others saw them to be, and it was not a pretty picture. During my interviews with friends of the couple, I heard more negative gossip than I'd heard on any previous job. Many of Candy's friends seemed like sycophants who cared more about Candy's wealth than her friendship. Edward's buddies had derogatory nicknames for his bride I'd never heard friends of the groom use before. Now, over two months later, my decision to hand over their story was still haunting me. I remembered the first conversation I had with Nickels Sr. after I'd sent off my final draft FedEx to Candy. Not even a day had passed from the moment I sent the final draft when I realized what I had done, so I decided to send the fifty percent deposit back as well. I knew I didn't deserve to get paid for what I'd written. Nickels Sr. was the first to call. I unsuspectingly answered my PDA. He started talking before I'd even said hello.

"I don't care that you sent the money back, Fixx. Candy has been crying nonstop ever since she got that piece of shit you call a love story. Candy means the world to me. If she's unhappy, I'm unhappy. I'll do whatever it takes to make sure everybody knows you're a complete fraud! Then I'm going to destroy your life."

In a foolish, futile attempt at gaining some lenience, I tried to explain to him that I was having trouble with my own love life, but he cut me off.

"They've called off the wedding, did you know that, you little maggot?"

I reacted to that information with silence.

"I hold you one hundred percent responsible for this, you piece of shit. I knew I never should have hired you. My damn wife thought your romance novella would be such a great gift. Edward's the one who cancelled the wedding, so I'm going to take care of him first, then I'm coming after you. I'm going to make sure you never write another story for anyone ever again."

Feeling weak in the knees, I tried to protest. "But Mr. Nickels, you can't pin that all on me. Maybe in the long run, this is all for the best. If Candy and Edward are having second thoughts—"

"Watch your back, Jon Fixx. I'm coming." Then he hung up.

Looking back on that conversation, I remember thinking it couldn't get any worse. Between my problems with Sara and my problems with the attorney general of California, how could my life become any more complicated or depressing? Then it did. Soon after Nickels made it clear to me he was going to ruin my professional and personal life, that's when Tony Vespucci came calling.

2
Early September
Los Angeles

With Vespucci, as with the Nickels family, it was my writing that got me into trouble. Not because it was so bad but because I'd written something good. Very good. My best in fact. Given my current state of mind at the beginning of September, though, I was in no position to take on a new client. But I met with Tony Vespucci for two reasons: 1) He said Cranston Jefferson—by far my most favorite client ever—had given him my name; and 2) Tony Vespucci was a New York Mafia boss. This was a man I couldn't turn down. He was also a man I didn't want to work for. Bit of a conundrum for me, if you will. On the phone he was cryptic in his request, only that he'd like to offer me a writing job. He mentioned that he'd read what I wrote for Cranston and Judith and was impressed enough to want to meet me in person.

How he was acquainted with Cranston Jefferson I couldn't imagine, but acquainted he was on an intimate scale, and so he was given access to the love story I'd written for the Jefferson's on their sixtieth wedding anniversary: "The Socialite and the Veteran." Their story was the stuff of legends. Judith was a New York socialite from one of the few wealthy East Coast families that was not financially ruined by the

Great Depression. Cranston was a war veteran. They had met in France at the tail end of the war, during the Battle of the Bulge and the Allies' final push across Germany. Cranston sustained a leg injury bad enough to take him back to the hospital on the French side of the border and into the care of a beautiful young nurse named Judith. He was in the hospital for only two weeks, but that was all he needed to fall in love. And he fell hard, as men will when they are all of nineteen, saving their country and risking life and limb each and every day. Then, as quickly as he'd come from the front, the Army saw fit to ship him back there. All Cranston actually knew about Judith was her name and she hailed from Manhattan. So when the war was over, he went to find her.

To both illustrate what I do and show you what Vespucci read, here's an excerpt from their story:

. . . and the greatest war in modern history came to an end. Finally, after a long delay, Cranston was sent stateside in December 1946. The trip home seemed prolonged and drawn out. After spending the last two years and three months on European soil, he wanted to be back in the United States, plant his feet on native ground, and feel home again. His need to get back as quickly as possible stemmed more from the incredibly strong feelings bound up in his chest than from his desire to see his country, though. He'd fallen in love exactly two years earlier, and not a day passed in his remaining tour when he didn't imagine the beautiful nurse who had tended to him when he'd been in the hospital. After being sent back to the front without even so much as a goodbye, he vowed that as soon as he arrived in the United States, he would search for this woman to the ends of the earth and would put his heart in her hands.

Then, it was up to Fate.

His ship came to rest at the docks in New York Harbor. He debarked, ignoring the crowds all around him, a singular line of thought directing him toward Manhattan. He'd never been to New York before. He stared up at the tall buildings and the close proximity of the bricks and mortar, giving him a feeling of bearing down. This was nothing like his hometown of Atlanta. In uniform, he took a taxi to the heart of Manhattan, straight to the high-rise apartment building in which the Steele family occupied the penthouse. During his long conversations into the night with Nurse Steele, she'd mentioned more than once where her parents lived and where she'd grown up, so Cranston had little trouble finding the place. He stepped out of the taxi, his chin tilted upward as he stared toward the sky to the very top of the building. "Was she there?" he wondered. His heart was racing. Standing before the entryway, the doorman eyed him curiously.

"You say you're here to see Miss Judith?" he responded when Cranston made his intentions clear.

Cranston nodded.

Uneasy, the doorman let Cranston pass through the gilded double doors into the lobby, following him with his eyes from his vantage point outside. Our soldier strode straight for the front desk, his head held high, sure of himself as he met the first line of defense of the upper crust. But Persistence is Love's Partner-in-Crime, and Cranston had spent many nights nearly freezing to death on German soil dreaming about this day. He would not be deterred. The haughty look of the man sitting behind the desk created the first nick of doubt in Cranston's otherwise iron will.

"I'm here to call on Miss Judith Steele."

The attendant didn't attempt to hide the disdain on his face upon hearing the question. "What is your business with Miss Steele?"

Cranston did his best to stay calm, keep his face neutral, polite. "That's between me and her."

The attendant didn't like that answer, and his face showed it. "I'm not sure if she's home."

An unmistakable bottled fury appeared in Cranston's eyes. The attendant retreated into his seat. Cranston seemed to grow in height as he spoke. "I just spent the last two years killing Krauts. I've seen the worst of humankind. I will not be turned away by you or anyone else. If you don't call her down here, I'll be going up that elevator over your dead body." Cranston placed his large hands on the counter before the attendant, leaning in for emphasis. "Call."

Clearly frightened, so much so he didn't even try to hide it, the attendant quickly glanced side to side, confirming the fact that he was very much alone in the lobby. Without hesitating, he picked up the phone and called the Steele residence, informing the person on the other end that Miss Judith had a gentleman caller. Once the attendant hung up the phone, Cranston stepped back from the desk, standing very still in the center of the lobby facing the elevator doors. Minutes went by. From outside, the doorman looked over his shoulder every few seconds, interested in what the soldier was up to.

The whoosh and crank of the elevator alighting filled the room. Without a moment's hesitation, Judith stepped into the lobby, as beautiful as the night is long, ringlets of black hair cascading off her shoulders, princess white skin, her curves highlighted by the black strapless evening gown she wore. She took one step, then stopped, stunned by the man she saw before her. She was clearly expecting someone else. She could not hide the shock on her face; it was written in bold. Fate was unfolding right in front of her, but she was frozen, unable to move.

They stared at each other, twenty feet of lobby between them. The energy in the air was palpable. Cranston, too, could not move. He couldn't get his muscles to work. He'd dreamed about this moment for so long, imagined the scenario over and over in his head, and now that it was happening he could barely believe it was real. He didn't know what to do. The woman standing before him was stunning, so beautiful, in fact, that for the first time in his journey homeward doubt crept into his heart. Did he deserve her? Was he worthy of her love and attention? Had Pride overridden Judgment? He was a war veteran with no financial prospects to speak of, at least not anything he could put on paper, and no formal education to fall back on other than his own life experiences. He definitely didn't have the family pedigree to qualify him as an acceptable suitor to Judith's father, Mr. Henry Thomas Steele. Up to this point, though, Cranston had not given any thought or weight to any of these things. Standing only steps from the woman he had dreamed about every night for two years, Cranston didn't know what to do. She wasn't moving either. Was that a good thing or a bad thing? He couldn't read her face. Whenever he'd imagined this moment, he thought he'd know exactly what to do, but he had not prepared for the impact of Judith's brilliance. He'd known she was beautiful in a nurse's uniform, her hair pinned up in a bonnet without the benefits of beauty products, and for those fourteen glorious days in the winter of 1944 that was how she appeared. But now, in an evening gown, she appeared untouchable, so gorgeous that Cranston nearly turned on his heel and ran out the door because there was no way on God's green earth that this magnificent woman would ever grant him even one day, let alone a lifetime. He couldn't breathe. He felt suffocated.

The attendant behind the desk stared, completely forgetting the manners required by his position. The man in military uniform standing in the lobby, who only moments before seemed so sure of himself, seemed hesitant, even scared. The attendant glanced at Miss Judith. She didn't look happy. From beyond the lobby doors, the doorman had turned away from the street, watching the scene unfolding inside, fascinated by what he was witnessing. He could not see the face of the man who'd entered so confidently, but he could see Miss Judith across the lobby. And she looked serious, almost stern. What was she going to do?

Judith looked at Cranston. She could not believe he was standing before her, that he'd tracked her down, that he was real. She'd dreamed about him many nights since those two weeks in December of '44. He looked even more handsome and rugged now than he had then. Over the last year, since returning to the States, she had been thrown back into the cosmopolitan world of New York City high life, and she was good at playing the role of the young ingénue, heiress to the Steele financial empire. Suitors came and went: rich men, handsome men, successful and intelligent and arrogant men—albeit some sweet—but not one of them seemed relevant to her life. She remained unaffected by their attentions to the complete and total dismay of Mr. and Mrs. Steele, who began to wonder if their daughter's war experience might have had a detrimental effect on her emotional health. Judith knew she was not emotionally unstable, but her time overseas had, in fact, had an irrevocable effect on her. Each time she entertained the possibility of a life with any of these men, the image of Cranston would appear in her mind, pushing all other thoughts aside. She would fantasize about having a life with him, about children, about sharing a family with the man who held her hand late into the night in the hinterlands of the French frontier and made her feel safe the only time during her entire tour on European soil. She had dismissed all these thoughts as nothing more than silly female fancy. Cranston had spent only fourteen days in her care, and she figured he had probably forgotten her once he went back to the front. He was nothing more than an innocent, unconsummated wartime fling, better left on the French-German border than brought back to the States. She believed her connection to Cranston was relevant only when it was tied to time and circumstance. A change in either, or both, of these essential components would render any existing feelings void of their original nature and leave the connection between them disappointingly less than worthy of future attention. But with Cranston standing there before her, Judith knew her fears were unfounded. Time and circumstance were two of the essential components for their initial love affair, but not the only two. The third and most essential component, which she had dismissed in his absence, was the spark between them that had started the fires burning in the first place. As she gazed at him, the spark reignited with such an unexpected ferocity that Judith had to freeze for fear she would lose complete control. She gazed at him, her feelings unbearably intense, sublime in their depth. Judith was unaware of everything and everyone around her except for the soldier standing across the lobby.

Cranston didn't know what was going through Judith's head. Neither did the attendant behind the desk. Nor the doorman standing outside. Nor did Mr. Henry Steele, who had just stepped out of the other elevator into the lobby to witness the scene unfolding before him. He also didn't have a clue about Judith's feelings for this soldier. All he knew was that Jimmy at the front desk had informed him there was a soldier standing in the lobby asking to see his daughter. Something in Jimmy's tone had alerted Mr. Steele, so he came down to see for himself. His steely glance homed in on the soldier standing across the lobby staring at his daughter. The four men stood frozen in place, held by the power of this woman.

Judith saw the doubt creeping into Cranston's eyes, but before it could grow any larger she whispered, though it sounded far louder in the silence of the lobby, "Cranston!"

Suddenly, the energy in the room shifted. Judith took a step and then another and another and ran into Cranston's open arms. Jimmy's mouth fell open, but he had enough sense to look down at his desk. Eddie the doorman turned back to the street, smiling wide, having just witnessed something he never thought he'd see in his lifetime. Mr. Steele looked on with disapproval bordering on horror at the impropriety of his daughter's behavior. Cranston and Judith were oblivious. They were locked in a tight, loving embrace, both knowing without a word spoken that neither of them would ever let go.

Mr. Steele, Mrs. Steele, and the rest of the Steele clan had nothing good to say about him. Their twenty-two-year-old Judith could do far better. Cranston Thomas Jefferson was from Georgia. He was poor. He had no prospects. He carried the name of a slave owner. He was black. Judith didn't care. She was madly in love. So she did what any rebellious, independent twenty-two-year-old woman in love would do. She ran away, leaving her family and her wealth behind.

That's the Jefferson's story, or at least part of it. I was brought in by the grandchildren to write their love story for their sixtieth wedding anniversary. I remember the day I presented the family with the finished product at the anniversary party. With six children, over thirty grandchildren, and eight great-grandchildren, they had a lot to be proud of. I developed a special affinity for Cranston, and the feeling seemed to be mutual. I stayed in touch with him after finishing the job, so it was easy to reach him after getting the call from Tony Vespucci, but his response to my questions provided little insight.

"Meet with him, Jon. No one ever got hurt from talking."

"Why does he want to see me?"

"To hire you. To write."

"Who for?"

Cranston had a coughing fit for a moment before answering. "I'm guessing his daughter. She's getting married."

"Is Tony Vespucci who the papers say he is?"

I heard Cranston's concern through the wireless connection. "Even more so."

"Cranston, how in the world do you know him?"

"The Italians are heavily involved in the textile industry." "Italians" was clearly a euphemism for Mafia. "And I knew Tony's father. We were good friends."

"So, I should meet with him?" I asked.

"Jon, if Tony Vespucci wants to meet you, saying no is not an option."

I didn't like the sound of that.

After getting off the phone, I scoured the Internet for everything I could find about Tony Vespucci. I discovered there was not much useful information available about him, though what I did read didn't put me at ease. "Apparently" and "allegedly" cropped up often in the news articles I read about Vespucci. He was the unofficial boss of the New York Mafia. Since the fall of John Gotti and the media circus surrounding him, some members of the Mafia seemed to take on a new, heavily enforced code of silence. At least that's what one reporter, Jim Mosconi, seemed to think was happening. He believed that Vespucci was better at enforcing omertà—the Mafia's strictly enforced code of silence—than most of his colleagues, the key reason the FBI had next to no useful information about Vespucci and his actions inside the Mafia. I paid special attention to Mosconi's articles because he seemed to be more in the know than any of his colleagues. He was the only reporter who thought Tony

Vespucci was the mastermind, or the enforcer, behind the New York Mafia's renewed code of brutally enforced silence. Even before I met with Vespucci, I knew that Jim Mosconi would be someone I'd be calling if I took the job. But I was getting ahead of myself. I didn't want to work for this man. What if he was dissatisfied with what I wrote? Would he react like Nick Nickels Sr.? Or worse? I didn't want to find out. I decided unequivocally I would turn him down when we met, regardless of what Cranston said.

The next day, during that first week in September, I found myself sitting across from Vespucci at a diner on Century Boulevard near LAX. Absurdly, I thought maybe if I did whatever Vespucci wanted me to do and he liked my work, I could get him to do something about Nick Nickels Sr. If I'd had any doubt about Tony Vespucci's profession over the phone, those doubts disappeared as soon as I was sitting across from him, doing my best to keep eye contact with him.

"But, see, Mr. Vespucci, I have a very defined process when I write these stories. I generally take on only twelve stories a year, and I require a minimum of six months to give a guarantee that the job will be completed on time and to my client's satisfaction." But my girlfriend is wreaking havoc in my personal life right now, so I'm not sure it's such a good time for me to be writing other people's love stories, I added silently.

Across the booth, Vespucci stared at me with intense coal-black eyes. I had trouble holding his look, but now was not the time to show any sign of weakness. I kept my eyes locked on his. He was and was not what I had expected. He had the dark features of southern Italian ancestry, the belly of a man comfortably moving into his mid-fifties, stood about five feet nine, and looked the part of a Mafia boss. But he didn't sound it. He was extremely well spoken, charming, his nature disarming and persuasive.

"Jon, I understand your hesitancy," Vespucci assured me. "If I'd known about you earlier, I would most definitely have called you sooner. But I only discovered your talents last week when I was in Cranston's office. I came across the novella you did for them while I was discussing business with Cranston. It was superb."

I gave him a slight nod, acknowledging the compliment. I was still having trouble understanding the connection between Cranston and Vespucci. Cranston, an above-board businessman who owned a large textile business, among other things, was not involved in organized crime. I got the impression Vespucci considered Cranston a friend first, but I had trouble wrapping my head around that as well. As far as I knew, Blacks and Italians didn't run in the same circles.

"May I ask a question, Mr. Vespucci?"

"Please, call me Tony," Vespucci said, flashing a magnificent smile at me. "What do you want to know?"

I heard a cough over my shoulder. My head swiveled around a little faster than I would have liked. Joey, Vespucci's only companion and, I assumed, bodyguard, sat in the booth behind me staring at the back of my head. I guessed he was watching the door for possible hit men coming to do ill to his boss. Built like a wrecking ball, he was about my height, but must have weighed at least two hundred twenty, most of it muscle. If ever I forgot Vespucci's background, I only needed to turn around and see Joey's eyes on me to remind me who I was dealing with. I slowly turned back to Vespucci, wiping the sweat off my brow.

"How do you know Cranston?"

"Over the years we've done a lot of business together."

My eyebrows must have shot up of their own accord because I was trying to keep my face as unreactive and neutral as possible, but I was having trouble doing so. Vespucci didn't miss a thing.

"I own a business that sells fabric. As I'm sure you know, Cranston makes clothing. Sometimes, we supply him with the raw materials."

I nodded. Oh, okay.

"But that's not all," Vespucci said. A faraway look crossed his face so quickly I almost missed it. "Cranston saved my papa's life during World War II."

"Really?" This was news to me. Cranston had never mentioned any of this the entire time I worked with him. Then again, he had no reason to. It wasn't relevant to his and Judith's story, and Cranston was far from a braggart, not one to highlight his own exploits.

"When my papa came to the States, one of the first things he did was track down Cranston Jefferson. When he found out he was married and living in New York City, he never let Cranston forget what he had done. I've known Cranston since the day I was born, you could say."

I sat in the booth dumbfounded. I considered myself a good researcher, exceptional at times, able to uncover the most intimate details about my subject's life. But this was all news to me. I suddenly felt like I'd been cheated, as if somehow Cranston had not been completely forthcoming. I made a mental note to call him first chance and give him a piece of my mind.

"Jon, my daughter Maggie will be getting married late in December. I'm sorry I'm not able to give you the normal amount of time you usually require, but Cranston speaks so highly of you I have no doubt you'll be able to get it done in the time allotted. I'll open my home to you, give you whatever you need, an open checkbook, if you will. And I'll pay you twice your normal rate," he said with a wink.

I put my hands up, palms out, in protest. "Mr. Vespucci, Tony, that's not necessary. It's not about the money."

"I know that. I'm offering you more money because I know you're short on time and will be forced to work outside your realm of comfort. I believe you should be reasonably compensated."

I didn't know what to say. I couldn't turn this man down. He projected immense power. At the same time, I didn't want to take this job. When I worked on a project, I had to complete numerous interviews with the family and friends of the groom and bride. In this case, I could only assume I'd be interviewing known thugs and felons and, dare I say, killers. Feeling Joey's gaze on the back of my head, I nervously looked back over my shoulder. Joey was not smiling. I was sure he'd killed people. I turned back to Vespucci. "Why me, why now? I'm assuming your daughter has been engaged for some time? Don't you think this is a bit late in the process?"

Vespucci nodded thoughtfully. "Good questions. As I said, I only discovered your talents last week. Cranston spoke so highly of you that it was impossible for me to ignore the opportunity. According to Cranston, you could have been a top investigative journalist with your sixth sense and your ability to uncover minute details about people, coupled with the discretion of a politician. My circumstances, shall we say, call for all of these talents. I need someone who will keep the whole story about my daughter and her fiancé inside the family, if you know what I mean."

Yeah, I knew what he meant. As far as I was concerned, that was the first implicit threat I'd received. A friendly smile was planted on Vespucci's face, but I read between the lines. The longer I sat across from him in the booth, the longer the distance between my thinking I would turn him down and actually doing so was growing. I sat silent, letting Vespucci's words sink in. He said he wanted the whole story. That phrase stuck with me. What did that indicate? Something he was not aware of about his daughter and her fiancé? Were they hiding something from him? Vespucci was studying my face.

"Jon, look. My children are more important to me than anything. I would offer my life in place of theirs if it came down to that. My oldest, Michael, already has kids of his own. He's married and settled down, on a clear track. Maggie, however, is my only daughter, and she's still finding her way. She's stubborn and she and I have not always seen eye to eye. I want to do something to let her know how much I care. I figured this would be one good way."

With years of interviews behind me, I'd learned to read the many different signs of the parents of the bride and groom. Tony Vespucci was not telling me everything about his motivation. There was more to it. If I could be sure of one thing when I left the diner, this was it. Instinct led to my next question. "I'm assuming you approve of the marriage?"

Vespucci didn't react. His facial muscles were frozen in place, but the look in his eye told me I was onto something. He answered my question with a question. "Jon, I've flown all the way to Los Angeles with one purpose—to meet you. Do you think I'd go to all this trouble if I didn't approve of the marriage?"

I responded with a nod, a noncommittal acquiescence. We stared at each other for a moment. Within the first three minutes of meeting a client, a parent, a friend of the clients, I always knew whether I liked them or not, and rarely did I change my mind. Reluctantly, and with a great deal of trepidation, staring at Tony Vespucci, I had to admit I liked him because I knew it meant I would not be able to turn him down.

"Can I be frank?" I asked.

Vespucci nodded.

"Given your unique position . . ." I didn't know how else to refer to it. I'd watched enough of *The Godfather Trilogy* and *The Sopranos* to know you just didn't blurt out that someone was in the Mafia, so I tried to be as circumspect as I could be. "Can you guarantee my safety?"

For the first time during our fifteen-minute interview, Vespucci started chuckling. "What do you think I do, Jon?"

I was about to answer the question when I realized maybe the question would be better handled as a rhetorical one. I shrugged my shoulders, an embarrassed look on my face.

Vespucci continued, the chuckle still in his voice. "Of course you'll be safe, Jon. All you'll be doing, for God's sake, is writing a love story for my daughter and her fiancé. Nothing you haven't done a hundred times before."

Trying to make myself feel less foolish, I smiled. "Of course, of course. Well, okay." Before I said it, I felt a tight, lightning-like sensation filling the lower half of my stomach, signaling that my actions were not at all in sync with my internal guidance system. "I'll do it, Tony."

A wide grin spread across Vespucci's face. "That's fantastic, Jon. I knew you'd agree." Of course he did. Who ever turned this guy down? Especially with two hundred and twenty pounds of muscle sitting behind him? "Joey will give you anything you need. I'm looking forward to seeing you in New York. Now, remember, I'm only springing this on everybody tonight, so when you arrive tomorrow, it will be a bit of a surprise, but I'm sure everyone will welcome you with open arms."

Tomorrow? What tomorrow? I was going tomorrow?!

"Tony, I'm not sure I can get a plane ticket for tomorrow."

"Don't worry, it's already done."

Oh, okay. "By the way, what is Maggie's fiancé's name?"

"Oh, I didn't tell you? It's Marco Balducci."

The anxious, lightning-like feeling in my gut expanded considerably. Balducci. I'd come across that name in my research, a name allegedly involved in heavy mob activity. I hoped Vespucci would leave before I got sick all over the table. Vespucci stood up, looking down on me.

"Jon, great to meet you. You're everything Cranston said you would be." He extended his hand. I reciprocated. "I'll see you in New York." With that, Vespucci disappeared out the double doors of the diner into the California sunshine, climbing into the black stretch limousine waiting for him.

Joey loomed over me, blocking my exit from the booth. With his left hand he reached across his chest, his hand disappearing inside his vest. Sweat appeared on my brow instantly. I tensed up. Joey's hand reappeared with a business card on it, offering it to me. I took it, noticing a long scar in the center of his hand as I did so. Joey saw my look.

"Hunting accident," he offered as an explanation.

He smiled for about one frame of film time, a flicker at best, and then it was gone. It was creepy. I wondered what he'd been hunting. Carefully, I took the proffered card. On the front, it said *Vespucci Construction, Inc.* with a New York address and exchange. On the back, in dark print was written two New York phone numbers. The first was Joey's, the second Maggie's. A plane ticket appeared on the table in front of me. I looked up at Joey.

"Tomorrow."

I nodded, the sweat on my brow trickling down.

"Relax. Tony's a great guy. You got nothing to be afraid of."

With that little tidbit of positive speak, Joey turned and sauntered out of the diner. As the door closed behind his right foot, I exhaled, realizing only then I'd been holding my breath. I sat back in the booth, thoughts swirling in my head. I could not do to the Vespuccis what I had done to the Nickels. Nick Nickels Sr. was clearly upset, but so far I'd only received threats and, deep down, I didn't believe it would go much further than that. Vespucci, on the other hand, would not threaten me. He would just make me disappear. What if his daughter didn't like what I wrote? What if Marco Balducci didn't like me? If everything I read was even only partially true, Marco was someone I needed to worry about as well. I dropped my head in my hands, exhausted just thinking about it. Tomorrow would only be the first trip. I would have to go back at least two more times before I gathered everything I needed. When working on a story, I found that three trips were necessary to get the whole picture. Some players involved, such as the friends of the family and distant relatives, needed to be interviewed only once, but because of scheduling conflicts, I was never able to complete all those interviews in one trip. I liked to interview the key players, the bride and groom and their immediate family, more than once. Plus, usually, I took Luci with me on at least one trip so he could get a feel for the couple. As my artistic designer, he put together the layout and gave the novella its look. He liked to meet the players and see where they came from. It influenced his decisions about the overall design. But Luci was in China until the end of the month, studying kung fu with his master. So I was alone on this one.

The logistics of it all were overwhelming, more than I could handle, given my emotional state that first week in September. I would have to tell Sara I was leaving town. Not that she'd care. My home life with her was becoming untenable. I just wanted it to go back to the way it used to be. The changes had rolled in during the summer, subtle at first, but more obvious as time passed. It started with small, minor inconveniences of love. The kisses before she left for work disappeared, replaced with a silent wave at the door. Hugs before bed became a rare item, given with a Spartan reluctance when I was upset about something, and only then in a patronizing, placating manner. Her lack of attention got so bad that sometimes I pretended to be upset just to get some human touch from her.

Ironically enough, I'd met Sara on business about two and half years before as the best friend of a bride-to-be. Little did I know when Sienna and Jeff hired me to write their love story how much it would change my life. A friend of a friend had told Sienna about my services, and she and Jeff hired me over the phone without a formal interview. I discovered after sitting with them for only minutes that Sienna and Jeff were one of the Chosen Couples, as I'd grown accustomed to labeling their kind, who made the Art of Relationship appear simple and easy. They had the easygoing attitude of a couple that could joke about indiscretions and stolen glances with the opposite sex with never a ruffled feather or cross word. They finished each other's sentences, had regular sex, got jealous only when absolutely necessary, and supported one another in their individual endeavors. They went overboard on my expenses to travel around the country to interview their college friends and nail down the early phase of their life together. In fact, they paid my airfare to fly me to Boston to interview Sara, even though she was the only person there I had to interview. Sienna deemed it necessary because Sara was her best friend from college and had been there from the start. Looking back, I think Sienna was playing matchmaker, though she never admitted it, then or later.

I remembered how quickly I'd fallen for her, like in the first few seconds. From the moment I said hello I didn't have a chance. She just clicked for me. After my trip to Boston, I had Sara on the brain. I could think of nothing but her. While writing the story for Jeff and Sienna, Sara was always hovering in the background. When they invited me to the wedding, I jumped at the chance to go, which I rarely did. During the first few years I'd written these stories, I would always attend the weddings, but over time, the weddings became more work than anything else. Everyone at the wedding knew me and it always became several hours of straight socializing, something I was neither good at nor enjoyed. So, I soon made it my practice to turn down all wedding invitations unless there were special circumstances, for which I would make an exception. Sara was the special circumstance and the exception. At the reception for Jeff and Sienna, late in the night, after the alcohol had been flowing for some time and the music was blaring, Sara came over to me and asked me to ask her to dance.

"Ask me to dance," she said.

So I did. The dancing led to more dancing, and then Sara asked me if I would accompany her back to her hotel, which was more of a request than a question. So I did. The rest of the night unfolded as I'd eagerly hoped but not expected. We had fast, sloppy sex the first time, and then better, more focused sex the second time around. Soon after, the first signs of sunlight showed through the blinds.

I was already hopelessly, madly in love and half asleep when Sara leaned into my ear. “Would you like to do this again sometime?”

I nodded.

“I just accepted an offer at a law firm in Los Angeles. I start in two weeks.”

And that was that. Sara and I became an item, and I was swallowed up into her world.

3
Early November
Los Angeles

But here it was almost three years later and I was no longer consumed by Sara's world. She'd booted me out. We were broken up and it was over and I needed to get my life together. October had come and gone and I had spent it doing absolutely nothing but mooning over Sara. As a direct result of my behavior, an overzealous FBI agent had just paid me a visit. I was working for the Mafia. The Chicago couple's project, "The Coffee Shop Lovers," was due by Thanksgiving and I hadn't touched that in months. I needed to shake this break-up lethargy, get my life moving again, stop feeling sorry for myself. I needed a jolt.

I needed something uplifting to draw me out of my miserable state. I crawled across the carpet to my computer, sat down cross-legged at my makeshift chair cum desk and went online to the *Los Angeles Times* website. I scrolled through the day's obituaries, scanning the newest dead people in town. Not finding what I needed, I scrolled back to the previous day's deaths but didn't see what I was looking for. I went backwards a day at a time until, bam, there it was. I grabbed a pen and wrote down the address for the memorial service.

I stood up, went over to the few clothes I had hanging in

my closet because the rest were all boxed up and grabbed my black suit, quickly changing out of my night's dirty outfit. I had my suit pants on when I realized I had not showered in days, so I went into the bathroom, turned on the light, and stared in the mirror. Dull eyes stared back. Out of respect for where I was heading, I hopped in the shower and rinsed off. I dried off quickly and pulled on a pair of underwear, grabbing my only black button-down shirt, noting how wrinkled it was. I checked myself in the mirror and spotted a stain center right. My suit jacket, once on, hid the stain. As long as I didn't take the jacket off, I'd be fine. I glanced at my computer clock, noting I had thirty minutes before the service started. I put on my pants, grabbed my shoes, and hustled out the door.

I hopped into the Regal, put my hand on the gearshift, and popped it in reverse. But the look in my rearview mirror stopped me. My eyes had a look I'd never seen before. Even to myself, I appeared unhinged. I blinked, shaking my head, the unhinged stare replaced with a deep, sad, empty gaze. I'd become so accustomed to seeing this look in my eyes I rarely noticed how pathetic I seemed. But with Williams' unsolicited help, I had taken a step that morning in a positive direction. He'd pushed me out of my sandbox of self-pity. I was now ready to move on from the breakup. I pulled out of the garage onto the street, turning right toward Beverly Hills and the Good Shepherd Catholic Church on Santa Monica Boulevard. I took Coldwater Canyon over the hill and with the light weekend traffic arrived at my destination with a few minutes to spare. Driving past the church around to the parking lot in back, I saw people dressed in black quietly filing in. I drove into the lot, noting the worried side glances my muscled-up Buick invariably received. At the end of the parking lot, I pulled in between a Cadillac Escalade and a Toyota Prius, the irony of L.A.'s schizophrenic nature on display. I parked, turned off the ignition, and climbed out of my car. As I straightened up, I realized I'd taken the last available spot. The place was packed. This was going to be a good one. I needed this. If this didn't take my mind off Sara and her new sleeping buddy, then nothing would.

I crossed the parking lot, gazing up at the pure blue sky as I moved toward the church. The sun was climbing strong in the east. Sunlight was streaming down, reflecting off the multicolored windows built into the archways of the three-story sanctuary, a beautiful day to honor someone's life. I trailed an elderly couple up the few front steps to the entryway toward a somber greeter handing out the deceased's condensed biography. As he handed me a program, I froze, getting the feeling I was being watched. I quickly turned, looking over my shoulder up Santa Monica Boulevard, then in the other direction, not spotting anyone or anything unusual.

As I turned back to the greeter, trying to make the look on my face match his sad semi-smile, something caught my eye. I turned toward the side road bordering the church, spotting a black Lincoln Town Car sitting in a yellow passenger-loading zone. The windows were tinted, so I couldn't see who was inside. Williams. Was the guy following me? What did Sara tell this guy? I felt a surge of anger toward Sara, her French boyfriend, and his asshole FBI-agent-cousin. I wasn't about to let anyone harass and intimidate me. Regardless of my somewhat erratic behavior, it didn't call for being followed. Here I was trying to mind my own business for the first time since the breakup, and I was not going to stand for this intrusion. I turned away from the proffered program and angled toward the Lincoln. Hustling across the sidewalk, I stepped off the curb and crossed the street to the opposite side, banging on the driver's side window with foolhardy disregard.

"Get out of the car! I let you go last night, but I'm not going to let you keep harassing me."

There was no reaction. The tinted windows were so dark

I couldn't tell what he was doing inside the car. For all I knew, he had a gun pointing at my forehead, but I didn't care. I tried to bait him. "What? Are you scared? Afraid of what I'll do to you out in the open?"

I was feeling completely irrational. Every second I stood in front of the car I was getting angrier. Something had unscrewed inside me that morning, the underlying, always-present human instinct for self-preservation hibernating somewhere deep in my subconscious. "Did you hear me? Get out of that car so we can talk man to man!"

Suddenly, the window opened. Instinctively, I took a step back and relaxed my body, preparing. As the window crack widened, I saw the top of a head covered with the glow of blond hair, then more blond hair cascading over female shoulders. Deeper into the car, I could see a second head of long blond hair in the passenger seat. Two pairs of deep, Mediterranean blue eyes, red with recent tears, were glaring at me, two cans of Mace aimed at my face. I stared at these women, frozen by my own foolishness. They were young, college-age, beautiful, scared. And high. My nostrils were hit with the strong smell of marijuana. My cheeks flushed red with my mistake. I smiled in embarrassment, raising my hands up.

"I'm so sorry! I thought you were somebody else."

The Mace cans were still held high, aimed at my face. I felt my behavior merited an explanation.

"See, my girlfriend broke up with me and the guy she's sleeping with now is related to a guy who's in the FBI who came over early this morning and warned me to stay away from her. He drives a Lincoln identical to yours so I thought he was following me and that's why I came over here. I'm real sorry for scaring you."

Nothing. Cans still at the ready.

"Well, um, okay. So."

Neither woman said a word. Standing there staring at them, I saw the same person twice. Identical twins. With my hands still up in surrender, I took a step backwards and meekly waved at them. With the Mace still at the ready, the windows climbed upward, shutting the blond twins behind a wall of tinted glass, leaving me standing in the middle of the street staring at my reflection. Feeling utterly foolish, I turned back in the direction of the church steps. I took the proffered program from the greeter, though I was not given the same sad smile. This time he took a long, hard look at my face. I smiled sheepishly and passed him into the church. So much for anonymity. I didn't like to be noticed when I came to these events. I wanted to observe, not be observed. Just as I crossed the threshold, I got that same feeling I was being watched, but this time I didn't turn around, not trusting my sixth sense or the reaction it might provoke.

I entered the sanctuary, a large Catholic church, now filled with mourners, row upon row of them, right up to the front steps of the altar. A large cross with a larger-than-life Jesus nailed to it hung on the front wall. I shuddered. The image of Jesus on the cross always scared me. I cut to the left and grabbed a seat in the last pew on the outside aisle. Soft organ music wafted through the air, filling in the empty spaces between and around the mourners. Many people had come to pay their respects to—I checked the program again—Carol Margaret Zefarelli. The picture on the cover showed a woman who had lived a long life; she looked old and near the end. In the picture, her hair was thinned, her skin saggy and sallow. I guessed she'd died from some kind of cancer, this picture taken while she was going through chemotherapy. She was Italian, born not long after the war to end all wars. Opening the program, the inside cover was the picture of a completely different woman, a woman in the prime of her life. She could not have been more than twenty at most. Her dark hair blowing behind her in the wind, she was standing on a bridge somewhere in Europe, the architecture in the background saying as much. Her hands gripped the railing, a provocatively sweet smile aimed at the camera. A conservative, formfitting dress circa the early '40s revealed a well-shaped body. The contrast between the ancient Carol and the young Carol on the inside cover was striking.

I turned to her biography. Born in Italy, she'd lived through the terrors of World War II and had fought in the underground resistance against Mussolini. After the war, she moved to the United States by herself, went to college, became a high school teacher, got married, had four children, and, after raising them, went back to law school and got her law degree to practice on behalf of the poor and underprivileged. She founded a halfway house for abused women in downtown Los Angeles that had now been open for over thirty years. She founded a scholarship fund at a prestigious local private high school for intellectually talented but financially challenged youth to attend. Carol and her husband were blessed with the ability to use their money to make more money, and they put it to good use. Her biography made it clear she had fought the good fight. Her track record spoke for itself. She wanted to help others. As I read more about Carol's life, I felt a tingle of inspiration. Long ago, I'd learned that memorial services were great places to go if I wanted to be inspired. I realized I'd been acting like a selfish prick over the last few weeks, moping around as if my life was over. But it wasn't. I was at a memorial service for Carol Zefarelli, and her life *was* over. It was a solid reality check.

My thoughts were interrupted by the beginning of the service. A priest walked to the front of the altar, solemnly looking out over the gathering. I looked around, realizing that my pew was now filled. I took stock of the entire room, noting that the place was packed with more mourners gathered along the back wall. It was standing room only. Father Murphy, as the program indicated, gathered his thoughts. He looked down at his hands for a moment, and then he looked back up.

"Let us pray."

In unison, all heads dropped forward, chin to chest. I did likewise, not wanting to stand out, but I found it impossible not to peek. I could see just over the heads of the crowd to the front, noticing several sets of shoulders silently heaving with the tears of loss and sadness. Up front, the extended family appeared to take up several pews. I spotted the blond twins seated to the side of what I assumed were their mother and father. I had not seen the blonds enter the church, so they must have come in from a door near the front of the sanctuary. On the other side of the twins was a young man head and shoulders above the other family members. Suddenly, he turned around, his gaze intently sweeping across the rows of mourners, searching, until his eyes found me. His look was as cold as ice. The twins must have pointed me out to him. I quickly dropped my head to break his gaze. Staring down at my lap, I wondered if maybe it would be a better idea if I left. Maybe it wasn't my day. Father Murphy's voice interrupted my thoughts.

"Ladies and gentlemen, we are gathered here today to celebrate the wonderful life of Carol Margaret Zefarelli."

All heads went back up. Slinking down in my seat so I was partially hidden, I looked up to the front but could no longer see from my lowered vantage point if I was being watched.

Father Murphy continued. "She was a woman of incredible fortitude, and an amazing, loving kindness with a tenacity and stubbornness beyond compare. Believe me, I know. If she disagreed with you and felt that her way was better, she let you know." Soft laughs rippled through the sanctuary. "Oh, so I'm not the only one." Father Murphy smiled. "And what made her so wonderful was that she used her attributes to help others in need. She had a clear, unbending sense of what is right. She championed the underdog and believed in fighting for the less fortunate with all the powers God gave her. We knew her as a loving mother, a doting grandmother, a faithful wife, a beautiful friend and, most of all, one of God's cherished children. And she loved our God with all her heart. She truly believed she was put on this earth to do His work."

He paused, looking out over the crowd of mourners. "As I see all of her many friends and family before me, I see you loved her as much as she loved all of you. Recently, I visited Carol at her bedside, and her spirits were very high, even though she was in a great deal of physical pain from her illness. She still managed to smile when I entered and asked me if I'd performed any good miracles lately." Scattered murmurs of laughter greeted the Father's fond memory. "She had a wit, no doubt. I sat down beside her and she took hold of my hand, smiling through her pain and said, 'Don't worry about me, Father, I'm going to be fine. I'm going home. But please look after my family.'" Father Murphy paused again, glancing down at Carol's family members with a sympathetic smile. He looked back over the crowd. "Carol was fearless." The sound of quiet tears increased, accompanied by sniffling and coughing. "I held her hand and we sat silently together, praying. Then Carol, always one for surprises, handed me a list of all the people she'd been watching over, people who needed food or care or a friendly visit every so often, and she asked me to take over for her." He looked to the ceiling. "Carol, I am honored to continue your life's work. Let us pray."

In sync, everyone's head went down, including mine. I'd been drawn in by the priest's words. I felt tears on my cheeks, tears of empathy for those around me and the grief they were experiencing. Father Murphy finished the prayer and called Carol's eldest child, Connie, the woman who'd been sitting beside the twins, to the altar.

Connie was in her early fifties. She stood before us, nervous. She cleared her throat. Shyly, she looked up at the crowd of mourners, then back down to her papers. "I promised myself I would not cry, so bear with me." She took a deep breath. "My mother was an incredible woman, feisty and proud and stubborn and very loving. She taught us to believe in ourselves and be the best that we could be and always to do the right thing. Our mother was a special kind of lady." Her shoulders shook, the tears falling down her cheeks, in spite of her promise. She dropped her head as she gathered herself. Many of the family members followed suit. I could see shoulders shaking in the front row. The giant man up front put his arm around one of the blond twins as she rested her head on his shoulder.

Connie proceeded with her eulogy. "Many of you may not know this story, mother wasn't one to brag. When we were very young living in Pittsburgh, my mother taught history at a prestigious prep school. One year, her favorite student was a shoo-in for valedictorian. My mother referred to him as one of Einstein's peers. I was only a little girl, but I remember her talking about this boy. At the end of the year, she discovered that another student was going to be given the valedictorian honor, and my mother got very angry." A smile crossed Connie's lips at the memory of her mother's temper. "There's nothing worse than an angry Sicilian woman. When she found out, she immediately left her classroom and marched through the school halls to the headmaster's office, demanding to know why the most qualified and deserving student in the senior class was not going to be valedictorian. The headmaster looked up at her from behind his desk, as my mother liked to tell it, saying, 'But Carol, he's a Jew. We've never had a Jewish student become valedictorian. We can't do that.' My mother didn't say another word to him. She marched out of his office, went back to her room, sat down at her desk, and typed up her letter of resignation, stating that as long as the school followed its tacit policy of bigotry, she was resigning effective immediately. She ripped the page out of the typewriter, marched right back to the headmaster's office, and placed it on his desk."

Sitting in my pew in the back, I was not the only one in

the congregation enthralled. The great room was silent, no rustling of clothing or coughing or ancillary noises. Everyone was keyed into the daughter's voice. In my mind's eye, I saw the story unfold: a young Carol, beautiful and vivacious, her dark eyes stormy in their anger as she shamed the headmaster for his discrimination. I envisioned the headmaster's reaction to her resignation, realizing he was going to lose his most prized teacher over reasons he could not address publicly. Maybe the headmaster had a secret crush himself on young Carol, and his fear of losing her was enough to galvanize him into action. Connie's voice pulled me out of my imagined reverie.

"My mother's resignation threw the school into an uproar. Later that same week, the headmaster came to our house, begging my mother to come back, telling her that the academic committee had reconsidered its position and reviewed each of the candidate's capabilities and realized my mother's favorite student was the one most deserving of the award and would be named valedictorian that year." Carol's daughter looked up with a proud, distant smile on her face, somewhere with her mother in a memory long ago. A murmur of satisfaction floated through the church.

I took my focus off the front for a moment, looking around at the mourners packed into the church, all ages represented in the crowd. Carol had a long reach, touching many people. There were even young adults in their teens and twenties interspersed throughout the mourners. I gave myself a mental pat on the back for picking such a good memorial service. This was exactly what I needed to bring myself out of my depression, to show myself there is good in the world. When I looked back at the altar, I watched as Connie took her seat to be replaced by the blond twins. I immediately slunk back into the pew, not wanting them to notice me from their heightened vantage point. I searched the program, discovering the twins' names were Francesca and Daniella. I watched over the shoulders in front of me as the twins positioned themselves behind the altar, their shoulders touching the entire time.

Francesca, or Daniella, started talking. "We're sure many of you knew Grandma was special."

Then Daniella, or Francesca, "She was one of kind."

Their voices even sounded identical. It was disconcerting to watch. They chimed in together, "We are going to miss you, Grandma, so, so much."

As if on cue, they started to cry, their shoulders heaving in unison, tears trickling down their cheeks. The young women standing before me at the front of the church appeared demure and innocent, not much like the two women I saw smoking pot and aiming cans of dangerous, debilitating spray at my face earlier. Then again, I had pounded on their car window like a crazy person at their beloved grandma's funeral, so what did I expect? After a moment, they took a collective breath and continued.

Right Twin said, "Grandma, we'll miss your stories about your childhood in Italy."

Left Twin, "And about your travels throughout Europe."

Right Twin, "And then when you came on the boat over to America."

Left Twin, "We'll miss your hugs and your love."

Right Twin, "We'll miss your advice on men."

At this, with a soft smile she looked over at head-and-shoulders sitting beside her empty spot in the front row. Left Twin looked over at him as well, but something pulled her attention farther into the crowd. I realized she was staring at me, even though I was buried down in my pew. Right Twin picked up some kind of mental cue, turning her attention to me also. Their stares made me squirm in my seat. It lasted for a second, then two, then three. They stood at the altar, their gazes like lasers focused on my forehead. I felt a bead of sweat trickle down my neck. I looked around to see if anyone else was looking at me. I slowly sunk down in my pew as far as I could to get below their sight line.

Suddenly, they turned to one another, and then they began to sob. Through their tears, they said, "Grandma, we love you."

Head-and-shoulders went up to the altar to guide Right Twin back to her seat followed by an older man who could only have been their father, who took Left Twin down from the other side. They returned to their seats in the front, but some rustling and confusion followed them after they sat down. As Father Murphy moved in the direction of the altar, the rustling pulled his attention, drawing him away from the altar toward the family. After quiet debate among the priest and Connie and a very elderly gentleman with a close-cropped, thin white head of hair, the priest and Connie helped the elderly man, ancient by any standard, out of his seat. As he made it up to the altar, Father Murphy and Connie made sure he was stable and settled before they returned to their seats. The man stared down at his feet for a moment. When he finally looked up at us, his eyes were swollen, his cheeks reddened from a trail of tears. I looked at my program to put a name with his face. Tomasso Zefarelli, the husband left behind. He took a breath to start talking but fell into a coughing fit instead. One cough turned into two, and the old man began to suck air, trying to pull in enough oxygen to stay upright, his body convulsing with the coughing. Both Connie and another woman near Connie's age, I assumed to be one of her sisters, hurried up to the altar to help him. Tomasso waved them off with an irritated, I-can-take-care-of-myself gesture. The sisters pulled up short on either side of their father, not sure what to do. The coughing subsided as Tomasso pulled in more oxygen, gathering himself together. Connie and her sister meekly returned to their seats, appearing a bit peeved that their father had scared them so. Tomasso looked out over us all.

"My family didn't think it would be a good idea if I spoke at my wife's memorial service. They weren't sure if my heart could take it." A sad, sly smile crossed his face. "But I can be as stubborn as Carol. Carol always said the children got their bullheadedness from my side of the family, so I don't want to let her down. This year we celebrated our sixty-second wedding anniversary. Carol was afraid she wouldn't make it, more worried about that than she was about what was happening to her. She put up with me for all these years, so that means she wasn't only special but also incredibly patient. When Carol was first diagnosed two years ago, we both hoped maybe it was just one more bump in a long life of little bumps, and that if we worked hard enough and prayed long enough, we could get over this one too. But this bump was too big for my darling Carol. She was the strongest person I've ever known, but this disease was stronger."

At this point, tears began falling from his eyes. He paused, overcome with grief. The silence in the sanctuary was deafening. Even at his old age, life was still precious and love lost was all consuming, debilitating, and painful. I watched this old man I didn't know mourning over the loss of his wife, and wondered what he was feeling inside, how he comprehended the death of his life partner.

Tomasso's tears subsided as he gathered himself together. "I can honestly say, folks, that in my many years of life, I have never felt this kind of pain. And it is the most wonderful, bittersweet pain. Carol was my wife, my true love, my best friend, and I feel lost without her. For an old grump like me, my life would not have been worth a damn if Carol had not held my hand and been my guide. But I know she's gone home and she's happy watching over us." Tomasso looked up to the ceiling. Sporadic sniffles could be heard throughout the church. "Don't worry, I won't be long in this life. I'll be with you soon."

Sobs followed his last words from family members at the front of the church. For the first time in any memorial service I'd attended—and I'd attended quite a few—I felt like an intruder, that I was witnessing something not meant for my eyes. Tomasso leaned on the altar, his hands spread out for balance, weeping shamelessly. Silently, Father Murphy stepped up to the mourning husband and whispered into his ear. Tomasso's sobbing subsided as Father Murphy looked down to the family. Connie also appeared to be crying, as did many members in the front row. Connie's husband gave his wife a reassuring hug and then stood to help guide his father-in-law back to his seat. Once Tomasso was settled, his daughters surrounded him and wrapped their arms around him. Father Murphy stood at the altar quietly, his eyes downcast so as not to bring any further attention to the mourning family and their intimate display of affection and sadness. The daughters held onto their father, and when the tears seemed to have run their course, the family found their way back to their seats.

Father Murphy looked up from the altar. "In our sadness, let's not forget that Carol has gone home, she's where she's always wanted to be. She confided to me not long ago that even though she was a little scared, she was excited to finally meet her Maker. Her faith never faltered. She credited all her successes in life to be not of her doing but that of the Almighty's. Carol's faith was boundless, and her joy for life contagious." Father Murphy paused. He looked at Carol's family. "In our pain, we must remember that Carol has started a new chapter and is looking down on us with open arms. Let us pray."

Father Murphy dropped his head. "Father, in your infinite wisdom, You have shown us your will, and we ask that You care for Carol as she joins You in her eternal resting place. Please lay your blanket of protection over her family and friends and guide us as we move through this difficult time of grief. Help us honor Carol's life by recognizing the faith that You instilled in her of your greatness and infinite love."

Everyone followed suit and a collective "amen" sounded

throughout the church. The rustling of clothing and people shuffling in their seats signaled the end of the memorial. Father Murphy invited everyone to join the family in the hall next door for refreshments. That was my exit cue. In the many memorials I'd attended, I never once stayed to eat. I'd gotten what I came for—inspiration—and didn't want to siphon any more from the family. People were filing out of their seats toward the front of the church to pay their respects to Carol's family. I went the other direction as unobtrusively as possible. I sidestepped several elderly people standing in the lobby, exiting through the front door of the church into the sunlight. People were milling around, some smoking cigarettes, the irony obviously lost on them. I passed them down the church steps to the sidewalk and followed the path along the side of the church heading toward the parking lot. I felt a little lighter than I had before going in. Silently, I looked up at the sky. Thanks, Carol, wherever you are. I had work to do, and now I felt like I could get started.

I was getting close to the parking lot, and as I expected, it was still full. The back of my neck tingled with the same feeling I had prior to the service. I was hesitant to trust my instincts, given my embarrassing encounter earlier, though not hesitant enough to look around. A car was tracking with me on the road, keeping abreast of me as I walked. It was another Lincoln Town Car with tinted windows. I decided God must not like me very much. I stopped. The car stopped. I started walking and the car began moving with me. I stopped. The car stopped. I took a step backward. The car backed up a foot. Real cute. Didn't Williams have something better to do? I turned and faced the car.

"What do you want?"

The window lowered to reveal Tony Vespucci's heavy, Joey. "Tony would like to have a word with you."

I suddenly felt a sick feeling in my stomach. I had not contacted Vespucci or his daughter since my second visit at the end of September. I'd been so wrapped up with Sara and the breakup and my own emotional turmoil that I'd totally ignored my promise to Vespucci. I stood on the curb stupidly nodding my head. "Oh, sure, sure. Does he want me to call him? Or do I need to fly to New York?"

Joey looked at me like I was a complete moron. He jerked his head, indicating I should get into the back seat.

"Oh, of course."

I hustled into the street and climbed into the proffered back door of the Lincoln, but I didn't see Vespucci anywhere. I closed the door, sitting back with a lead feeling in my gut. I had promised a solid draft of their story by mid-November so Maggie and Marco could review it and make the necessary changes couples always wanted to make. I had about ten days to go to meet this deadline and I hadn't even begun. With Joey staring at me in the rearview mirror, I did my best not to let him see me panicking, but the look in his eyes made me panic even more. I wondered if Vespucci was even going to let me live another two weeks. Joey turned in his driver's seat, throwing a friendly, sinister smile my way that quickly turned to a scowl. I looked at him dumbly, not sure what he expected of me. He jerked his head downward, indicating a flat screen monitor against the back seat. Vespucci's face filled the screen.

"Jon. How are you?" Vespucci's voice came from everywhere in the car, like the surround sound in a movie theatre.

A bit disconcerted, I responded, "I'm good."

"I hope Joey was polite to you."

I glanced at Joey now back to watching me in the rearview mirror. I answered with a vigorous nod.

"Oh, good. Sometimes he can be overzealous when I ask him to do something. Joey tells me you're at the funeral of Carol Zefarelli?"

I dumbly nodded. He said her name as if he were familiar with her.

"I wanted to attend her funeral but business kept me back in New York."

Nonplussed, I asked, "How do you know Carol Zefarelli?"

"She was my mother's best friend from childhood back in the Old Country, like family."

"Really?" I could not believe the coincidence. Then my mind started working. Why was Vespucci so concerned about my showing up here? He didn't seem very happy. I tried to imagine the odds of my randomly picking a funeral service for someone related to a client, and the chances seemed slim. But here I was and it had happened.

"Did you know that, Jon? That I was acquainted with Carol Zefarelli?"

"No, I didn't know that. Pure coincidence."

"I'm not a big believer in coincidences, Jon. What are you doing there?"

A slightly threatening tone had entered Vespucci's voice. I tried to convince myself I was imagining it. I started doing quick calculations, connecting one unattached thought to another, light appearing in my dark mind. Here I was, a hired writer who had been given an open door to interviewing and collecting information from a major Mafioso boss' daughter and her friends and family. Vespucci must be thinking I was looking into him. The absurdity of my researching a Mafioso boss made me inadvertently laugh. Joey looked over his shoulder at me like I was crazy. Vespucci was taken aback, more surprised than offended at my temerity.

"Something funny, Jon?"

"No, no, Tony. It's just, you're going to think it's funny."

"Try me." He wasn't smiling.

I quickly considered the reasons I went to memorial services, realizing it would sound strange, but I didn't want Vespucci to have any misconceptions regarding what I was doing at this particular memorial service. The last thing I wanted was for him to think I was somehow digging into his personal life. In short order, I explained to Vespucci my reasons for going to memorial services. When I finished, Vespucci stared back at me from the monitor with a strange look, not sure if I was making fun or, in fact, that maybe I was crazy. I glanced up from the monitor to check if Joey had grasped my explanation and saw the same look on his face.

I concluded my explanation. "That's why I go, Tony. I looked in the paper this morning and Carol Zefarelli's memorial service was listed. It looked like the right one. So I came."

Vespucci took a breath. "You know, Jon, that's about the weirdest thing I've ever heard." He smiled for the first time, apparently ready to move on. "Now that we've got that covered, then, was it a good service? Did they do Carol justice?"

"Oh, yes, sir. It was one of the best memorial services I've ever been to."

"Good. I'm glad." He stopped for a moment, lost in a memory. Joey turned back around in his seat, watching guests as they intermittently left the church. Vespucci took a breath and came back to me. "Now, Jon, onto the business I was calling about, Maggie and Marco. How's their story coming along?"

What was the safe answer to that question? I had not even started a rough draft. I had not organized my notes from my interviews in September. And I really needed to have another interview with Maggie and Marco to nail down the essence of who they were as a couple so I was clear on the direction of the piece. In effect, I had done nothing more than complete the first sets of interviews. But those interviews had left me with more questions than answers about the couple's relationship that I was not ready to discuss with Vespucci at this point.

"It's coming along fine," I said. "I've got my next trip planned to visit next week to tie up any loose ends and get answers to some questions I still have so I can put the final touches on the story. I'm getting close, Tony." Nothing I said was true. I had not booked a flight, and I was nowhere near having a first draft completed for them.

"Good. I'm sure I've made this clear to you, Jon, I don't mean to push you, but Maggie is my only daughter. As far as I'm concerned, even the best isn't good enough for her. Do you understand?"

I understood that meant no matter what I did, Vespucci was probably going to be unhappy with the finished product. Then what? What would he do? My only hope was to ensure Maggie was happy with what I wrote, a goal I felt would be a little easier to attain, given the way she and I had hit it off during my two visits in September.

I responded, "I understand how you could feel that way. Maggie is very special. There's no doubt about it." And I meant that. In my interviews with Maggie, she had been charming and personable, clearly intelligent, and it had been hard not to notice that she was drop-dead gorgeous.

"Great, Jon. I'm glad we understand each other. I know you'll take care to make sure she's very happy and if she's happy, I'll be happy. If you need anything, let Joey know. And, Jon?"

"Yes, sir?"

"I don't want you to leave any stone unturned. Find out everything."

"Don't worry, that's my job," I answered, though I considered it a strange order. No father had ever given me those specific instructions. In fact, no parent had ever said that to me. It gave me pause, but before I had time to ask him if he had anything he'd like me to focus on, the screen went blank. I looked up at Joey, catching his eyes on me from the rearview mirror. He turned around in the driver's seat.

"That's good. He likes you."

What in my exchange with Vespucci had led Joey to say that I could not tell, but it was better than Vespucci not liking me. I wanted to please this guy, not just because of who he was and what he could do to me. I realized sitting in the Lincoln with Vespucci's heavy that I liked his daughter quite a bit, more than I considered healthy. She had been nothing like I expected. She was straightforward and modest and bright and gave no indication that she was a Mafioso boss's daughter. Marco, on the other hand, had been arrogant and intimidating, seemingly doing the interviews with me more out of obligation as the groom than because he wanted to. Joey interrupted my thoughts.

"Here's cash for the ticket and anything you need for getting around. Keep receipts." Joey handed me a stack of one hundred dollar bills.

That was my cue to get out. I opened the back door and climbed out of the car. I stepped up to the driver's side window, attempting to hand the money back to Joey. "I usually just bill my clients at the end of my research, so there's no need for me to take the money now." I held it out to Joey.

Joey stared at me. He growled, "Take it."

Reacting to his tone, my hand immediately found its way into my pants pocket, stuffing the money inside. I nodded my head dumbly. "Okay. Thanks." I took a step back from the car, turning around. I realized now it must have been Joey's presence that had given me the feeling I was being watched before the memorial service. I looked over my shoulder back at the Lincoln. "Hey, Joey, why do you say he likes me?"

Without a response, Joey's face disappeared behind the tinted driver's side window, the Lincoln slowly pulling away up the street. I crossed the parking lot quickly, which was still full of cars. I got to my car, took my keys out of my pocket and was about to open my lock when, over my shoulder, I heard a deep voice.

"Is this the guy?"

Two high-pitched female voices responded in unison, "That's him."

Daniella and Francesca.

I turned around, my back to the car. The giant who'd stared at me during the service was standing right behind me. I immediately felt cornered. The blond twins were on his right, glaring at me. The giant was frowning, caught up in his own machismo. I offered them a smile, trying to defuse the situation. I took a quick glance around the parking lot, hoping the sight of a more reasonable person might be able to help, but the lot was empty of people.

The giant spoke again. "Who are you? How did you know Carol Zefarelli?"

I blanked. "Uh, I,"—I didn't want to lie—"I didn't."

Francesca, or Daniella, said, "He made—"

The other one finished the sentence, "—us cry."

The giant never took his eyes off me. His fist came up fast, taking me by surprise, and connecting with the bone above my left eye. I slammed against my doorframe, stumbling forward to the ground. For a second, I only felt numbness, and then the pain started rolling in. The skin around my eye socket began burning. I stayed low, trying to think. I didn't react immediately because I felt that maybe I deserved what I was getting. I had no right to bang on their window at their beloved grandma's funeral. I had been rude and belligerent.

The giant said, "Get up, or I'll kick you." I looked up from the ground. The twins' eyes were glowing with sadistic satisfaction. I looked at the giant's foot, deciding I didn't want to get kicked by his size fourteen loafers, so I shook my head, grabbed hold of the car and hoisted myself up. The blonds began speaking again.

Left (from my new vantage point) Twin, "He scared—

Right twin, "—us a lot."

I raised my hands in surrender. "Hold on, I can explain my—"

The left fist connected with my solar plexus from the side. The blow knocked the wind out of me. I doubled over, gasping for breath. My initial feelings of guilt were quickly replaced with anger. I would not take a third punch. Though I let Williams have his way with me, I knew my way around a fight—Luci had helped me with that—and if this testosterone giant prolonged his assault, I would have to fight back. Keeping my face down between my shoulder blades and chin tucked under for protection, I held my hand up indicating I wanted to speak. “Look, I’m sorry for scaring you. I thought you were someone else. OK?”

There was no response. I peeked up, ready to duck out of the way of another punch. The first thing I saw were the eyes of the blonds spread wide with fear. My eyes shifted front toward the giant, noticing another pair of shoes behind the size fourteens. I pushed my butt against the car for leverage, getting upright. Joey was standing behind the giant with a gun to his neck, his eyes on my face.

“You okay?” Joey asked.

I nodded. “Just a misunderstanding, I think.”

“Looked like more than that to me.”

I’m not sure who was in more shock, me or the testosterone junky and his girls.

“Looks like this guy has a problem with you. Should I have a problem with him?” Joey asked in a calm voice.

I had never seen fear up close, but staring into the giant’s eyes I saw how true fear manifested itself in the human body. His pupils had dilated to the point that all I could see was black with a rim of iris. I looked over his shoulder at Joey’s face. Joey was not kidding. He was doing what he did for a living.

"No, Joey. Just a misunderstanding. Right guys?” I said.

Three heads nodded in unison.

"Are you sure?” Joey wasn’t about to let it go.

“I’m sure.”

“All right. You three, sit down.” The giant was on his ass before Joey finished speaking. The twins followed suit. “Now close your eyes. Don’t open them until I say so. Jon, you go ahead.”

"Thanks, Joey."

I passed him an appreciative smile. My affinity for Joey and the Italians grew exponentially at that moment. There was more to Joey than I thought. I climbed into my car and stuck the key into the ignition. I looked down at the blond twins and their boyfriend, feeling a little sorry for them.

I leaned out my window. "Again, I'm sorry for the mistake." I looked up to thank Joey but he was halfway to his car. I looked back at the three figures on the ground, not one eye open. I was amazed at the power of fear. I'd never encountered anything like it. By the time I pulled out of the parking lot, Joey's car was already in the distance and the three friends were still sitting in their appointed places. I looked in my rearview mirror. My left eye was swelling up. It would be a good shiner.

I headed north on Beverly Drive up to Sunset and made a right turn, driving east through Beverly Hills into the hallowed territory of the Sunset Strip. As I drove into West Hollywood, I spotted the Whisky A Go-Go where the Doors played their first gigs and Jim Morrison found his voice, and moments later I saw the sidewalk in front of the Viper Room where River Phoenix took his last breath. Farther east on Sunset, I passed the Chateau Marmont where John Belushi ended his career and his life. Giants—all dead from a similar weakness. Their ghosts lived on in the minds and souls of all those who chased the same dreams these creative giants had. Some called L.A. a Fool's Paradise. Considering myself to be one of those fools, I could not disagree. I guided my car off Sunset, taking La Brea up to Hollywood and past the Walk of Fame. Tourists filled the sidewalks with their uncharacteristically L.A. outfits: Europeans with short shorts; Japanese with their ubiquitous Americanized sunglasses and digital cameras; and overweight Midwesterners with screaming kids in tow. The Chinese theatre crossed my vision on my left side, as I glimpsed a crowd of people watching a street performer finish up his dance routine. I kept driving, leaving the Hollywood morass behind me. I had to share the last twenty-four hours with someone and figured Luci and Izzy would be happy to see I had snapped out of my miserable, pitiful state. I reached Vermont and cut back to Sunset, driving southeast down through the Silver Lake Hills, palm trees haphazardly climbing into the sky on either side of the street. The mixed language of Spanish and English marketing signs passed me on both sides, old and new establishments mixed along the road. Echo Park was in the slow process of gentrification, money cozying up to the less fortunate, slowly squeezing them out of the picture in the name of progress and growth. I cut a left on Coronado, driving past the old California Craftsman style homes that dotted the flats of Echo Park and much of East Los Angeles. Up ahead, past the stop sign, I could see Izzy in the front yard tending to her flower garden. Slowly, I pulled up to the house and parked my car, the hum of the engine grabbing Izzy's attention. She turned my way and gave me her sweet smile, her body straightening up as she shifted in my direction.

For the first time in a long time, I was glad to know I was somewhere I was wanted.

4
College
Pennsylvania

I attended college but never graduated. My college years are significant for three reasons: 1) I met Luci Gardner; 2) I dated Jennifer Breaker; and 3) I stumbled into my future career path.

LUCI GARDNER

Luci entered my life during the spring of my sophomore year. College was not what I expected, mostly because I didn't know what to expect, though I expected something different. Rather than partying and wasting late night hours with meaningless socializing, I spent my time studying, working out, and smoking pot. My latent antisocial tendencies came to the fore early in my freshman year. I had trouble relating to the other students: their wealthy backgrounds, how they slid in and out of social networks with grace and pizzazz, the way they traded partners and friends without batting an eye. I quickly discovered I was best served by putting my energies into my academics and my newly found love for weight training.

By sophomore year, I made no attempt to hide my disdain for the social scene on campus, even willing to spend the little money I had on a local meathead gym rather than train at the school facilities so I didn't have to listen to the inane banter between the fraternity brothers and jocks. The off-campus gym equipment was more suited to my growing weightlifting habit while allowing me to self-isolate even further. Most of the clientele came in from the local factories, rough guys who trained hard and talked little. The gym was bare bones, no fluff. Weights, benches, bars, a single water fountain. That was it. With little chatter, and ne'er a woman to be seen—other than the owner's big-haired daughter working the front desk—all focus was on training. Aside from the local radio station blasting out of the jerry-rigged speakers hanging from the four corners of the room, the only sounds heard were metal on metal when a set finished or the occasional grunt while weight was being hoisted or squatted or dropped. I fit in perfectly, keeping my head down and my mouth shut. No one bothered me. As far as I knew, I was the only college student who trained there, though no one seemed to hold it against me. Most of these guys worked shift hours, so the gym was very busy from 5 a.m. to 11 a.m., the early guys needing to make their 8 a.m. start time, the later guys rolling in from the night shift and wanting to get their training out of the way before they went home to sleep. From 11 a.m. to 4 p.m. the gym was quiet, so I tried to fit my training in midday because I had unfettered access to the machines. Plus, there were fewer intimidating hulks standing around watching me put up my less than impressive amounts of weight.

One day I was training hard and feeling confident about my gains in strength over the recent months. Late in the morning the gym was empty, the last stragglers having left only minutes before. I had the gym floor to myself. I decided to attempt a 220-pound bench press, placing two 45-pound plates on either side of the barbell and locking them off with clips to secure them. This was a first for me, but I was sure I could handle it. Taking a deep breath, I lifted the barbell from its inverted V holders. Two seconds later, I found myself in the untenable position of trying to lift the bar off my chest. With all my strength, I pushed up, but to no avail. Gravity, the amount of weight, and reality were all working against me. The bar digging into my chest became more intense as each second passed. I cursed myself for putting the clips on. Otherwise, I could have tipped the bar in either direction to let the weights fall off. It would have made a terrible clatter and grabbed the embarrassing attention of the gym owner's daughter, but I figured that was better than being asphyxiated because I was an idiot. I was beginning to panic. I tried rolling the bar down my chest toward my stomach, hoping I could roll it the length of my body and let it fall over my knees onto the ground. But the bar was not cooperating. It was becoming entrenched on my chest, closing up my lungs. At that moment, two hands appeared from behind me.

A deep voice followed, "Need a lift?"

I looked over my head, noticing only a head of shoulder-length dark hair.

"On the count of three, give me what you got. One, two, three!"

Simultaneously, I pushed up as he pulled, both of us exhaling with the strain. I had very little to give, but the guy above me had no trouble lifting the bar off my chest and placing it back in the bench prongs. As soon as the bar was in place, I sat up and turned to him, forced to take several deep breaths before I could speak. For a few moments, stars danced before my eyes. When the eye show finally disappeared, I addressed my savior.

"Thanks, dude. Appreciate that." I felt embarrassed and thankful at the same time. "That's never happened to me before."

"No problem. Glad I was here to help." He tilted his head toward the front desk. "If Stacy was the only one here, you'd have been a pancake."

Stacy was her name? I needed to get better about that.

He chuckled. "Happens to the best of us. I've been there." I doubted that, but I appreciated his attempt to make me feel better. "It's part of the initiation into hard-core training." How did he know I was new to hard-core training? "My name's Luci."

I held my hand out. "Jon, Jon Fixx."

Rather than shake my hand, he held out his right hand bundled up in a fist. Flustered, I quickly bundled my fingers together, not wanting to seem uncool as if I didn't know the correct way for guys to say hello, and knuckle-bumped the outstretched fist.

"Germs. The more hands you shake, the more germs you gather," he offered as an explanation. "The Japanese have it right with the bow."

I instantly liked him. He was on the positive side of six feet and lean, muscles everywhere, the long mane of dark hair settled comfortably on his shoulders. I had trouble matching the name Luci with the guy in front of me.

"Luci, is that a nickname, short for something?" Lucius? Lucifer? I raised my eyebrows in a question.

"Nope. Just Luci, 'i,' not 'y.'"

Oh, ok. "I haven't seen you in here before. Do you usually come in at this time?" I asked.

"No, I'm usually here early in the morning, but I had a project to finish for an afternoon class, so that took priority."

"You're at the college?" It wasn't a big school, so I was surprised I hadn't seen him walking on campus. He cut a striking figure, hard to miss.

"No, I'm in my first year at the Pennsylvania College of Art & Design downtown."

I nodded. I'd heard of the college, though I'd never been there. "I'm a sophomore over at F&M, but their gym sucks, so I come here."

"I've been there. You're right, not that great."

As we talked, I noticed something about his eyes. They were different from most guys, but I couldn't pin it down. Then I realized I thought his eyes were pretty, like a woman's. The thought made me immediately uncomfortable. Why am I thinking that?

Luci said, "When do you usually come in here to train?"

I was stuck staring at his eyes, delaying my response. Suddenly, I realized Luci was wearing eye makeup. My initial affinity receded a bit. Was he hitting on me?

"Whenever I can. I don't have a set schedule."

"You should change that. Muscles need to be shocked, so mixing it up is good, but you need to allow your muscles to prepare. When you train the same time every day, your body knows when to get ready, revved up so to speak. You'll get more out of your workout because your body is naturally warmed up and ready for it."

"I didn't know that. Thanks." I stood there a moment, not sure what to say. I was dying to ask this guy why he was wearing eye makeup, but I didn't want to offend him.

Luci broke the silence as he took a step backwards. "I've got to finish up. Nice to meet you, Jon."

"Good to meet you, too."

Luci walked away. I moved over to the abdominal machines and knocked out a few final sets of crunches to finish my training day. By the end of my session, I'd grown more curious about who this guy was. I figured he was gay but, hey, what the hell? As long as he didn't hit on me, I couldn't care less. Plus, I was lonely at college, and living in the self-imposed isolation I'd worked so hard to create for myself was taking its toll on my psyche. I grabbed my bag from the corner, still mulling over whether I should approach Luci. I definitely didn't want my interest to be misconstrued. But before I had turned around, the strap of my gym bag over my shoulder, I heard my name called out.

"Hey, Jon, I'm heading next door to grab a protein shake. Care to join me?" Luci yelled across the gym floor as he finished up a set of curls with 60-pound dumbbells. The guy was not screwing around.

I automatically nodded. I didn't care if he was gay or not. I'd cross that bridge when necessary. For now, I was craving a friendship more than anything, and I had a good feeling about this guy.

Sipping on his wheat grass and greens-filled smoothie at the juice bar next door, Luci provided some insight into how he ended up at the art college. I figured he was a couple of years older than me because he'd been at Penn for two years before dropping out and entering the Pennsylvania Art College. As I self-consciously drank my not-so-healthy chocolate-peanut butter protein shake, I asked him why he'd left Penn, not an easy school to get into. Very smart, wealthy people went there.

"I didn't enjoy the formal structure of higher education. That, coupled with a desire to sculpt and draw, pulled me out of school for a semester while I figured out what I wanted to do. Eventually, as a lark, I applied to the College of Art & Design and got in. Izzy, my girlfriend, is still at Penn. She's planning on going to med school. We trade off visiting each other. This weekend it's her turn, so she'll be rolling into town soon. You should meet her. I think you'll like her."

As I listened to Luci, I had trouble grasping who this guy was. He didn't fit into any easily identifiable stereotype. He had an effeminate name and he was definitely wearing eye makeup. The light in the juice bar was much better than in the gym, so there was no mistaking it. I'd been hit on by guys before, so I knew what it was like and how to handle it with a polite but firm "not my thing," but it didn't seem Luci was doing that. However, Izzy could go either way as a male or female name. I wondered if maybe Izzy was a transvestite. All these thoughts were swirling around in my head as Luci spoke, and I could not decide whether any of it mattered, or if I even cared. I was craving a friendship, and

I had liked Luci the moment we met. He stopped speaking, staring at me. Then, he asked, "Do you like the college?"

I shrugged, not sure how to answer or why he was even asking me that.

"Are you lonely there? Don't feel like you fit in?"

I looked away, embarrassed that he could read me that easily. When I turned back to Luci, he was staring at me, genuinely interested in my response.

"I don't have any friends on campus. I've never been a social animal, and I don't fit in over there. Kinda sucks."

"Well, you can't say that anymore. Now you have a friend here." Luci held his right hand out. I wasn't sure what he intended, thinking about the whole germ thing, but he held it out a little farther, indicating he wanted to shake my hand. I grabbed hold of his hand in a strong, firm handshake. "Nice to make your acquaintance, Jon Fixx. I think we're going to be great friends."

Remembering there was a rave party happening that night and there would be free alcohol, I blurted out, "You said your girlfriend gets into town soon?"

Luci nodded.

"Want to come with me to a party tonight? It's a rave. Should be fun."

Luci demurred, indicating the party scene was not his cup of tea. I promised him we could go, check it out, get some free drinks, and then go somewhere else if he and his girlfriend weren't comfortable. He considered it a moment, and then agreed.

That night, Izzy and Luci showed up at my on-campus apartment around nine o'clock. When I opened the door, I was struck simultaneously by two glaring facts before me. First, Izzy was a stunning six-foot redhead with alabaster skin and piercing green eyes. She reminded me of an elven princess from *Lord of the Rings*. She was thin, wearing a tight-fitting, long black skirt and snug, black sleeveless t-shirt, no bra, and thick three-inch platform heels, which placed her at least two inches taller than Luci. Her smile was dazzling. For a moment, I couldn't think. Luci saved me.

"Jon, this is my girlfriend Izzy. Izzy, this is Jon Fixx."

"Hi, Izzy," I said straight to her nipples.

"Nice to meet you, Jon."

She reached out to shake my hand when I realized I wasn't looking at her face, so I glanced up. She shook it with a bright, caring smile that washed down on me like warm rain. Maybe Luci was on to something with his eye makeup. When I invited them in, the second thing I noticed was Izzy wasn't the only person wearing a skirt. Luci had on a long, flowing flower-print, Grateful-Dead-groupie-type skirt with large, black Doc Marten boots underneath. Up top, he had a loose fitting blouse reminiscent of Shakespeare's time.

Noting my reaction to his outfit, Luci said, "If a person doesn't live his truth, he is a slave to the world around him."

I smiled. I liked Luci more every moment. We smoked a joint together and drank some cheap wine. I discovered that Izzy was waiting to hear from the top-notch medical schools she'd applied to. I told her if she were my doctor, I'd try to get sick all the time. Once we finished smoking, we headed to the party. We passed small groups of people on the street, mostly students out looking for fun. They gave Luci sideways glances, some openly leering at him. Luci took no notice. Our banter continued all the way to the party. Both were intelligent, good conversationalists, and for the first time since I'd entered college, I felt at home with some people my age.

The party itself was not far from campus, and given the chatter I'd heard about its being a retro rave party, the majority of partygoers would be bigger fans of the Cure than N'Sync, more geeks than athletes, so I didn't worry much about Luci's impact there. However, things changed quickly as soon as we arrived at our destination. I'd clearly been misinformed. I saw a group of several guys standing near the entrance. The party was being held in an old warehouse, and I'd been to one party there the year before. I recognized a couple of the faces from the college's weight room. A few of them had football jackets on. A couple more were wearing long-sleeved shirts emblazoned with the letters of their fraternity. Luci and Izzy didn't seem affected by what we were seeing. We walked past the group of guys near the front door. Loud bass was pounding through the walls. The warehouse was three stories high, and all the windows were blacked out, giving it a creepy, Halloween feel. A trim, young guy stood at the front door holding a clipboard. I hadn't expected this. Off to our left, a group of young women wearing short skirts and tight tops were smoking cigarettes. I heard giggles and glanced over my shoulder to catch the women staring at Luci. I looked toward Luci and Izzy, nervous about how they'd react. Their faces betrayed no emotion, both of them oblivious to the stir they were creating. I approached the gatekeeper, mustering as much friendliness as I could. He stared back. No emotion. Nothing.

"I'm on the list," I said.

"Name."

"Jon Fixx."

He found my name, indicating with a jerk of his head that I could enter. I motioned to Luci and Izzy to follow me and we stepped through the doorway. The gatekeeper held his clipboard out as Luci reached him, barring them from following me.

"Your name?"

I quickly turned back. "They're with me."

"So?"

"Well, since I'm on the list, can't they come in with me?"

The gatekeeper glanced over at the crew of jocks we'd passed coming in. A short, dark-haired guy standing in the center of the group shook his head with an almost imperceptible movement. He turned back to me.

"No."

I looked at Luci and Izzy, embarrassed and apologetic. Before I could say anything, Luci smiled. "Jon, it's okay. Let's go. We'll do something else."

But I wasn't about to walk away that easily. "C'mon, man. What could it hurt if you let us in? Isn't this an open party?" I asked the gatekeeper.

He got serious. "Does it look like an open party? It's a Kappa Sigma sponsored event and you have to be on the list to get in. Sorry."

This was news to me.

I felt Izzy's hand on my shoulder. Quietly, she said, "C'mon, Jon, it's okay."

Defeated and feeling a little humiliated because I'd invited my new friends to a party I couldn't get them into, coupled with a deeper feeling that I was a loser, I turned my back to the loud, thumping music. Luci and Izzy followed suit. We had not moved even two steps when a voice barreled toward us from the group of guys standing nearby.

"Anyways, we don't let faggots into our parties."

Luci froze mid step, as did I. My head snapped in their direction. Luci, however, stared straight ahead. The biggest guy in the four-man group took a step forward. He looked like a gorilla-sized linebacker with wide shoulders, a large head, pugnacious nose, and military-type crew cut. A dumb, vindictive grin formed on his face, the dim look of too much alcohol. The other three guys were smirking, waiting to see how this would play out. From the corner of my eye, I could see the guy at the door squirming. He seemed uncomfortable with what his fraternity brother had just said, but he wasn't about to call him out on it.

Having invited my new friends to this party, feeling the embarrassing sting of being turned away, only then to be coupled with bigoted ridicule aimed at them, I couldn't take any more. I was going to make this right if it was the last thing I did. I took a step toward the linebacker. Seeing my advance, he squared up with me, stepping forward with anticipation. Luci's hand shot out, grabbing my wrist with an iron grip, stopping my advance.

Izzy's voice broke the silence. She turned to the linebacker. "I have a lot of gay friends. They always tell me it takes one to know one."

I laughed out loud in spite of myself. The fraternity brothers froze. The linebacker looked like his head was about to explode.

Luci, always the pragmatist, as I would learn in time, gave a small tug to my arm and said, "Jon, let's go." He stepped away from the group, pulling me with him. Izzy followed suit. I was still seething that I didn't stand up for my friends.

"That's right, faggot. Get out of here, and take that trannie with you."

Luci slowly turned his head, his eyes focused on the linebacker. The guys standing around him appeared unsure how to react. Luci's withering stare wiped the smile off the linebacker's face. Even through the dimming effects of alcohol, the linebacker didn't miss the clear threat in Luci's eyes. They were filled with supreme self-confidence and an underlying pain, and they said, "I'll hurt you." Then, Luci just turned away and kissed Izzy on the cheek. Together they took another step, expecting me to follow. I turned back to the guys, the grins returning to their faces. The alcohol and marijuana in my system gave me a false sense of bravado and impaired my judgment. Before Luci could stop me, I quickstepped to the linebacker who was still squared off at me, his feet planted firmly on the ground. I stopped directly before him. His grin disappeared, replaced with a threatening scowl. "What are you gonna do, pipsqueak?"

I pointed at his friends. As his eyes followed the direction of my finger, I kicked him square in the groin. The crunching sound of my foot connecting with his crotch was sickening. He uttered a loud bellow, falling to the ground with a thud. The other brothers stared at him in shock, but only for a moment. I was as surprised as they were at how decisively the linebacker fell.

Then all hell broke loose.

Their recovery time was faster than mine. Three of them were on me instantly. A right cross caught me on the chin, and though I didn't see the assailant's face, I did see his shoes as I fell to the ground. But it wasn't his Nike sneaker that connected with my stomach. It was a work boot that knocked the wind out of me. I was dragged to my feet, tied up in a full nelson, my arms locked behind my back with my face sticking out ready to be pummeled. I struggled to get loose but was too weak from the kick.

I yelled out, "I'll never tell you! You can do whatever you want, but you'll never get it out of me! You'll have to kill me first!"

This gave them pause, confusing them for a moment. From the corner of my eye, I saw two more guys exiting the warehouse door to help their buddies. The guy with the clipboard stood frozen. Amid all the tumult, I heard Luci say above the din, "Let him go."

The guy holding me in the full nelson turned me in Luci's direction. The other guys, now five in total—six to be accurate, the linebacker still laid out—turned as well. From my vantage point, even though Luci was tall, it did seem a little funny that a guy wearing a skirt and a fluffy blouse was warning these guys off.

The new blond leader lunged at Luci with a right cross. Luci swayed easily to the left as the attacker fell off balance, landing on the ground face first. Two more fraternity brothers rushed in from behind me. My captor was nice enough to continue facing in their direction so I could watch the fight unfold. Luci blocked a punch coming from the right. At the same time, his left foot sent the other attacker into the air, knocking him on the grass ten feet back. The attacker curled up into the fetal position, holding his midsection. To his right, Luci followed the blocked punch with a rabbit shot to the other attacker's face, finishing with a cross that laid him out on the ground. Luci turned to deal with the first assailant who'd come after him, but the guy was now standing beside the gatekeeper, unsure how to proceed.

Luci turned back to my captor, "Let him go." Suddenly, my arms were free. I quickly turned to the guy who'd been holding me captive. He backed up in a hurry, already five paces away from me. I looked at Luci in amazement, crossing the distance between us quickly to put him between our attackers and me. Eye makeup and skirts and a girl's name masked Luci's masculinity. This guy was like Bruce Lee.

The fraternity brothers were in varied positions of defeat. The linebacker who'd started it all was on his knees staring at Luci, though still unable, or unwilling, to stand up. Another lay on the ground curled up in pain. The fraternity brothers who remained standing had fearful, confused looks on their faces. All eyes were on Luci, their sense of reality thrown into turmoil. The look on Izzy's face was unreadable. I couldn't tell if she was angry with me for starting the whole debacle, or if she was angry with the fraternity brothers for acting like such ignorant creatures. Or maybe she was proud of Luci for taking care of business.

Luci took a step toward the guy laid out on the ground. The rest of the guys warily moved back. He leaned over and picked the guy up from the ground, helping him to the door frame and leaning him upright. Then Luci turned away, showing them he was fearless, and walked over to Izzy and me. He stopped a few steps before us and turned around. "Don't mess with something you don't understand. The trouble you get into will be inversely proportional to your lack of wisdom."

Wordlessly, we turned our backs on the warehouse and walked the way we'd come. Izzy placed her hand on the back of Luci's neck, caressing him affectionately. We walked along silently, lost in our own thoughts. I later discovered that Luci had been studying kung fu since he was a young boy and had, at the time I met him, already earned the title of master.

"Jon, you need to remember something. There will always be people out there who don't like you. And they don't know why. You have to let them discover why on their own. You can't shove it down their throats."

I was being reproved, though far more gently than how the bigoted ignoramuses had been. I glanced over at Luci sheepishly and apologized. "Thanks for saving my ass."

Always generous, Luci said, "I didn't save your ass. You could have handled those guys. It just might have taken longer."

Izzy turned her beautiful, green elven eyes on me. "Thanks for standing up for us." She leaned over and kissed my cheek.

I remember feeling one of the proudest moments in my life after hearing those words. I had new friends, and I'd shown them that they could count on me. We strolled through town back to my place. I have always remembered that night clearly. The moon was hanging low in the sky, guiding us home. As we walked, we lit another joint and talked about life and our dreams, about our favorite music and favorite books, and what we loved to do when we didn't have anything to do.

Over the next many years, Luci took me on as his student and taught me his martial arts. An expert I would never be, but over time, I learned to hold my own. Throughout college and after, whenever something really good or really bad happened, Luci was my go-to guy, Izzy even more so, depending on the topic. My first two years in Los Angeles were probably my loneliest years there. I was busy with work, having no trouble taking my Love Story business to the next level, but without Luci and Izzy, I felt like a piece of my life was missing. The happiest day in my adult life was when Luci called and told me that Izzy had decided to do her residency at Children's Hospital Los Angeles.

But I'm getting ahead of myself. I need to tell you about Jennifer too. In an ironic, perverted twist of logic, you could say Jennifer put me on my professional path as the purveyor of Love Stories.

JENNIFER BREAKER

College was expensive, and I was on a full academic scholarship, one key reason I never felt like I fit in. I didn't have the money most of my fellow students had, or more accurately, their families had. I entered the school feeling like an outsider, and this feeling grew with each passing semester. My disaffection with the whole institution and its inhabitants—both students and professors—mounted each year, while at the same time my friendship with Luci grew. I spent more and more time off-campus, an unusual habit for a student attending a school with such a small, insular population. But in the fall semester of my junior year, I met Jennifer Breaker in an upper-level anthropology course, which was my major and an area of study for which I was a shoo-in to receive departmental honors when I graduated. She clearly had a chip on her shoulder about life in general and her parents specifically. She did her best not to fit in, and dating me worked perfectly. I was madly in love with her. She was upper middle class, on partial scholarship, smart, and with an off-center attractiveness. There is no need here to describe the ups and downs of our relationship, but it is important to point out that it lasted exactly one year, literally. On our first anniversary, when all I could think about was what we'd be doing at the end of the evening, Jennifer was in a completely different frame of mind, and body. I thought things were going great. She didn't. Apparently, a recurring pattern in my life.

On that fateful night, Jennifer told me she was having personal problems, she needed some space. I couldn't understand what personal issues she was talking about because

I knew all about her personal life. We were in college, we spent almost all our time together, and we had even decided to take another anthropology course together. But she said she needed more space than she could find within the bounds of a relationship.

"It's not you, Jon. It's me," she said with a sad frown and a tear in her eye.

So on the night of our anniversary, I became a blubbering idiot, saying all kinds of overly dramatic things like, "God, I love you so much, I don't know what I'll do without you," and "I've never held someone's hand the way I've held yours," and "You are the most special person I've ever been with, I'll be lost without you." But the capper, said in my attempt to be a bigger man than I truly was, dribbled out of my mouth. "If this is what you want and what you need for your own personhood, then I want this too because I want what you want. I want what's best for you."

At the time, I meant every word I said. At least I wanted to believe I did. I knew that last bit was a load of crap, but it sounded good. I was trying a weak attempt at reverse psychology, which failed miserably. What I really wanted was for her to shut up, stop saying the things she was saying, and have sex with me. Instead, she said, "Jon, are you okay with this? I know you're super sensitive and tend to blow everything out of proportion."

That one hit so close to home I got defensive, but I knew I couldn't show it. I had to be careful. I looked into her eyes with all the sincerity I could muster and said, "I truly want whatever is going to make you happy." A look of guilt and relief crossed Jennifer's face, and then it was gone, covered with sadness. Suddenly, I wondered if there was more to this than she was admitting. Was there somebody else? So I asked.

"Jon, c'mon. Look at me. I love you. This doesn't have to do with anybody else. I just need space. I have a lot going on personally in my head." What was she talking about?

This was the first I'd heard about stuff going on in her head. "Well, you know, with my parents and everything." Her parents had been divorced five years. "And I just feel like I can't give you what you need right now." I could not understand what she was talking about. Mostly what I needed was sex. It wasn't that complicated.

But Jennifer was intractable, and nothing I said could change her mind, so we broke up. On our anniversary. I spent the rest of the week going to classes like a zombie. On Friday, we shared Anthropology Theory class with Professor Benedict, one of the few professors I actually admired. I got to class late and sat in the front row. She gave me a sympathetic, pained smile from the second row as I walked into the room. My return smile was a failed imitation.

Dr. Benedict patted me on the back as I passed him on my way to my seat. "How you doing, Fixx?"

I nodded to him. I'd taken other classes with Benedict, liking him so much that I picked him to be my advisor. Benedict was in his early thirties, very bright—and cocky—but an atypical professor, nonetheless. He was handsome, charming, and had a loose teaching style. Many of the coeds had crushes on him. I'd heard stories but I didn't much care, because his classes were some of my favorite. I listened to Dr. Benedict's lecture and heard nothing he said. I could feel Jennifer's presence on my skin. The minutes ticked interminably by on the clock hanging high up in the front of the room. Class was ninety minutes long, and I felt every one of them. Inadvertently, I would glance over my shoulder at Jennifer, who seemed completely rapt with Benedict's lecture on the development of anthropological theory in the early twentieth century, fully engaged, taking notes, intently listening. I was overcome with the urge to scream at the students sitting there, at Jennifer, at Benedict. They all looked so smug and content hiding in this little cocoon of costly higher education.

"Jon, you have a question?" Dr. Benedict was staring at

me. He'd stopped talking. The rest of the class had their eyes on me as well. I realized I was standing up. My urge to scream had propelled me out of my seat. "Uh, no, no. Just stretching. Sorry, Dr. Benedict."

I sat down, embarrassed, frustrated, overwhelmed. I ducked low in my seat, staring straight ahead, keeping my focus on the front blackboard as best I could and off the woman one row back and four seats over who was creating an emotional storm inside me. I didn't really know how to behave. Jennifer and I were no longer together, no longer a couple, but we were sitting twenty feet apart in a classroom we would share for the rest of the semester—eight more weeks! The thought of it made me sick to my stomach.

Then I heard a rustling behind me. The students were packing away their notes and books, getting ready to move on. I looked up at the clock: 10:20 a.m. Class was over. Benedict wrapped up his lecture, leaving us with a question for the next class. Students headed out the door. I didn't move. If I left first and didn't say goodbye to Jennifer, then I'd feel like the bad guy, but if I waited for her to leave and she left without saying goodbye, I'd feel like crap. So I did nothing. I left the decision in Jennifer's lap.

"Jon."

I looked up from my backpack. She was standing beside me, her voice dripping with sympathy. What did that mean? That she felt sorry for me? That she wasn't having any trouble with this?

"Hi."

"How are you doing?"

"Fine."

A moment of uncomfortable silence followed. The final few students filed out of the classroom. Dr. Benedict was just finishing packing up his briefcase. He looked up at me from the front of the room.

"Jon, we still on for tomorrow to discuss your thesis?"

"Yes."

"Great. Look forward to it. Bye, Jen."

Jennifer smiled and waved to him. "Bye, Professor Benedict," she tittered, the sympathetic tone gone completely for a moment. Then she turned back to me, the brief smile replaced with a sad frown. "I just wanted to say 'hi.' Hi."

"Okay."

"I'm sorry about all this, Jon."

I nodded, looking out the window for fear my emotions might take over and I would either start to cry or grab her by the neck and throttle her right there in the classroom. I stared at the East Coast autumn, trees with leaves of deep reds and light purples and soft greens visible beyond the window frame.

"Well, I'm going to go now. I have to get to my next class."

I nodded without looking at her. She turned her back to me, walking toward the door, but hesitated after three steps and looked back over her shoulder. I gazed out the window. She sighed and turned away from me. As she reached the doorway, the urge to speak to her was so strong, I couldn't stop myself.

"Jennifer."

She stopped in the doorway and turned to me. "Yes?"

"Are you okay?"

She smiled sadly. "I'm okay."

The smile made my heart skip. "Good. Just wanted to make sure you're okay." I nodded uncomfortably, indicating I didn't have much else to say. Jennifer stood silently in the doorframe for another moment. I shrugged my shoulders, trying to get comfortable with my body, still unclear how to act. Jennifer realized I had nothing more to add, so without another word between us, she left.

"Bye, Jennifer," I muttered.

I remained in my chair at the front of the lecture hall. I stared at the large oak tree outside the window, the first leaves of winter dropping before my eyes to the ground. Lost in my reverie, I missed the students entering for the next class, and before I knew it, I was listening to a lecture on the history of modern dance in the United States with the focus that day on Twyla Tharp. Unwilling to bring attention to myself, I sat through the class, feigning note taking. The only fact I took from the class was that Twyla Tharp, a dancer and choreographer, had written and published two books, one her autobiography, the other a guide on living the creative life. "If Twyla Tharp can get published," I muttered, "so can I." By that point, I'd been working on my first novel since the summer before entering college, figuring I should be able to finish it once all this college work was out of the way. I was hoping to be like Brett Easton Ellis, but at the rate I was going, it looked like I was going to be the next Jon Nobody.

When class ended, I unobtrusively made my escape and wandered off campus down the small city street to my apartment. As a senior, I had the luxury of being able to live off-campus and I much preferred it. I lived in a one-bedroom conversion above a garage that I'd found for cheap in the back of a four-unit apartment building. It was far less than I would have paid for campus housing, and the location was private, so it worked for me. The garage backed up to a junior high school parking lot cum playground. My day from 8:10 a.m. to 3:10 p.m. was defined by the bell system of the junior high's class schedule.

Arriving at the front of the fourplex, I took a look up and down the street. An occasional car passed in both directions. I looked at my watch. It was almost noon. Other students filtered down the street, ostensibly heading for their domiciles and lunch. I looked up at the sky, blue as could be, the temperature moderate, somewhere in the high sixties, a beautiful East Coast October day, but I felt empty and lost. I crossed the backyard and climbed the stairs to my small apartment. Once inside, I grabbed a beer from the fridge, dropped on the couch, and started drinking, doing my best to think about nothing.

But Jennifer's face kept crossing my mental screen no matter how hard I tried not to think about her. At some point, I passed out, many beers already down my throat. I woke with a start. I must have been asleep for hours, because it was almost dark outside. My reality quickly jumped to the foreground of my thoughts as I stared at the ceiling, Jennifer's face etched across the smooth surface. Hoping to distract myself, even though I could tell I was still inebriated, I grabbed a rolled joint from the kitchen drawer where I stashed them, and lit up. I tried to relax as the joint slowly burned away, but it was all to no avail. My head began to spin.

What was she doing at that very moment? We often spent Friday nights at her apartment, watching movies. Like me, she didn't like going to parties; she felt they were juvenile. Like me, she was not a big fan of the college drink fests. Her schoolwork came first and everything else came second. Including me now, I guess. Overcome with a wave of loneliness, I moved over to my bed, staring at the ceiling as the fullness of the evening darkness filled my room. Luci was visiting Izzy in Philly, so I couldn't call him for emotional support. My digital clock across the room read 8:42 p.m. I knew there was only one salve for my loneliness. Jennifer.

In short order, I logically convinced myself that Jennifer missed me, that even if she wanted to remain broken up she'd be happy to see me. She was probably at home right now mooning around in her room just like I was. Once the idea entered my mind, the decision to go was a *fait accompli.* It would have taken gargantuan self-discipline on my part to take a contrary action. I was craving a fix, and Jennifer's face was both the drug and the antidote. With purpose, I threw my jacket over my shoulders and headed out the door. I crossed the yard to the alley. I could hear an amalgam of male and female voices coming from one of the apartments above, music underlying the chatter. I walked down the alley at a brisk pace, turning the corner at the front of the house, heading east. There was a slight chill in the air. I shuddered, the cold seeping under my skin, my drunken high not keeping me as warm as I expected. I was shivering and moving a little faster with a slight sway to my stride. Jennifer lived six blocks down and four blocks over, ten minutes at best. I covered the first few blocks at a fast clip, slowing down as I got closer, suddenly reconsidering my approach. What if she didn't want to see me? What if she told me she wanted to date other people? What if. . . ? I came within a block of her apartment duplex.

I kicked the negative thoughts out of my head. Of course she'd be glad to see me. She might be mad at first, but that would change once we started talking. I took a deep breath and walked the length of the last block, passing the duplex and fourplex apartments lining the street. I stopped in front of the light blue, East Coast traditional that was Jennifer's. She lived in the four-bedroom unit on the first floor with three roommates. The second story was an identical unit, also full of students. The house was dark and the lights out. Obviously no one was there.

Jennifer was not home.

Doubt crept into my mind. I walked around to the side walkway between the houses and crossed down the middle. Over the last year, I had developed a habit of climbing into Jennifer's bedroom through her window so I wouldn't disturb her roommates' rabid reality television viewing. They were usually sprawled out in the communal living room, watching TV, and I had to cross in front of them to get to Jennifer's room. Over time, I stopped using the front door altogether. Jennifer left the window unlocked, so I never had trouble getting in.

As I reached her window, my heart rate increased. I stepped off the path onto the large brick I'd placed there and reached up to the windowsill. I laid my hands on the bottom of the window, gripped, and pulled up. The window slid easily. I smiled, pleased with myself. I took this as a sign that Jennifer wanted me to do this. She'd intentionally left the window unlocked, hoping I'd come over.

Quietly, I slipped inside and closed the window behind. I looked around her room. It looked exactly as it had when I'd last been there less than a week before. The vanity mirror and chair in the corner, the television on top of her tall dresser in the other corner, pink accents throughout, and a large four poster with a white bedspread and a bunch of extra-large pillows at the head of the bed. I stood still, taking it all in. I could smell the soft citrusy scent of Jennifer's lotion. I closed the window and crossed over to the bed, taking a seat. I reached down and untied my shoelaces, setting my shoes on the floor beside the bed. I laid my head back on the pillows and tried to get comfortable. But I couldn't do it. I felt uneasy, like an intruder. What if she came home and completely rejected me? But how was that possible? How could she do that, considering everything we had shared over the last year? Could a few days apart wipe away those feelings? I decided it wasn't possible. I settled back in the pillows, only slightly satisfied with my thoughts, the uneasy feelings lingering. But as the minutes ticked by, my muscles relaxed and I was seduced by the soft feel of the bedspread coupled with the effects of the alcohol and marijuana in my body. I fell into an easy stupor. I yawned, glancing at the clock: 9:10 p.m. I turned my eyes back to the ceiling, and before I knew it, I was asleep.

I woke to voices. My head was fuzzy. At first I couldn't remember where I was. I turned to the clock: 10:11. Suddenly my head cleared and I remembered what I was doing, realizing immediately something was wrong. The voices were getting closer, coming down the hallway toward Jennifer's room. I could discern Jennifer's voice, and I realized that the voice answering her was male. They were almost at the door. I panicked, grabbing my shoes and slipping them on without tying the laces. I stood up, looking across the room at the window. Jennifer was at the door. I heard her pull her key out. She always locked it because she didn't like her roommates having access. The key was in the lock. I calculated the time it would take to cross the room, open the window, and climb out. I'd never make it. The key rattling in the lock sounded like a bomb going off in my ears. Frantically, my eyes jumped around the room searching for an escape, suddenly landing on the closet door. As quietly as I could, I slithered across the room, grabbed the closet door handle, opened it and slid inside. I heard the hallway door opening as I pulled the door shut. I held my breath, wondering if Jennifer had seen the door or heard me moving about. I slid as far back into the closet away from the door as I could. I stood tense, waiting to be discovered. But that didn't happen. I relaxed a little, only then overcome with a wave of immense jealousy. It was past 10:00 p.m. on a Friday night and she had a guy in her room. A date! I'm at home getting drunk and high to assuage myself, and she's out getting it on with someone else. Their voices pounded on my ears through the closet door, the male voice familiar to me. He spoke with the intelligent tone of an older man, not the swallowed vocabulary and slang of a student. "Are you sure your roommates will not be home soon?"

"Allan, I'm sure. They're at an all-night Kappa Sigma party. I won't see them again until tomorrow. We're completely alone. Anyways, I asked them for some privacy."

What?

"You did?" The male voice seemed alarmed. "I hope you didn't tell them why."

"No, silly. Geez, you're such a worrier. Just relax."

"We have to be careful, you understand."

I knew the voice but couldn't place it.

Jennifer giggled. "Don't worry, Professor, you're secret's safe with me."

It clicked. Dr. Benedict! Son of a bitch! There was silence, then the rustling of clothing. I took a step forward. There was no way I was going to allow this to go on any further. I pushed the clothing out of my way, about to grab the door handle when Dr. Benedict interrupted their festivities.

"Did you hear something? Are you sure no one's home?"

There was a pause.

"Allan, you're so jumpy. Stop worrying, there's nobody here."

I considered bursting out of the closet and scaring the hell out of both of them and tell my lying, backstabbing advisor that I knew his dirty little secret and was going to make sure the entire world knew it as well. But in the next instant, I considered the bigger picture, and that's where my best choice of action became fuzzy. I would have to explain what I was doing in the closet because, technically, I was breaking and entering. In addition, the thought of what the student population would think of my actions gave me pause. There would be no end to their contempt. I would not be able to hold my head up again any time I walked on campus. "There goes the guy who hid in his ex-girlfriend's closet." I could hear them laughing.

So my fear of being considered less than a man by the general population kept me hiding in my ex-girlfriend's closet, listening to her and my college advisor become intimate. The sounds of sexual excitement emanated through the closet door. Jennifer exhaled passionately. I knew that noise. She made it whenever I kissed the back of her neck. It had taken me six months to discover that little trick. This guy had it in one night? Unless . . . how long had this been going on? There was a soft thud. They were on the bed. I didn't feel my fists clenching nor did I realize my fingernails were biting into my palm so hard they drew blood. Sounds of them rolling around on the bed filled the closet with a claustrophobic air. I was close to hyperventilating. I was not sure how much more of this I could take. The sound of shoes dropping onto the wood floor followed. I heard zippers unzipping, more rustling. I felt shame and anger, jealousy and despair, so many conflicting emotions flowing through me all at once. I wanted out of that closet. Suddenly, the most disturbing sound filled the room. Jennifer gave a high-pitched squeal, part exhalation, part excitement. Up until now, whenever I heard it, I knew my own release was not far behind. But it was so strange, foreign, to hear the noise from afar, knowing it was another man's action doing the work. A dissonant feeling of excitement joined the many other feelings coursing through my body.

I dropped to the floor, pulled my knees to my chest and sat back against the wall, resigned to the fact this was real and I would have to endure the whole thing. I looked at my watch. It read 10:36. I'd been in the closet for twenty-five minutes. Jennifer had always been loud. I always wanted to believe it was because of what I did for her. Sitting in the closet, I learned I was wrong. Jennifer's moans filled the room, that and the creaking of the bed. Every so often, Dr. Benedict would grunt. He sounded stupid. I heard feet on the floor. The creaking of the bed ceased. The groaning continued. That meant they were on their feet. Their positions flashed across my brain. This was more than I could take.

"Oh, right there. Ohhhhhh."

A wave of numbness washed over me. I felt myself splitting off, moving up to the top corner of the closet, and watching myself listen to the activities happening beyond my hiding spot. Suddenly there was a thud and the bed started creaking again.

"Don't stop! Don't stop!" That was Jennifer's pre-orgasm declaration. She didn't say that to me all the time, only when she was unbearably excited. Until that moment sitting in that closet listening to Jennifer's moans of ecstasy, I foolishly believed she and I shared a unique sexual DNA coupling. But it appeared that Benedict and I had the same DNA. Jennifer's moans subsided.

My mind instantly refocused on my predicament. I still needed to get the hell out of the closet without discovery, a quandary I was not sure how to solve. Would they leave? Fall asleep? But wait—what was that noise? They weren't done. It appeared Benedict had not finished his end of things. Jennifer's moans resumed, but with more intensity, taking on an insistent eagerness in tone I'd never heard before, a greedy call for more.

"Oh my God, Allan, you're incredible!"

Propelled by her declarations, the thumping and slapping of flesh increased with frequency and sound. I tried to rid my head of the images the sounds were creating, but visions of Jennifer and Benedict in coitus filled my vision. I looked at my watch: 10:59. The sex continued. I took a deep breath and exhaled slowly. I rested my head against the back of the closet settling in for the long haul. Benedict's grunting turned into extensive groans. He and Jennifer had found a rhythm, his groaning and her moaning overlapping. Now 11:15. He was adding insult to injury. Forty-five minutes was my record with Jennifer. I shifted in my crouched position. I was beginning to feel cramps.

The dress hanging above me brushed my head. I looked up. In the semi-light, I realized it was the very same dress, a pink flower print with spaghetti straps that suggestively hung just above the knees, that Jennifer had been wearing when I met her the year before. My memory was interrupted by screams from the bedroom. Jennifer was on the point of a huge climax—her second, something I'd only been able to accomplish once—making noise on a measure beyond any scope I'd ever caused, all accompanied by loud grunting from Benedict.

"Oh my God! Oh my God! Oh oh oh oh! Allan! Again! Again!"

And like an orchestra hitting the final note in one large crescendo, my ex-girlfriend and my thesis advisor climaxed in one final coupled scream. Then silence. Well, I'd come over looking for some kind of answer as to why Jennifer wanted so much space and I found it. Now all I wanted to do was get out of there as quickly as possible. I hoped they would leave and I could exit quietly, undiscovered.

"That was incredible," Jennifer sighed.

The torture continued.

"I agree." A pause. "So what's going on with you and Jon Fixx?"

I sat up ramrod straight.

"Oh, Allan, you are so crass. Do we have to talk about my ex-boyfriend right after we do it? Geez. I broke up with him. He's really sweet. Just too intense for me. And there was you." For the first time that night, I felt tears burning my eyes. I realized that up to this point I'd been thinking of everything I'd heard as just sex. But it was more than that. Jennifer was over me.

"Are you sure your roommates aren't coming home?"

"I'm sure."

There was silence. Moments later, the sounds of quiet snoring crossed my closet threshold. Benedict had fallen asleep. I checked my watch: 11:45. I waited. The snoring continued, and I heard no movement or rustling. I stood as quietly as possible and slowly pushed my way through the clothes to the front of the closet. Silently, I placed my hand on the doorknob. As softly as I could manage, I turned the knob and guided the door open, peeking out. Benedict was sprawled on his stomach, his left leg crooked, his right arm hanging over the side of the bed. The guy sure knew how to make himself comfortable. Jennifer lay on her back, her eyes closed, her breathing regular. Carefully, I inched the door open and stepped into the room, trying to keep my eyes on the path to the window. As I crossed in front of the bed, my eyes fell on Jennifer's painted toes peeking out from beneath the loose sheet. I followed the outline of her legs up over her stomach across her breasts to her face. She lay there, looking innocent in repose. Her eyelids fluttered, then opened. Her face registered silent shock. She inhaled. I imagined a scream would follow. I raised my right index finger to my lips instructing her to stay silent. We locked eyes for a moment. She sat up slightly on her elbows. I kept my finger at my lips. Benedict stirred in his sleep, then settled back into the bed. I stared at her for a moment longer, then turned away, quickly crossed the room, and opened the window. Without looking back, I climbed out and left.

That night I went back to my apartment, packed up all my belongings and moved out the next morning. I found a generic apartment in a working class part of town, void of college students, rent paid by the hard-earned wages of those living there, not by bourgeois parents. The neighborhood had an element of roughness. I formally dropped out of college the following Monday. I never spoke to Jennifer again. Prior to the end of the term, with the use of my computer and the local library, I finished the thesis I'd started with Benedict, probably the best research paper I'd ever written in my college career. I sent it to him in an anonymous envelope with no return address. I tacked a note on the front of it that said, "God knows your sins and so do I. Revenge belongs to the righteous." At the time, it sounded powerful. A few years later, Benedict was driving home from a night out with another young female professor—I guessed he'd decided it wasn't wise to keep tapping the undergraduate population—and their car was struck by a drunk driver running a red light. Both professors were killed instantly. By that point, I held no ill will for Benedict, too much time had passed, and I felt sadness for his family, wherever they were. A few days after the accident, I received a phone call from Jennifer, the only time she tried to contact me before or since. To this day, I don't know what his death signified for her, or why it motivated her to call me, but I didn't care. Unlike my feelings for Benedict, Jennifer I had not forgiven. I didn't call her back.

In the long run, though, Jennifer's betrayal was a boon of sorts. I have no idea where I would be if I'd finished college, graduated, then tried to figure the next step in my life. My choices may have ended up generic and mundane, maybe graduate school, or a nine-to-five. As it was, Jennifer's action forced me to think outside the box, to push my creative envelope to find out what I was made of, which, with the help of a little serendipity, led me to my current profession. It all began with the first job I scored after leaving college.

MY FIRST LOVE STORY: ZACHARY & NICOLLETE DICKERSON

When I dropped out, I had to get a job immediately. I'd been working on campus as part of my scholarship, but my job was inextricably linked with my attendance at school: no more school, no more job. As soon as I had my living situation handled, I hustled for a few days looking for a waitering position, finally landing one as a server at The Bordello, a local high-end joint serving an eclectic mix of Cajun Americana. I spent my days training with Luci and writing, working on my interminable novel, as well as short stories I sent to *The New Yorker, The Village Voice,* the newly formed *n+1,* and many other internet and print media sources, all to no avail. Bret Easton Ellis I was not.

While honing my writing skills during the day, I spent my nights serving food and learning about people. I enjoyed the job because it provided me ample opportunity to study human behavior. I learned what good waiters do—become invisible. The less aware the clientele are of your presence, the better your tip. Don't make mistakes in the order, keep the drinks filled without asking, deliver the food on time, get the table cleared immediately after the food has been ingested, and talk only when the clientele ask you a direct question. I learned how to fade into the background. As fate would have it, though, Nicollete Dickerson, the daughter of the owners, took a platonic sort of liking to me. One night, while I was sitting out back behind the restaurant on my break and writing in my notebook, she stepped up to me after lighting a cigarette and pulled the book out of my hands with that ubiquitous look of charming entitlement wealthy American children carry throughout their lives. After a few minutes of reading my words, she said she liked my style and wanted to know if I had more. So I gave her my manuscript, at least what I had up to that point, and she liked that too, which made me like her all the more. Just the fact that she was willing to read my writing was enough for me.

Over the next couple of weeks, over her cigarette breaks behind the restaurant, Nicollete and I became good friends, sharing stories of our past, our families, and our love life. My Jennifer-tale garnered a great deal of sympathy, though I left out the finale, unable at that time to talk about it. Nicollete was in the throes of preparing for her wedding, which was coming up in just shy of three months. Most of our conversations centered on the planning of the wedding: the choices she had to make about colors and designs and, of course, the wedding dinner reception.

One night, I asked her how she'd met her fiancé, Zachary. I was surprised to learn that she'd met him while backpacking in Ireland. It had been a whirlwind fling that lasted only a week. Zachary had just finished college and taken a job as an elementary school teacher, but he was also a semipro rock climber and hardcore outdoorsman. On the weekends, he was a guide for tourists on nature hikes and entry-level rock climbing missions. Nicollete said she fell in love the first day of her trip as she watched Zachary scramble up the side of a sheer cliff to show his charges how it should be done. The next week, they spent every waking and sleeping moment together, right up to the second she disappeared inside the hull of a 747 headed back to the States. But one month after Nicollete got back, Zachary showed up on her doorstep, holding a bouquet of roses and a ring.

I made an offhanded comment that their story would make a great movie romance. Nicollete turned to me and asked, "Will you write it?"

"Write what?"

"Our love story. Will you write it? Zachary has gone back and forth between here and Ireland while we work out his green card situation, and many of my extended family and even some of my friends haven't had a chance to get to know him. This would be a great way for everyone to see why I fell in love with him."

At first, I dismissed the idea out of hand, saying I had neither the ability nor the wherewithal to do something like that. But Nicollete was adamant. She grabbed my hands, pleading with me. "Oh, Jon, c'mon. Of course you could do it. You're a great writer. Zachary and I will tell you everything, and all you have to do is take notes and then write it up in a story."

I shook my head, indicating I didn't think I could do it. But once Nicollete had the idea, she would not take no for an answer, and she quickly began to run down all the reasons I could benefit. She'd talk to her father to make sure I was properly compensated. It would be a way to get a lot of people to read my writing. At least all her wedding guests would. Wasn't that the goal of a writer in the first place? She had a lot of cute friends, and she'd make sure I met every single one of them at the wedding and be introduced as the guy who wrote the beautiful love story. Finally, I conceded, agreeing to think about it. For a week, Nicollete hounded me. Then her father called me into his office before the dinner shift, handing me a check for more than I made in two months and telling me it was a deposit if I would do what Nicollete was asking. That was my first lesson about fathers who want to please their daughters and will do whatever it takes. The push coming from the Dickerson clan was too great and I finally succumbed, agreeing to fulfill Nicollete's wishes. Mr. Dickerson agreed to cover all costs, on top of paying me for my services, basically setting the blueprint for my future business model.

So, after almost three months, many interviews with family and friends—not part of the initial plan but something I realized was necessary after interviewing Nicollete and Zachary to get third-party perspectives—and one trip to Ireland, I found myself at their wedding with lace-bound copies of "The Whirlwind Romance of Nicollete and Zach" floating around. Nicollete's friends were all tittering when they found the novella placed at every dinner setting. On the cover was a reproduction of Nicollete and Zach cuddling together at the top of an Allegheny peak while on a hike. The pure novelty of it struck such a chord, especially with Nicollete's friends, that almost overnight I was able to quit my job as a waiter and start writing full time. It wasn't exactly the writing I had envisioned, but I had nothing to complain about. Without an argument, I accepted job offers from two of Nicollete's friends who were recently engaged, and thus went through my first major adulthood change. I learned very quickly—first amazed, then dismayed, and finally just begrudgingly thankful because this fact kept me employed—people not only love to talk about themselves but truly believe that other people will find what they have to say important. All of this because one night, smoking a cigarette behind her parent's restaurant, Nicollete Dickerson had the brilliant, unique, narcissistic idea of seeing her love story in print. And she wanted me to write it.

But never once, from the moment Nicollete made the fateful suggestion that night many years back, did I think I'd find myself one day flying to New York to interview the daughter of a Mafia don from the Five Families of New York, the most powerful wing of the United States organized crime syndicate known as La Cosa Nostra. Back in early September, on that first flight to New York, I knew I was in over my head. But just how much, I had not the slightest clue. I was about to find out.

5
Early September
New York – 1st Trip

The plane was riding high in the sky somewhere over eastern Pennsylvania with about an hour to go. I stared out the window at the white clouds below. I could see squares of green and tan on the ground, indicating the trade-off between pasture and farming. With less than twenty-four hours to prepare for my departure, I had to scramble to make sure I didn't forget anything. Sara came home so late and tired she passed out in bed before I could explain to her why I had to leave on such short notice. Anxiety kept me awake most of the night, but at some point I fell into a restless sleep and dreamed Sara and I were on our honeymoon in Hawaii, both so happy that I woke with a start when it ended, disappointed and troubled by the divergence between my dream world and our reality.

My thoughts were interrupted by the pilot's voice announcing our descent into JFK International airport. My focus shifted from Sara to my task ahead. I was more worried about the Vespucci clan than I wanted to admit. With Luci gone to China for the month, I couldn't use him as my sounding board, or for protection.

After leaving Vespucci at the diner, I'd gone straight home to find out exactly what I was getting into. Nothing I read put me at ease. Throughout the 1980s and '90s, the FBI and the federal government had done a good job of neutralizing the Italian Mafia's power base in the United States with the use of the customized RICO—short for Racketeer Influenced and Corrupt Organization—laws, created in the early 1970s for the specific purpose of prosecuting known Mafia members. By the beginning of the twenty-first century, the Mafia seemed to be limping along, barely. But then, a few years back, there was a shift. The New York power base quietly re-emerged. New blood had found its way in and up, slowly taking over the straggling ties of the infamous Five Families and reconnecting them to gain influence, power, and finances. The first obvious signs of resurgence, according to the sources I was reading, were the occasional Italian guys with names like Jimmy "the Tank" Romano, Mikey "the Grill" Ciotola, and Nick "Knuckles" Tatone showing up with bullets in the backs of their heads, execution style, on the side of the road, in an alley trashcan, at a highway rest stop. At the same time, it appeared the FBI was having newfound difficulty infiltrating the newly organized Five Families of New York. It seemed the organization as a whole had been baptized anew with the generations-old code of omertà—silence or death.

From time immemorial through the 1960s, it was unheard of for a made man, a member of the Mafia, to rat out his own. But as the FBI began infiltrating the mob using cutting edge technology in conjunction with good old-fashioned street smarts, the sacred code of omertà began to crumble as the RICO-inspired lengthy sentences were handed down. After Joseph Pistone, aka Donnie Brasco—the FBI agent who infiltrated the highest echelon of the Bonanno wing of the Five Families—helped bring that borgata to its knees, the code of silence or death lost its ironclad hold. Over the next two decades, the FBI slowly took apart each Family, all with the begrudging assistance of high-level Mafia players who decided losing their honor and turning government witness was less painful than spending the rest of their lives in prison. But as the first decade of the millennium wound down, the FBI hit a wall.

The reporter named Jim Mosconi was the only member of the intelligentsia I could find who seemed to have a good handle on the current situation of the Mob hierarchy. He was employed by the *New York Post,* but curiously, none of what he wrote about the Mafia was published in the newspaper. It was all in a blog he'd created about the subject. It appeared that the New York public had gotten bored with the Mafia after the incarceration of John Gotti, the Dapper Don. Post-Gotti, no one colorful enough within the Mob appeared to keep the public interested, and the papers did little to follow the much weakened organization after that. If his blog was any indication, though, Jim Mosconi was fascinated, maybe even obsessed, with the Mafia. His blog included a family tree of the Five Families of New York, starting with the modern creation of the Mafia in the 1930s and leading to the present. Lucchese, Bonanno, Genovese, Colombo, Gambino—all represented the power base of the Mafia in the United States. Prior to meeting Tony Vespucci, I had, at best, a modest knowledge of the Mafia, based mostly on what I'd seen in *The Godfather* and *Goodfellas,* so I was not surprised to discover that the Mafia was a violent organization. But the reality was far worse than I had imagined. As I dug deeper, the body count grew at an alarming rate, clearly illustrating to me that the dangerous reputation of the Mafia was based solidly in a blood-and-guts reality.

According to Mosconi, Vespucci became the acting boss of the Genovese family after Vincent "Chin" Gigante died in jail in 2005, leaving a vacuum that many Mafia experts still don't feel has been filled, contradicting Mosconi's own assertions. The Genovese Family was considered by many to be the most powerful Mafia family in America, its genesis dating back to the godfather of the modern American Mafia, Charles "Lucky" Luciano. A few other sources named

Vespucci as a power player in the New York Mafia scene, but only Mosconi seemed to think Vespucci was a boss. The FBI and the U.S. District Attorney's office were silent on the issue. From my standpoint, it didn't matter what Vespucci's overall position was in the hierarchy. He was in the mob. That was enough. But it wasn't. I quickly discovered that the groom-to-be Marco Balducci and his father Giancarlo were well entrenched in La Cosa Nostra as well. As best as I could figure, Giancarlo worked with, or for, Vespucci. I figured it was safe to assume, then, that Marco was a made man as well, a soldier at the least, most likely a capo with his own crew. I couldn't imagine what he and Vespucci would do to me if they were displeased with my work. I shuddered at the possibilities. The only person whom I knew nothing about was Maggie Vespucci. Given what I'd learned so far about my client's family, I can't say I was all that excited to meet her, nor was I expecting much.

My plane hit the runway. I was in New York. I took a deep breath as we taxied toward the airport. Though Vespucci was Mafia, I was here to write his daughter's love story for her impending marriage. I had a job to do, and I knew how to do it because I'd done it so many times before. I just had to stay focused and not let my underlying fears interfere with my judgment. I powered on my phone as the plane pulled up to the chute for us to disembark. I hit the "S" button for Sara's quick dial, hearing her voice almost immediately. Straight to voicemail. I looked at my watch. It was 2:30 p.m. in Los Angeles, so she was probably in a meeting. I left her a message, telling her I'd arrived safely and would call later to say goodnight. I grabbed my bag from the overhead, slung the strap over my shoulder, and followed the passengers in front of me off the plane into the frenetic energy of the JFK International Airport and New York City. I never traveled with more than one small carry-on for clothes and my computer bag, so I didn't have luggage to wait for or allow the airline to lose. I tracked with the other exiting passengers into Terminal 3, walking toward the diminishing light of a New York evening.

At curbside, I stepped to the closest taxi. A hip-looking black guy with long dreads and arms crossed leaned against the passenger side door. Reggae drums emanated from inside his cab. He looked at me, not saying a word.

"Greenwich Village?" I asked.

He nodded, coolly pushing up off the car, taking my bags out of my hands all in one fluid motion. He opened the trunk, my items disappearing inside. I climbed into the back passenger side door, settling in for the long ride ahead of me. Peter Tosh spoke to me from the back speakers, a remake of Chuck Berry's "Johnny B. Goode" at a considerably slower pace than Berry's original version. I reached into my pocket and pulled out a piece of paper with the address of my destination.

As the car pulled away, I said, "I'm heading to, uh . . . 25 Waverly Place. In Manhattan."

The driver hit the gas and the taxi jumped off the curb into the crowded traffic exiting the airport. I tensed for a moment as he swerved past a Lincoln Town Car, only to wedge us between two passenger buses. I looked at my driver's name under the mirror and was about to tell Jamal I wasn't in any rush but he beat me to it.

"Relax, mon. I'll get ya dere safe."

Jamal glanced back at me in the rearview mirror. His dark eyes reflected calm and cool as he cleared the buses. I decided I had enough to think about, so I settled back into my seat, watching the New York cityscape pass me by. Before leaving Los Angeles, I'd had a brief conversation on the phone with Maggie, introducing myself to her and explaining what my itinerary would be. I asked her to make a list of people I could set up interviews with immediately after landing. I didn't want to spend any more time in New York than absolutely necessary. Maggie volunteered to be my first interview, so I told her I'd come straight from the airport to meet her in Greenwich Village.

The taxi wound its way onto the expressway. In the distance, I could see the Manhattan skyline. I was surprised my first interview would be there because I had assumed Brooklyn was the New York stronghold of the Italians. Though Manhattan had the history of Little Italy, those years were long gone. I had no idea what to expect from Maggie, but from the moment Vespucci mentioned his daughter while we sat in the diner, I envisioned Marisa Tomei from *My Cousin Vinny:* short skirt mid-thigh, tight blouse with bosom flowing, big hair, a gum-smacking smart-ass, solid Brooklyn accent. But the Maggie I spoke to on the phone was sans accent, polite but curt. She gave me the address and the suite number, saying we could talk more when I got there.

As Jamal and I closed in on Manhattan, the buildings looked like they were stacked one on top of the other. Coming from Los Angeles, I had a hard time reconciling New York and Los Angeles, two of the most populous cities in the country. Downtown L.A. seemed like a tiny island of tall buildings in comparison with New York. Here, it was many taller buildings squeezed together, owning the space both horizontally and vertically. I rolled down my window, wanting to inhale the smell and sounds of the city. Having lived in Los Angeles for several years, I knew that L.A. didn't have the palpable energy of New York. Downtown Los Angeles was like a side note to the rest of the city, a far cry from the heart and soul that Manhattan was for New York. In fact, Los Angeles didn't have a center. It was more like a huge sprawl of small cities bleeding into one another. I had never before considered how different the two metropolises were, but as we closed in on Greenwich Village, I noted that Los Angeles and New York were antithetical to each other, opposite in both layout and structure.

Jamal slowed in the traffic, and pulled up to 25 Waverly Place. I looked out the window at a building with the title Rufus D. Smith Hall. I glanced up and down the street. I turned to Jamal. "Is this New York University?"

"Ya brother, dat it is."

I paid him and then stepped onto the street and grabbed my bags from the open trunk. I could hear the fading sounds of Bob Marley as the taxi disappeared into the early evening traffic. I turned and stared at the building before me. Hitching my bags up over my shoulder, I pulled the note out of my right hand pocket: suite 324. I stuffed it back into my pocket and stepped through the double-door entryway on my way to my first interview for the Vespucci-Balducci wedding. A couple of undergraduate students passed me in the lobby, an air of freedom surrounding their every movement. I couldn't remember ever feeling that way at any time in my life, not even in college. Maybe one day I would know what it meant to flow from day to day without a feeling of impending doom. From somewhere behind me, I heard a chant, "Sara! Sara! Sara!"

Startled, I turned around to see who was behind me, scaring a young woman entering the building. Embarrassed, I stepped aside and let her pass, mumbling an apology. I told myself Sara was not the problem here—I was. Sara was being Sara, distant and aloof right now, and Jon was being Jon, or Jon was being me, depending on who was talking. I was the one who couldn't give Sara the room she needed to work out her issues, thereby forcing her to focus her energy on me rather than on herself. If I could only learn how to give her the space she needed, our relationship would be better. Probably. I pulled out my cell phone and quick-dialed Sara's number, hoping she would pick up, but it went straight to voicemail again.

"Hi. I just wanted to call and tell you how much I love you. I know we've been fighting a lot lately, but I promise when I get back to L.A. I'll make it up to you." I paused a moment, at a loss, then "I love you. I'll call later."

I hung up, realizing a bit too late I had done exactly the opposite of what I had just berated myself for doing. Frustrated, I put the phone in my pocket and walked through the large foyer, passing NYU paraphernalia hanging on the walls. The hallway smell carried me back to my college days with the musty scent of old buildings, books, and academia. Coming out of the foyer into a large hallway, I spotted the elevator. I stepped inside and pressed the number three button. As the door closed, I heard heels sounding off the marble floor, a voice echoing in the hallway over the clicking noise.

"Could you hold the elevator, please."

Just as I caught a glimpse of a long skirt and black blouse, the door closed. I heard curse words coming at me from beyond the elevator doors. I pressed the "door open" button. An irritated frown changed to a friendly smile on the face of the woman before me who was carrying a stack of stuffed folders in her left arm.

"Thank you so much. This elevator is so damn slow. I didn't want to wait for it."

I smiled back in the goofy way I always did when near a beautiful woman. "I just pushed the button. The elevator did all the work."

"But the important thing is you pushed the button."

I nodded, now at a loss for words as the elevator door closed, shrinking the size of our world considerably. I gave her a sideways glance. I couldn't place her, but I could swear I'd seen her before. "Are you a professor here?"

"Assistant professor." She opened the top folder in her hand, focused on a paper inside it.

"In what field?"

"Postmodern anthropology."

"Is that like Van Gogh drawing cave men?"

She laughed at my joke.

I took the opportunity to get a closer look. Dark, brown eyes well set, small nose, beautiful pale skin, high cheekbones, full lips. The déjà vu cleared. I'd never met her before, but I did know her. Sort of. Realizing who she was—or, more accurately, who she resembled—I froze.

During my childhood, I spent most of my time with my nose in a book, but my love for reading didn't do me any favors in my social life, mainly because I found my books far more interesting than my peers. Maybe as compensation for my lack of social interaction, or just because I was an odd child, I developed the unusual habit of befriending the heroes and heroines in the books I read. When I was done reading, often before bed, I would spend a lot of mental energy describing the appearance, facial features, hair color, physical shape, and human tics of the main players featured in whatever book I was currently reading. I went into great detail with my visualization so that as I read, my characters' images would come fully alive in my mind. My ability to create a life-like mental image of these characters grew with age, and it had the strange side effect of lulling me into feeling that these literary characters were an essential part of my life.

I never shared this secret life with anyone. Ever. My favorite book was *The Count of Monte Cristo* by Alexandre Dumas. I've read it many times over the years, the characters from the story jumping off the page because of how often I'd imagined them. Dante, the main tragic hero, was engaged to the most beautiful woman inhabiting my fantasy world of book characters, Mercedes, which is saying something because I had read an average of five books a month since I was seven, so she had a lot of competition. Over time, Mercedes became the ideal against which all other female characters—and the women in my life—were measured. As far as I was concerned, Mercedes was perfectly beautiful, or beautifully perfect. I'd never run across any woman in my real life that came anywhere close to matching her beauty.

Until now.

Because if Mercedes had stepped off the page into my life, she would have looked exactly like the woman standing beside me in the elevator. The realization shut down my vocal chords and my nerves took over.

Pulling her eyes away from the paper, the smile carrying to her eyes, she looked at me. "It is something like that."

I was unable to meet her gaze, staring at the doors, wishing they would open up. Rather than be happy to see my fictional world come to life, I panicked. I didn't know what to say to her. The seconds ticked by slowly, the quiet creaking of the elevator filling our ears. Finally, the doors opened and she exited first onto the third floor where I needed to go, but my feet wouldn't move. As the doors began to close, she turned back toward the elevator.

"Nice to meet you."

Stupidly, I just nodded, my lips stuck together.

As the elevator doors closed, she turned on her heel and I caught a glimpse of her muscled calves just visible below the hemline of her skirt, flexing as she walked.

When the doors shut, I got my voice back. "You, too." But I was on the way to the fourth floor. Flustered, I gathered my senses, pushing the third floor button, hoping the elevator would go back down quickly enough for me to get one more glimpse before I had to start my interview with Vespucci's daughter. When I stepped onto the third floor, Mercedes was gone.

I had to believe the encounter was a fluke, not to be dwelled on or judged an omen. It just was. Yet, I felt guilty because of Sara, trying to rationalize it away because I hadn't done anything measurably inappropriate. I just looked. Sara could have nothing to be upset about.

Getting back to task, I looked around for room numbers, but didn't see any, so I took a right, the direction my elevator mate had taken. Passing office doors, I saw an occasional light on inside the rooms, though the majority of them appeared vacated for the day. Near the end of the hallway, I spotted number 324 over the final office door on my left before the hallway turned right. I was disappointed I had not caught a glimpse of Mercedes, but I did my best to forget her and focus on my upcoming interview. I squared off at the door, about to knock, faltering at the last moment. This would be the official start of the project. There would be no turning back. I took a deep breath, knocking with a sure hand.

A female voice from within said, "Come in."

I pushed the door open, stepping inside. Large bookshelves sat at right angles, taking up two walls in the back corner. I immediately noticed Mercedes standing on her tiptoes, reaching up to pull a book down from the top of one of the bookshelves. Her right hand was extended high above her head, her blouse riding high and pulling away from her long skirt, revealing pale skin and a tiny waist. I stood in the doorway staring once again at her flexed calves as she strained to pull the book down, close to hooking the top seam of the spine. For the moment, I was frozen. My Mercedes was Maggie Vespucci. Or rather, Maggie was Mercedes. Or Mercedes was an invention of my mind, and Maggie was Tony Vespucci's daughter, and I was deeply in over my head. Forcing myself into action, not wanting Mercedes-Maggie to think I was gawking at her, I averted my gaze just as she hooked the back of the book with her finger. The book fell on her head and then to the ground with a smack. She leaned down to pick it up, turning toward me with an embarrassed smile.

"My mother always said I was a bit clumsy."

I didn't know how to respond to that. We stared at one another. I blushed. Maggie appeared to be running calculations in her head.

"I'm Dante."

Maggie looked nonplussed. I mentally kicked myself in the butt.

"I mean, I'm Jon, Jon Fixx," I added hastily.

Maggie inadvertently glanced at the book in her hand, then back at me. "You're the wedding writer."

I nodded.

"Please, come in."

I took a few steps into the office, hesitant. That nervous feeling was back, throwing me off balance. I never got nervous on interviews. This was a first. I became hyperaware of my surroundings, of my every move, of Maggie's reactions. Feeling disoriented, my feet followed Maggie's offer to sit in the chair facing the large office desk, and I dropped into the seat with a thud. I tried to reorient myself, having a little success now that I was off my feet. To take my mind off the woman before me and to collect my thoughts, I glanced around. The bookshelves, the desk, the small sofa against the wall were the only pieces of furniture. Above the sofa, I saw a framed photograph of a beachside city built into cliffs overlooking the ocean.

"Sicily. Palermo," Maggie volunteered. She was sitting on the edge of her desk, her legs crossed and I could see her small ankles, just as I had imagined Mercedes' to be. Then, standing up, she shook my hand and said, "Glad to meet you, Jon Fixx." It was a strong, sure grip. "Thanks for taking us on as clients. It was my father's idea. When he told me what you do, I was intrigued. Then I read the story you wrote for Cranston and Judith Jefferson and I was sold. It was so beautiful."

"Thank you," I said, a little too modestly. I didn't do well with compliments.

"I was surprised he was able to get you here so fast, considering he only told me about his plan yesterday."

"Your father can be very convincing," I said.

"He was nice, of course?"

"Of course. I just mean he made it clear he only wants the best for his daughter—you—and would spare no expense," I said in my best salesman voice.

Maggie was nothing like I expected. She had undeniable intelligence reflected in her Mercedes-like eyes. She smiled. "That sounds like my father. He won't take no for an answer. Ever."

I nodded. I had discovered this Vespucci characteristic

firsthand. I glanced around the office, hoping to change the subject. Nothing caught my eye to comment on. I returned my gaze to Maggie, unable to ignore her beauty up-close. I was feeling a raw, visceral reaction toward her. It took all of my self-control to keep myself in my seat, putting every ounce of energy I could muster to keep my voice normal, my face neutral. Feelings of guilt washed over me, Sara's face looming large.

"Are you okay?" Maggie asked.

I was breathing heavy. Trying to get it together, I said, "Oh, sure. Sorry. I came straight from the airport. I should have eaten something."

"Jon, please. We can do this later. Would you like to get something to eat?"

The soft lilt of her voice calmed me. I threw my best smile at Maggie. "No, no. I'm fine, just got a little dizzy. I don't want to waste any time. So please, let's continue."

The visceral pull had been so powerful that I'd felt a sharp pain in my gut, accompanied with a strong desire to grab her, pull her close, and touch her intimately. I tried to look at the reaction objectively, but there was no place for objectivity here. I kicked my thoughts into autopilot. "So, I'm assuming you got your Ph.D. in anthropology here at NYU?"

"That's right. I finished my Ph.D. last year. When I was done, the powers that be offered me a position to teach here in the Anthropology Department for two years as an assistant professor."

"Wow, that's an honor. I'm guessing not many of your classmates were given the same opportunity."

She shook her head. "Thank God I was given the offer, because when I first declared my major in anthropology as an undergraduate, my father couldn't understand the point. You know, what kind of work it would lead to."

"I imagine it must be very hard to get a job in the field with only an undergraduate degree in anthropology. I can see why your father would be concerned. You'd really have to see it through to a Ph.D. to get the payoff for time spent. Right?" I realized I must have sounded patronizing.

Smiling, Maggie responded, "I'd have to say you're right. Where did you go to school?"

"Franklin & Marshall College. In Pennsylvania."

"Good school."

I gave a noncommittal shrug.

"What did you major in?"

"Anthropology."

"You're joking?"

I nodded. "Yep."

"Really? What a coincidence. So you speak from experience. Did you go to graduate school too?"

"Never finished. I left in my senior year. Unforeseen circumstances of life."

She was silent a moment, considering. Then, "May I ask what kind of unforeseen circumstances?"

As a rule, I never shared personal information with my clients. I decided early on it muddied the waters. But something in Maggie's look made me want to confess. Up to this point, I'd never told anyone other than Luci the story about Jennifer. "I discovered my thesis advisor in bed with my girlfriend a week after she dumped me."

"Oh." Whatever she was expecting to hear, that wasn't it. "How did you catch her in bed if you were split up? Did you live together?"

"It's a long story, so I won't bore you, but in short order, I went to her apartment unbidden on a Friday night, stole into her bedroom, and waited for her to come home because I was working under the foolish misconception that maybe we could work it out."

"What happened?" Maggie asked.

"She came home with my professor and I had no way to sneak out. So I hid in the closet."

She stifled a laugh. "Oh, I'm sorry, that sounds terrifyingly, tragically funny. How long were you stuck in the closet?"

"About two hours, during which time I got to discover they'd been having an affair for some time." I gave Maggie my best cover-up smile. "I'm sorry. I shouldn't be talking about me. That's not why I'm here. I'm here for you and Marco, so let's talk about you."

But she wasn't ready to let it go. "Did you report him?"

"No. I dropped out of school that same week. Moved across town. Got a job. Just walked away."

"Oh, that's horrible. You didn't go after the guy?"

"In a way, I've learned to accept what happened as fate. If Jennifer hadn't cheated on me, I don't think I would have found my way to this," I answered.

"Is that why you do this?"

"Do what?"

"Write other people's love stories?"

I had never thought about it. Was that why I did this? Because I couldn't get it right in my own life? I deflected her comment with a laugh. "That's funny. No one has ever asked me that before, and I've been doing this for eight years. I'm in a serious relationship now, so if that was my original motivation, it has changed since. But we're not here for me. We're here for you. That's why I flew to New York."

But she couldn't take the hint. She pressed on. "So, who's going to write your love story when you get married?"

I was getting annoyed. I had never encountered a client who wanted to know about me. Usually, my clients were more than happy to talk about themselves for unconditional lengths of time if I allowed them to. "I don't know. I guess I'll have to wait and see." I changed the subject. "So, what was your thesis for your Ph.D.?"

"Early Italian settlement in New York City and the long-term cultural and financial impact their settlement had on the City. The crux of my thesis, though, was about what New York would have looked like if the Italians had not come here en masse. That was the truly interesting part for me.

Trying to create a New York City with no Italians. Raised a lot of eyebrows when I made my final submission."

"Sounds fascinating." Of course, Italians. I wanted to ask her if "early Italian settlement" was code for Mafia, but I needed to discover the lay of the land before I asked anything even remotely connected to her father.

"Since I wasn't sure what I wanted to do by the time I finished my program, the offer for this teaching position seemed like a good idea." She looked around the room. "I wanted to meet you here before you met the rest of the family."

At the mention of the word "family" my heart rate sped up. I would have to get myself together if I wanted to see this project through. Maggie noticed my reaction.

"Don't worry. It will just be my immediate family. My parents, grandmother, brother and his family. And Marco, my fiancé. It shouldn't be too overwhelming for you." A conspiratorial look crossed her face. "My father told them all to be on their best behavior. So, good luck!" She glanced at the clock. "We should go if we don't want to be late." She grabbed a colorful wrap hanging on the back of her chair and hung it around her shoulders. I stood up and followed her out of the office.

"Will Joey be at dinner?"

Surprised, Maggie asked, "How do you know Joey?"

"I met him when your father flew out to Los Angeles to meet with me. I got the impression your father doesn't go anywhere without Joey."

Maggie didn't say anything, staring at me a moment, considering what I said. Then, "C'mon, let's get out of here." We took the elevator down to the lobby and walked out onto the New York streets.

As we stepped onto the sidewalk, I blurted out, "So what exactly does your father do?" I immediately regretted having asked the question and wished I could take it back.

Maggie frowned.

I worried I'd crossed the line. Maybe it didn't matter what he did for a living. Maybe all that mattered was writing Maggie's love story, because the sooner I finished it, the sooner I could be on my merry way back to Los Angeles to work on repairing my own love story. After several moments, Maggie responded in a flat tone, "He's an entrepreneur. He dabbles. Raw fabric, dry cleaning, commercial real estate, the restaurant business. He's got it all."

"Oh." Simple as that. I decided I would not spend any more mental energy on her father's almost guaranteed mob involvement.

Maggie looked at me. I was unsure if she was warning me off the subject, or if she wanted to make sure I believed her. She spun around, hailing a taxi. Moments later, a taxi screeched to a halt and we climbed in.

A dark-skinned Sikh asked, "Where to?"

"Dyker Heights, 82nd & 11th," Maggie said. As the taxi pulled away, she explained she had left her car at her apartment. "So, rather than go back to get it, I figured we could just take a taxi to save time. Otherwise, we'll be late for dinner."

"I thought your father lived in Brooklyn?"

"Dyker Heights is part of Brooklyn, southwest section. More like a suburb of Brooklyn, though. We moved there when I was in high school. I grew up in Bensonhurst on 61st near Bay Parkway. Dyker Heights was a step up, as far as my father was concerned. A little more chichi, if you will."

Maggie caught my blank stare. "How many times have you been to New York?"

"Only a few times." I felt excluded from a special club. Throughout my life, I'd met a number of people who were not native New Yorkers but had spent more than enough time in the Big Apple to engage in an educated discussion about streets and neighborhood intersections. I, however, knew little more about the city than what I could locate on a map.

Maggie laughed. "So, I'm speaking a foreign language to you?"

"Basically." I laughed with her. It was an ice-breaking moment. "I thought Bensonhurst was where the Italians lived."

"True while I was growing up there, but it has changed quite a bit. A Chinese immigrant influx started in the 1990s, part of the reason my dad wanted to move, though I didn't agree with him. I think he wanted to live in a house that reflected his financial success, one that would be good for the family in the long run."

As we headed south through Manhattan, I took in the low-rise buildings we were passing, noting the hustle of early evening rush hour around us. "Will we be crossing the Brooklyn Bridge?" I asked Maggie.

Maggie nodded.

"I've never been on it." As we passed through the intersections, I leaned forward to note the street signs. We were heading south on Bowery, passing Canal Street. "This is Little Italy, right?"

"That's right. Though it's a bit of a misnomer now. Not a lot of Italian heritage left here. Except for one of the best Italian restaurants in the City. My absolute favorite place to eat. Funny enough, though, an Italian doesn't own it. Your friend Cranston does.

"He never told me he had a restaurant," I said, surprised.

"It just opened up last year. The restaurant, or rather the building, has a colorful history. It was once owned by Carlo Gambino."

I perked up. I knew from my research that Gambino had been a major Mafia player from early in the organization's history.

Maggie said, "I think Cranston bought the building several years ago. Eventually he booted out the shoe store that was where the Ravenite club had been. Do you remember John Gotti?"

"Of course."

"That was his hangout."

"The Feds bugged that whole joint. It's how they busted him."

Maggie lifted her eyebrows in mock surprise. "So, you know the story of John Gotti?"

"Hard to miss. Remember, he was always in the newspaper. Growing up, I only knew two Mafia names: Don Corleone and John Gotti."

"I think that's why Cranston did what he did. He knew the infamous attachment of the spot alone would bring business, but it's his pizza that brings everyone back. Best pizza in Manhattan, and I'm a native New Yorker, so that's saying something."

"I'll have to check it out before I leave town."

I looked out the passenger window, watching New York life pass by. We were closing in on the Brooklyn Bridge. "Mind if I ask you some general background questions?"

"Shoot."

Over the course of our ride, I learned Maggie was born and raised in Brooklyn. Every so often I heard traces of the unique, defining Brooklyn accent one expected when speaking to a native, though I hadn't noticed it at the university. She obviously worked hard at dropping it. She attributed her desire for higher education to her father, whom she said was always pushing her academically. I was surprised to hear that Vespucci had a voracious appetite for books, especially history, and that Maggie had inherited her father's love for reading. When she had declared her major in college, both her parents were disappointed she had chosen anthropology, hoping she would pick something more practical, like premed or business or prelaw—like her brother Michael, who was an attorney. When she went abroad to Italy as a junior to work on her first research project and returned speaking fluent Italian, both Vespucci parents warmed to Maggie's choice. Now, with her teaching position, the Vespuccis were fully on board. Maggie stopped talking to point out the window at the East River. We were crossing the Brooklyn Bridge.

"In 1883, at the time it was built, it was the longest suspension bridge in the world and considered one of the wonders of the world," Maggie informed me.

I gazed at the East River, spotting the Statue of Liberty in the distance. Dusk was settling in, the floodlights on the bridge highlighting the most famous Lady in the United States.

"My first time crossing the Brooklyn Bridge. Now, I feel like an honorary New Yorker," I said, and looked at Maggie.

"Happy to be of service," she replied.

My discussion with Maggie had been no different from the multitude of other interviews I'd had with past brides-to-be, except that she seemed more intelligent and more down-to-earth than my average client, as well as more respectful when she spoke of her parents. At the same time, the Vespucci's apparent desire for their daughter to succeed, and concern for the path she took, seemed in line with other American middle-class parents, at least according to the way Maggie described it. Nothing in her self-described biography so far intimated any connection to the dangerous, illicit sphere in which I presumed her father to be a controlling interest. Maybe I was wasting my energy worrying about who Tony Vespucci was or what he did for a living. Did it really matter to me that he was connected to the Mafia? I was not here to write his story. I was here for his daughter. I snuck a peek at Maggie looking off into the distance, her profile backlit by the streetlights. One aspect of Maggie Vespucci did set her apart from all my other clients, though. She was flawlessly stunning. There was no denying the fact. I quickly looked away, afraid she would catch me staring at her.

We were well into Brooklyn now, traveling on the I-278. I asked her for more detail about where she grew up, whatever came to mind.

"We lived in a brownstone in Bensonhurst, but when I was about sixteen, my father bought the current place. I love it, but the brownstone was my favorite. It was my first house. I guess that's why. Childhood, you know?"

"Where is your fiancé from?" I asked.

"Marco? We grew up in the same neighborhood. Went to the same schools. My family has known his family as far back as I can remember. When we were growing up, people would make jokes about us getting married." Maggie looked out the window at the passing brownstones as our taxi closed in on our location. I waited. Over the years of interviewing, I learned that the less I questioned and probed, the more I got. Maggie continued. "We sort of dated in high school, but it didn't last long. More like a brief test run than a real relationship."

"He was your first love, then?"

"I don't know if I'd say that. But maybe." She paused, looking at me intently. "My father told me you'd be perceptive."

I shrugged off the compliment. I was already finding my hook for their story: Childhood True Love Rediscovered. Maybe this would be easier than I thought. "So, what happened?"

"We went our separate ways. I went to college and then graduate school. I dated but never met anyone else who came close to being the one. At least, not really. Then, last year I ran into Marco at a neighborhood party. I hadn't seen him since high school, so it was a bit of a shock."

"I thought you said your families were really close? Why hadn't you seen him since then?"

"He went to Italy to help run his father's business. He was there until last year."

"Was he in Italy when you were there?"

"Yes."

"And you didn't cross paths?"

"He wasn't on my radar at the time. I was so focused on my studies that the idea never came up."

I wasn't sure how to interpret that. "When you met again here in New York, did you still feel that spark?"

"Yes. At the party, he told me he came because he'd heard I'd be there. I don't know if that was just a line, but he insists to this day it wasn't."

I had a nagging feeling. Something she said bothered me. They'd broken up in high school. There was more to that breakup than Maggie admitted. But that wasn't what was bothering me. I looked out the passenger window. Tony Vespucci's face loomed large in my mind. His words came back to me. "'I love my daughter more than anything. Nothing is too good for her.'" How did he feel about his daughter marrying a guy who broke her heart once already? "Your father must be so happy you're marrying your first true love," I said.

I could have sworn I saw her face darken, but the look was so fleeting that I couldn't be sure. Maggie smiled. "My father is glad I'm getting married. He thinks I'm getting old."

We shared a laugh. Vespucci was not the first parent I'd come across with old world sensibilities who felt that an unmarried woman past the age of twenty-five was on her way to becoming an old maid. Suddenly, the taxi came to an abrupt halt. Living in Los Angeles, I never used a taxi, and given my experience so far, I was glad I didn't have to.

"We're here, Jon." She looked at me with a pretend concerned look. "You sure you're ready for this? Old school Italian families can be loud and overbearing. My family is no exception."

By this point, I'd been around every type of family possible. I'd seen happy families, grumpy families, families that gossiped about one another in each other's presence, close-knit families. But I had to admit I had never encountered the Family, so this definitely was a first. I hesitated. As long as the taxi was here, I could still leave. I took a deep breath, pushing myself out of the car. Before I'd even shut my door, the taxi driver was gunning the engine. I watched it speed away.

"You get used to it. Taxi drivers are their own kind."

I turned toward the house. What I saw before me was like nothing I had seen in Manhattan. I was standing in front of an oversized, walled compound, large weeping willows and oaks towering high above the walls. I glanced up and down the street, noting that the other houses were single dwellings on large lots, all two or three stories, but Vespucci's house was the only one with a stonewall guarding it. I followed Maggie through the iron gate into the large courtyard, open and lush with trees and bushes. As we reached the landing front door, I felt a sudden, intense stinging on my left arm. I jumped sideways looking down at my arm. "Ouch!" I yelped.

Maggie turned around. I felt like I'd just been stung by a bee or a spider, but I couldn't see what had bitten me.

"My nephew," Maggie said, annoyed. In a sterner tone, she said, "Mikey, get out here." Nothing. "Now!"

I spotted a ten-year-old carrying a BB gun skulk out from behind some dense bushes. Slowly, he crossed over to us. He was small for his age, had dark hair and a round face. His piercing blue eyes almost glowed in the early evening light. Maggie pointed her finger to a spot directly in front of her without saying a word. Mikey blinked his blue eyes, weighing his options, but a shift in the look on Maggie's face convinced him to stand before his aunt. She grabbed hold of his ear and pulled. "What did your father tell you about shooting your BB gun at people?"

Mikey didn't answer, though I'm not sure if he was being defiant or he couldn't speak because his ear was being pulled off his head. Finally, Mikey forfeited, his pitch a couple octaves higher than I assumed was his normal ten-year-old voice. "That it's dangerous."

Maggie wasn't through. She pulled a little harder. "What do you say?"

"I'm sorry. I'm sorry!" he said, looking in my direction.

Maggie let go of his ear. Mikey's heels dropped back to the ground. I figured I wasn't the first person Mikey had used for target practice. He was probably just preparing to join the family business. Covering his ear with his hand, Mikey hugged his aunt and Maggie wrapped her arms around him.

"Are your mom and dad inside?"

Mikey nodded. "Can I go now?"

"No more shooting anyone."

"I know, Aunt Maggie. Please don't tell Dad."

Maggie smiled, and Mikey picked up his gun and went off to hunt more, hopefully, nonhuman, prey.

"Sorry about that. He's already a handful. Can't wait to see what he's going to be like when he's fifteen."

I couldn't wait to see what kind of gun he'd be shooting at fifteen, but I didn't say anything, just nodded my head in agreement.

I followed Maggie into the Vespucci's home. On my right was an office, a giant mahogany desk sitting in the middle of the room. To my left was a spacious living room filled with antiques, a vintage I didn't know, and on the walls were outsized landscape oil paintings, obviously worth a lot of money. The fireplace was blazing, and I was struck by the nostalgic smell of burning wood.

"Mikey is your brother's son?" I asked Maggie.

"My older brother Michael, yes."

"No other siblings, right?"

"Just Michael. He's seven years older. Got the marriage thing down quicker than I did. He was twenty-five when he settled down."

I followed Maggie along the hallway into the kitchen, and I was suddenly hit with multiple, savory aromas. The stove was alive with activity, differently sized pots and pans competing for attention. Two large saucepans emitted steam from their loose tops. Meat was sizzling in two frying pans, side by side. I started salivating. I noticed two women were preparing dinner. The younger one was of the post-World War II generation, and the older one was post-World War I. I guessed, correctly, that I was looking at Maggie's mother and grandmother. Post-World War II grabbed Maggie and gave her a big hug. "Oh, good, Maggie, you made it in time for dinner!"

"Hi, Mama." Maggie exchanged kisses on the cheek with her mother, and then she turned to me. "This is Jon Fixx. Jon, this is my mother, Barbara."

"Good to meet you, Mrs. Vespucci."

"Don't be silly, Jon. Mrs. Vespucci is for my mother. Call me Barbara."

"Sure, Barbara." I liked Maggie's mother immediately. She had a friendly energy about her. I was already being lulled into a sense of familiarity with the Vespuccis, and I had not been there even five minutes. I made a note to myself not to drop my guard.

Barbara grabbed hold of my cheek. "My husband told me you were a good writer, but he didn't tell me how handsome you were." I was too busy blushing to say anything to her. "Maggie, have you been behaving yourself with this boy?"

Now, it was Maggie's turn to blush. "Mama, stop it!" Maggie turned to me. "Ignore my mother, Jon." Maggie walked over to her grandmother, placing a kiss on each cheek. "And this is my Grandma Jean."

"Nice to meet you, ma'am."

"You too, young man."

"Is Marco here yet?" Maggie asked.

"He's in the back with everyone else," Barbara said, as she scooped pasta into a large serving bowl. From where I stood, I couldn't see much of anything in the backyard.

"Here, Jon, can you carry this outside?" Barbara asked. I suddenly found myself holding a steaming bowl of spaghetti with meatballs.

"This way," Maggie said, as she followed her grandmother

out the side door, me in tow, the three of us laden with different dishes of food including a large bowl of risotto, braciole, lasagna, and a huge multicolored salad.

Around the outside corner of the house we went into a gigantic backyard filled with pines and maples brightly lit by overhanging lights running from the house to the trees and back to the house. An oversized picnic table was in the center of the yard. I spotted Joey first. He was throwing horseshoes in a horseshoe pit in the corner of the yard, flanked on either side by two younger guys.

Maggie slowed her pace to fall in step with me. "Don't be overwhelmed, they're all friendly," she said.

Behind me, Barbara called, "Everybody sit. It's time to eat."

I followed a step behind Maggie to the massive picnic table. Vespucci was reading to a young girl who didn't look any older than five years of age and resembled Mikey Jr. minus the BB gun. When Vespucci spotted me, he picked his niece up from his lap, carefully setting her down beside him on the long bench.

"Jon Fixx, you made it in one piece. I'd like you to meet my beautiful niece, Sabrina."

Sabrina smiled up at me.

"Hi, Sabrina."

Precociously, she responded, "Hi, Jon Fixx."

Vespucci chuckled. "This one, smart as a whip. Glad you made it in time for dinner."

Maggie leaned over her father, giving him a hug and kiss on the cheek. "Hi, Papa."

"You and Jon have a chance to get acquainted?"

"We did." She smiled over at me reassuringly.

The family was closing in from all sides and behind me. Within moments, everybody was standing around the table, and I quickly picked out who was who. Maggie's sister-in-law Caroline was standing beside her holding Mikey Jr.'s hand. Joey was to the left of Mikey Jr., flanked by the other two guys who'd been playing horseshoe. Maggie's brother, Michael, tall and thin with an open, friendly face, stepped over to Maggie, giving her a kiss on the cheek. By process of elimination, that meant the remaining guy was Marco. The scowl on his face aimed in my direction told me everything I needed to know. Vespucci stood up, putting his arm around me. Awkwardly, I set the bowl of spaghetti down on the table.

The family fanned out around the dinner table. Vespucci indicated I should sit in the seat on his right. Joey sat down across from me. Out of the corner of my eye, I watched my principal clients greet each other. Maggie exchanged a small kiss with Marco. He was still staring at me, probably wondering who I was and why I'd shown up with his bride-to-be. From the head of the table, in a friendly, authoritative voice, Vespucci bellowed, "Marco, Maggie, grab a seat. I'll explain everything in a moment."

Reluctantly, Marco guided Maggie to the two remaining seats between Joey and Grandma Jean. I may have been mistaken, but I could have sworn the scowl on Marco's face had deepened. To my left, Vespucci cleared his throat. "For Maggie and Marco's upcoming wedding, I want to give you both a very special gift. I have to apologize to you, Marco. I kept this a secret from everybody because I didn't want to spoil it. Maggie only found out yesterday, in fact." Marco and Maggie exchanged looks. Vespucci looked down at his granddaughter, pointing at me. "Sabrina, who is this?"

Sabrina responded, "Jon Fixx." All eyes turned to her in surprise. No one else at the table had heard our initial exchange. Caroline and Michael smiled with parental pleasure. Sabrina reveled in the moment. Mikey Jr. squirmed in his seat, not appearing to enjoy the attention his sister was receiving.

"That's right, Sabrina. Everyone, this is Jon Fixx. He writes real-life love stories," Vespucci announced, but it sounded like such an eccentric thing to do that I expected the men at the table to laugh at me.

"So Maggie, Marco," Vespucci continued, "Jon is my gift to you both." There was silence at the table. Vespucci looked at me. The rest of the table followed suit. Everyone stared, waiting. I wanted to crawl under the table. I wasn't sure what I was supposed to say. I looked at Tony for some help. He flicked his chin at the rest of the table. "Tell them what you do."

Unsure, I turned to the rest of the faces. "Uh, I write couple's love stories."

Little Mikey piped up, "Grandpa said that already."

Sharp little kid. Unlike his sister's comments, Mikey's crack didn't inspire laughter from anyone. In fact, his mother gave him a smack in the back of the head. Mikey Jr. closed his mouth tight, stewing in his seat, staring at me. I figured that his ten-year-old mind was envisioning various ways to end my life.

I explained the best way I knew how. "I usually get hired to write the love story for a couple before they get married. I interview the couple and their family and friends, then I write the story and put it in a book with pictures and mementos and other items of a romantic nature."

The table was silent. "Think *Bridges of Madison County*, only personalized." And with that, heads started nodding. I heard positive murmurs around the table. I hated that I had to compare my writing in that manner to get it understood.

Vespucci looked around the table to make sure everyone had heard what I'd said. He clapped me on the back. "Doesn't that sound fantastic folks? Marco, you and Maggie will have your very own love story." Everyone looked at Marco, and I looked at him as well. He smiled, though his smile looked forced.

"This sounds fantastic, Tony. I couldn't ask for a better gift," Marco said, as he looked at Maggie who was beaming.

Vespucci smiled. "Good. So everybody, make sure you give Jon your contact information before he leaves tonight so he can schedule a sit-down with you." He raised his glass of wine. Everyone followed suit. "To Jon Fixx and his ability to put true love on paper." The table collectively sipped their glasses.

A moment later everyone was filling their plates with spaghetti and meatballs, salad, and hot bread. For a few moments no one spoke, the food more important than talk. I was hesitant to put too much on my plate, but Vespucci encouraged me to fill it up. "You must be hungry after your trip. Don't be shy. Take as much as you like."

I filled my plate with far more spaghetti than I could eat.

"Tony, where did you find Jon?" Caroline asked. "I mean, it's such a unique thing that he does. I've never heard of it before."

"Cranston Jefferson, my textile guy," Tony answered. "I was in his office a couple of weeks ago and saw his sixtieth wedding anniversary book on his desk. There was a photograph of a much younger Judith and Cranston on the front cover."

I knew that picture. Luci and I had agreed it should go on the cover. The picture was taken in front of the first home they shared together. The two of them are standing stiffly before the camera, Cranston wearing a dark brown suit circa 1947, Judith wearing a long, slim, formfitting dress with a red-flower print that carried just below the knees. I made a mental note to make sure I had a sit-down with Cranston before I left.

Maggie asked, "When did you write the book for the Jefferson's?"

"About two years ago now."

"I got the impression from Cranston, Jon, that you're in regular contact with him. Is that true for all your clients?" Tony asked.

"Not generally, no. But Cranston is a special person, and we hit it off." I felt I was revealing too much, though Tony seemed satisfied with my answer.

Caroline responded, "That's really neat. You must learn so much about people."

With a clever smile, I said, "More than I ever thought possible."

Out of the corner of my eye, I caught a frown forming on Marco's face in response to my words, but when I turned his way to make sure I wasn't seeing things, it was gone.

As random talk resumed around the table, I took the opportunity to watch Maggie and Marco as they ate, my sixth sense making noise in the back of my head. Marco had said very little, and I could tell he was going to be a hard nut to crack. As I considered the possible outcomes of a one-on-one interview with him, he turned my way, catching me staring at him. I blinked and shifted uncomfortably in my seat. His eyes reflected power, intelligence, danger.

"So, you're like Don Juan's ghostwriter?" Michael asked.

"Without any of Don Juan's abilities," I responded.

Everybody laughed, except Marco.

Maggie's mother chimed in, "Surely, Jon, you've got somebody back home. How does she feel about having such a hopeless romantic for a boyfriend?"

"How does she feel? Uh . . . " How does she feel about having a hopeless romantic writer for a boyfriend? I didn't know the answer to that question. "I don't know how she feels about it, to be honest with you. We never talk about it."

The women at the table exchanged surprised glances.

"She must love it. I can't see how she'd feel otherwise," Barbara responded.

At that point, the conversation steered away from me, to my relief. Family matters were taken up. Mikey Jr. and Sabrina were discussed at length. I didn't talk much through the rest of dinner, listening instead to the rise and fall of the family chatter. If I had been unaware of Tony Vespucci's alleged position in the Mafia, I never would have guessed it while sitting with his family at dinner. From all angles, they didn't seem much different from the many other families I'd spent time with. In fact, by the end of dinner, I found myself liking them more than I usually did when I first met a family. I waited until dinner was over and the dessert had been served before looking across at Maggie and Marco and asking if they could sit for the initial interview. Maggie looked to Marco who, after the briefest of pauses, nodded in agreement. The table was cleared and we moved inside.

Maggie led me to Vespucci's wood-paneled study. The walls were lined floor to ceiling with bookshelves. I wasn't sure what I had expected from Tony Vespucci, but it sure wasn't a library stocked with highbrow literature. I walked over to one bookshelf, looking at the titles. Plato. Aristotle. Socrates. Camus. Sartre. A shelf full of philosophers.

"That's my father's favorite section. He loves philosophy," Maggie said. My face must have revealed my surprise. "All of these books and no formal schooling beyond high school, completely self-educated."

"Wow, I never would have guessed. This is a serious collection of books for anyone."

Maggie smiled. I glanced back at the numerous books, hardcovers, all in pristine condition. Grudgingly, I felt a sense of admiration for Tony Vespucci, his collection of literature clearly put together with intention. I glanced at Maggie as she pointed out her father's favorite books. Picking one book in particular off the shelves, Maggie stepped closer to me as she stared down at the pages of the novel in her hands. I took in her raven black hair, the curve of her shoulders, her tightly fitted blouse presenting the curves of her breasts. A wave of attraction flooded over me. Panicked, I turned away from Maggie, shoving my face into the covers of a group of leather-bound books. As soon as Maggie was out of my sight, I was overcome by a wave of guilt—Sara's face again, looming large. My emotional self-chastisement was interrupted by Maggie's voice.

"Jon, this is my father's favorite book."

She held out an old book, its edges frayed. "It's an original copy signed by the author, Alexandre Dumas." A copy of *The Count of Monte Cristo* rested in Maggie's hands. She held it almost reverentially, like any true book lover would.

"This is your father's favorite book?" I couldn't hide the surprise on my face. Was this coincidence? Was fate playing some kind of trick on me? How could my favorite book be Tony Vespucci's favorite book? I wondered if he thought his daughter looked like Mercedes too.

"What?" Maggie couldn't avoid noticing the shocked look on my face.

"Have you read the book?"

"Sure. Good story."

Before I could respond, I was interrupted by Vespucci's voice from the doorway.

"Good story? It's the best revenge story ever told. But that's not why I like it. I like it because it clearly illustrates how God works. God helps those who help themselves. Edmond was a righteous man. Villefort, Danglars, and Morrell conspired to take away what God had given him. Therefore God gives Edmond the ability to educate himself, enrich himself, and return to enact the Almighty's vengeance on the men who tried to ruin him."

With Maggie close by, I was having trouble focusing, but I knew the story well enough to speak intelligently about it. "But, in the end, after Edmond gets his final vengeance and all three conspirators have been destroyed, he is surprised by his own reaction to his success. Rather than joy and pleasure at what he has accomplished, Edmond finds only a feeling of empty, disheartening, dull satisfaction."

Vespucci smiled. "And so goes life, Jon. It's never perfect or clear-cut or black and white. It's messy and cloudy and ambiguous. Perfect righteousness is for the angels. Here on earth, we have to slog along and do our best, and hope God likes what we're doing." Vespucci glanced around the room. "Where is Marco?"

"He's making a phone call," Maggie said.

Vespucci looked irritated. Maggie took his hand in hers and pulled him onto the sofa beside her. It made for a good picture. Proud father and doting daughter. Maggie turned her attention to me, her dark brown eyes focused on mine. Again my thoughts strayed into the guilty zone. I felt her beauty in my body, inside my gut, down in my belly. She locked eyes with me, a genuine smile on her face, her father beside her. I began to feel overly nervous. I couldn't take my eyes off Maggie's face. I felt like I was bugging out, as if I was having a bad trip. I took a deep breath, trying to get a handle on my physical reactions. Vespucci was staring intently at me. He knew what I was thinking, I was sure. I heard Sara's voice, "'Jon, are you mentally cheating on me? Do you want to have sex with her? Is that why we're having problems? Because you want to be with another woman?'"

Maggie's voice interrupted my thoughts. "Jon, are you okay? You're sweating. Do you need some water?"

I shook my head to clear it out. Sara's face disappeared. I realized Marco had entered the room during my embarrassing episode and was standing beside Vespucci, a curious look on his face. I took a deep breath and got my bearings. "I'm sorry, I just got a bit lightheaded. I haven't had much sleep the last couple of days, and I think the travel today just wore me out."

"You want to call it a night and pick up tomorrow?" Vespucci asked.

Feeling unprofessional, I responded, "No, no. I'm fine. Let's get started." I looked toward Marco and Maggie for confirmation. "That is, if you two are up to it?"

Vespucci answered for them, "Of course they are. Let the fun begin." Vespucci gave Marco a parting hearty slap on the back. Marco grimaced in response. Vespucci leaned over and kissed his daughter on the cheek and walked out of the room. I pulled my mini-recorder out of my pocket and set it on the coffee table between us.

Marco eyed the recorder. "You have to record us?"

"Well, as long as you don't mind. It allows for a better flow if I don't have to take notes. I hope that's okay?"

Maggie gently pulled Marco onto the sofa with her. "Of course it's okay." Marco seemed irritated by Maggie's show of affection as he sat down beside her.

"Let me explain how this works," I said. "I'll interview both of you tonight to get an idea of how you two first met and ended up together. After tonight, I'll meet with each of you individually to fill in the gaps. After that, I'll interview as needed. Will that work?"

Maggie looked at Marco before answering, taking his nonresponse as a yes. She turned back to me, nodding her head. I began questioning them about their history together. Initially, they talked more about their fathers than themselves. How Vespucci and Marco's father, Giancarlo Balducci, had grown up in the same neighborhood, went to the same schools, worked the same jobs after high school. Balducci now owned and operated two foundries, one in New York and another in Italy. Marco was his second in command. Marco was five years older than Maggie, so when they were growing up they had little crossover in school and had a different set of friends. But because their fathers, and their families, were so close, they saw each other whenever their families got together, which was often. They dated briefly when Maggie was sixteen, but the relationship ended before it became serious. When Marco turned twenty-one, he went with his father to Italy to assist in opening their factory and didn't return to the States until a little over a year ago. As circumstance would have it, Maggie and Marco had not seen each other during the many years he ran a successful business over there, which also included a cozy relationship with the prime minister of Italy.

As I sat listening to their story, I noted that Marco was a big player in his own right. His Italian business included some heavy-hitting contacts, not easily made or lightly ignored. I made a mental note to do some research on the Italian political landscape. Marco had been on U.S. soil only about a month before running into Maggie at a large family gathering. This is what I wanted to hear about.

"Was it love at first sight?" I asked.

The couple looked at each other. Maggie answered first. "When I saw Marco, it had been over ten years. He looked the same, just a little older. Yeah, I'd say there was a spark. Definitely on his side, because the first thing he asked me was whether I had a boyfriend." Maggie gave Marco a flirtatious squeeze on the arm.

Marco didn't respond either to the question or to Maggie's flirtation.

I prodded him, "So there was a spark?"

Marco nodded.

"How long before you formally asked her out?"

"That same night."

Maggie smiled. "He didn't waste any time."

"And how did your families react when you started dating?" I asked.

Marco answered first. "My parents were happy, especially my father. Having his son marry his best friend's daughter was more than he could hope for."

Maggie said, "My father's never been an effusive man." She left it at that. Marco gave Maggie a sideways glance, annoyed by her response.

"Well, he obviously approves now," I added with a smile.

I shifted gears and asked them about their courtship, what they liked to do together. In just over two hours, I got a clear idea of what their romance was like and who they were as a couple. I paid close attention to how they interacted with each other, how much they touched or interrupted one another, and how they added to each other's thoughts. When Maggie started yawning, I called it a night. I had gotten an adequate amount of material to work with. After making plans to meet with each of them individually—Marco in the morning at the foundry and Maggie in the afternoon at a coffee shop near NYU—I said goodbye to the Vespucci clan. Maggie's brother and his family had left earlier. Barbara gave me a hug at the door, and Maggie kissed me on the cheek. Vespucci walked me out to my waiting taxi. I spotted the ever-present Joey hanging back.

"Jon, thanks for doing this. I will owe you a debt of gratitude when you're all done."

I felt his praise was a bit presumptuous, given my current track record. The whole ordeal with the Internet Lovers and the phone calls from Attorney Nickels Sr. flashed across my mind.

"Don't thank me now. Wait till I'm done, just to make sure you like what I do. You won't owe me anything other than what we agreed to." For some reason, I felt more like I owed him something than the reverse.

"I like humility, Jon. But I know you're very good. I didn't just depend on Cranston's word. I did some checking on my own."

Knowing Vespucci had checked on me was anything but comforting.

"I'll do my best," I said.

"I know you will."

Over Vespucci's shoulder, I saw the shades open in the colonial windows to the left of the front door. I spotted Marco standing in the first window, watching me talk to his soon-to-be father-in-law. He'd been friendly during the interview, but the sinister look on his face now was anything but. Vespucci glanced over his shoulder to see what I was looking at, but Marco was gone. I wondered if he had actually been standing there or if my jumpiness was playing tricks on me.

"See something?" Vespucci asked.

"No. Just tired, that's all."

The taxi pulled up and I hopped inside. My driver was nothing like the Jamaican dude. This guy asked no questions, played no music, and, in fact, didn't say a word the entire trip back to Manhattan. I had gotten a room at the Washington Square Hotel, right in the middle of NYU, figuring it was in a hip area near enough to Greenwich Village that if I had any spare time on my hands I could take a short walk to entertain myself. Dropping me at the hotel, the cabbie pointed to the fare meter. I paid him the fare plus a tip. He nodded and was gone as soon as I climbed out of the car. I stepped up to the gold-inlaid front doors, an attendant opening them and welcoming me to the hotel. As I checked in, I picked up French, Italian, and what I believed to be Norwegian being spoken in the lobby. The hotel was a mid-scale affair, nothing too fancy but more than enough for my modest upbringing. Having spent little time in hotels growing up, I never tired of the pleasure of sleeping in a room I didn't need to clean, the pleasure increasing twofold because I rarely paid for my room since it was part of my fee. The desk attendant handed me my hotel key, pointed me toward the elevator, and said I should call if I needed anything. I thanked him and found my way up to my room.

I was on the fourteenth floor, facing south, so when I entered, the lights of New York lit up my room. Taken with the view, I dropped my bags on the floor and flopped down on the bed, staring out the window at the New York nightlife. Out of nowhere, Maggie's smiling face appeared before me, followed by a quick tightening in my belly. I blinked and she was gone. I immediately chalked up my attraction to my client as nothing more than a symptom of the distance between Sara and me. I figured as soon as Sara and I were able to repair the problems we were having, my attraction to Maggie would disappear as fast as it had come.

I pulled my computer out of my bag and opened the Skype program. The hotel clock read 9:32 p.m., so Sara was still at work. I double-clicked on the call button, happily noting Sara's Skype was on, though I couldn't put much weight on that because she set many of the programs on her computer to automatic start-up. After only two rings, I heard the pickup ping, and soon saw Sara's face. I met her image with a big grin, making sure I was centered in the camera's eye.

Before I could even say hello, Sara spoke, irritation in her voice. "Jon, not a good time. I'm working on a rebuttal I need to finish before I leave tonight. Has to be handed in tomorrow morning. Glad you got there safe."

"Oh, I understand, sorry to bother you. Just wanted to say goodnight."

"Got it. Goodnight. Sleep well. If I get this done sooner than I think, I'll give you a call. Okay?"

I could see the stress lines across Sara's face. Those only appeared when she had a lot on her mind. Her blond hair was pulled back in a tight bun, giving her face a more severe look than she usually had.

"Can we talk in the morning before you go to work?"

"If I have time, yes. I have to go."

"Good luck getting it done. Don't stay too late at work. I love you."

"Me too. Sleep well."

Click. That was that. I stared at the blank computer screen, closing the Skype program and powering the computer off. I stared at the twinkling Manhattan night, wondering how many other couples out there in the city were having similar problems. I decided going to bed would be the best choice. I knew there was little chance Sara would call me later. I went to the bathroom, washed my face, brushed my teeth, stripped down to my boxers, went back into the main room, and climbed into bed. I lay down, but sleep felt far off. I went back through the evening's events. Dinner had gone far better than I expected, Vespucci's family much more likable than I thought they would be. I began to think maybe this would be a lot easier than I had envisioned. The only wild card I could clearly identify was

Marco Balducci. During my interview with Maggie and him, he'd been friendly enough, but the sight of him in the living room window just before I left for the evening gave me pause. I had an appointment to meet him at 9:30 a.m. the next morning at his factory in Brooklyn. I would be alone. I felt a chill run through my body. Instinctively, I pulled the covers up a little higher.

But Marco was not my first appointment of the morning. I'd set something up earlier with a man I hoped would give me some insight into the Vespucci family that I was sure the Vespucci family would not give willingly.

I fell into a fitful sleep, but just before the void of unconsciousness swept over me, Maggie's warm, smiling face appeared, a twinkle in her eye. The sound of rushing wind filled my ears, Maggie's image knocked aside by Marco's grimace. I woke with a start, sitting straight up in bed.

Sleep was not going to come easy on this trip.

6
Early September New York – 1st Trip

I found myself sitting in a nondescript coffee shop near the corner of 4th and 11th, about a ten-minute walk from the hotel. I had arrived fifteen minutes before the scheduled 8:00 a.m. appointment. I ordered a cup of coffee, took a seat near the front window and waited, watching the foot traffic, mostly students, roll in and out of the shop. I was one of only a few patrons sitting at the six tables in the small establishment. In the back corner, a wiry, dark-haired man in his mid-forties, with sunken cheeks and pale skin, sat alone, like me. Every time I looked in his direction, I caught him staring at me. When I realized that he wasn't accidentally making eye contact with me, I got up and walked to the back.

"There a reason you're staring at me?"

"Jon Fixx."

It wasn't a question. Suddenly I felt foolish, realizing this must be Jim Mosconi, though why he'd sat there for so long without saying anything I couldn't fathom.

"That's right. You must be Jim Mosconi," I said.

He nodded.

"What do you want from me?" He got right to the point.

Doing my best to match his all-business tone, I sat down

across from him, spilling my coffee across the table as I did so. He shot back from the table like a man on fire, avoiding the spilled coffee. He was wired.

"Sorry!" Grabbing several napkins from the dispenser, I mopped up the mess. I reached behind me, dumping the napkins in a nearby trashcan and returning my attention to Mosconi. He slowly pulled his chair back to the table.

I said, "I've always been interested in the Mafia, and I've read everything I can get my hands on about the history of the criminal syndicate in the United States. Recently, you seem to be the only reporter who has a good handle on the current status of the Mafia in the U.S. Since I was coming to New York for vacation, I was hoping to pick your brain on the subject."

I fell silent, not sure where to go from there. Mosconi stared at me, waiting, his look bordering on contempt.

"That's it?"

"Yes."

He shoved his chair away from the table and stood up to leave. I immediately reached out to grab his wrist, my aggressive action surprising both him and me. At my touch, he yanked his arm away.

"Where are you going?"

Mosconi almost hissed at me. "If you're going to lie to a reporter, given what you do for a living, you better work on your poker face. I'm sure you know when your clients are lying."

I sat dumbfounded.

He asked, "Who's getting married?"

Mosconi was no dummy. Or maybe I was just too much of one. His question threw me for a loop, but I started running calculations, realizing that he must have researched me as well. I hadn't used a pseudonym. I needed to work on my spy skills. "You have to understand, everything we discuss is strictly off record. You can't use any of it in future articles. Deal?"

Mosconi nodded. "I know why you're here."

"You do?"

"The marriage of Maggie Vespucci and Marco Balducci. Right?"

"Yeah, that's right." Was he guessing, or did he know for a fact? By that point, I wasn't sure it mattered.

Calmer, Mosconi returned to his seat. "Did you think I wasn't going to do my homework on you?" He paused, scanning the sidewalk in front of the coffee shop. "Does he know you're talking to me?"

"Who?"

"Who do you think? Tony Vespucci."

"I don't think so." I was sure Vespucci would not be happy I was talking to a reporter. I felt sweat drip down the back of my neck.

"I recommend you keep it that way. I'll keep anything we discuss out of print as long as you keep our meeting confidential. Otherwise, this will be the only time we meet."

"Agreed." I looked straight at Mosconi.

"Why are you so concerned about the Mafia?"

"It's important to know everything I possibly can about my clients," I answered.

"Is Tony Vespucci your client?"

"He's paying me."

"But you're not writing about him, right? Your story is about his daughter and her fiancé and their romance."

"That's correct."

"Once you write their love story, then you'll be done. After that, you have no further obligation. Is that correct?"

"More or less."

"Then I recommend, Jon Fixx, you do your job and not worry about anything else. Don't dig any deeper than you need to get your job done and leave it at that."

"This advice coming from an investigative journalist?"

Mosconi stared at me for several moments, considering. Finally, "What do you know about the Mafia?"

I shrugged. "Not much more than what I've read recently. I've seen the Godfather movies, *Goodfellas,* you know, the standard fare."

"That's it?"

I nodded.

Mosconi leaned forward. "I grew up in Brooklyn. My older brother hung out with made guys. He helped run numbers when he was in his teens. He had ten years on me, so I didn't see much of it. He was shot and killed when he was twenty-two, working for a mob guy. My interest in the Mafia is personal. The violence and killing you see in those movies doesn't come anywhere close to the reality. Made guys kill for a living. They steal, extort, torture, and take all in the name of La Cosa Nostra. This is real life. You understand me?"

I nodded. I wasn't feeling so good about my upcoming appointment with Marco. "Look, I contacted you because you seem to be the only reporter who has any handle on the status of the Mafia right now. Going back to the '80s and '90s, I was able to find a lot of articles on the subject but very little in the last decade. You're the only person I could find who can give me an idea of who I'm working for. That's all I want."

Mosconi considered my words, interlacing his fingers together and placing his palms on the table. "How much do you know about the history of the Mafia in the United States?"

"The basics. I know the history of the Five Families, I can even name them: Genovese, Bonanno, Gambino, Lucchese, and Colombo. I don't have many holes there, at least not up to the millennium. But since that time, I've been able to find very little of anything useful."

"You've done your homework. The RICO laws almost obliterated the strength of the Mafia. Starting with Giuliani when he was a federal D.A., the government dismantled the leadership of every family. You probably know most of this,"

Mosconi said, impressed with my understanding, as limited as it was. He continued. "Staring at long prison sentences across the board, almost all of La Cosa Nostra royalty were struck with what I aptly named the Canary Syndrome. The strength of the Mafia's code of omertà lost all hold on the individual. As each of these mob bosses and their underlings stared at the possibility of life sentences, they started singing like canaries." Mosconi smiled at his own ingenuity. "By the late '90s, it appeared they were on their last legs. Then 9/11 happened. State and federal money and time got redirected toward fighting the new enemy—Muslim fundamentalism—so over the last decade the Mafia has been slowly, and carefully, rebuilding."

I acknowledged I'd heard and understood all he'd said, and then I waited for him to continue. But he fell silent, staring out the window. Something had caught his eye. Suddenly, he leaned forward, quietly asking me, "Were you followed here?"

The question threw me by his sudden change in demeanor. "No. I don't think so," I said. "Why would I be followed? Who would follow me?"

I felt Mosconi's eyes bore through my head. "You're sure?"

"Yes."

"Tell me, has Vespucci confided in you? Given you any reason to think he's in the mob?"

"Of course not."

"And you're sure he hired you only to write his daughter's love story?"

"Why else would he hire me? That's what I do for a living. Before last week, I didn't even know who Vespucci was."

Silent for several moments, Mosconi kept looking through the front windows of the coffee shop, noting the passersby. Satisfied, he turned back to me. "Look, I know you want information on your employer. The best advice I can give you is to do your job, learn as little as you have to about Tony Vespucci, Giancarlo Balducci, and his son Marco Balducci, and then go back to Los Angeles."

"How am I supposed to do that?" I asked, questioning Mosconi's advice. "Marco is marrying Vespucci's daughter. I have to interview him. In fact, I'm meeting him this morning."

"You heard what I said. I've got to go. Good luck with your project." Mosconi stood up to go, but I blocked his path.

"Wait a minute. You haven't told me anything about Tony Vespucci. That's the reason I called you."

"Fine, I'll give it to you in short order. But I'm warning you, Jon Fixx. The more you know about Tony Vespucci, the less you're going to want to know." Mosconi sat back down.

"I got it."

Mosconi glanced at the front window and then turned back to me, launching into a short history lesson. "You know Joey Massino?"

"Name sounds familiar."

"He became the boss of the Bonanno borgata officially in 1991. The Bonanno clan were like pariahs for a while within the Five Families because of the whole Donnie Brasco affair."

"I'm familiar with that. An FBI agent infiltrated their inner ranks."

"That's right. For a while, the Bonannos were on the outs with the other Families. Then Massino took over in 1991. And by '95, with the other major bosses taken down by RICO convictions, Massino had put the Bonannos back on top, even renaming the borgata after himself. At that time, he was the strongest boss around, and what made him different from the others who'd come before him was how careful he was. The FBI could never get him on tape, nothing on surveillance. In fact, they couldn't get anything directly linking him to a crime. Unlike his predecessors, he never frequented clubs, he passed orders through only one underling, and he often had his meetings on frequent trips outside the United States. The only reason the FBI was able to bust him was because the Canary Syndrome hit some of his crew in the late '90s, and then things started falling apart."

"What does this have to do with Tony Vespucci?"

"Vespucci makes Massino look like an amateur. Vespucci is barely on the FBI's radar, even though I believe he is the new boss of the Bonanno-Massino clan. He's got legitimate businesses pulling heavy income, and he uses these businesses as a convincing front."

"How do you know all this??"

"I've been studying mobsters since I was a little kid. Developing sources since I was twelve."

"Did you grow up near the Vespuccis? Did you know Maggie Vespucci when she was a kid? Marco?"

"No. But I kept my contacts in the old hood. That's how I know."

Mosconi stood up. "I have to go. Piece of advice, kid. Tony Vespucci is a master chess player, genius smart, had a reputation for his skills in the old neighborhood when he was growing up. His moves are calculated and always intentional. You're just a pawn. Don't step out of your role. Just do what you're being asked and nothing more. A pawn is the weakest piece on the board, so it's the easiest to get rid of." He stepped around my chair and headed for the front door but suddenly stopped and turned back to me. "Honestly, Jon, Tony Vespucci is not the guy to be afraid of. Marco Balducci, on the other hand, he's the one you should worry about."

After dropping that warning in my lap, Mosconi turned and was out the door before I could stop him. I sat in my chair, stunned. I was looking for answers, but now I was more confused than before. At the moment, though, I was focused on Mosconi's parting shot about Marco. What did he mean? From the corner of my eye, I caught the clock on the wall above the cash register, realizing it was close to 9:00 a.m. I was supposed to meet Marco at his factory in Brooklyn in thirty minutes. I dropped a couple of bucks on the table to cover the coffee and tip and hustled out of the shop onto the busy Manhattan streets.

I flagged a taxi, hopped in, and gave the driver the address Marco had given me the night before. Stuffing the piece of paper with the address back in my pocket, I leaned against the back seat, trying to clear my mind. As the taxi crawled through Manhattan toward Brooklyn, I mulled over the meeting with Mosconi. I couldn't shake the uneasy feeling his words had left me with. He'd been jumpy from the start. Why would he think I'd been followed? And by whom? Even more troubling was his warning about Marco. Why should I be more worried about Marco than Vespucci?

Round and round the questions swirled in my head for the next thirty minutes as the taxi wound its way through the busy streets. Before I could come up with any good answers, I was already at my destination, an industrial section of Brooklyn. As the taxi drove away, I was standing before a drab, two-story factory that took up a large city block. Two wide chain-link gates leading to an expansive front parking area appeared to be the only way in. At either end of the chain-link fence, a large, twelve-foot cement wall topped with barbed wire encircled the factory. Cameras were perched at the top of each corner of the gates, one peering directly down on me, the other pointing inward, toward the courtyard. If anything, this security seemed like overkill, especially considering the factory was only a foundry. I'm not sure what anybody could steal from a foundry. But what did I know?

I stood before the gates trying to figure out how to get in. Looking up, I felt the invisible eyes behind the camera staring down on me. I glanced up the street in one direction, then in the other. Nothing. It was deserted. Across the street sat a large, three-story warehouse, the windows dark. I couldn't see any activity. Turning back to the front gates, I finally spotted a small call box on the wall. I stepped over to it and hit the button. After a few seconds, I heard a buzz. Tentatively, I pushed on the gate door and slowly stepped inside the courtyard cum parking lot, staring across the hundred feet of cement to the factory entrance. I could faintly hear the crack and sputter of moving machinery. I assumed I'd hear more action and noise from a foundry. Blackened Victorian windows, evenly placed across the front of the building, didn't look all that welcoming. Cars lined the sidewall of the lot. I crossed to the front door, but it was locked. I knocked, waiting, looking over my shoulder at the gate through which I'd come, realizing it was shut.

"Follow me."

I jumped sideways. Turning back, I saw Marco standing in the doorway staring at me.

"You seem nervous, Jon. I find that people on edge are usually hiding something."

I was embarrassed by my reaction and realized he was baiting me. Rather than answer directly, I deflected, laughing, "Right, right. Sorry. I just drank too much coffee this morning. Always puts my nerves on edge."

Marco's face flatlined, my answer not what he was looking for. Without a word, he turned his back to me and stepped inside the factory. I followed him into the dimly lit recesses of metal production. As I crossed the threshold, I realized the two-story structure wasn't what it appeared to be from the outside. The main room was actually two stories high, but the upper level consisted of catwalks zigzagging throughout the massive space, apparently used to service the many large machines spread across the factory floor. The movement of the machines and the many men tending them, wearing variations of overalls, hard hats, and plastic safety glasses, caught my eye. As if an afterthought, Marco stopped in the middle of the room, turned, and tossed me a pair of plastic goggles. His own pair rested on his neck.

"Put those on."

Just as quickly, he resumed his walk toward the bowels of the factory, briskly moving between the maze of dirty molding machines and leading me through an extra wide doorframe into a second workroom, this one even larger than the entry room. Gas torches illuminated the smoke-hazed room. From where I stood, I could see a large magnet moving raw metal from one large bin to another. An older man in dirty overalls, with heavy work gloves on his hands and large goggles covering his eyes, worked the controls of the magnet from a corner of the room. As we passed him, he gave us a curt nod, nothing more. If Marco acknowledged the nod, I missed it. Moments later, I followed him up a set of stairs leading to a catwalk that ran the perimeter of the room, leading off to all corners. I could see an orange glow coming from somewhere as I walked up the stairs, unable to spot its origin. I followed Marco silently. He seemed uninterested in talking. As we reached the center of the catwalk, Marco stopped, pointing down to a large furnace that was at least ten feet deep and five feet wide. The tub was filled with a molten liquid. Even high up above where we were standing, I could feel the heat emanating from the orange glow below.

Marco turned to me. "Do you understand what we do here?"

I shrugged, shaking my head.

"We take raw metal, melt it down, and then pour it into castings. These castings in turn make car parts, airplane parts, military components, stuff like that. You've never been in a foundry before?"

"No," I answered.

"Down there," he said, pointing to the molten material in the pit below. "That's the centerpiece of a foundry. It's the power source. That metal bath is twenty-eight hundred degrees Fahrenheit. What I call raw power. Can be very dangerous."

He turned and looked straight at me, waiting to see my reaction. He stared at the red liquid, then reached down and grabbed a piece of cold metal twice the size of his fist and dropped it into the furnace. As the metal hit the molten bath, sparks erupted. Before I had time to react, tiny molten liquid balls flew up at me, burning small holes in my jacket and leaving tiny burn marks on my neck. I jumped back from the edge of the catwalk, slapping my neck in reaction, though it did little to take away the pain. Two thoughts immediately crossed my mind. First, I didn't like Marco very much. Second, I needed to steer clear of him as much as possible because he could be dangerous. I'd been with him less than five minutes and that's all the time I needed to reach this conclusion.

His voice dropped a notch, conspiratorially. "Imagine what the pit would do to a human body."

I gave Marco a nervous, sideways glance, wondering why he was trying to intimidate me. Over the years, I'd had more than one future husband who felt threatened by my access to his fiancé, the misdirected jealousy leading the paramour to make sure I was clear about what he would do to me if I got out of line, usually after one too many drinks. This felt different. Why would Marco feel threatened by me? At the moment, I couldn't figure it out, so I stored away the question for later.

He continued with his intimidating act. "Only, you can't just dump a body in the pit when it's fired up. Since the human body is made mostly of water, the water component of the body would boil when it hit the liquid, and the body would explode. So, you'd have to turn the pit off, let it cool, and dump the body in. Then turn the pit on, let it heat up, and bam, the body disintegrates, bones and all. No sign it ever existed. Pretty ingenious way to get rid of someone without a trace, wouldn't you say?"

I nodded. That feeling of foreboding I'd felt when first

meeting Tony Vespucci was coming back strong. I should have followed my instincts and turned Vespucci down for this job. I amended my earlier thought about Marco from "could be dangerous" to "is dangerous."

Attempting to change the subject from Marco's successful murder scenario, I said, "Where would you like to do the interview?" Marco stared, assessing me. There was something going on in the bigger picture that I was unaware of. Maybe Marco didn't want to do the love story and this was his way of letting me know. I figured I would discover more in the afternoon when I interviewed Maggie. Trying to keep my face as neutral as possible, I returned Marco's stare with a mask of indifference and slight deference, a useful tool I'd developed over the years.

Done scaring me for the time being, Marco turned and walked away. High above the floor, we crossed the length of the large workroom and descended a set of stairs on the opposite end, crossing through a dimly lit hallway into a set of office spaces. Marco led me through the reception area into an alcove office. A large metal desk sat near the back of the small office. A large picture of Marco and a man I assumed to be his father, Giancarlo Balducci, hung behind the desk. Based on the background of mountain and seascape, I assumed it had been taken in Italy. The desk was a mess, papers strewn about, pens, stapler, and scissors mixed in the piles, and a large laptop sitting atop all of it. I noted no pictures of Maggie anywhere. Marco motioned to me to take a seat in one of the two cushioned chairs in front of the desk. I pulled out my recorder, set it on the desk, and looked at Marco. He was staring at me, unresponsive.

"Do you mind if I record our interview?" I asked.

"Jon, let's be clear on where we stand with one another. And this stays between us. Do you understand?"

"Sure."

"I'm doing this only because my fiancée wants me to make her father happy. I'm a very private person and don't like sharing my life with anyone, especially a stranger."

This was not the first time I'd heard this speech, or some variation on it, but this was the first time I'd heard it from someone in the Mafia.

"If you tell Maggie or Tony what I just said, I'll make sure you pay for it."

I tried to take it in stride, responding with as neutral a tone as possible. "No problem, we're on the same page." My agreeable nature didn't seem to placate him. I chose to ignore his malevolent stare. "So," I said in my most chipper voice, "ready to do this?"

"If I find out you're sticking your nose anywhere it doesn't belong, I guarantee you'll regret it."

Mosconi's warning suddenly rang loud in my ears. He said Marco was the one to worry about. Now, sitting before him without family around, alone, on his turf, my well-being began to take precedent over my desire to fulfill my job requirements. Doing my best to maintain eye contact with Marco, I inhaled slowly and centered my thoughts. I decided I was being foolish to think he would harm me, especially here. Everyone in the family knew where I was. The thought fortified my mental position, allowing me to push back. A little.

I said, "Love is a serious matter, and I get paid to write about it. At the moment, your future father-in-law hired me to write about the love between you and Maggie. So I have to do what I'm doing. I'm sorry you're an unwilling participant, and if I didn't have to do this, I wouldn't. But Mr. Vespucci cuts a rather imposing figure, as far as I can see, and I'd rather do everything in my power to make sure I satisfy his demands."

Sitting back in his chair, Marco was silent a few moments. Finally, "How long have you known Tony?"

"I just met Tony this week when he asked me to write about your and Maggie's courtship."

"Do you know what Tony does?"

I wondered where Marco was going with this. Made men never discussed either the Mafia or their membership in it. The subject was taboo. I clearly could not trust Marco, and I didn't know what his agenda was, so I chose the safe route. "Sure, he's an entrepreneur, a businessman. Clothing, textiles, dry cleaning, internet sales, stuff like that."

Marco smiled in spite of himself. "Right, that's Tony." I sensed a sudden shift in his attitude. "Okay, let's get this over with."

And so it went. I started by asking him about his early years and his involvement with Maggie when they were children. I tailored all my questions around Maggie only, and steered clear of any questions about the rest of her family, especially Vespucci. I got the impression from Marco that Maggie was more like a little sister to him when they were younger. Until she hit sixteen. Almost overnight, it was impossible not to notice her. And Marco wasn't the only one. A lot of boys were vying for her attention. As he put it, Maggie signaled she was interested in him and they started to date. But before anything serious developed, his father sent him to Italy to help start the family business. As Marco put it, he "found his legs" there. Once his father felt comfortable with the budding ventures, he left Marco to oversee everything, a very heady position for a man in his early twenties, I thought. More than once, Marco mentioned the name of the Italian prime minister in relation to their business dealings.

Marco gave a detailed account about Italy and his family's growing involvement in Italian-American trade and the Italian political landscape, but I wanted to know about the more recent past. I'd already covered most of this material the night before. Having done these interviews for enough years, I knew that Marco's time in Italy, though important to him, would be a paragraph at best in the final product, so I saw no point in spending any more interview time on it than was necessary. Nudging him toward the topic of Maggie, I noticed the timbre of his voice changed slightly, a subtle shift at best, but a shift nonetheless. I wasn't sure of the significance of this, but he seemed on more secure footing when talking about business and Italy than when talking about Maggie and her family.

I led him through their last two years together with my normal set of questions. What they did on their first few dates. What it was like dating her. After all, he had known her since childhood. At one point, I asked him what it was like to ask Tony Vespucci for his daughter's hand in marriage. I assumed that given their culture and background, it was a foregone conclusion that Marco would do this. He gave me a guarded look of mistrust.

"I didn't ask Tony first. This is not the Old Country, Jon."

His answer provided insight into the possible tension I'd sensed between Vespucci and Marco the night before. I had no doubt Vespucci felt slighted Marco had not asked him for Maggie's hand.

After close to an hour of questioning, I had enough information from him to work with, figuring I could fill in the blanks with Maggie and the other family interviews. "I think that's enough, Marco. I appreciate you taking time out of your day to see me." I hit stop on my tape recorder and placed it in my pocket.

Marco leaned forward in his chair, placing his hands on the desk and said, "We have an understanding?"

I nodded, not exactly sure what the understanding was, but having no further interest in talking to Marco, I aimed for placation. "I'm sure I'll see you again before I go," I said, as calmly as I could.

"Good. You can find your way out?"

I stood up. "Sure."

I turned for the office door but Marco's voice stopped me.

"Be careful on the catwalk on your way back. We had a guy fall into the pit last year. It was ugly. Left little for his family to bury. Very tragic," Marco warned.

Not for the last time, I wondered what the hell I was doing here. "I'll be careful. Wouldn't want to fail you and Maggie and not finish your love story before your nuptials."

Without waiting for a response, I turned and quick-stepped it back the way I'd come. As I crossed over the pit on the catwalk, I slowed to take a good look at the orange molten liquid below. I shuddered at the thought of falling to my death in that pool of fire. If I needed to interview Marco again, it would not be here. I turned and moved even more quickly toward the exit and was momentarily blinded by the sun when I stepped through the door. I crossed the distance to the fence in seconds and found myself back on the street.

I looked in both directions for a taxi, but the street was deserted. I started walking past tall warehouses and anonymous storage buildings toward a busier intersection. About halfway down the block, I passed a black Ford Taurus parked across the street. As I passed, I glanced over at the driver. A man not much older than me looked my way. I turned away, minding my own business. I walked a few steps before turning back, but he wasn't paying attention to where I was heading. As I reached the intersection, cars were now passing at regular intervals. From the corner, I hailed a taxi and jumped in, giving the driver directions to NYU. As the taxi pulled away from the curb, I looked back down the street from where I'd come. I could just make out the fence line of the foundry. The Taurus was gone. As the taxi passed through the busy streets of Brooklyn, I called Sara on my cell, with no success. The phone rang several times and went to voicemail. I left a message, then hung up and texted her, just to be sure.

A terse response came back. "In Meeting. Will call later."

I was beginning to feel the tinges of real panic about our relationship. I tried to look at it objectively, an impossible feat for me, I knew, but if I took a step back and began noting all the little things happening, and not happening, between us, it didn't add up to a promising outcome. When I got back to L.A., I needed to sit down with her and do some serious talking. I didn't know what the problem was, but I was going to figure it out and fix it. My thoughts were interrupted by the cab driver's voice announcing our arrival and my fare in one breath. I paid him and climbed out of the car, back at the same building where I had met Maggie the day before. It seemed so long ago. I went inside and took the elevator to Maggie's floor, finding my way back to her office without incident. Her door was slightly ajar. I pushed it open and saw her organizing paperwork on her desk. She gave me a welcoming smile, a far cry from her fiancé's non-welcome earlier. It was impossible not to notice the flutter in my stomach and my increased heart rate. I felt my cheeks redden.

"Hi, Jon. Found your way with no trouble, I hope?" Maggie asked.

"Just fine."

"Everything go okay with Marco?" Sure, except your fiancé's a psycho. "Went great. No problem."

She looked up from her desk. "Really?"

"Yeah, gave me a tour of his foundry and everything."

That seemed to satisfy her. She finished up with the shuffling on her desk as she stuffed a few loose documents into her shoulder satchel. "Have you eaten yet?"

I shook my head.

"Mind if we grab some lunch while we do this? I'm starving."

"Not at all. That'd be great."

"Good."

Maggie crossed from her desk to the door. I couldn't help but notice her outfit, a casual sleeveless formfitting dark print dress, elegant and attractive, sexy yet understated. I inadvertently took a step back to give her more room as she passed through the doorway and felt her breasts brush against me.

"C'mon, Jon Fixx, I'm going to get you some of the best food in New York."

"Where are we going?" I asked.

"It's a surprise. Mind if we walk? It's not that far."

"That'd be fine. I do enough driving in L.A."

As we walked, I reflected on the night-and-day difference between my interview with Marco and my time thus far with Maggie. Maggie was amenable where Marco was obstructionist. Maggie seemed like an open book, and her behavior was loose and relaxed with me, as if we'd known each other for a while, not the twenty-four hours it had been. As we walked down the streets of Manhattan, Maggie seemed to have Tony's perceptive sense.

"You're wondering why I seem so comfortable with you?" she asked.

Caught off guard, I started to protest but shifted gears immediately. "Well, yes and no, to tell you the truth."

"For starters, Jon, I can see why you are so successful in your line of work. You have an easy, friendly nature. It's unassuming. Makes people comfortable to talk to you," she said. I could feel the warmth in her smile.

I shrugged.

"Oh, c'mon. I'm sure people have volunteered some of their deepest, darkest secrets during your interviews. Yes?" She looked askance at me.

I smiled in spite of myself. "That has happened on occasion."

"Have you ever had to hide information you've discovered from one fiancé to the other?"

"I don't call it hiding. To me, the term "hiding" denotes a level of self-involvement that I don't feel is accurate. I am a third-party neutral observer, nothing more, so I can't be responsible for hiding information. My job is solely to report what I've been hired to report. It's a subjective venture, and the outcome is predetermined," I responded, as accurately as I could. "I write the love story the way the participants—and their families—want it to sound, not always the way it unfolded, or is unfolding in some cases."

"So you do hear all the juicy details?"

I laughed. "Between the couple, their parents, the siblings, and the best friends, I almost always hear something I shouldn't. And it never appears in the final copy. Because if it did, there wouldn't be a final copy."

"Never?"

"Ever."

"Tell me about one time."

"When I discovered something I shouldn't?"

She nodded eagerly. Rarely did my clients feel comfortable enough to ask me about my past clients, so I wasn't sure what to say. "Well, remember, the confidentiality agreement I signed for you is something I do for every client," I said. "I have to be careful discussing past clients' indiscretions. I'm kind of like a therapist, or attorney, in that regard."

We walked on in silence. I glanced over at Maggie, noticing a mischievous look on her face. "Okay, Jon Fixx. Then tell me this. Hypothetically, if you found out something about Marco that would hurt me, what would you do with that information?"

My insides froze. A client had never asked me a question like that fraught with such weighty implications. My work involved people's feelings, the future of their lives, marriage, which was a 'til death do us part type of experience. Secrets were sometimes better left unrevealed, at least better left unrevealed by me. But in this case, on the one hand, I had Tony Vespucci, who I was pretty sure had the means to disappear me, and, on the other hand, I had Marco Balducci, who had just shown me how he could disappear me, if necessary. I answered in the safest way possible. "I'm sure that scenario won't present itself."

A serious look crossed Maggie's face. "Was Marco truly friendly and forthcoming this morning?"

I forced a relaxed smile. "Most definitely. He's excited about this whole process. At least that was my impression."

Maggie's eyes locked on mine, searching. I kept the smile planted on my face. She turned away. Suddenly, her mood seemed to lighten and she shrugged off whatever thoughts had been weighing her down. "Then, I guess we'll have to see if you give me the same courtesy. I may just pass you a few secrets that Marco doesn't know, and we'll find out how honorable you are."

"You won't have to worry. I'm like a vault," I promised.

"I'm not worried," she replied, laughing.

We'd gone almost eight blocks when she prodded me with her elbow in a playful nudge. "C'mon, just tell me about one big indiscretion you discovered, no names of course, confidentiality and all."

I decided there was little harm as long as I kept the story anonymous, so I told her about a couple from Atlanta where the groom had been having a long affair with the bride's maid-of-honor. During my interview process, the terrible secret was discovered and the wedding never happened. When I finished, Maggie had a pained look on her face.

"Oh, how terrible. Did they ever reconcile?"

"The groom ended up marrying the bride's best friend, so maybe in the long run it was best for everyone. But they didn't hire me to write their story. I'm not sure they wanted everyone to read about how they had been dating on the D.L. for almost a year, both cheating on their mates."

Maggie laughed. "No, I can understand why they wouldn't want that. What an unusual job you have. It really must be interesting."

Suddenly, Maggie stopped in her tracks. I stopped as well, not sure if I'd done something wrong when Maggie pointed to a building before us and I realized we were at our destination. A green awning hung over a small, quaint Italian restaurant. "Fanelli's" was printed across the door of the establishment. The place was packed, tables jammed together. I could see servers rushing in and out of the double doors in the back of the restaurant.

I glanced over at Maggie. "Cranston's place?"

"This is it."

I couldn't hide my excitement. "Is Cranston usually here?"

"Sometimes," she replied. "Maybe we'll get lucky."

We stepped inside Fanelli's and were hit with the hustle and bustle of the lunch hour. I followed Maggie to a two-seater just vacated by men in suits. A busboy cleared our table as we sat down.

"This okay?" Maggie asked.

"This is great," I said, as I looked around, impressed with Cranston's business acumen.

An attractive young woman hustled to the table, handing us menus. "Hey, Maggie, good to see you, darlin'," she said, leaning over and trading kisses with Maggie on the cheek.

"Hi, Janene. Meet my friend Jon Fixx," Maggie said, smiling at me from across the table.

"Hey, Jon Fixx, glad to meet you." Janene quickly looked back at Maggie. "Where do you find these good lookin' boys?"

I blushed.

"And he's modest. Good combination," she added. "Your usual, Maggie?" Maggie nodded. "And you, Jon Fixx, what do you want to drink?"

"I'll take a Coke."

Janene disappeared to get our drinks.

When she was out of earshot, I said, "She's a piece of work."

"She's great. Been here since they opened. Want to split a pizza with the works, make it easy on Janene?"

I hesitated, thinking about a bride eating pizza before her wedding. Most brides were usually so consumed with losing weight that I barely ever saw them eat while I was interviewing them, and they would definitely not eat a pizza.

"Don't feel obligated. We can get something else," Maggie said, apologetically.

"No, no," I protested. "Pizza with the works sounds great. I'm accustomed to my brides eating like a bird before their wedding."

Maggie laughed. "That's never been my style."

"Plus, Sara hates pizza, so I rarely get to order it."

"Sara, the lawyer?" Maggie asked, curiously.

"The same," I answered.

"So what if she doesn't like pizza. Why can't you order it for yourself?"

I shrugged. "I don't know. When you're eating out, pizza is something you want to share with someone."

"I never thought of it like that, but I guess you're right. It's not a food you want to eat solo."

I added, "This is one of the deep, philosophical facts I've learned on my journey writing love stories."

Maggie leaned forward conspiratorially. "Will there be a Jon Fixx love story about you and Sara one day?"

I wanted to answer with a definitive "yes" but suddenly admitted to myself for the first time that given the current Sara-Jon state of affairs, the best I could say was "I don't know." Instantly uncomfortable at this realization and knowing Maggie would not stop questioning me if I gave her room, I immediately put the spotlight back on her. "I'm not the one getting married in a couple of months. So we should be talking about you and Marco."

"But it's so much more fun talking about the Love Doctor's own love life."

Love Doctor. Online, one of my past clients had referred to me as the Love Doctor in a review of my business. It had stuck. I hated it.

"I read some of your samples on your website last night. I wanted to be prepared for our interview today," she said, giving me a smile that captivated me.

Janene appeared at our side, setting our drinks on the table. "What'll it be?"

"The works."

"Good choice. Best pizza in the whole state of New York. After you eat this pizza, you can die."

"I don't have any plans on dying soon, but—"

"Don't worry, darlin', it's just a saying." As she turned away, she said to Maggie, "He's literal, this one."

"In more ways than one," Maggie said, as she touched my hand, ever so briefly. "I knew you'd like this place."

"Jon?" A familiar voice interrupted Maggie.

I looked up to see Cranston Jefferson standing over my shoulder. I stood up and hugged him. "Cranston, so good to see you!"

"Well, well," he said as he looked from me to Maggie. "Your father told me he'd be calling Jon to write your love story, but I wasn't sure if he was serious." Cranston gave me a wide smile. "So, Tony talked you into doing their story, huh?"

"He can be very convincing."

"Yes, he can."

"Why didn't you tell me about this place when I was working with you?" I asked Cranston.

"The restaurant wasn't open yet," Cranston replied. "I owned the building, but I had to find a way to get the old tenants out without any fuss." He glanced down at the table and quickly looked up. "Where's that famous little tape recorder, Jon? Or are you off the clock? Have Maggie's charms swept you off your feet, you giving her a little extra attention?"

"Mr. Jefferson, if you were only a little younger," Maggie said, flirting with the old man.

"Maggie, I'm eighty-five years old, and you know what I've learned in that time? You can never give a beautiful woman too much attention." Then, turning to me, he said, "Jon, did you move on from that girlfriend of yours?"

I was at a loss, not expecting him to ask me about Sara. Coming right after Maggie's question, Cranston hit a nerve. After a moment I forced a smile. "We're still together."

Cranston put his hand on my shoulder. "Well, then, you two enjoy your lunch. And, Maggie, be careful, dear. You'll be telling him your deepest, darkest secrets before you know it."

"Thanks for the warning, Mr. Jefferson," Maggie said, standing up to kiss Cranston goodbye.

"Jon, stop by the office, if you have time to visit," he said. "You know where it is."

"I'd love to," I answered. "Time with you, Cranston, is always time well spent."

Cranston wandered off to attend to his other patrons. Then, Maggie and I settled back down at the table.

"After you left last night, my father told me Mr. Jefferson has a deep affection for you. Now I see what he meant. That's why I wanted to eat here."

"And I have a deep affection for him and Judith," I replied. "You could make a movie about the Jefferson's story." I suddenly found myself reminiscing about the hours I spent with him and Judith taping their story that led me to be sitting across the table with the daughter of a Mafia boss, in Cranston's restaurant, no less.

"I agree. Did my father tell you how they know each other?" Maggie asked.

"He mentioned it, but not in great detail."

"My grandfather served in World War II, my father's father. He and Mr. Jefferson crossed paths somewhere near the tail end of the war. As the story goes, Mr. Jefferson saved my grandfather from a German ambush. I'm not sure of the specifics."

"Wow, Cranston is full of surprises. In all the hours I spent interviewing him, he never mentioned that once." I pulled out my small tape recorder and set it on the table. "Now, can we focus on you? Are you ready?"

"Sure," Maggie said agreeably. "Shoot."

Over the next hour, Maggie filled in the many holes left by her fiancé from the morning's interview. Growing up, she saw Marco several times a year when the families got together over the holidays. She'd always had a crush on him. All the girls did. As a teenager, Marco had a bad-boy danger about him that the girls found attractive. He was five years older than Maggie, and he wasn't interested in her until she turned sixteen and nature took over. Literally. Just like Marco had said. All the boys at school noticed her. Her boy's body, as she described it, seemed to change overnight into a young woman's. Requests for dates started coming and her father was suddenly interested in her social life. On her sixteenth birthday, he sat her down and told her that boys were going to be interested in her for more than just her mind. Therefore, any boy who wanted to date her had to meet Vespucci face to face. I laughed out loud. The thought of wanting to take Maggie out but having to meet her father first would have put a solid restraint on my desire. Once word got out about Vespucci's rules, the dating requests almost came to a halt. At school, the boys still flirted with her, but few were brave enough to take the next step. At the same time, Marco's attentions ramped up. Suddenly, at family functions, Marco was spending more time attending to Maggie's needs. Maggie couldn't say whether her father noticed, but she did and she liked it. I asked her why it never got serious. She stopped, considering her answer.

"It did get serious."

Her voice had changed. I perked up. "We always spent New Year's Eve with the Balduccis and a couple of other families. Marco asked me to meet him at a party somewhere else that night. My father would not let me go out un-chaperoned, so I lied to my parents and told them I was staying at my girlfriend's house."

"Your father was old school. Did you rebel against him

often?"

"Are you kidding? No way. I did not argue with my father, at least not in a disrespectful manner. That was something neither Michael nor I ever did. We just weren't raised that way. We were taught to respect our parents. Period. Plus, in the neighborhood, he had a reputation."

"Reputation?" Of course he did.

She was trying to put the right words together. "He was known as the enforcer, as the guy who always did whatever he said he would do. Never an empty promise. That reputation has served him well in business."

I'll bet it has. "Your dating life suffered because of it, though."

Maggie laughed. "But Marco was different. He didn't seem to be intimidated by my father."

The back of my neck started tingling. This is what I was looking for. Hints of a possible conflict between father and future son-in-law.

"That night on New Year's Eve," Maggie continued, "Marco and I figured my parents would stay at his parents' house until well past midnight. That's what they always did. But it didn't turn out that way. I'm not sure why, but my parents left the party early and came home. They walked in on us in a compromising position, mostly an undressed compromising position. My father was beside himself. I've never seen him so angry before or since. My mother and I had to stop him from beating Marco to death on the spot."

"What happened after that?"

"My father made me go to my room. I heard him call Giancarlo as I was heading up the stairs. After that, I don't know what went on between them. For a while, I tried to find out, but my father wouldn't talk about it. Marco wouldn't talk about it, either. Even now."

"How did you and your father handle seeing Marco at the family gatherings after that?" I asked, aware Maggie was talking about a sensitive issue between her and her father and Marco and I wanted to keep her on track.

"We didn't. Marco went to Italy to open their foundry. I didn't see Marco again for almost ten years."

"What about your father and Giancarlo? Was there a falling out?"

"Not that I'm aware of. We still saw the Balduccis at family gatherings a few times a year. Only Marco wasn't there. But since we got engaged, his parents have been really happy." Maggie glanced down at the tape recorder, suddenly realizing all that she was revealing. She leaned forward and said in a whisper, "Jon, please don't write about this. I don't want my father and Marco to know I've told you this."

So this was the root of the tension I picked up between Vespucci and Marco. Vespucci still didn't trust Marco, and Marco was still angry with Vespucci. There was a battle going on between them, I was sure of it.

Before I could respond to Maggie's request, she said, "Jon, you have to understand my father's background. He operates according to the values of the old country. He's a practicing Catholic. He interprets church doctrine literally. It's old-fashioned and I don't adhere to it, but a woman's virginity before marriage is sacrosanct. After all, I'm his only daughter. So, until I went to college, I did what he told me to do. You can't write about this, and you can't let Marco or my father have any idea you know about it."

"I understand. Don't worry, it won't leave this table," I promised.

Maggie leaned back, relieved.

"How did you feel after Marco left?" I asked her, gently.

Maggie looked at me and sighed. "You're looking for the long-lost love angle, I guess."

I laughed. "I'm just trying to get all the facts so I know how to write the best, most truthful story I can for you and Marco."

"Well, I'd love to say I was heartbroken and that it was a Romeo/Juliet scenario. But I was sixteen and curious and very attracted to Marco. Beyond that, I wouldn't say I sat at home and pined for him. I had crushes on a couple of boys at that time, so it was more like a page in a story than a whole chapter."

"What did your father do after Marco left?"

"That was the worst part. He grounded me for a month. When word got around about that night, I didn't get asked out again by a boy until my senior year."

The idea of a beautiful teenage girl going dateless because of her father's reputation made me chuckle. In the next moment, though, my laughter disappeared when I reminded myself that the man who instilled enough fear to override teenage boys' hormones—a feat of gargantuan proportions—was also the man who had hired me for this job.

"It's not funny, Jon," Maggie admonished me. "For a sixteen-year-old girl not to get asked out, ever, it can do a number on a girl's ego."

"Oh, c'mon, you can't have thought there was anything wrong with you. You're so beautiful, how could you think that?"

I suddenly wished I could pull the words back. The compliment was over the professional line between polite and flirty.

Maggie's head tilted slightly as if she was looking at me in a new light, if only for a moment. Then she smiled. "Thank you. I wish you'd been around my senior year. Without any attention from the boys, a girl can begin to feel unattractive."

I grabbed my soda and took several long sips to avoid having to respond. Thankfully, Janene arrived with a large steaming pizza covered with pepperoni, sausage, mushrooms, onions, and a couple more items I wasn't sure of. She set the pizza on the round insert on the table, adroitly slicing it into even pie sections.

"Enjoy. Don't eat too fast!" she quipped and placed more

paper napkins on the table and left.

Maggie and I looked at the pizza, then one another.

"Looks fantastic," I said, as I admired the pizza and Cranston even more.

"Ready?" Maggie asked.

"I am."

We each grabbed a slice and spent the next few minutes silently eating. Maggie raised her eyebrows as I took a bite. My mouth was too full of the best pizza I had ever eaten, so I could only nod. I would have to tell Cranston when I next saw him.

After several slices were gone, I started the interview again. "What happened when you and Marco reconnected? How did your father react?"

Maggie hesitated a moment. "When you write these love stories, you practice maximum discretion, right?"

"Of course," I assured her.

"When Marco and I met last year, we were adults and my father couldn't interfere the way he had when I was a teenager, which gave us a lot more room to get involved. At first, we kept it light. Over time, it grew more serious. I didn't tell my father about our relationship right away because I didn't think it would go anywhere. I assumed we were just having fun, taking care of a childhood crush that was never resolved. But Marco was serious about our relationship almost from the start. He was the one who suggested we be exclusive. In fact, if I'd left it up to him, we'd be married already. I wasn't sure how I felt at first, but when he finally bought the ring and made the official proposal, I had no reason to say no."

I was having trouble matching the story Maggie was telling me about her fiancé with the guy I'd interviewed earlier in the day. As she described the progression of their relationship, it appeared she was not as taken with him in the beginning and that Marco, not Maggie, had been the driving force from day one. This all came as a surprise to me. Up to this point, based on past experience, if I'd been made to guess how their relationship had unfolded, I'd have reversed the roles. I made a mental note to go over this again when I had more time. I circled back to my original question.

"And your father. What was his reaction to all this?"

"My father was funny when I told him about Marco. I assumed he would be happy for us, because Marco is his best friend's son."

"But what about when you were sixteen? You didn't think he'd still be upset about that?"

"Jon, it had been almost ten years since that happened, and I hadn't seen hide nor hair of Marco in that time. We were just teenagers, kids at the time. If my father still had an issue after all that time, he would have said something." She paused. "But when I told him we were dating, his response was nothing. Not happy for me. Not upset. He never said much of anything. After I thought about it for a while, I realized Papa usually keeps his own counsel. When it's something important, he doesn't share his thoughts or feelings until he's made a decision. He never said anything, and I never asked." She smiled. "But I think hiring you was his way of giving us his approval."

I nodded, smiling back, although I didn't agree with Maggie's assessment of her father's actions. My sixth sense was quietly ringing a bell. Something was not right about all of this. Families didn't usually hire me if they weren't in total support of the upcoming nuptials. Even if either or both members of the engagement couple had a strong desire to bring me in, it only happened when the parents writing the check were behind it. It was even more rare for the initial request to come from a parent of the engaged. First contact with me was almost always made by the bride-to-be, less often by the groom-to-be, and rarely by the parent of either principal. But in this case, Tony Vespucci was so intent on having me write his daughter's love story that he flew out to

Los Angeles to meet with me personally without the knowledge of his daughter or anyone else, as far I knew. Then, even with my protestation that I would not have enough time to do my best job, he was adamant. Maggie interrupted my thoughts.

"Excuse me a moment. I'm going to use the ladies room." Maggie stood up from the table and headed to the back of the restaurant toward the restrooms. I watched her walk, disappearing down the narrow hallway.

"She's beautiful, isn't she?"

I jumped in my seat, jerking my head around. Cranston was standing at my side. I quickly gathered my composure. "She is," I answered, trying not to betray my feelings.

"Have you met her fiancé yet?" Cranston asked.

"I have. He's charming," I said with a hint of irony.

Cranston eyed me. "Has Vespucci been treating you well?"

"So far, yes. But I've only been here one day," I said with a wry smile.

"Well, Jon, I feel responsible for you being here, so I want to make sure you're taking care of yourself."

"What do you mean?" What did he mean? Take care of myself?

"Tony heard about you through me, but I didn't actually think he'd hire you," Cranston answered.

"Getting a job's not a bad thing, Cranston," I said. "Or in this case, is it?"

Cranston shrugged his shoulders. "Whether something is good or bad depends on where you're standing." He paused, and then asked, "How much do you know about Tony? I'm assuming you've done your usual, exhaustive research."

"I've done enough to know Tony Vespucci is not someone to cross."

"Nothing could be more true, my friend," Cranston said, but the way he said it sent a chill down my spine. "I've known

Tony a long time. Been doing legitimate business with him for years. But Tony has his hands in a lot of different ventures. Some of them are, shall we say, under the radar."

I lowered my voice to just above a whisper, "He's connected, right?'"

Cranston brushed his index finger against his nose, indicating yes. "Just keep your eyes and ears open, and if you do what Tony asks you to do, you should be fine. If you need anything, call me."

"Thanks, Cranston." I stood up and gave the old man a hug. Although he was doing his best to reassure me, all the concerns and fears I had tried to dismiss rushed back to the surface and, for a moment, I panicked. I wanted to run out of the restaurant, hop on a plane, and go back to Los Angeles.

Cranston's voice intruded on my flight scenarios. Noting the look on my face, he placed his withered, surprisingly strong hand on my shoulder and said, "Tony is a man of his word. You do right by him and he'll do right by you. Just do your job the way you have always done it and he'll be more than satisfied." Cranston nodded to me when he saw Maggie walking down the hallway towards us.

"But I'm not worried about Tony, Jon. I'm more worried about what's going on around him. Just keep your eyes open and watch your back." As Maggie approached, Cranston added, "Now she's a catch. Marco doesn't deserve her. He's the bully in the schoolyard, always has been."

Before I could respond, Maggie sat down at the table.

"Young lady," Cranston said to Maggie, "give your father my regards, and tell him he should take good care of Jon here. Can you do that for me?"

"I will happily pass on the message, Mr. Jefferson," Maggie said, and then looked at me, as if to say, "Of course, we wouldn't think of doing anything less."

"You two enjoy the rest of your lunch," Cranston replied, as he patted me on the back. I watched him as he casually walked away from the table. He had accomplished so much in his lifetime and he was still going strong.

Maggie was watching me watching him. "Amazing what he does at his age."

I couldn't agree more but I was still working over Cranston's warning. I couldn't help but feel I was getting in deeper and deeper and wasn't prepared for what lay ahead. It felt surreal. I felt surreal. I turned my attention back to Maggie.

"My father is a good judge of character," Maggie said. "It's made him very successful. He doesn't like a lot of people, but I can tell he likes you. The same way Cranston does."

Her father liked me. At least for now. That was a good sign.

Maggie leaned forward. "But you like to keep your distance. You don't let anybody get too close to you, do you?"

Maggie fell silent, waiting for an answer. I tried to get a grip on the tangle of thoughts and panic scrambling through my brain and body, doing my best to clear it all out and get some control.

"Is that a rhetorical question?" I asked her.

Maggie responded, "Deflection. See?" She sat back, disappointed.

"I'm sorry, Maggie, it's just the tools I've learned to keep the ball rolling forward in my interviews. I have to keep the focus always on the principal to gather the information needed," I explained. "In this case, the principal is you. Over the years, I've found that if I talk about me, it muddies the waters and colors the responses I get to questions that need to be asked. I'm sure you'd understand that because of your anthropology background."

Reluctantly, she said, "Yes. Okay. Focus back on me. Fire away."

As the restaurant emptied, we ate our dessert, a tasty gelato with a sharp espresso. Slowly, we got off the subject of Maggie and Marco's relationship and talked about Maggie's

Ph.D. studies, her family, and what she loved about New York. The conversation ebbed and flowed. As we talked, my fears and concerns about Vespucci and Marco and what I was getting wrapped up in disappeared as I became more interested in Maggie herself. Finally, after almost two hours of recording in the restaurant, I stopped the tape and realized the restaurant was almost empty. As if on cue, a busboy cleared our table and we waited for Janene to hand me the check.

"Mr. Jefferson sends his regards," Janene said, hovering over us. "He had to go, but he asked me to tell Jon Fixx he was serious about stopping by to see him and Mrs. Jefferson. Lunch is on him." She gave me a big smile.

I wasn't surprised by Cranston's gesture. "Please tell Cranston thank you, Janene, and I'll do my best to see him and Judith," I said. Then, Janene gave Maggie a hug before clearing our table.

We left the restaurant in mid-afternoon, and instead of taking a taxi back to Maggie's office, we walked a roundabout way, taking our time, lost in our own thoughts. Maggie broke the silence. "Mr. Jefferson said you usually take a minimum of six months to work on a project." She paused and looked at me. "Then why did you take on our story? You've got only a little over three months."

"Let's just say your father can be very persuasive."

"My father threatened you?" she asked, apprehensively.

"No, no," I said and immediately regretted putting it that way. I gave her my best smile, scrambling to recover. "He was very convincing. And it helped that Cranston Jefferson gave your father my name."

Maggie scrutinized my face as I spoke. She seemed satisfied with my answer. "It's just sometimes my father can be pushy in his business dealings, and I want to make sure you are completely here of your own accord."

"Of course," I said, emphatically, so Maggie would not get suspicious that I had initially turned her father down.

I wondered in that moment if she knew or had any idea of what her father was capable of doing if someone made him unhappy. I pushed the thought aside and tried to lighten our conversation. She asked me general questions about my business, and I answered as best I could. It dawned on me as we walked that we could have been good friends in another life, maybe more. As soon as I had the thought, I dismissed it, realizing it would get me nowhere.

We said our goodbyes when we reached the university.

"So, Jon Fixx, I'll see you again before you leave, right?"

"I think so. I'll do the rest of my interviews in the next few days with your family and friends and then try to see you and Marco, if time permits before I leave."

"Will be done as soon as I get upstairs," Maggie assured me and gave me a hug. "Jon, I hope your girlfriend in Los Angeles knows what she has. I see why Mr. Jefferson likes you so much." She studied me a moment longer, then turned and disappeared through the double doors.

I stared at the university building long after Maggie was gone. I wasn't sure what to think or how to react. There had been only one time before when I had been strongly affected by another person while on assignment and that was Sara. Not only had I never felt such a strong connection with a client before, never had a client tried to delve into my personal life. While trying to shake myself out of the daze I was in, I waved down a taxi, directing the driver back to my hotel.

Sitting in the taxi, I slowly reviewed the last twenty-four hours, and what I had discovered during this time led me to three hypotheses. First hypothesis: Maggie and Marco were not in love as much as they'd like me to believe. There were definitely chinks in the armor. Of that I was sure. This was not to say they weren't in love at all, or not in love enough to get married. I'd seen couples on par with Maggie and Marco who got married and were fine. However, they didn't fall under the category of head-over-heels.

Second hypothesis: I presented some kind of threat to Marco, at least he saw it that way, though I couldn't fathom what that threat could possibly be. Often, when I found a principal who presented me with an unwelcome attitude, the principal was hiding something.

Third hypothesis: The man who hired me, the man who was paying me, the father of the bride, didn't like his soon-to-be son-in-law. I was as sure as anything that Tony Vespucci had never forgiven Marco for his earlier transgressions, and I guessed that if I dug deeper there was more to it. But did I want to dig deeper? I heard the voice in my head shout a resounding *No!*, but I had no choice in the matter. I had taken this job. I was not about to tell Tony Vespucci I was changing my mind. I'd just attempted to do that for the first time in my career with the Nickels clan. For obvious reasons, that had not gone over well at all. I knew I still had not seen the last of Nick Nickels Sr. and when it came to the Intimidation Factor, he had nothing on Tony Vespucci. Walking away was not an option.

As I stepped out of the taxi in front of my hotel, I came to the unsatisfying decision that I would have to keep the rest of my interviews on an innocuous level, just enough to get the information I would need to write Maggie and Marco's love story. And then I would get out as quickly as I could. That was that. I took the elevator up to my floor, and walked down the hallway to my room. I felt Maggie's hug again, her body tight against me. The feelings tingling just under the surface made me uncomfortable. Though I'd decided just moments before to finish this job as quickly and safely as possible, one thought kept nagging me. Why did Vespucci hire me? I didn't get hired by fathers who didn't like their daughter's fiancé. Maybe I was reading the whole situation wrong; maybe Vespucci and Marco made their peace with each other when Marco got back from Italy. As I thought about it, I knew I could not find out the real reason Vespucci hired me if I approached it head on. If I wanted to know what I was doing here, I would have to play it out. Would I be safe? I would have to take my chances, I decided.

I got to my room, my thoughts flip-flopping back and forth. I reached for the handle of my hotel room door, but the door opened at my touch. I stood there, surprised, then cautious. I pushed the door open, flipping the light switch just inside the entrance. From my vantage point, nothing seemed out of place. I stepped inside the room, pulling the door shut behind me. My overnight bag rested beside the bed in the same place I'd left it earlier. I figured the maid must have left the door open by accident after she cleaned my room. I went back to the door, stepping on the outside and pulling it shut to ensure the lock worked. It did. This time, I needed to slide the card to unlock the door. I stepped back inside, noticing the blinking light coming from the phone on the nightstand beside the bed. I crossed the room and picked up the receiver, hoping Sara had left me a surprise message instead of calling my mobile. I punched the appropriate buttons and heard the automated voice prompts telling me I had one message. My guts tightened as I listened to Nick Nickel Sr.'s voice.

"Jon, soon you will understand the great resources I have at my disposal. You don't become district attorney for the state of California, which by the way is the fifth largest economy in the world, without knowing how to keep an eye on someone. I know where you are each minute of the day. I have eyes everywhere. One way or another, you will pay me back for embarrassing me like you did in front of my daughter. Candy still cries herself to sleep because of what you wrote. Welcome to my world, Jon Fixx. I'm going to make you a permanent fixture. I'll be seeing you."

I erased the message and hung up the phone. Nick Nickels was tracking me. This was something new. By now, I was used to the threatening phone calls, the yelling, and the like from the Nickels clan. But those messages were emotionally driven. They didn't worry me so much. This one was different. Nickels Sr. sounded calm, sinister. In addition, he was putting time and money into tracking me. The unlocked door suddenly took on a whole new light. I jumped up, rushing through my small hotel room into the bathroom, through the step-in closet, under the bed, checking any space that would be large enough to hide a man. Or a bomb. Or something. But I found nothing. I was getting paranoid. Nickels Sr. was all talk. I had given him his money back so he couldn't pursue me legally. He wanted to harass me, and he was doing a good job. I didn't think I could become more unsettled than I already was. But now I had Nick Nickels Sr. to contend with as well, even here in New York. This was all becoming more than I could handle.

Thinking over all my troubles reminded me I had not had a substantial conversation with my girlfriend since I had arrived in New York. I grabbed my PDA from my pocket. No missed calls. She hadn't even called me back. I sat on the side of the bed, staring at my phone. I was a fool if I thought this was just a phase. I couldn't deny the emotional distance between us. I felt isolated, in limbo, never clear where I stood. I grabbed my phone, hitting the speed dial for Sara's number. The phone rang a couple of times. Then I had Sara live.

"Hello."

"Hi, lover. Just checking in."

"Dammit, Jon, I'm on the other line with a really important client. You know the drill when you're on the road. I'll call you tonight when I'm ready for bed."

"Oh, okay."

"Bye."

"I just wanted—" Click. I kept the phone to my ear. "—to tell you I love you." I put the phone on my lap. That was that. Momentarily defeated, I stared at the wall, empty.

Finally, I shook my head, figuring the best thing for me to do was work. I grabbed my laptop out of my bag, powered it up, and logged into my email. Good to her word, Maggie had already sent me a list of family members and friends I needed to contact. I immediately set to making phone calls and sending emails, lining up the rest of my time in New York. I was a bit disappointed because the two key people I truly wanted to talk to were unavailable. Tony Vespucci and Giancarlo Balducci had both left town on unexpected business trips, so I'd have to wait until my next trip to interview them. In the interim, I'd have time to sketch out Maggie and Marco's story, and anything new I discovered on the next trip could be added in. Once I'd outlined my interview time frame, I ordered room service and passed out with the television on.

The rest of the week was uneventful. I didn't receive any more disturbing calls from Nick Nickels Sr., though I was sure I hadn't heard the last of him. I made no headway with Sara. The few conversations we did have were lackluster and short. I made my way through the interviews with most of the remaining family members on Maggie's side, realizing they didn't seem to have the same issues with Marco that I guessed their patriarch did. In fact, by the time I was done, I began to question my own instincts. Not a hint of negativity about Marco. Maggie's mother, her brother and sister-in-law, and even her nephew all seemed to like Marco and think the marriage was a wonderful godsend for the Vespuccis and the Balduccis. I also interviewed several aunts and uncles and cousins, getting the same story from all of them. They thought it very romantic, considering that Maggie and Marco were childhood friends. Maggie's friends—Vanessa and Sonia—considered Marco to be a true catch, handsome as the devil and charming. But I was surprised by the short list of friends Maggie gave me to interview. She was more of a loner than I would have initially thought. I saved Marco's side for the next trip, wondering if I would get the positive attitude toward Maggie that Marco got from her relatives.

I was able to pay my respects to the Jefferson's at their

penthouse in Manhattan. Judith and Cranston served me dinner. Cranston didn't mention his earlier warning to me, and I didn't ask. But before I left, Judith asked me how it was going with the Vespuccis. I told her it was coming along fine. "You just take care of yourself, you hear?" she advised me, and sent me on my way with a kiss on the cheek.

Vespucci had sent Joey to take me to the airport, and after four full days of interviews and not getting anything that supported my feelings about Marco, I figured I'd ask Joey about him. Joey wasn't on my interview list, but I was sure he had an opinion about Marco and Maggie's upcoming nuptials. It took most of the drive for me to summon up the nerve to ask the question I wanted to ask. I saw the signs indicating the final approach to JFK and gathered up the courage.

"Joey, can I ask you something?"

Joey looked in the rearview. We hadn't spoken much on the drive.

I took a deep breath. "Why did Mr. Vespucci hire me?" We were at a red light as the words tumbled out of my mouth. I looked up to see his eyes boring into me from the rearview mirror.

"What kind of a question is that? He wants to make his daughter happy." The light turned green and the car jumped forward, Joey's eyes back on the road.

Since I'd already opened the door, I figured I might as well walk through it. "It's just, I don't know. I don't think Mr. Vespucci likes Marco very much. That's all."

Joey hit the brakes and jerked the car over to the side of the road. My heart rate doubled. Clearly, I was onto something, but now I wasn't sure if I would make it to the airport. Joey stared at me in the rearview. It was very disconcerting to talk to his back. "Why do you say that?"

I weighed my answer, realizing I didn't really have any hard facts. "Just a hunch, I guess."

Joey considered my answer a moment before responding.

"Let me make a recommendation to you, kid. Do your job. Keep your hunches to yourself. Understand?"

I nodded, my heart rate slowly returning to normal when I was sure Joey wasn't going to do anything else. Suddenly, we were back on the highway, rolling into the airport drop-off moments later. I climbed out, my overnight bag in tow. I stood there as Joey pulled away. I watched his Town Car disappear into the traffic, Joey's warning ringing in my ears and leading to two thoughts. First, I would be best served to follow his advice, as I'd originally intended. Second, his reaction led me to believe my instincts were right on target. I was onto something. But at what cost if I pursued them? Not wanting to answer that question, I turned my brain off as best I could, picked up my bag, and headed into the terminal.

7
Early November
Los Angeles

As Izzy wiped the sweat off her brow, I opened my door and climbed out.

"Jon Fixx. We've been looking forward to the day you would snap out of it. Luci's in back. Can you stay for lunch?"

"What do you think I'm doing here?"

I crossed the street into the front yard. Izzy stepped away from her flower garden, taking off her gardening gloves as she bent over to give me a peck on the cheek. She froze midway when she spotted the damage on my face. "Jon, what happened?"

"Just a misunderstanding," I said, trying to pass off the bruising on my forehead and face as nothing worth discussing.

"Looks like more than that." She took a step back and stared at me, her green eyes scanning my face. Always tactful, she didn't push the issue. Instead, she smiled and said, "I'm really happy to see you!"

"Thanks, Izzy."

"Luci's working out. I'll finish up here, and then you can tell us what happened to your eye."

"Thanks, I appreciate it." She gave me a gentle push toward the house. I walked up the three steps leading onto the porch and pulled the screen door open. The house was a refurbished five-room Colonial Craftsman circa 1919. Luci and Izzy had bought the house not long after they arrived in Los Angeles and had slowly brought it back to life. I crossed the threshold, stepping onto the original wood floors which Luci had resurfaced himself on his hands and knees one square foot at time. A Batchelder-tiled fireplace anchored the room, built as the focal point at the center of the living room wall, off to my left. Two large foursquare wood-framed windows were placed equidistant on either side of the fireplace, two more again at the front of the house, filling the room with daylight. To my right, directly across from the fireplace, there was an entrance to the hallway leading to the bathroom centered between two equally sized bedrooms. I could see the retro, original matching white-tiled floor and counters in the bathroom. An open doorframe led from the living room into the kitchen bordering the back of the house. There was no television visible in the living room. They didn't have one. A futon couch rested against the front wall. A waist-high bookshelf ran the length of the back wall filled with esoteric books about world religions, metaphysics, spirituality, history, and medicine. Two armchairs offset the fireplace, a small end table between them. Izzy and Luci were true minimalists. The home was sparsely furnished and free of any clutter, clean and humble and simple, like its owners.

I paused in the living room, slowly glancing around at the walls. The living room appeared schizophrenic because of the strange, ill-matched color scheme Luci had created. Each of the four walls was painted a different color: A deep red covered the wall with the fireplace; a light brown took up the wall directly opposite; a deep purple drew attention to the back wall bordering the kitchen; and a light mauve spread across the surface of the front wall.

As I crossed toward the kitchen on my way to the backyard, I noted the black light installed above the bookshelf at the intersection of wall and ceiling, perfectly centered midway. I looked around to see identical lights on each of the other three walls. These black lights were part of Luci's living room art piece. When he had first shown me the color scheme of his living room walls, I made a joke about the mismatch. Luci responded with a smile, "Just wait."

A couple of months later, he invited me over for dinner and a show. It was sometime in the summer, and we had eaten on the front porch as the sunlight slowly faded. When night lazily settled in around us, Luci stood up and led me into the living room, indicating I should sit on the couch against the front wall. Izzy sat down beside me, the look on her face telling me she knew what was coming. As I soon discovered, Luci had installed blackout curtains over each of the windows to make the room extra dark. He turned off the overhead lights and the room was enveloped in black. I raised my hand in front of my face but I couldn't see it. I heard the sound of a switch and the room was filled with the blue glow of black light. I looked up and around, spotting the black-light frames. Then my eyes dropped from the light sources to the back wall below. At first I was so taken with what I was seeing that the images didn't register.

Slowly, my eyes adjusted. The back wall was filled with images of horses and buffalos and Native American Indians engaged in the hunt, galloping, hair streaming in the wind, bows and arrows held at the ready. The images were so lifelike I thought they were actually moving, the glow of the black light playing tricks on my mind. Over to the left side of the mural, a group of hunters were astride their horses, one with his hair pulled back tight in a long ponytail, the wind from the speed of his horse whipping against his cheeks. Another hunter had left his hair loose and long and black, flying free as his pinto horse took the lead in the chase. Most of the men on horseback were bare chested, small loincloths covering their groins. Lean and lithe, they laid out low over their horses as they galloped onward, the horses' muscles straining with their flight, clearly pushing the limits of their abilities. I counted over twenty Native Americans spread out on this side of the tableau, working hard to gain ground on the buffalo stampeding away from them.

My eyes traversed the pictorial in a slow scan, noting too many buffalo to count at first, many of them about to run right off the wall into the kitchen. Closest to the floor, the scene was bound by a deep blue river, the water gushing into the distance. A large mountain range covered the top of the wall, the highest peaks nipping the ceiling. A lone black panther with green eyes stood guard over the scene unfolding below him, but he was not watching the hunt. He was staring directly at me, his gaze unnerving. I looked away for a second to get my bearings, noticing Luci was watching me, a satisfied grin on his face, his white teeth glowing in the black-light. I looked back to the panther, his hard gaze still upon me. I got up from the sofa and walked over to the wall, looking up at the panther seated on the mountain two feet above me. No matter what my vantage point, he was staring at me, alone, watching, studying, waiting.

"He's our guardian, watching over us."

Without turning around, I nodded. That he would.

Luci's maternal grandmother was a full-blooded Cherokee. Growing up, he had spent many summers on the reservations of different Native American tribes throughout the Southwest. His Native American roots had influenced Luci, shaping his personality and conscience. Of his grandparents, he'd been closest to Grandma Peshlaki, as I knew her, and I assumed this was a tribute to her. Since the time he first showed me his black-light art, he had covered three of the four walls with Native American themed murals, floor to ceiling. Every so often, I'd take a joint to their place, and Luci and Izzy and I would turn the lights out and smoke, watching the murals come to life before us. I made the mistake of taking Sara over there one night after we'd been dating for about eight months. Afterwards, she said she didn't get the point of the murals. I tried to explain to her it wasn't about a point, but that was too illogical for her. Izzy and Luci were not fans of my ex-girlfriend. They were not going to miss her.

I crossed the living room doorway into the kitchen and took the few steps I needed to reach the back door. Through the screen, I could see Luci in the small backyard going through one of his martial arts routines, wearing his ubiquitous free flowing white gi, his feet bare. The gi was his outfit of choice most days now. Since moving to California, his cross-dressing days were a thing of the past, something he left back in Pennsylvania. He swept an invisible foe's legs out from under him, followed instantly with a round kick to the face, then finished with a jump and a 360-degree turn in the air, his other leg whipping around to take his opponent's head off. Luci landed on both feet, took a breath, and turned around.

"Jon."

I nodded hello.

Luci acknowledged my black eye with a silent stare, assessing me as he moved across the yard for a better look. "Finally crawled out of your cave. How are you feeling?"

"Getting better."

"Been out picking fights, I see?" He leaned in, inspecting the damage. "Nice solid hit. Please tell me you didn't get this from Sara's new boyfriend."

I shook my head.

"I'm assuming there's a story behind this?"

"Sort of."

Luci raised his eyebrows. One of the benefits of a best friend is that he understands understatement. "I just lost a bet with Izzy. I said it would be two months before you left your apartment. She said you'd be out before that."

"Thanks for the vote of confidence."

"Izzy didn't see your place." Luci passed me in the yard,

grabbing a towel from the back of a lawn chair, wiping the beads of sweat from his brow. On his way back to the center of the yard to pick up his kon, a large wood staff, he patted me on the back. "I guess this means you're ready to start your life again."

"If the last twenty-four hours is any indication, my life is going to go on whether I want it to or not."

"I wish you could remember that all the time."

Luci carried his staff into the garage, waiting for me to explain myself further. I followed him into the garage that Luci had converted into a training space. The entire floor was covered in a one-inch thick, soft rubber, nonslip padding. A punching bag hung from a rafter in one corner, a self-standing, canvas-striking bag in another. A double-end striking ball tethered to both floor and ceiling was attached in the corner nearest the entrance. Luci used the double-end bag to increase his punching speed and agility. When he worked on it, the bag looked like it was invisibly attached to his fists with a cord, moving back and forth with the impact of blows without ever wavering off path, almost too fast for me to track. Sometimes, I would try to work the double-end bag but my semi-coordinated efforts amounted to a jumble of missed punches and always ended in profanity. I didn't think I'd ever be able to master it. There were two benches, a flat bench and incline bench over to one side, a full rack of dumbbell pairs from five pounds all the way to one hundred pounds against the back wall. A squat rack was screwed in near the front where the garage door had been. Luci used the room for his private clients who studied under his tutelage as a kung fu master. However, as I learned in time, Luci hated to fight, and he preached pacifism as a way of life. Fighting was a last option for him. He often said the winner of the fight is the one who walks away without ever throwing a punch.

From the kitchen screen door, I heard Izzy say, "Lunch will be ready soon."

"I'll get cleaned up," Luci responded.

Izzy disappeared back into the kitchen.

"I finished the mock-up for the Chicago couple. I've been waiting for your call to get it over to you." Seeing the peevish look on my face, Luci said, "You're not done with it, are you?"

"No."

"Final copy is due in a couple of weeks."

"I know."

Over the years, as I tested new and better ways to improve my business, I discovered that the story alone was not enough to please the overanxious eyes of my brides-to-be so concerned with the aesthetics of a wedding. They not only wanted a fairytale storybook to describe their romance to their friends, they also wanted the finished product to be an eye-catcher. So, to give it an extra punch, I needed a more elaborate finished product, but I had no visually artistic ability to speak of. Enter Luci. I asked him to design the jacket covers and give each story a unique look that matched the couple. When Luci finally agreed to help, he did me one better and suggested that I begin asking clients for romantic mementos that I could include in the book: love letters, favorite pictures, a CD of favorite songs, a lock of hair, the menu of the first restaurant they ate at, movie stubs, and the like. Then Luci took these romantic mementos and created a unique canvas as the centerpiece for the story. The response from clients to Luci's artistic touch was overwhelmingly positive; he took my business to a whole new level of success.

Over time, I developed a tiered pricing sheet so clients could choose how detailed they wanted the book to be and how much money they wanted to spend. The basic package included only the story and a cover design. The most complicated, multimedia package meant Luci had to spend a great deal of time designing the layout of the story while incorporating all the different paraphernalia the couple wanted to include in the final product. Within a year of his involvement in my business, Luci had become an essential partner.

Sitting down on the weight bench, I asked, "Does the name 'Tony Vespucci' mean anything to you?"

He shook his head while wiping down the bench. "Great mobster name, though."

"Funny you should say that."

Luci looked up at me from his squatted position, my tone peaking his interest. "Really? Mob? As in Mafioso?"

"Yes."

"Please don't tell me he's responsible for your black eye? If he is, you need to leave now, because you're putting Izzy and me in danger."

I smiled. "He's our latest client."

Luci stopped what he was doing. "I thought the Chicago client was your last client of the year."

"That was the plan, but it got changed. While you were in China in September, I went to New York."

"And you're only telling me now?"

"By the time you got back, I wasn't really thinking about my work because of Sara."

"That's your reason for not telling me?"

"Well, and I wasn't sure if I wanted to get you involved in this one."

Luci gave me a sidelong glance, resuming his cleanup. "Tell me."

"That first week in September, Vespucci paid me a visit. I didn't know how to say no to a Mafioso crime boss." I stood up, kicking my shoes off and walking over to the punching bag, throwing a half-spirited kick low on the bag. I turned to Luci. "I didn't want to get you involved until I was further along." Luci watched me, giving no indication what he was thinking. I switched legs and kicked from the other side. "Then Sara destroyed my life, and I forgot about everything."

"When does it need to be done?"

"Late December."

"Not a lot of time, Jon. Especially since you just burned a month hanging out in your apartment." Luci straightened to a standing position, wiping down the barbell resting on the benches V cups. "Is it an anniversary or a marriage?"

"Marriage. His daughter. Maggie."

Something in my voice got Luci's attention. He stopped wiping for a moment, checking out my face. "Maggie, huh. What's this Maggie like?"

"Just finished her Ph.D. at NYU."

Luci took that in, silent a moment. "Please tell me she's marrying an accountant."

"Guy's name is Marco Balducci."

"Mob, too?"

"Yeah. Before coming back to the States last year, he spent ten years living in Sicily, running a foundry for the family business. He even got friendly with the prime minister."

"The Italian prime minister? That guy's dirty as they get. He's all tied up with the Italian mob."

"I know. I've been doing my homework."

Both of us silent, I watched Luci finish wiping down his equipment. Finally he stood up, moving over to his set of dumbbells lined up on a rack against the wall. He picked up one at a time. "You tried to turn him down, didn't you?"

"Yep. Wouldn't take no."

"Figures." Luci mulled that over a moment. "So, you've just been sitting on this since you and Sara broke up. Have you written anything?"

I shook my head.

"What about interviews?"

"Started them in September. I've got initial notes, but I need to go back next week to finish my interviews and tie up the loose ends. Mr. Vespucci paid me a visit this morning to make it clear he would not be happy if I didn't do my job."

Luci quickly turned to me. "He gave you that black eye?"

"Yes, I mean no. Well—"

"Which is it?"

"It's complicated. It started with the FBI agent—"

"What FBI agent?"

"—then more happened at the memorial service."

"What memorial service?"

Izzy's voice interrupted us from the kitchen, "Let's go, boys."

We both looked toward the house, then back at each other. Luci raised his finger. "Stop. I want you to start from the beginning and explain everything, and I want Izzy to hear this."

I nodded, following him as he walked out of the garage and crossed the yard to the kitchen steps. Izzy had already brought a couple of dishes out to the table, so Luci and I went inside and grabbed what was left to carry and took it out to the table. As we sat down, I stared at the spread, realizing I had not had a good meal, other than Izzy's care packages, in weeks. I'd lost over ten pounds. I wasn't a big guy to begin with, so I was sure the weight loss showed. Lately, when I looked in the mirror, I had noticed the hollowness in my cheeks.

Before me was a vegetarian's paradise. Neither Izzy nor Luci ate meat, and they avoided processed foods, so I knew I could eat whatever was on the table without regret. They tracked the days of the farmers' markets in the different areas of the city and made sure to hit at least one every two to three days to buy fresh organic vegetables. A plate of large, juicy red tomatoes sat directly in front of me. Beside it was a large spinach salad with black olives, avocado slices, and pine nuts sprinkled across the top. A plate stacked with a dozen ears of steamed yellow corn, a large bowl of steamed brown rice, and a pile of veggie burgers completed the spread. I looked at Izzy with gratitude.

"I figured you'd be hungry," she said, smiling.

Izzy was right. I was starving. I filled my plate with tomatoes and salad and rice and two veggie burgers. I ate with a rapacious vengeance. As I stuffed food in my mouth, Luci and Izzy watched me for a few moments before they began to eat.

Luci broke the silence. "Jon has some explaining to do, so I'm going to ask him to start over because he was talking a bunch of nonsense in the garage and I'd like him to explain it to both of us."

Two sets of eyes turned to me.

I had to wait a moment as I chewed my food before I began. "A guy from New York hired me to write the love story for his daughter's wedding."

"A mob guy," Luci added. Izzy's eyes opened wide.

"Yeah, a mob guy," I repeated. I stopped eating, sitting back, taking a breath, trying to decide where exactly to begin. "The last twenty-four hours have been . . ." I paused, trying to gather the words, ". . . well, if it hadn't happened to me, I don't think I'd believe it."

"I would," Luci responded. "Trouble must have a willing participant. It follows those who seek it."

"Tell us," Izzy said gently, admonishing Luci with a look.

Between bites, I went back over my previous twenty-four hours. Luci and Izzy sat quietly, their faces revealing first amusement, then surprise, and then shock as I moved through the turns in my story. I recounted my entire night, from meeting Donovan at the rest stop to my run-in with Ted Williams to the whole debacle at the memorial service. When I finished, I took a deep breath. "And then I decided to come see you guys," I finished with another deep breath. "That's everything."

Izzy spoke first. "Let me get this straight. So Ted Williams is Sara's new boyfriend's cousin? And he's an FBI agent?"

I winced at the mention of her name in connection with another man. I nodded.

"But why would he threaten you if last night was the first time you called her?" Izzy asked.

I looked away sheepishly. "Oh. I forgot to mention I've made a few more phone calls from the phone down the street over the last few weeks."

Izzy stared at me, waiting, knowing there was more.

"And I may have parked outside her place a couple of times at night just to make sure she was okay."

They shook their heads in unison. I shrugged my shoulders.

"Then you went to a memorial service, scared the dead woman's granddaughters, got beat up by a big boyfriend, and was saved by a mobster's bodyguard?"

I grinned at Izzy. It sounded so crazy I couldn't help it. "Yeah."

Izzy looked at Luci, who had been sitting quietly watching me. He appeared to be perusing the damage on my face. "The black eye came from the guy this morning, right?" I nodded. "Where did you get the bruise on your forehead?"

Inadvertently, I raised my hand to my forehead, having completely forgotten about the bruise, the night seemed so long ago. I pushed gently against my forehead, pain shooting into my skull. The bruise hurt. "Oh, I left that part out," I said, embarrassed. "I couldn't get the voice in my head to shut up, so I banged my head against the phone booth at the rest stop. Knocked me out for a minute."

Luci and Izzy exchanged a look. Silently, Izzy stood up from the table and crossed to the house. Luci stared at my face. Neither of us spoke. A few moments later, Izzy returned to the yard with her medical bag. She pulled out her penlight, sat down beside me and pointed it at my eyes. "Hold still. Look left. Now right," she instructed.

Protesting, I said, "I'm okay, you guys." But I enjoyed the attention, nonetheless.

Izzy put the penlight away, satisfied with her examination. "You aren't showing any signs of the effects of a concussion."

Luci cut in, "Jon, you said the guy kicked you while you were lying on the ground?"

I nodded. Luci indicated to Izzy to check my ribs. She immediately placed her hands on my midsection. As she felt around my rib cage, I winced as she prodded my left side. More gingerly, she felt around the sore area. "You've got two bruised ribs, but nothing worse," Izzy said. She pulled some aspirin out of her bag and gave me the bottle. "Take this for the next couple of days. It will ease the pain when you breathe and bring the swelling down."

"Thanks, Izzy," I said.

Izzy shook her head as she packed her stuff away. "Jon, why can't you find yourself a nice girl? Enough of this." She stood up, carrying her bag back inside.

"Are you going to leave Sara alone?" Luci asked.

"Yes."

"Because, Jon, the FBI doesn't just pay random visits to ex-boyfriends to warn them away. This guy isn't answering to anybody above him. He was working off-duty, which means he doesn't have any oversight, so he may not be as guarded about his actions as he would be under normal work circumstances." Luci checked my gaze to make sure I was listening. Izzy came out the back door and took her seat beside Luci. "You understand?"

I did understand, but I wasn't sure if I'd mind another visit from Williams. The guy had made me feel small and insignificant, throwing his weight around my small apartment and I'd done nothing wrong. I would not be so accommodating the next time, if there was one.

"I'm serious," Luci said, concern in his voice.

"I know. I agree," I answered.

But I didn't. Luci knew I didn't agree, but he left it there for now. He would wait to make his point at a more opportune time. Over the years, Luci had trained police officers and military personnel and government agents because of his martial arts background, so he wasn't speaking out of turn. He knew how these guys operated.

"Jon, we worry about you," Izzy reiterated.

"Oh, c'mon. I'm going to be fine. I always am," I said, a bit defensively.

She pointed at my face. "Obviously."

"Tell us more about Tony Vespucci," Luci said, changing the subject.

"Believe it or not, I'm not so worried about Tony Vespucci," I answered. "I'm more concerned about his soon-to-be son-in-law. I've been to New York twice, have completed almost all my interviews with the key players and core family, but there's something going on that I can't pin down."

"Jon, what does that matter? All you have to do is write the story and you'll be done with it," Izzy said.

"But that wouldn't be fair to Maggie if I didn't do my job and get the whole picture."

"Maggie, the bride? What do you owe her? Before September, you didn't even know her," Luci responded.

Luci and Izzy's eyes locked on me. I tried to meet their gaze but had to turn away. Suddenly Izzy sat back.

"Oh, Jon, do you have a crush on your client?"

"What? No!" I countered.

Izzy and Luci exchanged looks, the concern registering on both their faces.

"You guys, c'mon, I'm a professional. I don't have a crush on Maggie Vespucci. She's the daughter of a Mafia boss. Like I could ever fall in love with a mob daughter."

Neither of them was buying my rap.

"Seriously, you guys, I'm just telling you there are things that don't add up, little things. I was hired to write a love story, but it's my job to find out everything there is to know so that my story is as truthful as possible. Some things just don't add up."

"Like what?" Izzy asked.

"For starters, I don't think Tony Vespucci likes his daughter's fiancé."

"So? That's not a news flash. How many couples have we worked with who had the same issue?" Luci responded.

"But Vespucci hired me to write the love story."

"He just wants to make his daughter happy," Izzy added, smiling.

I fell silent, realizing as I spoke to them they were right. I had no proof to justify my distrust.

"Honestly, Jon, don't you think it best you just finish the interview, write the story, and be done with it?" Izzy added. From inside the house, the whistle of the teakettle interrupted Izzy's next words. She pointed her finger at me, warning me, "Wait 'til I come back. I don't want to miss anything." She hurried inside.

Luci looked questioningly at me. "You said, 'mob boss.' This guy is actually a 'boss,' as in 'Don Corleone' status?"

"As far as I can tell."

Izzy came back with the tea before Luci could say whatever was going through his mind. She set the tray on the table and poured each of us a steaming cup of chamomile tea. She resumed her seat, looking at me expectantly. "What did I miss?"

I paused, waiting to see if Luci would say anything, but he didn't, so I shook my head. "Nothing."

Luci picked up his cup and blew on his tea. "So what have you done so far?"

"I've interviewed everyone in the family except for Vespucci, have had multiple sit-downs with the principals, and interviewed a few of Maggie's and Marco's friends. I've almost got enough to write a story, but I need to go back at least once more to figure out my hook. I don't have much of a handle on Marco's side. He basically warned me that if I dig any deeper I'll regret it. He's made it very clear he doesn't like me."

"Why don't you say something to his fiancée?" Izzy asked. "Or this Vespucci character?"

"It's more complicated than that. I don't know where I stand with each of these players, or whom I can trust. Before I start banging on the hornet's nest, I want to know if there are any hornets inside."

"Good point."

Luci cut in. "Have you worked on this story at all since you got back from your second trip to New York?"

I shook my head.

Izzy asked, "Not even given this Vespucci guy an update? That's not good."

Luci added, "And he sent a guy out here this morning to check on you?"

"Yes."

Izzy was about to speak but Luci interrupted her. "Are you intent on finishing this project?"

I considered Luci's question, wondering if I even had a choice. Though Vespucci seemed to like me, I was sure he wouldn't take kindly to my telling him I was quitting the project. Then, there was Maggie to consider and the unresolved questions about her and Marco's relationship. "Yeah, I'm going to see it through to the end. I don't have a choice."

Luci and Izzy accepted my response silently.

I stared at them, considering what was ahead of me. After a few moments, I said, "I'm going to go home right now and get working on "The Coffee Shop Lovers" and do my best to finish it before I have to go back to New York. That way, I can get it to you so you can do what you have to do. I'm leaving town on Monday to finish up my interviews with Maggie and Marco." I saw the concern on their faces. I smiled, trying to seem more confident than I felt. "Don't worry guys, I'll be fine."

"And Sara?" Izzy asked.

"I'm over it."

"No more phone calls?" Izzy again.

"And no more nightly visits to check out who's at her

place?" Luci asked.

"No more," I finally said.

Izzy stood up, placing her hand on my shoulder. "Anybody want dessert?" she asked.

Luci and I both nodded. Once she was out of earshot, Luci leaned toward me and said, "I'm coming with you to New York."

"Luci, that's not necessary. I can handle this."

"I know. It sounds like you've done a great job so far."

I smiled.

"I just want to come along for the fun."

I knew I would never be able to talk him out of it. I didn't say anything further. There was no need.

Izzy returned carrying an apple crumble made with all natural ingredients, I was sure, and a stack of small plates. Luci took the plates from her, placing one in front of each of us. He kissed Izzy on the cheek while she placed the dessert on the table and cut it into large portions. The exchange between them was inconsequential, something I'm sure they did everyday, but to me it was a flash of insight. It was so easy for them. They flowed together, moved in the same direction with ease. They didn't have to work at it, or if they did, it didn't appear like work to me. This is what a good, healthy relationship looked like. They had what I wanted but incapable of finding.

I took a big bite of the crumble. "Izzy, this is fantastic!"

Izzy smiled. I suddenly realized we had spent the last two hours talking about me, and feeling like I had been rude, I asked Izzy, "How's work going?"

"The hours are killing me," she answered.

"And me," Luci chimed in. Izzy patted him on the shoulder in mock sympathy.

"But it's going well. I'm almost done with my residency."

"She's getting job offers from all over the country," Luci added.

"What?" I sat up straight. This was the first I'd heard.

"Are you going to take a job somewhere else?"

"No, no," Izzy said. "Luci just likes to tease you. I'm considering either joining a local practice or starting a private practice. I'm not sure yet. There are several factors to consider." I breathed a sigh of relief.

"Jon, do you really think we'd leave you here? You wouldn't know what to do with yourself if we left. Do you know what Izzy said the other night?" Luci paused, looking at Izzy to see if she was going to stop him. She didn't, so he continued. "The job offers started rolling in, and I asked her, 'What is the biggest factor you will consider in deciding which job to take?' She looked at me and said, 'Well, it has to be in L.A. We can't leave Jon here alone.' Believe that? You've got more power over my girlfriend than I do."

I glanced at Izzy and blushed.

"But don't get any ideas, Jon."

I shook my head vigorously. Luci stood up, picking up the plates and silverware off the table. I followed suit, with Izzy right behind me. Together, we moved our discussion into the kitchen and washed the dishes. Luci informed Izzy he'd be going to New York with me. Her response was short and simple.

"Then, be careful. Jon, bring him back in one piece."

"I'll do my best."

I made plans with Luci to check in with him on Sunday and gave Izzy a hug. They were standing on their porch, watching me drive away. I headed back up Sunset Boulevard through Echo Park, driving past the Spanish and English billboards. Sunset carried me over to Vermont, which I took north to Franklin Street. I could have hopped on the freeway and gotten home quicker, but I was enjoying being outside again. I'd been cooped up physically and emotionally for so long that it felt good just to be outside without an agenda connected to Sara. The weight on my shoulders had lessened. I felt lighter in spirit. For the first time, I knew I'd be able to move on, that I was going to make it. I made a left turn from Vermont onto Franklin, the street narrowing as I did so. The sun was riding low in the sky. It would be dark soon. With my windows down, I felt the hint of evening on my face, the air cool and crisp, the smell of fall in the wind.

I reached the 101 North exchange at Franklin and Argyle, again debating freeway versus surface but decided against it. I drove below the freeway underpass, continuing on Franklin and crossing over Cahuenga Boulevard, old brick and block apartment buildings lining both sides of the street. I reached the Highland exchange, where the traffic picked up, large shops and stores to the south bordering the eastern crush of the famous section of Hollywood Boulevard. The Hollywood Bowl sprawled out just to the north and west of me, invisible from the street, and only the wide, long driveway indicated its existence. I'm sure from above it looked like a bottleneck, Highland narrowing from several lanes as it merged northward onto the 101 Freeway. I was glad it was the weekend, because during the week this entire area was chaos. I jogged on Highland for a moment, cutting across a couple of lanes, watching a BMW, then a Lexus, scurry out of the way of my oncoming, gangbanger Buick. I'd become accustomed to this reaction by other drivers when they saw my car in the rearview, an unexpected benefit I never would have imagined when I reluctantly purchased it soon after I arrived in Los Angeles.

The Buick was a gas guzzler and not the most reliable car, but it had a unique style and the smoothest ride I'd ever experienced. The suspension system was fine-tuned to make passengers feel like they were floating down the road. The car, however, provided a misleading indicator of who I was. In Los Angeles, probably the most car-dependent, car-obsessed culture in the world, your car defined you. Many people spent more time in their cars, driving to and from work, running errands, and going to recreational activities than they spent sleeping. A person's first impression of you was often based on the car you drove, not on the clothes you wore or the first words you spoke. Considering I was a writer by trade, a geek in most circles, a matching car would have been a Toyota Camry, a Ford Escort, or a Honda Accord. But as fate would have it, I didn't choose my car. It was chosen for me.

When I first moved to L.A., I rolled into the city on the train at Union Station downtown, with two large suitcases and a destination to Hollywood. At the time, I believed everyone who was anyone lived in Hollywood. No one was there to pick me up—I didn't know a soul—so I jumped on a bus. The Los Angeles public transportation system is not known for its efficiency or user-friendly ways, as I quickly discovered on my trip to Hollywood. By the time I reached my destination, I'd been on six buses and missed my connecting bus three times. Five hours later, after getting a good tour of the east side of Los Angeles, I decided that getting a car was the first order of business. Back in Pennsylvania, during college and after I dropped out, I'd gotten along without a car, but here in L.A., my needs had clearly changed. I spent the night at a cheap motel in Hollywood on Santa Monica Boulevard east of Vine, watching transvestites trawl the streets for business.

In the morning, I went looking for a car. As far as I was concerned, a car should be inexpensive and effectively get me from point A to point B. A few blocks past the motel, I came to a small mom and pop car dealership, tucked in beside a mobile phone shop on one side and an electronics shop on the other. There were only about forty cars on the lot, but I knew I'd rather give a small business my money than some large corporate-owned dealership. As soon as I crossed from the sidewalk onto the lot, a squat, round Mexican woman rushed out to meet me. She had a flat, wide nose, her hair poking out from her head in all directions, making it unclear whether her hair did that of its own accord or if she intentionally styled it that way. Her eyes sparkled. "*Hola buenos dios, mijo!* Come in." She smiled at me, and though I was on guard having just arrived in the city, I immediately liked her.

"Hola," I said with a heavy gringo accent. I do speak Spanish. It was one of the few truly utilitarian values my education had left me with.

"Usted es nuevo en la ciudad?"

I cocked my head to one side, surprised. How did she know I was new to town?

She smiled a little brighter at me. *"Se sienta en su cara, mijo."*

I nodded.

"Usted necesita un coche."

"Yes, I just want something that won't break down and is safe."

"Of course, *mijo,* of course. *Mi marido tiene el coche perfecto para ti. Usted va a encantar. Mi nombre es Maribel."* She looked over her shoulder, whistling, and then turned back to me. *"Mi marido se fuera derecho."*

Taking a quick glance around the lot, I noticed the cars appeared at least a few years old, nothing new, but the price tags on them were what got my attention. All were within my financial grasp. I spotted a light-blue four-door Honda Accord a few cars over that looked manageable, respectable, and reliable. My eyes moved away from the Honda down the line, but not seeing any other options, I looked to the other side of the lot and spotted a couple of older model Toyota Camry's that would suit me just fine—dependable, reliable, unflashy.

"Mijo, aqui esta mi marido," Maribel said.

For a moment, I was confused. I didn't see a man anywhere. Then my eardrums were hit with a deep bass voice.

"Down here," the voice instructed.

I looked down to see a Mexican dwarf standing beside the woman, his eyes sizing me up. I did my best to hide my surprise. He did his best not to notice my unintended bewilderment. He addressed me in English.

"You want a car?"

"Yes," I answered. His voice seemed to come from deep within, as if he had a voice synthesizer box strapped somewhere to his body. His gaze fell down to my shoes, slowly moving up my body to my face. I grew uncomfortable as he sized me up. I glanced nervously at Maribel. She gave me a reassuring smile.

"Don't worry, darling. Stan *es muy bueno en juego la gente con los coches,"* she said.

I looked back down but Stan was gone. His deep bass traveled at me from my side, so close I jumped. He was standing on the hood of a Ford Taurus just behind my right ear. He stared at me intently.

"What's your name?"

"Uh, Jon. Jon Fixx."

"All right, Jon Fixx, I'm going to hook you up with a car that will change your life. It will fill in the holes of your existence. It will take away any inadequacies you have, imagined or real. It will make you feel like a real man for the first time in your life."

I almost asked him if he was a friend of Tony Robbins. I couldn't hide the doubt on my face. "Mr. Stan, I'm just looking for a car.'

"Drop the mister, just call me Stan." He studied my face, his eyes digging deep into my gaze. "You don't know anything about cars, do you?"

I hesitated. Horror stories about used car dealerships and the immoral snakes that ran them began flooding my mind. I guess my thoughts seeped over into Stan's mind as well because his voice took on an edge of tired irritation.

"Son, stop worrying. I'm not going to screw you with some piece of shit that breaks down on you two days later. You ever want to bring the car back, bring it back to me and I'll hand you exactly what you paid for it. I'll put that in writing."

I nodded, confused. I wasn't sure exactly what was going

on. Maribel was beaming.

"Follow me." Stan jumped off the hood of the Ford. "Show me what you think you'd like," he said. "Every car on the lot has been tweaked to meet the state smog standards, so you won't have to do that."

"Well, I'd like something that will get me around without much trouble, reliable, dependable," I told him. Now that the words were out in the open, not in my mind, they sounded kind of geeky. I glanced at Stan to see his reaction, a look of stern dismissal lingering on his face, as if at any moment he might decide I was too nerdy to even sell a car to. I stopped him at the Toyota Camry. "I like this one."

Stan's face broke out in an amused smile. "Jon Fixx, you don't have the *cojones* to drive this car. Forget it. Let's keep moving."

What the hell did that mean? Wasn't I the one buying the car? I had never encountered this sales tactic before. I wasn't sure I liked it very much. As we walked down the line of cars in the small lot, I noticed another Honda Accord I hadn't seen at first. It was in my price range, looked to be in good shape, so I stopped in front of it. Stan was ahead of me but didn't stop. I called to him, "Uh, Stan, sir, I like this one."

Stan didn't even turn around. He just waved me forward with his right arm in the air, motioning me to follow. I looked over my shoulder at Maribel, hoping she could talk some sense into her husband. She shooed me forward with her hands to keep me moving. I turned back, reluctantly following Stan down the line of cars to the back end of the lot near a small, single story house cum office. Having reached the end of the line, Stan didn't stop. He kept moving, disappearing through the office door. I stopped underneath the tin overhang, covering what would have been the porch. Unsure what to do, I stood at the office door considering my options. What if this dwarf Stan and his wife Maribel were serial killers? What if they had a basement underneath their office space where they kept prospective buyers they didn't like and locked them down there, stole their possessions, stripped them of their clothes, tortured them? My overly dramatic, fearful thoughts were interrupted by Stan's abrupt entrance back through the front door.

"Do you want your car or not?" Stan demanded, as he reentered the house. "Like I said, white boy. *Cojones*, that's what you're missing."

I glanced over my shoulder one last time at Maribel. Her soft smile reassured me, so I steeled myself and followed Stan into the house. The living room had been converted into an office space with two desks, a fax machine, computers, a large printer, and marketing-related literature covering the wall behind it. A life-size portrait of Maribel and Stan on their wedding day, both wearing mariachi outfits, hung prominently to my left. An entryway in the wall to my right presumably led back to the bedrooms. There was a small archway directly across from where I had entered, leading into the kitchen. I could see the backyard from my vantage point, apparently filled with more cars. I saw the screen door at the back of the kitchen slamming shut just as I entered. My nostrils were overcome with the pungent smell of Mexican cooking. My mouth started watering. The smell of cooking food relaxed me a bit, allowing me to drop my guard. I hesitated briefly as I took in my surroundings, then followed Stan out to the back. As I passed through the kitchen, I could see that the gas stovetop was covered with frying pans and steaming pots. I slowed as I passed, realizing I'd been traveling for the last several days and hadn't had a good meal in over a week.

Stepping into the backyard, I immediately noticed the cars were more expensive. The yard was at least one thousand feet deep, all cement, and surrounded by a six-foot stonewall. The wall was topped off by rounded, intimidating barbed wire two feet in diameter. There was a large metal gate leading out to an alley in the back corner of the lot. There were Porsches and muscle cars and Mercedes. Stan was standing in front of an old Buick Regal that had been refurbished into something considerably more interesting than it would have been when first coming off the lot back in its production year. The paint job wasn't original. It looked as if someone had stripped the car down, lifted the frame up with a crane, and dropped it into a large bucket of black paint. It was jacked up in the back, with extra wide tires, and the windows were tinted so dark I couldn't see inside from where I was standing. The car looked tough. However, no matter how interesting the car appeared, it was missing the qualifiers I was looking for: reliability, dependability, and efficiency.

Stan reached up, slapped his hand down on the front hood, and announced, "This is your car."

I started laughing self-consciously, shaking my head. "Stan, I'm sorry, I can't buy that car. That's not right for me. I need a Honda or a Toyota. I need something that won't break down, that—"

Stan stared at me, disgusted with my reaction, his face stern. "What did I tell you, Jon? If the car doesn't work for you, bring it back. Come over and take a look at it."

Hesitant, but not wanting to make him angry, I did as he asked, crossing ten feet of cement to the driver's side door. I opened it up. It was long and heavy.

Stan smiled, obviously enjoying himself as he described the car. "It's got an 8.0L quad-turbo W16 engine with 1001 break horsepower."

I had no idea what he was talking about. I just nodded my head so I wouldn't look too ignorant.

"This is as powerful as a Bugatti Veyron without the cost. You could race this thing if you wanted to." Stan stopped speaking, staring at me, then added, "You, of course, would never do that, but the option's still there. Plus, it has one of the best suspension systems ever built."

All I could do was stare at the car, unsure how to respond. I had no idea what a Bugatti Veyron was, but I figured it must be something powerful.

Noticing the doubt on my face, Stan added, "Look, Jon, I specifically hunted this car down for you."

I stared at him in disbelief, smiling uncomfortably. "How can you say that? You just met me ten minutes ago."

"Maribel is psychic," Stan said with obvious pride. "She described you to me last week, told me you'd be coming soon. So I went out looking for this car. It matches your needs."

I've never been one to go for that psychic stuff, but I've always been of the mind that if you can't disprove something, then the possibility that it exists can't be dismissed. So whether Maribel was truly psychic or not, I had no opinion, but standing in the middle of Hollywood on the day after my arrival with a Mexican dwarf used-car salesman telling me he specifically went looking for a car for me prior to my arrival was far more than I could swallow. Dumbfounded, I tried to find the words that would extricate me from the situation as quickly and easily as possible. "You're telling me that you've known I was coming so you went and located this car for me before I even walked onto the lot?"

Stan nodded with pleasure. "That's right."

I stared at the car, trying to buy a little time, not sure what to do. This was getting far too weird for me. I just wanted to leave, mostly because I knew that if I stuck around much longer I'd end up buying the car because I liked Stan and his wife Maribel. My feelings would override any good sense I had. "I think I'm going to have to think about this," I said. I stepped back from the Buick. I turned to go back inside.

"Let me tell you something, son. If you don't buy this car, then you don't buy a car here." Stan waddled over to me, looking up at my face. "Jon, you think you're the first guy off the boat that's been through here, rolls into town looking for that intangible something they think will make their life worth living? At least with the right car, part of the search becomes tangible."

I looked back at the Buick. The interior was a dark brown and in good shape. I asked, "Why this car?"

"*Cojones*, son. *Cojones.* You got 'em. You just don't know it. This car will help you find 'em."

Behind me, I heard the screen door open. Maribel was carrying a large tray full of tacos and quesadillas and salad. "Jon, will you join us for an early dinner?" she asked.

Two hours later I drove off the lot in my new used Buick Regal with a full stomach and new friends. I discovered over time what Stan had meant. Driving on the L.A. freeways and streets, I never had trouble making a lane switch or pulling into a long line of traffic. Drivers usually conceded space to my car with very little protest. I rarely got cut off. However, the routine police stops got to be annoying after a while. The first came about a month into my ownership. I'd been going forty-one miles per hour in a thirty-five mile speed zone. After pulling over, I sat at the side of the road, watching the police sit in their car behind me for several minutes. What they were doing I couldn't tell, but then suddenly, all hell broke loose. Three more LAPD cars pulled up on the opposite side of the street. I guessed this was not routine protocol for a traffic stop. I began to wonder if Stan had sold me a stolen car. Flashes of Rodney King getting beaten flashed across my mind. The officer on the passenger side of the cruiser got out but hung back, his hand on his gun. In my side-view mirror, I watched the other officer slowly approach my driver's side door. To show them I was friendly, I figured maybe I should get out of the car so they could see me. I reached for my doorknob, opening my door. The motion of the door swinging open ignited a firestorm of activity around me. As if a starter gun had fired, the police officers reacted simultaneously.

The officer closest to me shouted, "He's moving!" A split second later his gun was pointing at me.

The officers across the street were scrambling out of

their car, guns drawn in my direction. I froze. I saw movement out of the corner of my right eye. The officer on my passenger side was squatting down with his gun pointed directly at my head.

"Slowly climb out of the car, hands first! Lie down spread-eagle on the ground!"

I did as I was asked without looking around. I lay like that for several minutes before I finally found the courage to look up. I heard someone yell out, "False alarm."

Moments later, I saw black police shoes milling around me. Suddenly, I was hoisted to my feet. The police officers explained without apology that a car with an identical description as mine had been involved in a fatal drive-by gang shooting earlier that week. With a few pats on the back and accompanying guffaws from the officers for being a good sport and a few uncomfortable smiles from me, I was on my way. My first run-in with the L.A. police cops left a bad taste in my mouth. I didn't drive away a fan. Over time, I got used to the traffic stops and felt secret pleasure when the police discovered I was white and relatively square, as far as they were concerned. I grew to love the Buick and take extra good care of it. Having few friends in Los Angeles, I became good friends with Stan and Maribel, and they became one of my regular stops every so often, Maribel always stuffing me with wonderful home-cooked Mexican fixings.

The memory of my first few days in Los Angeles, all the promise they contained, brought a smile to my face. I'd come a long way, even if I was going through a bit of a rough patch. I passed Whitley Heights to my north—a bunch of old houses built on the steep hills right up against the Hollywood Bowl with stair access only. I followed Franklin until it dead-ended at an out-of-place cemetery. My only option was a left turn onto Sierra Bonita, a small street that led me down to a stretch of Hollywood Boulevard, far from the commercialization and tourism of the storefronts and street performers and panhandlers further east. This section of Hollywood Boulevard was marked by semi-expensive homes on the north side and multi-unit dwellings on the south side. The road narrowed to two lanes, one of which was taken up with parked cars on the weekends and nights. As I passed the cemetery, I wondered if anybody famous was buried there.

A short trip on Hollywood led me to Laurel Canyon Boulevard, one of the key canyon pathways to the Valley. I turned right and followed Laurel upward, traversing its winding narrow path. I'd read stories about Jim Morrison when he was living in his Laurel Canyon apartment with his on again, off again lover Pamela Courson. He didn't have a car and depended on rides from others to get places. His drinking bouts were legendary. He would often wander down Laurel Canyon from his apartment to get drunk at one of several bars on Sunset, making the bar his home for the night as long as they'd let him stay.

Soon I was descending Laurel Canyon, northbound into the Valley. I made a left from Laurel onto Ventura Boulevard, entering an architecturally much less interesting section of Los Angeles. I drove west on Ventura, passing the various storefronts and businesses lining either side of the road as I made my way back to my apartment. As my car closed in on the apartment, for a moment I considered driving over to Sara's house and taking apart her new boyfriend as payback for what Williams had put me through. I pulled up to the light on Woodman and Ventura. If I made a right turn, I'd be home in one block. Or I could keep going. The light turned green and I didn't move. A driver behind me sounded his horn. I was frozen. Then I heard Izzy's voice, "You promised." I took a breath, turning the wheel clockwise toward my apartment.

I pulled into my garage, my thoughts moving in a productive direction, now on my writing. I'd shoved Sara deep into a mental corner, sure she'd pop up again soon enough. I wanted to get to work on "The Coffee Shop Lovers" and finish it before I had to fly back to New York. I was about to open my door, when the last twenty-four hours rushed back in a flash. I figured it wouldn't hurt to look around to make sure no one was lurking in the garage or up in my apartment. I poked my head out of the Buick, but seeing nothing out of place, I climbed out and exited the garage to the exterior stairwell leading up to the first-floor hallway. I entered the building without incident, almost expecting Williams to be standing at my door again. He wasn't. I opened my front door and stepped inside. I looked around the room, making sure it was in fact empty, which it was. I knew I was being neurotically cautious but, strangely enough, a tingling sensation told me I was enjoying the fear. I went to my computer, turned it on, and headed to the fridge, the interior light welcoming me home. The fridge was empty except for a few cans of soda. I grabbed a can, popped it open, then went back to my computer and sat down. I took a deep breath, opened the Chicago couple's story and stared at it. The preliminaries were done, but I had a lot more to add, plus a solid cleanup of what I had already written. I stared at the screen, took a breath, put my fingers to the keyboard, and asked God's creative muse to grace me with His Presence.

I started where I had left off.

8
Late September
New York 2nd Trip

My second plane trip to New York was more relaxing than my first for two reasons: 1) I had less anxiety about what, or who, was waiting for me there—I had no intention of meeting Marco alone again; and 2) the night before I left, there was a momentous shift in my relations with Sara.

After returning from my first trip, nothing much had changed between Sara and me. She remained aloof and distant most of the time. If I tried to discuss our relationship, she dismissed the subject with a wave of her hand. A few nights before my second trip, she spurred me into a heated one-sided discourse. My outburst lasted for several minutes and included the phrases "I love you so much" and "You're the love of my life" and "I'm nothing without you" and "How can we survive like this?" I fell apart, dropping any pretense of pride or ego.

"Jon, nothing in life is perfect. This is how things are right now. Can't you just accept the status quo?" She patted me on my head and gave me a kiss on my cheek. "I'm going to bed."

I tried justifying her behavior. She'd been working long hours, and, if the stars lined up for her, she would make partner within the next twelve months, becoming the youngest and only female partner in her law firm. I begrudgingly gave her behavior a wide berth. But that understanding did nothing to ease the ever-present fear that any day Sara would do something drastic. By mid-September, I had become hyperaware of my fear-filled discontent. I was analyzing every single interaction we had, whether at home or on the phone, in an email or a text message. Something had to change. I couldn't handle the suspense much longer. I needed to take control. Then, the night before I left on my second trip to New York, Sara threw me for a complete loop.

She showed up at home after a company function, dressed in a sexy skirt suit, plopping down beside me on the couch. With my computer on my lap, I was working on "The Coffee Shop Lovers," but, as usual, having a terrible go at it. I could tell she was tipsy, her movements loose. She tossed her purse on the coffee table where my bare feet were propped. I dropped my feet to the floor by force of habit. She hated it when I put my feet on the furniture.

"Hi, Jonny Boy."

She hadn't called me Jonny Boy in over a year, a nickname she laid on me early in our romance.

"How's your writing coming along?"

I was taken off guard by her affectionate nature. She leaned her head against me, one hand on my shoulder, her left leg resting suggestively on my thigh. I sat frozen, not wanting it to stop but afraid if I said the wrong thing she would stand up and disappear into the other room.

"It's fine. Been stuck on this couple's story, just can't get the hook."

"Oh, don't worry, you will. You always do." Her right hand was fondling my ear, her left hand moving slowly back and forth on my left thigh. "Do you want to have sex?"

Of course I wanted to have sex! But I feared she was teasing me. I gently leaned forward, setting my computer on the coffee table, then slowly reversed directions, settling back into her embrace. I stared at her, nodding, not saying anything for fear the sound of my voice would break the spell. A moment later, she was unbuttoning her blouse with her right hand and getting me excited with her left. Not even a minute later we were naked on the couch fully engaged in passionate love play. It occurred to me that Sara was probably closer to drunk than tipsy, but I didn't care. We were having sex. It had been so long that I was unable to sustain myself, hitting my climax before she did, but Sara barely seemed to notice. She led me to the bedroom, laid me down, and started engaging in several methods of excitement that worked me back up to a level of proper use. As our bodies worked on each other, I couldn't stop the thoughts running through my mind, that now things would get better, Sara had turned a corner, our downhill slide was over. In the throes of passion, as Sara reached her second climax, I had an epiphany: I needed to buy a ring.

Sara fell asleep with her naked body against mine. When I awoke the next morning, she was gone. A curt note said she went to the gym, and then work, that she loved me. Nothing about the night before. I would be on a plane soon, so I couldn't say goodbye to her. But it didn't matter. Things were going to improve. I could feel it. Both my drive to the airport and my flight east went by in a blur, and I was lost in the pleasing haze of the night before.

Later, standing on the curb at JFK, waiting for Joey to pick me up—Vespucci had insisted this time, claiming Barbara had given him a dressing down for not doing so on my first trip—I could still smell Sara's perfume, see her naked on top of me. A self-satisfied smile crossed my lips. Expecting a Lincoln Town Car and lost in my reverie over the night before, I didn't notice the Mini Cooper pulling up just in front of me at the curb. I was gazing at the oncoming traffic when, from the corner of my eye, I saw a mane of dark hair climb out of the driver's side door. Maggie caught the grin on my face as I turned her way.

"Happy to see me instead of Joey?" she asked, as cheerful as ever.

Flustered and blushing, I couldn't speak at first. My tongue wouldn't work. My smile had been for Sara's naked body, but the sudden surge of emotion I felt when spotting Maggie made me feel instantly guilty.

I blurted, "No."

Maggie's smile faded.

"I mean, yes, I'm very happy to see you." This wasn't much better, considering Maggie was my employer. "I mean, sorry, I was lost in my thoughts. I didn't get much sleep last night." I mentally kicked myself, basically insinuating I'd been having sex.

"My father needed Joey's driving skills, so he sent me in his stead. I'm your chauffeur. I hope that's okay." Moving around to the back of the car, she opened the trunk. Mechanically, I tossed my bag in the back.

Maggie looked more stunning now than she had on my first trip. Her hair was loose, carelessly hanging on her shoulders, a black formfitting t-shirt and similarly worn denim jeans accentuating the curves of her waist, hips, and legs. I was flustered, my stomach doing the same somersaults it did the first time I'd met her, unable to understand what was happening. She was a client, clearly spoken for, taken. I could still feel Sara's touch on my skin. The whole thing was absurd. I took a deep breath, trying to manage the physical gyrations occurring in my body. I rallied, getting my feet planted securely beneath me, pulling it together.

"What a great surprise," I said. "You're way more fun than Joey. He never talks."

"Joey's not a big one for chatter," Maggie replied, laughing.

I laughed with her and climbed into the passenger seat.

"How's the prince of romance?" she asked.

"Prince of romance?"

"My colleagues at work gave you that nickname after I told them what you do."

"I wish it were accurate, but I'm sorry to say it's not even close."

Maggie pulled away from the curb, navigating her Mini Cooper in and out of the mass of traffic flowing thru JFK.

"How's the planning coming along for the wedding?" I asked.

Maggie's look told me all I needed to know. Like many brides I'd met over the years, she was hitting the burnout point. Even with her mother and sister-in-law handling most of the planning, Maggie said the minutiae of it all was getting to her. She tried to brush off my question with a wave of her hand.

"I don't want to talk about the wedding. It's completely in my face at the moment. All I think and hear every day is wedding this and wedding that. I need a bit of quiet on the matter. I can't say that to any of the family. But you're not family. And you won't tell, right?" she said with a conspiratorial look.

"As long as you don't tell your father I wasn't doing my job," I added.

"Deal."

This was not the first time I'd heard something along these lines from a bride. As the impending date loomed closer and closer, I'd seen brides and grooms express their stress and concern in many and varying ways. Maggie's phone erupted noisily between the two front seats. She glanced down at it.

"Oh, geez, it's Caroline. She and my mother want to use pinks and blues for the wedding colors, and they're putting in the final orders but they need my approval. I hate the color pink. Maybe you should help me pick the colors."

"No can do. I make it a point never to interfere in any way with my client's decisions regarding the wedding. It's a personal safety issue," I answered.

Maggie laughed. "A personal safety issue?"

"I'm serious. Weddings tend to bring out the best, and worst, in those involved. There is a heightened awareness of the importance of opinion and hierarchy. I've learned that, in the end, my opinion falls at the bottom of the hierarchy, even if the bride herself asks for my suggestions. Mother, mother-in-law, maid of honor, sister, sister-in-law, the wedding planner, maternal grandmother, paternal grandmother, father, father-in-law, groom, brother, cousin, other friends, usually in declining rank of order. I'm last on the list, below those aforementioned people. If I make my opinion known, then I will surely anger someone in that group. If you've ever been punched in the nose by a grandmother, you'd understand why I'm careful."

Maggie didn't notice the light change from red to green because she was laughing so hard. A honk from behind motivated her to punch the gas. "You rolled that list off like you had it memorized."

"I've seen that list in action. I'll never give my opinion, even if you twist my arms behind my back."

"Don't worry, Jon Fixx, I won't ask you for any wedding advice. But I don't think my grandmother will punch you. Not her style." With a pause, she added, "She'd use a gun."

I laughed, imagining Maggie's grandma holding a gun. My laugh faded when I suddenly wondered if she was half serious. Unexpectedly, images of my lovemaking session with Sara flashed across my mind, pulling my attention away from the close quarters of the car, away from Maggie and our conversation. I tried to squelch the thoughts. As pleasant as they were, they were too distracting to allow me to stay focused on Maggie's words. I glanced out the passenger window, taking a deep breath, hoping to empty my mind of images I would rather enjoy while alone. Without warning, the images of my lovemaking session became ever more vivid, my fingertips tingling with the feel of Sara's skin, my eyes traveling up her naked body, past her tight tummy across her breasts up past her breastbone suddenly settling on Maggie's face. I reacted by clenching my fists, falling into a coughing fit to cover my discomfort.

"Are you okay, Jon? Do you need some water? I've got a bottle here." She handed me a bottle of Evian from between the two front seats. "Here, drink this."

I stuck my hand up palm out, protesting, pointing at the bottle, then her.

"Oh, don't be silly. Drink it," she insisted.

In that moment, I realized I could no longer ignore this attraction I had for Maggie. Sooner or later, I would have to figure out why I was having these feelings. I dismissed the possibility that I was considering Maggie as a possible mate. Not once in my life had I been interested in a woman who was spoken for. It was not my M.O. and it made no sense for that to change now. Maybe I was testing my faithfulness to Sara with someone I knew I could never have. I took a deep swig of Maggie's water, trying to clear my head.

"Thank you," I said, trying to explain away my coughing fit. "Not sure what that was, just felt like I got something stuck in my throat." I looked out the window and stared at the pedestrians crowding the streets.

Maggie's voice pulled my focus back into the car. "Mind if I ask you something personal?"

"Sure."

"Why aren't you married yet? I mean, given what you do for a living, one would think by now you'd have that all locked up."

Before I could stop myself, I blurted out, "Funny you should ask that. Before I left L.A. last night, I decided it's time to take the next step. I'm buying a ring when I get back to Los Angeles. I'm going to propose."

"Really? Have you and Sara discussed it?"

"No, we haven't discussed it yet. I don't believe that's the way to do it. A man should just propose."

"So you're sure she'll say 'yes' ?"

I confidently nodded, though I had no idea if that was true. I hadn't given much thought to what Sara would say. In fact, I hadn't given any of it much thought, but I wanted to turn the previous night with Sara to my advantage. Strike while the iron's hot.

"I'm sure it's what she wants," I said.

"You don't sound so sure," Maggie answered, perceptibly.

"It's the right time."

I realized I felt defensive, but I wasn't sure why. I decided to change the subject, but before I could do that, Maggie asked, "Where did you meet Sara?"

"At a wedding."

Amused, Maggie asked, "A client's wedding?"

"Yup."

"I thought you kept an objective distance from your clients."

"I do. Sara was the bride's best friend. When I interviewed her for the novella, she nearly threw herself at me. When I was invited to the wedding, I figured I should go just to give her a chance."

"Really?"

"No, but it sounds good."

By this point, we had arrived in Brooklyn, closing in on the Vespucci compound. Suddenly, I realized we'd spent the entire drive talking about me. I was disappointed for wasting the time blabbering about myself rather than getting useful information from Maggie.

"I have to apologize. I shouldn't have been running my mouth the whole time. We should have been talking about you and Marco," I reminded her.

"Don't be silly, Jon. I want to know about you. I find you interesting. Talking about Marco and me can get boring. We'll have more than enough time to talk about what you need to know to get our story done."

"Okay. But do you mind if we keep what we talked about between us?" I asked.

"Deal."

We pulled up to the entrance. Maggie reached out of the car and punched a code into the call box, setting the large iron gate into motion. We pulled inside the driveway, the gate closing behind us. She parked and we climbed out of the car and headed into the house. The commotion of my first visit was absent this time. It was late afternoon, not the dinner hour yet. Vespucci had imposed on me, adamant that I stay with them rather than in a hotel. It was rare for me to stay with a family, though this would not be a first. I followed Maggie inside as she led me to the second floor down a long hallway to my bedroom. I carried my small overnight bag, setting it down on the floor beside the rocking chair. The room was cozy, a full-sized bed in the back of the room and a small dresser directly across from the bed on the wall where we had entered. In the corner, a door led into a small bathroom. On the wall was a large, rectangle photograph of a modest, nicely shaped duplex that looked to be somewhere in New York City. A young Maggie, maybe ten years old, was standing on the porch with a big, open smile aimed straight at the camera.

Maggie noticed my interest in the photograph. "That was the house I grew up in. My father loves that picture. I like it because it brings back a lot of great memories."

"You look happy."

"I had a lot of fun growing up in that house." We both stared at the picture until the moment passed and Maggie broke the silence. "I hope this room is sufficient."

"This is great."

"Then I'll let you get settled. I'll be downstairs in the library working. Come get me when you're all done."

"I will do. Thanks."

Maggie disappeared into the hallway. I picked up my bag and set it on the bed. I turned around, plopped down, and stared at the picture of the young Maggie. She looked like a normal, happy ten-year old. The duplex looked like an average, middle-class American home. There was nothing in the picture to indicate that Maggie's father was a major player in the New York Mafia. I looked around the bedroom, noting the nicely appointed wood furniture, the understated taste of the room. There was nothing extravagant or extraordinary about it. Yet, here I sat in the bedroom of an alleged Mafia boss as a civilian employee delving into his family's life, and even though I was going to write about the romance between Marco and Maggie, it still felt strange and at odds with everything I'd learned about the absolute secrecy of the Mafia. No matter how I looked at it, I couldn't shake the feeling that Vespucci's hiring me was outside the norm for a member of the Mafia.

I heard Maggie's voice inviting me down for an early dinner, interrupting my ruminations. By this time I knew enough about Barbara and her hospitality that I shouldn't have expected any less. I changed into clean clothes, hustled into the bathroom to freshen up from my trip, and went downstairs. There were three generations of women—Grandma Jean, Mrs. Vespucci, and Maggie—sitting at the informal kitchen table when I joined them for an informal meal of spaghetti and meatballs and Caesar salad. I asked where the rest of the family was, and Barbara explained that Vespucci was in a business meeting he couldn't get out of but had sent his regards. I asked about Marco. Maggie said he'd had production problems at the factory and would have to stay late to deal with it. I saw an image of Vespucci and Marco together at the foundry with a guy tied up in a chair hanging over the hot molten liquid.

"Would you like one or two meatballs?" Barbara asked.

"Two, thank you," I replied.

Once the food was served, Barbara began discussing the wedding plans, but Maggie cut her off. Nothing would be decided while they were sitting there and she wanted a break. Barbara took the request in stride and chose instead to educate me on Maggie's childhood adventures, telling one story after another about the trouble Maggie used to get herself into. Maggie protested each time her mother began another episode, but Barbara ignored her daughter's protests with a smile. Grandma Jean added colorful images to fill out her daughter's storytelling. By the time I was too stuffed to eat anymore, I had a clear picture of Maggie as a child: precocious, stubborn, independent, but clearly daddy's little girl.

After dinner, Maggie had to go back to the city for a study session with her undergraduate students, so I spent the rest of the evening watching television with Grandma Jean and Barbara. Eventually, Barbara excused herself to finish her nightly chores before it got too late. I remained on the sofa, alone in the room with Grandma Jean, the quiet rhythmic creak of her rocking chair keeping time with her motion. She must have been at least eighty-five years old, but she still moved around with a nimble dexterity. With the television voices humming in the background, we sat silently, staring at the screen, lost in our own thoughts. I was only half paying attention to what was happening on the screen.

"My daughter and my granddaughter seem very fond of you," Grandma Jean said, her voice bringing me out of my reverie.

"That's good. It makes my job easier," I said, taking the compliment in stride.

Grandma Jean fell silent again. I didn't want to be rude and ask her questions while her show was on, so I remained silent. I had interviewed Grandma Jean during my first visit, but I'd been pressed for time and the interview was much shorter than I would have liked. I had gained insight from her memories about Maggie's childhood and what she thought about Maggie's career choice. But she hadn't mentioned Marco even once, and I'd run out of time before I could ask her any specific questions about him and Maggie's relationship. I figured now was as good a time as any to fill in the gaps. I waited until a commercial break.

"Grandma Jean?" I asked, hesitantly. (She told me to call her "Grandma," though it sounded foreign to my ears every time I said it.) My voice broke her rocking, and the rocking chair slowed down. I took that as a cue to continue. "Mind if I ask you a few questions I didn't get to ask during our first interview?"

She nodded.

"Are you as excited as everyone else about Maggie and Marco's wedding?"

She resumed her rocking. The commercial break was over, so I thought I wouldn't get an answer. Instead, she began, "People get married for a lot of reasons. Some people get married out of convenience, some out of necessity, some because they don't know what else to do. All say they get married for love, but that's the folly of youth. When you've been around as long as I have, you realize so many other forces are at play and love ends up being an excuse rather than a reason. A marriage based on true love is the rarest kind."

"That's a cynical view of marriage," I said. I had no idea where she was going with this.

"Cynical, yes. But true. In the Old Country, the best marriages were arranged. It was a contract between two families. They didn't always work, but most of the time they did. That's all marriage is, a contract, an agreement between two people to spend their lives together and raise a family while they do it. The man and the woman each understand their role, what they are responsible for. Do you know why arranged marriages worked so well?"

I was not aware that they did. I didn't know much about arranged marriages—I had never worked for a couple who had an arranged marriage—but even with my lack of knowledge on the subject, I believed arranged marriages to be an archaic institution developed countries had evolved out of because it was generally misogynistic and backward. But here was a woman telling me arranged marriages worked.

"You doubt what I'm saying," Grandma Jean said, with authority.

"It's not that. I just don't know how you can say arranged marriages worked better than modern day marriages," I replied.

"That's because you're young. You can't see it any other way. Nowadays, as soon as things get tough, people get divorced. I don't see how you can call that working. The problem is they think because they made the decision to get married they have the right to make the decision to get unmarried if they want. Arranged marriages worked because there was no leaving. The arrangement wasn't just between the man and woman, it was also between their families. The families committed themselves to one another, and if the husband and wife separated, it also caused a serious rift between the families. There was far more at stake." She picked up the teacup sitting on the side table near her rocker and took a sip. "You young people place so much importance on love," she continued, "as if it will cure everything, will carry you through all the fights and tough times and rough patches. Let me tell you something. Love is about as powerful as a candle in the wind. One strong puff and the flame goes out. But in an arranged marriage, there's none of this fantasy about love. The husband and wife come to the marriage without any expectations. They must learn to love each other. Do you see?"

I really didn't see, but I was listening. Flashes of anthropology courses about ancient cultures crossed my mind. I responded, "To be honest, Grandma Jean, I'm not sure I see."

She gave me a wistful smile, the wrinkles on her face curling up for a moment. "When you get to my age, you'll understand. If you get married because you're in love, what do you do when you're no longer in love?"

I was not sure how to respond to that. But the thought that love always had to disappear from a marriage didn't sit well with me. "Not every married couple falls out of love."

"Of course they do," she answered. "That's why marriage doesn't work anymore. All you young people live with the fantasy that marriage is about being in love, about being attracted to each other, about always wanting to jump into bed. As soon as the going gets tough, your generation runs away because they don't know what to do. Because that special feeling isn't there anymore, then something must be wrong, they must have made a mistake when they decided to get married, their feelings must have fooled them. But see, that's when the real marriage starts, when the man and woman have to learn how to work together, how to work as a partnership. The romantic fantasy life is over. They have to trust that their parents' decision to put them together was made with a great deal of thought and consideration. This is why arranged marriages work. It's a contract. The man and woman each understand their roles. Arranged marriages don't end in divorce."

What she said made logical sense, but I didn't like it. She was challenging everything I believed about relationships, about my relationships, about my career, about Sara and me. But I only had to consider the current divorce rate to know she was onto something. The romantic in me was unwilling, though, to let go of the notion that romance and love had no legitimate place in a successful marriage. "Were you and your husband in an arranged marriage?"

"Yes, we were. I learned to love that man, God rest his soul, with all my heart. He was a good man. We never spent a night apart during our entire marriage."

She was speaking from experience, so I had to give everything she said serious consideration. The thought brought me full circle to what I had originally asked her. "Does this mean you don't approve of Maggie's marriage because it's not arranged?"

Grandma Jean turned to me. "My granddaughter is in love. Whoever made a rational decision based on feelings?"

I wasn't sure if she was looking for an answer.

She stopped rocking, leaning forward for emphasis. "If Maggie marries this man, she will be cursed. Marco Balducci is a bully and a thug, and he doesn't have any of my granddaughter's good sense or strength."

I stared at the aged matriarch, taken off guard by her candor. At the mention of Marco's name, I inadvertently ducked, looking around the room to make sure we were alone. Invariably, in my line of work, sooner or later I heard someone from one side of the aisle bad-mouth the other side. More often than not, it was a sibling or a close friend who didn't like the groom or the bride, but I usually didn't hear it from a parent or grandparent, and definitely not with such conviction.

"Does Maggie know how you feel?" I asked in a low voice.

"I've never told her. But she knows."

Our discussion was cut short by Maggie's sister-in-law Caroline and her daughter, Sabrina. At the sight of her great-granddaughter, Grandma Jean instantly switched gears. She threw a knowing look my way, shaking her head once, warning me off any further discussion, as well as making it clear to me that what we had discussed was to be kept between us. As Sabrina ran across the family room toward her great-grandmother, Grandma Jean opened her arms wide and gave her great-granddaughter a hug.

After spending some time socializing with Caroline and her daughter, I excused myself for bed. As I settled down in my room, I realized I was exhausted. I lay back, staring up at the ceiling. Grandma Jean's words about Marco echoed through my mind. Before I formed any further opinion about what all this could mean, I passed out in my day clothes, shoes still on, legs hanging over the side. I awoke in the middle of the night, my back aching from the position my body was in. Half awake, I stumbled around the room, trying to be quiet while I undressed, and then I found my way back to the bed, immediately falling into a dreamless slumber.

I awoke the next morning to a silent house. Reaching for my mobile, I hopped out of bed when I spotted the time at the top center of the screen. I was interviewing Giancarlo Balducci at 10:30 a.m., in less than sixty minutes. I scolded myself for not remembering to set my alarm. As I exited the bedroom and headed toward the bathroom, I spotted a note taped to my door from Barbara. It said that everyone was on errands or at work, she had left breakfast on the table, and Joey would be back before noon if I needed a ride anywhere. Smiling, I stuffed the note in my pocket. Mafia or no, my affinity for the Vespucci family was growing. Maybe my worries about this job, about the Vespucci's, about the Mafia were baseless. I showered and dressed, then went downstairs to the kitchen to find a bowl of fruit salad, granola, and a glass of orange juice waiting for me. I quickly ate my breakfast, calling a cab while I did so. Ten minutes later I was on my way to Bayside, Queens, one of the more affluent areas within the five boroughs.

About twenty minutes later, I climbed out of the cab in front of a nicely dressed three-story house in sync with the surrounding neighborhood. I wasn't sure what to expect from Balducci the father, but for some reason he didn't elicit the same feelings of trepidation I had for his son. I climbed the few steps to the front door, knocked, and waited only a few seconds before a balding, rotund man swung the door open with a big smile.

"Jon! I've been waiting to meet you. If what Maggie says about you is true, I'm gonna have to be careful so as not to reveal any secrets," Mr. Balducci said, welcoming me into his home.

I met these compliments with my most winning smile. A bear paw of a hand pulled me into the foyer and guided me past a cozy, expensively designed living room, past the formal dining room, then the kitchen, finally leading me into a large, open family room lined with bookshelves of DVD's and the biggest flat screen television I'd ever seen mounted on the back wall.

"Grab a seat. Want anything to drink?" Giancarlo asked.

"No, thanks. I'm fine," I answered.

"All right, sit. Tell me what I can do for you."

After my time with his intimidating son, I was taken unawares by Balducci's enthusiasm and openness. I found myself liking this man the same way I liked Tony Vespucci. He was funny, charming at times, though apparently lacking Vespucci's sharp intellect. As we spoke, I discovered Balducci's strong feelings for his longtime best friend from the old neighborhood. In addition, Balducci seemed truly excited to have his son marrying Vespucci's daughter. Sitting across from him, I realized I had expected Balducci to be lukewarm, at best, about the impending nuptials. In that moment, I discovered how strongly I believed that Vespucci didn't like Marco, and this belief was spilling over into the other areas of my research.

From all my reading, I knew Balducci was as much a player as Vespucci, but by this time, I had accepted the fact that my clients were part of La Cosa Nostra. I figured as long as I didn't ask any questions about said organization, I would be safe. Sitting across from me in his large recliner, puffing on an expensive cigar, Balducci looked like the consummate Mafia player from the movies, his large belly reaching over his waistline, his dark Italian features supporting the image, the large Cuban hanging between his fingers.

"Like I was saying, Tony and I were inseparable. Everyone knew in the neighborhood that if you messed with one of us, you was messing with both of us. That's how it should be, don't you agree?"

"Absolutely. Loyalty is everything in friendship."

Balducci turned his head away from the window, his face squared on mine. "That's right, Jon. Maggie told me I'd like you. In friendship, marriage, life, God, it's all loyalty. Everything follows from that. You understand?"

"Loyalty helps you make the right decision every time," I agreed.

"Exactly, Jon!"

"Is that one reason you're excited about Maggie and Marco getting married?"

"Yeah, I guess. I didn't think about it that way, but yeah. It's a show of loyalty to the importance of our two families. It'll tie 'em together with blood, with grandchildren. I'm real glad Marco and Maggie found each other. She's almost too good for him," he said with a sly smile. "Did you know I'm Michael's godfather?"

"Maggie's brother? No, I didn't know that."

"Yep, Michael was the first one to be born between Tony and me. Tony always seemed to be ahead of me."

His comment illustrated how close Vespucci and Balducci were. As I questioned him, Balducci spoke at length about Marco's time in Italy and his help in getting their business off the ground by working hard and making all the right political and business connections. But not once did Balducci mention the episode from Maggie's teenage years between Marco and her that so enraged Vespucci. I had to assume it had been more than just a blip on their radar. My thoughts were brought back to Balducci as he explained that one of his happiest days was when Marco came home one day and said he'd run into Maggie.

I saw my opening, and figured I'd slip in, damn the consequences. "Did they pick up where they left off?"

Balducci fell silent, staring at me. For the first time in our interview, I saw a dark cloud cross his face, a look that said everything I needed to know if I questioned this man's ability to do damage. "What do you mean?"

"I've gotten the impression that Maggie and Marco had a little something between them when they were teenagers," I said, diplomatically.

Balducci considered my words. Finally, he said, "My son can be a bit impetuous. He doesn't always know what's good for him." He paused, looking at his cigar for several moments. Then, he said, "I sent Marco over to Italy to become a man, to learn how to run a business. I figured if I threw him to the sharks, he would either learn how to swim or get eaten. But he also needed to learn the ways of the Old Country. Learn what it means to respect his elders, to respect the order of things. There are things you do and things you don't do. Period. At twenty-one years old, my son didn't understand that. He understands that now."

I wondered how much of his decision to send Marco to Italy had been his and how much Vespucci's, but I wasn't about to ask that. I was as far out on the limb as I wanted to be and finished the interview soon after. When I said goodbye, he walked me to the door, a friendly look on his face.

"Jon, if you need anything else between now and the wedding, don't hesitate to call. I'm excited because this wedding will connect our two families for life."

I said I would call if I needed anything further. I walked down the steps into the affluent Bayside neighborhood, deciding to stroll past the houses before calling a cab to head back to Brooklyn. As my mind traced back over the interview, I tried to be objective, but I was having trouble. Why was I so concerned about what had happened between Maggie and Marco when they were younger? Did it matter now? Did it matter if Vespucci didn't like his future son-in-law? Or vice versa? Why was I so hung up on the turmoil that I sensed was just under the surface?

As I dug down, I realized for the first time that my interest in the Vespuccis went well beyond what I'd been hired to write. In my line of work, it was almost impossible not to take sides, to form judgments of which I had to be hyperaware so they didn't affect the outcome of the final product. Sometimes, I liked the bride more, sometimes the groom, and sometimes I didn't like either. If I let my personal feelings interfere with my writing, it always got me in trouble. "The Internet Love Affair" and the Nickels clan were perfect examples. In the same vein, I worked hard at not getting attached to the players involved. Again, this was difficult to do, given the time I spent with my clients and the intimate discourse I shared with them. I became very good at presenting a welcoming persona while I kept my feelings at a safe, objective distance.

But the Vespuccis were getting under my skin, and in more ways than one. My feelings toward Vespucci's career choice were ambivalent at best. The Mafia killed people. But so did the U.S. government. I decided as long as Vespucci didn't hurt me, I didn't care what he did for a living. Then there was Maggie. What were these feelings I had for her?

Not wanting to think about the answer to that question, I shifted mental gears, grabbing my PDA out of my pocket and checking the schedule for the next three days. I had several interviews with bit players, cousins on the Vespucci side, a couple of Maggie's friends, and secondary family on the Balducci side. My final interview was scheduled with Vespucci the night before I left. But how far could I push him? Did I dare ask Vespucci directly if he liked his best friend's son? Did I ask him how he felt about old man Balducci these days? Would I ask him what happened between Marco and him when Maggie was a teenager? Should I ask him if there was more to his hiring me than just the obvious? The thought of actually uttering these questions in Vespucci's presence filled my gut with dread. I'd never have the courage to ask them. And what did it matter anyway? The Vespucci-Balducci story was a puzzle I didn't need to figure out. All I had to do was write their love story, and then I could settle back down in Los Angeles, propose to Sara, and live happily ever after. Right?

The next few days went by quickly. My interviews with the extended family members were innocuous, providing little new information about Maggie and Marco. I didn't see much of the nuclear Vespucci clan. Most of them were gone during the day when I was at the house, and many of my interviews with the extended family and friends were held over the dinner hour, so I didn't get to eat with the Vespuccis. Nothing much of note happened until the morning of my last day in town when my interview with Vespucci was scheduled for that evening. I'd slept in, waking up late with a monster hangover. A couple of Maggie's cousins asked me to meet them at a local bar the night before, and then they convinced me to do shots with them during the interview. The cousins were far more seasoned drinkers than I was. By the end of the night, I found myself stumbling into the Vespucci house, barely able to walk.

As I sat up in bed, my ears were ringing with a low hum, the outer edges of my head thumping. I had nothing on the slate until Vespucci's interview in the evening, so I figured I'd try to sleep it off. I laid back down falling into a dreamless slumber until close to noon. By that point, my head was feeling better, though my body still felt ragged and off-kilter. I set my feet on the floor and inadvertently grabbed my head, realizing I was not nearly as recovered as I had hoped. I sat on the edge of the bed regretting my night. I knew there was a reason I didn't like drinking. Slowly standing, I prepared to take steps down to the kitchen to eat. I wasn't sure what was best for hangovers, but I figured an empty stomach didn't help. I walked downstairs and noticed no one was home, so I found my way toward the kitchen. As I neared the hallway leading to Vespucci's study, I heard voices. My stomach tightened, which didn't help my hangover, and neither did the sound of Marco's voice. Immediately recognizing that eavesdropping would not be viewed as positive, I turned back toward the stairs when Marco's voice went up a notch, his words suddenly distinct.

"I don't understand you, Tony. I've been putting up with this guy all month. He's a civilian, and you're letting him run around askin' questions about us. I don't like it."

I froze. Throwing caution to the wind, I leaned forward, straining to hear all I could.

"Careful with your tone," Vespucci admonished him. "I hired the guy because I knew my daughter would love the idea of having her own story. It's romantic. You have a problem being romantic for my daughter?"

"Of course not. But I don't like him. He's trouble. I don't like the way he looks at Maggie. Have you noticed? He's got a thing for her."

What?

Vespucci's low rumble responded, "You should expect that from most men. Maggie's stunning. Is that the reason you came over here, to tell me that?"

"Dammit, Tony, you're missing the point. This guy's askin' questions he doesn't need to be askin', and he's talkin' to people he don't need to be talkin' to."

"Marco, unless you've got something to hide, I don't see anything to worry about. He's only asking questions about your and Maggie's courtship and the upcoming marriage. That's it."

"Then why's he going to visit Jim Mosconi?"

Marco's question was met with silence. My heart was racing. How did he know I'd spoken to Mosconi?

So quietly I could barely hear him, Vespucci responded, "How do you know that?"

"I put a tail on him. That reporter is nosy. He doesn't know when to leave well enough alone."

For a moment, no one spoke. I'd heard enough. My feet were burning with the desire to get out of that hallway but Vespucci's voice stopped me.

"Your concern is noted, but for now I want you to show Jon Fixx all the hospitality expected of us. He's my guest. Understood?"

Several moments passed. "What about Mosconi?" Marco was not happy.

"What about Mosconi? He's just a reporter. He's no

threat to us."

I heard the scraping of a chair. My feet were moving. I'd definitely heard far more than enough. Realizing I didn't have time to get back up the steps, I hopped back several feet, then began walking forward, putting my hand to my head as if in hangover pain, which didn't take much acting on my part, my eyes directed at the floor. I slowly retraced my steps when I looked up to see Joey in my path, staring. His eyes revealed surprise, but his face showed nothing. We eyed each other, Marco's visage suddenly appearing behind Joey's in the hallway. Unlike Vespucci's bodyguard, Marco was unable to hide his reaction, first surprise, and then anger at my presence in the hallway. "What are you doing here?" he growled.

I responded with a slight wince, raising my hand to my head. "Maggie's cousins took me out drinking last night while we were doing the interviews," I explained. "I just woke up. I was heading to the kitchen to see what I could find to help with the pounding."

"Jon, that you?" Vespucci called from the study. "Come in here."

Joey returned to the study ahead of me. I awkwardly turned sideways to pass Marco in the hallway and had to sidle past him with my back to the wall so as not to touch him. Vespucci sat behind his desk, his face like stone, revealing nothing. Joey stood to one side of the door behind me, as Vespucci made a quick motion with his hand, signaling for me to come closer. Marco followed suit, blocking the doorway. My heart was now pounding so hard against my chest I was sure they'd hear it, but I did my best to keep a calm face.

"I didn't know you were home, Jon. I thought you were meeting Maggie in the city," Vespucci said.

Through the haze of my hangover, I suddenly remembered saying something to Maggie the day before about meeting her in the afternoon. "Oh, right," I answered.

"Last night's drinking put a hole in my memory."

Vespucci studied my face. I remained as impassive as possible, doing my best to meet his gaze without faltering. I knew he was trying to read my thoughts, to gauge if I had caught any of their conversation, so I became a blank slate, not a difficult task at the moment with the thumping pushing on the edges of my skull. I had no idea what he was thinking, but I did my best to appear unafraid. I made the mistake of glancing at Marco, whose ugly scowl made me blink, then wince at the pain in my head. It took all of my willpower not to lift my hands to my head to allay the pounding. That would have been a sign of weakness, and I was unwilling to give that to Marco.

"I can't meet with you tonight, Jon. I have some business I have to attend to."

At this turn of events, I felt a mix of relief and consternation. Now, I would not have to ask my patron the difficult questions about Maggie and Marco. Now, I would not get the answers to the difficult questions I so badly wanted to know. Now, I would have to plan a third trip. Doing my best to seem unfazed, I responded, "I understand, Tony. But I won't be able to finish the story without your input. You're almost as important as the groom." I looked over my shoulder, trying to make a friendly gesture toward Marco. I was met with a threatening glare. At that moment, I realized Vespucci's good will was the only thing keeping me safe. I quickly turned back to Vespucci.

Vespucci smiled. "Of course, Jon. I'm sure we'll have time to sit down before you have to write the finished product. Go take care of your hangover," he directed me. "And don't be embarrassed. You're not the first man my nieces have put down for the count. Joey, can you show Jon what we've got in the kitchen to help a hangover, maybe one of your famous subs? Marco and I have some unfinished business to discuss."

Joey led me out of the office and closed the door. I had

to pass Marco as I left the room. I could tell Marco was furious, could feel his eyes on my back as I disappeared down the hallway. I followed Joey to the back of the house and into the kitchen. My heart was still racing from the close call, and I wasn't sure if Vespucci knew I'd overheard them or not. If he did, I figured I'd know soon enough and there was nothing I could do about it now. I did my best to set my worry aside as I watched Joey pull the sub ingredients out of the fridge. Silently, I watched him throw together several professional looking submarine sandwiches and set them on the table. Then he grabbed three Cokes from the fridge, sat down at the table, and started eating.

Joey looked up from his plate. "They're not gonna get up and walk over to you."

I grabbed a sub, realizing as I did how hungry I was. My hangover was already receding.

"Thanks, Joey. It's really good."

Joey didn't respond. A moment later, Vespucci stepped into the kitchen.

"Joey, you should have opened a sub shop," Vespucci remarked.

"I agree," I said, my mouth full.

Vespucci settled into his seat, popping his Coke open, taking the last sub.

After a few moments, the nervous energy still rolling through my system needing an outlet, I asked, "Marco's not joining us?"

"Do you want him to join us?" Vespucci asked.

Surprise must have registered on my face. I was not sure why he had phrased the question that way.

Before I could think of an appropriate response, Vespucci said, "He had to go back to the factory. They're working on a big job right now that needs a lot of babysitting." Vespucci then shifted gears. "So you've met with enough people and gotten enough information that you must have an opinion now. What do you think of Marco and Maggie?"

Not sure what Vespucci wanted to hear, I immediately went to safe ground, answering with as innocuous a response as I could. "I think they'll give you beautiful grandchildren, Tony." Over the years, I'd learned the strong desire for grandchildren was a near universal among the parents of the bride and groom.

"That's not what I mean, Jon. I want to know what you think about their relationship. You've been around a lot of engaged couples, right?"

"Yes, I have." Joey was staring at me.

"Are they good for each other? That's what I'm asking you."

I felt the ground move beneath my feet. At this point, I wasn't sure who intimidated me more, Vespucci or Marco. Before I could stop myself, I was looking over my shoulder to see if Marco was lurking in the hallway, if Vespucci was setting me up for a trap. Vespucci's voice snapped my head back forward.

"Jon, as Maggie's father, I have concerns about them and I want to put my concerns to rest. You've spent a lot of time with soon-to-be newlyweds and you must get a good idea of which couples are right for each other and which aren't." Vespucci paused. "I want to know what you think. It won't leave this table."

I nodded, trying to gather my thoughts so I wouldn't say anything I would regret later. "I haven't seen anything out of the ordinary, if that's what you're asking. Maggie and Marco seem like most engaged couples before the wedding."

"Do you think they're in love?"

Of course they were in love. Wasn't that why I was in New York? "Don't you?"

Vespucci's eyes never left my face. "Of course I do. But I'm not the expert. That's why I hired you." Abruptly pushing his chair back, Vespucci stood up. Joey followed suit. "I have to go. I'm glad you don't see any issues." The frown on his face indicated otherwise. He walked toward the hallway entrance, Joey one step behind.

I felt like I'd just angered Vespucci, though I wasn't sure why. But I didn't want them to leave without saying something. I tossed out, "Thanks for the sandwich, Joey."

"Anytime."

Vespucci stopped at the kitchen doorway, his voice nonchalant, and said, "Jon, you sure you didn't hear us talking in the study?"

My heart skipped a beat, but I did my best to remain calm. "No. Did I miss something good?"

"Not really. But if you had heard anything, we'd have to kill you."

With his finger pointing at me like little kids do, Joey took aim and fired, a deep "boom" escaping from his mouth. I jumped up in my seat, embarrassed and frightened at the same time.

Vespucci chuckled. "Just kidding, Jon." He turned to go, and then suddenly stopped, as if the thought had just occurred to him. "Jon, why do you think my future son-in law dislikes you so much?"

"He doesn't like me?" I asked weakly.

In response, Vespucci stared at me for several moments, then disappeared down the hallway, Joey in step behind him. I realized I was holding my breath. I exhaled, wondering what the hell had just happened. I wasn't sure if his questions about Maggie and Marco indicated simple fatherly concern for his daughter's happiness, or something more. Why did he tell me Marco didn't like me? Did he know I'd overheard them? Was he playing Marco and me off each other? Glancing at the clock, I decided to make an unplanned visit.

After taking a quick shower and changing from the clothes I'd slept in, I headed for the nearest subway station. Given what Marco knew about Jim Mosconi, I had to assume he'd had me followed and I guessed it would be easier for me to spot someone if I used the subway rather than a taxi. The pain in my head had diminished considerably as the sub digested into my blood stream. The train ride went by quickly, and I didn't spot anyone suspicious.

I stepped through the doors onto the platform in Manhattan and walked up the stairs into the sunlight, the hustle and bustle of city life all around me. There was a slight chill in the air that I hadn't noticed before, reminding me that I missed the fall of the East Coast, having lived in Los Angeles for several years now. Before going straight to the offices of the *New York Post,* I walked a few extra blocks, traveling in a circle to make sure I wasn't being tracked. I was more than a little panicked by what I'd learned earlier. Why was Marco so concerned about Mosconi? I was hoping he might be able to shed some light on my ignorance.

With one last glance down both sides of the sidewalk and satisfied I was alone, I stepped through the large glass doors into the lobby. A desk attendant was guarding the entrance to the elevators, so I waited several moments until he was distracted by an older man needing directions and I slipped past his desk to the elevators.

Thoughts swirled around in my head in an attempt to decipher the implications of the conversation I'd overheard earlier between Marco and Vespucci. A flash of my exit from the factory when I interviewed Marco the first time crossed my mind, and I recalled the man sitting in the car across the street. By the time I was at the end of the block, the man had disappeared. Did Marco put him on my tail?

As the elevator doors slid open, dropping me out into a small lobby, I cleared my head to focus on the task at hand. A young woman seated behind a mammoth desk greeted me with a peremptory, "Yes?"

"I'm here to see Jim Mosconi," I said.

She typed on the keyboard, glancing down at her computer screen. She responded, "He's on assignment. Out of the country."

I didn't expect that. "Could you tell me where he went?"

"Italy."

The word "Italy" unfolded at a snail's pace inside my brain.

I muttered, "Thank you" and turned toward the elevator.

Mosconi was in Italy. I was sure he was working on something related to the Mafia. I took the elevator to the ground floor and exited the building onto the busy street. I started walking, not sure where I was going, just wanting to think. I pulled out my PDA, typing a short, succinct email. "What are you doing in Italy?" Then I sent it to Mosconi.

After walking for a couple of blocks, my mind running in circles over my morning, I found myself standing in front of a jewelry store display window staring at sparkling engagement rings, instantly distracted from my troublesome thoughts.

Sara. Ring. Propose.

I looked into the brightly lit shop, noting the expensive woodwork detail lining the walls. A woman stood behind the counter, busying herself with inventory, methodically moving pieces around within the casing, pretending not to notice me staring in the window. About to enter, my hand on the door handle, I stopped. Why this store? Before I allowed myself time to think it through and change my mind, I called Maggie to see where she wanted to meet and if she could help me with something. She told me to come to her office in an hour.

I started walking, figuring it would take me about forty-five minutes. The noise and vibrancy of the cars and pedestrians and city life did little to slow down my thoughts, which cycled back and forth between what I was about to do for Sara and what had happened during the day with Vespucci and Marco and Mosconi. Given what I'd overheard, Marco and Vespucci clearly knew who Mosconi was. Did that mean Mosconi posed some kind of threat? And if so, what did it mean that I had met with him? It was clear to me that Vespucci was heavily invested in the American netherworld of crime, but nothing remotely concrete had been pinned on him by officials. Of all the literature I could find, Mosconi was the only author who had given Vespucci Godfather status without question. No ambiguity there. Suddenly, I stopped in my tracks. Something I'd read in one of Mosconi's last articles popped into my head. Mosconi had implied that the Balducci business enterprises in Italy were a conduit of sorts between the Italian and American Mafias. But he'd done nothing more than that. I could only assume Mosconi was in Italy to research this possible connection further. If Mosconi was on to something, he definitely posed a threat to the Balduccis. And, in turn, to the Vespuccis.

And now Vespucci knew I had met with Mosconi. If my suppositions were correct, I was in a far more tenuous position than I had originally thought. I glanced around, looking for a tail, but there were too many pedestrians going in both directions on either side of the street for me to see if someone was following me. Anyway, unless the tail raised his hand to indicate who he was, I really had no idea what to look for. After several moments of furtive looking about, I began to feel foolish. I understood I had to speak with Mosconi to find out what he knew. If he was sitting on an incriminating story regarding Vespucci, I needed to be careful. I didn't want to find myself implicated in Vespucci's eyes because of my interaction with Mosconi. But until I spoke with Mosconi, I realized there was nothing more I could do, so I tried to focus on the task at hand: finding an engagement ring. This would finally turn the tide in our deteriorating relationship, I was sure. In the dark recesses of my mind, though, my altar ego's Voice was playing devil's advocate.

Are you sure this is the right thing to do? Maybe you're reading this wrong. I'm not so convinced Sara wants to marry you. Maybe you should reconsider these actions, wait until you get back to Los

Angeles, have a sit-down with Sara, and discuss your decision with her. Screw the surprise! Take the safe route.

Shaking my head violently, I tried to shut my Voice down. I didn't need indecisiveness. Besides, the surprise was the best part of the equation. It would show Sara I wasn't afraid of her answer, that I'd come to this decision on my own, that she was worth the risk of going out on a limb to express my love for her. I took a deep breath, silencing my Voice with "Enough. I'm doing it." I startled an old woman passing by on the sidewalk. Sheepishly, I shrugged. "Sorry, ma'am."

I walked the last couple of blocks to Maggie's building and saw her standing on the sidewalk, waiting for me. With her hair down, blowing in the September breeze, a tight sweater showing off her curves, she looked more like a model than an assistant professor. She was engrossed in a book and didn't notice me. She was as beautiful as the day is long. I stood frozen. I just stared at her. Glancing up from her reading, she spotted me and waved. I got my feet moving so she wouldn't know I was gawking at her. I returned the wave, though my stomach was doing the same somersaults that seemed to occur every time I saw Maggie. I heard my Voice whisper, *See. You're a dummy. I'm done helping you.*

"Hi, Jon. You walked?" Her warm smile washed over me.

I nodded, the combination of my lingering hangover and the somersaults making it hard for me to respond.

"I got done a little early and figured I'd wait for you out here, get in a little personal reading," Maggie added.

I recovered my voice enough to squawk, "What are you reading?"

She held the book up to show me Stieg Larsson's *The Girl With the Dragon Tattoo.*

"Oh, you're in for a treat. It's wonderful," I said.

Maggie smiled. "I know. I've already read it once. This is my second go round."

"Larsson was brilliant! He died before the first book was

even published. Funny how life works."

"Shall we walk?" she asked.

"Why not?" I was just glad to be with Maggie so I could clear my head of the fraught scene at Vespucci's house.

Maggie stuck *The Girl with the Dragon Tattoo* into her handbag and pulled out a light, colorful shawl. Wrapping the shawl around her shoulders, she started walking and I fell in step beside her.

"Can I ask you a question about my fiancé?"

"Sure, shoot." Talking about Marco made me nervous.

"You can be honest with me, Jon. I'm not blind. Marco hasn't been very nice to you in all this, has he?"

"Well, I would say he's made it clear he doesn't like being interviewed."

Maggie nodded. "I'm sorry about that. But I know I can trust you, Jon. I've spent enough time with you to know that." She stopped talking and looked away. Then looking back at me, her eyes locked on mine, she said, "I don't know what it is, but I feel as if we've known each other most of our lives. There's a familiarity between us."

I had trouble holding her gaze it was so intense. "I agree." Then I looked away, afraid of what my eyes might reveal to her.

"Does that happen with most of your clients?"

I shook my head in response. We walked in step for a few moments. Then I asked, "Why Marco?"

Maggie turned to me. "Do you ask all your clients that question about their partner?"

The tone in her voice warned me from full disclosure, so I backpedaled. "No. In fact, I rarely ask it. Usually, I can tell. But with you and Marco, on the surface, I get it. I was just hoping you could give me a deeper understanding. Then, I could use your own words and I wouldn't have to make up my own when I'm writing your story."

"Well, I wasn't totally honest with you before when I told you about our history."

"From your teenage years?"

Maggie responded, "You could say that. Marco and I were more than a casual fling, or at least we had the beginning of more. We kept it quiet because we both knew how my father felt about me dating. You have no idea, Jon. When he caught Marco at our house, I thought he was going to kill him. I didn't see Marco again from that night until I ran into him ten years later. After Marco went to Italy, I asked my father what he did to Marco, but he wouldn't discuss it. I knew my father well enough to know not to ask him the same question twice."

"What do you think happened?" I asked, gently probing around the edges.

"I don't know. I've learned not to dwell on things I can't change. Whatever happened between my father and Marco and Giancarlo is between them, and it's been left in the past. As long as they're comfortable with that, so am I."

"Marco was more than just a crush?"

"He was the first and only boy I ever fell in love with. In the old neighborhood, all the girls had crushes on him. He was incredibly good looking, still is, and he had this dangerous aura about him. The girls loved it. I did too. Plus, Jon, ever since then, the men I've dated over the years have bored me. I could never seem to meet another man who had an edge to him. Marco has a sharp edge. I'm sure you've noticed."

"I have." No doubt about that. He would kill me if he could.

"My father didn't raise me to be weak, so he shouldn't be surprised I'd want to be with a man who's powerful like Marco is." Suddenly, Maggie stopped talking, embarrassed.

"Why didn't you look him up when you were in Italy during college?"

"I wasn't sure how he'd react to me, given what had happened. Plus, I was seeing someone back here and that was enough to keep me from making contact with him."

"So, when Marco showed up one day here in the States, all those feelings came back?"

"Like the snap of a finger."

"Is he any different now than he was then?"

After considering my question for a moment, Maggie said, "I'd have to say he's probably more guarded now, more careful about what he does, before he speaks. Other than that, I'd say he's the same."

"Do you think your father approves of you two getting married, given what happened in the past?"

"He hired you, didn't he?"

That I couldn't deny. But was it for the same reason every other father hired me?

"Jon, can I trust you? Completely?"

I said, "Of course. I gave your father the same vow."

"Do you know what my father does for a living?"

Her question took me off guard. I didn't expect her to broach this subject. I stared into Maggie's distinct hazel eyes, not sure how to answer. I glanced away down the busy Manhattan streets, watching the cars and buses passing in both directions. I gained nothing if I was untruthful. "I do."

Unexpectedly, Maggie appeared relieved. "I figured you did. Kind of hard to miss if you do a little digging."

"Giancarlo and Marco are of the same ilk."

"They are. Does that put you in a moral dilemma?" Maggie asked.

"Not my place to pass judgment. But can I ask you something?"

"Of course. We've dropped all other pretensions, haven't we?"

"Do I need to worry about my self-preservation, if for example, your father doesn't like my finished product?"

Maggie laughed. "Jon, this is not a movie. There is a code. Rules. You're a civilian. Anyway, I'm sure what you write will be wonderful, though you can't write anything about this conversation."

"I understand. I have no intention of doing that."

We walked in silence, the ramifications of our discussion slowly sinking in on the two of us. I was now bound to Maggie by her trust in me, and the mutual knowledge we shared. I was on the inside.

"I'm assuming you don't discuss your father's business with many people?"

"Not many. Some are in the know, but they don't ask. Most people don't know. Ever since John Gotti died in prison, things changed. "

"What about Michael?"

"He's a legitimate lawyer. My father didn't want either of us in the business, so he worked hard to make sure that didn't happen."

"Then, how can you say he approves of you marrying a man like Marco?"

"My father is wise enough to know his daughter is cut from the same cloth that he is. I love my father to death," Maggie said, "but I'm a grown woman now, and unlike when I was sixteen, he no longer gets to make my decisions for me. He understands my love life is off limits now. It's not something he wants to battle with me about."

"So you're not sure he approves of you marrying Marco?"

Maggie fell silent. She glanced at me, her face appearing sad even though there was a smile on it. "If my father had his druthers, he'd have me marry a professor. He thinks professors are safe and boring." Suddenly, Maggie switched gears. "Okay, enough about me and my family. Let's talk about why you asked me for help."

The flood of new information about Vespucci's history had made me momentarily forget why I'd wanted to meet Maggie in the first place. Wait. I needed her help to get a ring. "I'm going to propose when I get back to Los Angeles. I need your help picking out a special engagement ring."

"You're sure she's the one?"

I inadvertently looked away and then back to Maggie,

nodding.

She studied my face for several moments. Finally, she said, "I know the perfect place. It's the best jewelry shop in all of New York, though many people don't know about it. Let's go."

She took hold of my hand, pulling me over to the curb as she waved down a taxi. We got in and Maggie gave the driver an address. He just nodded, gunning the taxi down the street. For several minutes, only the rise and fall of the taxi's engine filled my ears. I stared out the window, not focusing on anything, lost in my thoughts.

"You're ready to spend the rest of your life with her?" Maggie's voice pulled me back.

Was she asking me that question specifically, or was she also asking it for herself? I considered the question, not sure of the answer, the scope of an entire lifetime beyond my comprehension. "Did someone ask you that?"

"My mother. She went over the good Italian Catholic thing, placing emphasis on the fact that Catholics, especially Italian ones, do not believe in divorce."

"Your mom's old school just like your dad."

"Old Country through and through. When I pointed out that several of my mom's friends from the old neighborhood were divorced, she crossed herself and told me not to bring them up. They weren't good Catholics." Maggie laughed at the memory.

"Did your mother's questions raise any doubts?"

"You've seen a lot of people get married, Jon. Don't they all have doubts?"

I shrugged my shoulders. "Most, yes. But, to be honest, I've never seen a correlation between the level of doubts and how it defined the future marriage." Maggie was weighing my words carefully. "I've seen couples where neither person seemed to have any doubts, and they were split within a year. Other couples, where both bride and groom were a dithering mess, are perfectly happy. I think it is part of the natural process. Be kind of weird if you don't have doubts, don't you think?"

Before she could answer, the taxi came to an abrupt halt. I leaned forward and paid the driver what we owed. We were on a narrow side street, an alley perpendicular to the road just ahead of us, with many low-rise shops on both sides of the street.

"Follow me," Maggie said.

I fell in step with Maggie, following her down the street, turning into the alley, passing several backdoor stoops before we stopped before an iron-mesh gate. She knocked on the door. A moment later a tall, lean guard with an unexpected smile on his face greeted us, inviting us into what turned out to be a stunning display room full of jewelry. There were large glass cases running along four walls. Assorted necklaces and pendants, earrings and bracelets hung from the walls, and bright lights danced around the room reflecting off the expensive glitter.

"What is this place?" I asked, curiously.

"The best kept secret in all of the five boroughs," Maggie replied. "A business run purely on word of mouth and referrals."

"And that's the way we like it."

Maggie and I turned toward the gravelly voice coming from the back of the room to see an ancient woman walk out from between a dark, red, silk curtain. Hunched over with age, the old woman still gave off a lively air, though I couldn't have counted the wrinkles on her face even if she'd let me. I guessed she was of Jewish origin, somewhere in Eastern Europe. I'd spotted a mezuzah on the doorpost as we entered.

"It's been a long time, young lady," the old woman said as she slowly made her way out from behind the counter to come around and kiss Maggie on the cheeks. Maggie leaned into her, returning the affection. "And who is this handsome young man you're toting around?"

"Mrs. Goldschmidt, this is Jon Fixx. Jon, Mrs. Goldschmidt."

"Well met, young man," Mrs. Goldschmidt said, as she shook my hand.

"To you as well, ma'am."

Maggie added, "My father got my mother's ring here from Mrs. Goldschmidt."

I smiled, convinced Maggie had brought me to the right place.

"And now you two have come to continue the tradition?" Mrs. Goldschmidt asked.

Maggie and I both shook our heads at the same time, stumbling over each other to correct Mrs. Goldschmidt. Before either of us could say anything intelligible, she reached out and grabbed Maggie's left hand, visibly upset by the engagement ring she saw there. Maggie's cheeks flushed red.

"Where did this come from?" Mrs. Goldschmidt reprimanded her.

Maggie answered quietly, "My fiancé didn't ask me first."

Mrs. Goldschmidt looked at me. "You're not her fiancé."

She wasn't asking but I shook my head anyway.

"Who then?"

"Marco Balducci."

"And your father is okay with this?"

"Times change, Mrs. Goldschmidt. What could my father say?"

"Did this boy not ask for your father's permission first?"

Maggie shook her head.

A string of Yiddish epithets erupted from Mrs. Goldschmidt's mouth, but her look of displeasure quickly transformed to one of resignation and sadness.

"You young men, all boys. You grow up, but you have forgotten what makes a man a man. Your generation forgets where they've come from. No respect for tradition, for the past, for what has come before. To honor your future, you must honor your past."

I couldn't respond, tongue-tied as well as fascinated by this strange old woman who owned this expensive jewelry store in a Manhattan side street. Maggie clearly regarded her in high esteem.

Maggie spoke before I could think of anything to say. "Mrs. Goldschmidt, I agree with everything you've said, and that's why I'm here. I can't change what my fiancé did, but Jon wants to buy a ring for his girlfriend. She's back in Los Angeles."

Mrs. Goldschmidt turned her hawk eyes on me again, studying me so thoroughly that I began to squirm. Unable to hold her gaze, I looked away. Finally, without a word, Mrs. Goldschmidt turned around, slowly walking back behind the counter. We stepped up to the large glass container.

"My family has been selling jewelry for over three hundred years," she said. "You learn a few things when you've been doing something that long. Knowledge gets passed down through the generations, along with the business." Mrs. Goldschmidt paused a moment for emphasis. "You can be with someone all your life and never know them. And you can meet someone for a day, and you've known them all your life."

Maggie and I stared at Mrs. Goldschmidt's wrinkled face, turning to each other as if we were acknowledging as one what she had said.

"It's important for people who are getting married to understand that."

Then, Mrs. Goldschmidt shifted gears. Over the next several minutes, she showed me several different kinds of diamond rings and gave me the price of each, describing their special features in turn. Then, she stopped and looked at me. "Your girlfriend does not know you're coming back with a ring? Have you asked her father for permission?"

"Her father died when she was a teenager. Her mom died four years ago," I answered.

Mrs. Goldschmidt took that all in, then stopped showing us the rings she had in her hand. Quickly shoving them back in the case, she stood up from her stool and walked behind the counter to the opposite side of the shop. Before either Maggie or I could see what she was doing, she had pulled a diamond ring out of the case and held it up before us. I didn't know much about rings, or jewelry in general, but I knew this ring was special.

"Oh, my God, this is stunning," Maggie whispered.

I was sure I couldn't afford the ring.

Mrs. Goldschmidt looked at the ring and then at Maggie. "I was keeping this for you, Maggie, but you don't need it any longer."

Maggie's face registered surprise, then a mixture of sadness and regret.

Mrs. Goldschmidt turned my way. "Jon, this ring is for you now."

I coughed, trying to cover my dismay. "Thank you, but no. I couldn't do that." I wasn't about to buy a ring Mrs. Goldschmidt had intended for Maggie.

Maggie protested. "Oh, Jon, this ring is unbelievably beautiful. You have to buy it for Sara. She'll be so happy."

"That's her name, Sara?" Mrs. Goldschmidt asked.

I nodded to Mrs. Goldschmidt. Staring at the ring, I was sure Sara would think it was gorgeous. There was no way she could say no if I had this ring, but I knew it was more than a little out of my price range. I said, "I appreciate your choice, Mrs. Goldschmidt. It's amazing, but I think this is more than I can afford."

She asked me how much I was planning on spending. I told her. "Then that's the price."

I stared dumbly at her. Even Maggie seemed surprised at the low number. Mrs. Goldschmidt waited for my answer, but then she grew impatient.

"Jon," she said in an authoritative voice, "an opportunity is called an opportunity because it has an element of time attached to it, and when that time has expired, the opportunity has passed." She glanced behind her at the clock on the wall, the minute hand about to hit 6 p.m. "Closing time is in thirty seconds."

"I'll take it."

As we concluded the final details of the purchase, Maggie and I didn't talk much. I paid the amount Mrs. Goldschmidt had asked, and she enclosed the ring in a special case. Maggie said her goodbyes, hugging the old lady before we exited. Just as we were about to leave the shop, Mrs. Goldschmidt called out to me, "I'm glad we met, Jon Fixx."

"Me too, Mrs. Goldschmidt," I called back to her.

A moment later we were back on the street, Maggie and I exchanging a look.

"Thank you," I said to Maggie.

"I'm glad I could help," she answered, giving me a big smile.

"That was a unique experience."

"I agree."

"Shall we walk back?" Maggie asked.

"Yes, we shall," I said.

In lockstep, we found our way back the way we came. The remainder of the night was uneventful. Most of the family was out, so I found myself packing alone. Maggie had plans with Marco, so I said my goodbyes during the evening. In the morning, I got up extra early, not wanting to bother anyone. A car from the airport was waiting for me. I got to the airport and onto the plane without a hitch. The ring was stuffed in my inside jacket pocket close to my chest. Just before shutting my PDA down for the flight, I noticed a new message in my email with the heading "Priority." I opened it up, not recognizing the address.

It read:

"Jon, Don't contact me again. I'll contact you. Following a hunch. Be careful. You're exposed. JM"

Jim Mosconi.

What the hell was he talking about, "You're exposed"? I wrote him back, ignoring his instructions. The email was immediately kicked back to me, indicating the email address didn't exist. As the plane took off, I fell into a fitful sleep, images of Marco and Sara and Nick Nickels Sr. and Maggie dancing like aboriginal shadows around a large bonfire with an extra-large version of the engagement ring I'd just bought hanging down. When I landed in Los Angeles six hours later, I felt anything but rested. The next day, Sara ruined my life. At least for a while.

9
Early November
Los Angeles

"The Coffee Shop Lovers," the story for my Chicago couple, was taking shape. Several days had passed since my visit to Luci's house, and I was feeling better than I had at any time since the breakup. I'd been writing day and night. In fact, for the first time in months, my writing was back on track. I was able to put Sara and Michel and Ted Williams on the emotional back burner while I worked. Serious about delivering a finished product on time, I locked myself in my apartment, knocking out a first full draft for "The Coffee Shop Lovers" in two days, a new record for me. I turned my cell phone off. I even put the Vespucci clan on hold for a few days so I could finish my commitment to clients who had come along earlier. But thoughts of Maggie and Marco and Mosconi entered my mind far more often than I liked. I couldn't stop thinking about them. I hadn't found the key to Maggie and Marco's relationship, if there was one. If I couldn't find the key—the connection that made their relationship special—it usually meant the difference between a generic love story without a backbone versus a unique love story that lived and breathed its main characters. In addition, as I was finally letting go of Sara, I found my feelings for Maggie becoming like those of an irrational schoolboy—all fantasy with no basis in reality. From a professional standpoint, I was afraid these irrational feelings would interfere with my objectivity, making it impossible to write a story in which Marco didn't appear to be a jerk. I already disliked Marco, and knew how he felt about me. My irrational feelings for Maggie were not helping. This was new territory for me, and I wasn't sure how to deal with it. I figured the best way to manage my feelings was to disqualify them, understand that my feelings for Maggie were not organic but rather a result of my breakup with Sara.

I didn't leave my apartment for several days while I worked on the project. I'd bought meat and peanut butter and jelly for sandwiches to tide me over while I worked. Luci checked in every day, showing me his progress on the visual side of the book, looking for my input—and approbation. During one visit, I asked him to read the first draft of "The Coffee Shop Lovers" because he always gave me constructive criticism that improved my final draft. I had become dependent on his feedback. That particular day, I turned on my phone for the first time in days to check messages. Nothing from Sara. Nothing from New York. I had only one message. A male voice I didn't recognize came through the speaker without a hello or introduction of any kind. "You think because I haven't called that maybe I've forgotten what you've done. That's too bad, because I haven't. You're going to pay. One day. By the way, you're an asshole." Click.

It was Nick Nickels Jr., the creepiest one of the Nickels clan. When I interviewed him, I had gotten weird vibes. The way he and his sister interacted reminded me of a book I had read in junior high school called *Flowers in the Attic* that a girlfriend made me read as a way to prove I liked her. The story was about a brother and sister locked in an attic for a long period of time. They fall in love, commit incest, have a baby, and do a bunch of other terrible, taboo things. Nick Jr. seemed more like a jealous ex-lover than a brother.

This message renewed my concern about the Nickels clan. Of the family members, Nick Jr. seemed to derive the most pleasure from leaving me harassing messages.

Luci didn't like any of it, advising me to call the police, something I wasn't willing to do. With Nickels as the attorney general for the state of California, I didn't think I'd get very far calling the authorities. Second, they hadn't actually done anything to me, and I knew the law did nothing to a stalker until they actually tried to harm you. I had done my research and the laws were very specific. I didn't tell Luci about the newest threat either, because I saw no reason to worry him. I figured I'd just have to keep my eyes and ears open. Plus, if I didn't leave my apartment, there wasn't much anyone could do to me.

After a few more days of straight rewriting and taking Luci's notes into account, I sat back from my computer screen. The creation of the romantic relationship between Scott Michaels and Anna Jensen had taken final shape. I was close to putting the finishing touches on the story and feeling good about what I had. I did my best writing in long jags, so when I got on a roll I didn't like to break the flow. I would write until I felt it coming to an end, which sometimes lasted for a week or longer. But this last writing session felt extra satisfying because it had been many months since I'd been able to do it. Patting myself on the back, I got up to stretch, realizing my stomach was grumbling. I looked at the clock. It was past 9 p.m. and I hadn't eaten anything since early morning. I wandered over to the fridge, finding it almost empty. The craving for a hot slice of good pizza hit me hard and fast. I grabbed my jacket and keys and was out the door. As I exited the building, the sky was dark, the street lamps on. The pizza place I'd been ordering from since I moved into my tiny apartment was only a couple of blocks away. I walked down Woodman toward Ventura Boulevard, the streets busy with cars. The pulse of life reverberated all around me. For the first time in a while, I felt alive, my body waking up, as if from a long, unsatisfying slumber. I had hit bottom during my tenure in the Cave, but I was finally on my way back up.

I spotted Vitello's Exchange across Ventura, a sign with a huge slice of pizza standing high above the one-story dwelling. My pace quickened as I thought about salty cheese melting in my mouth. I reached the intersection, the traffic lights in my favor, the walk sign beckoning me to cross. Moments later, I reached for the door handle about to step inside the pizza joint, when unexpectedly, I heard my internal Voice.

By the way, just a friendly reminder: Be careful.

I cringed, afraid my Voice was going to spin me into another episode like what happened at the rest stop off the I-10 freeway, something I could no longer stomach or desired. But the warning came as a surprise.

Careful about what?

But there was no response. Silence. I took note of the warning, passing through the doorway to fulfill my craving. The redheaded, pimple-faced teenager behind the counter took my order without a word. He turned around and threw two slices into the oven. I took a seat at one of the booths lining either side of the center aisle. Aside from the youngster at the front, two older guys hustled around farther back in the kitchen making pizzas. A fourth guy came in from the back door with a light jacket on. He checked a stack of pizza boxes waiting near the rear entranceway, exchanged a few words with one of the pizza makers, then grabbed the stack and disappeared through the rear exit. I recognized his old, weathered face because he had delivered quite a few of those pizza boxes to my apartment over the last several weeks. The other guys were new to me. After a few minutes, the redhead pulled my slices out of the oven, dropped them onto a paper plate, and set them on the front register counter. He caught my eye. I grabbed my food, returned to my seat, and chowed down. I was hungry.

Long writing jags did that to me. I savored every bite, my taste buds craving grease and fat.

The pizza was gone in less than ten minutes, so I finished the last bit of Coke in my cup, and got up to take an easy walk back to my apartment with the intention of putting the finishing touches on the Chicago couple's love story. The process of writing their story had helped pull me out of the terrible coma I'd been in since breaking up with Sara. I'd begun to worry that my Love Story writing career might be coming to an end. But now, I was back.

I was about a block and a half away from my apartment, my full stomach making me unobservant and careless. The tackle came from behind. In a split second, I was on my back in the shadows of an alley running through the center of the block off Woodman. I could make out two bodies standing over me. I quickly scrambled to regain my footing. My thoughts were in free-form as I tried to gain a defensive stance. Why would Williams bring a colleague to beat me up in the alley? Did the FBI beat people up in public areas? What did I do this time? I was on both knees, then had one foot planted, when a shock paralyzed me, coursing through my body and dropping me back to the ground. I saw one of the shadows step back, his right hand holding a Taser. A solid kick took me in the midsection, a sharp pain racing to the circuits in my brain telling me I probably just broke a rib.

The shadow who kicked me stepped in close, leaning near my face. I was rolled up in the fetal position, protecting myself as best I could. I heard a voice in my ear, "This is just the start, Jonny Fixx-it. You piece of shit! Any time. Any place. You turn around and I might be there."

The voice sounded vaguely familiar. I tried to make out the face before me, but I realized both antagonists were wearing ski masks. They wouldn't get far in southern California without drawing attention to themselves. I ruled out Williams. Not his M.O. This guy wanted to hurt me but stay anonymous. Williams had no need to be anonymous. That shortened the list of possibilities by one. Someone connected to my Italian contingent? But why? That didn't make sense. My life had become one long string of surreal moments. This was my third beating in a week. First Williams, then the funeral, and now this—whatever this was. And it didn't seem to be over yet. I needed to hire a bodyguard. Maybe I would tap into my emergency retirement fund. The absurdity of it all made me smile.

"Why are you smiling? I wouldn't be smiling if I was you."

Another kick in the ribs wiped the smile off my face. I gasped, desperately gulping for air.

"That's better."

He leaned over, getting close to me again. I noticed my other antagonist hanging back. "You won't know when or where, but at any moment I could be there, ready to make your life a living hell. Eye for an eye, you hack piece of shit."

Living hell. Hack. Those phrases rang a bell in my cloudy mind. I'd gained my breath back. I figured I'd throw a dart and see if I hit a bullseye. "Gotta be careful in this day and age. Election year coming up and all. What would the press do with a story about an abusive son, obsessed with his sister—"

I'd hit a bullseye! The kicks came in on my body hard and fast. The voice and foot bruising my body belonged to Nick Nickels Jr., I was sure. The other antagonist stepped in, trying to pull his partner off me. Nick Nickels Jr. shrugged his partner off, coming at me harder. Better prepared for the onslaught, I'd curled into a tight little ball, protecting my rib cage as best I could. The kicks hurt, but weren't doing a lot of damage now. Headlights from the opposite end of the alley revealed a car turning down it in our direction. The kicks abruptly ended.

"This isn't over by a long shot," Nickels Jr. yelled at me as the two attackers retreated in the opposite direction from the car, disappearing around the corner onto Woodman.

Using my heels for leverage, I pushed myself up against the wall of the building. Taking a deep, jagged breath, I did a body check, surveying the damage. My body would be covered with bruises by morning. As I exhaled, I could hear a slight wheezing. Broken rib, most likely, probably the same one the man-boy from the funeral had started on. The headlights stopped halfway down the alley, long before reaching me and turned into a parking space. Hands on the ground, I shoved my back against the wall to stand up. The movement took more energy than I expected, so I stood there stooped over, my butt against the wall for support, waiting for my breathing to slow. After a few minutes, I gathered myself up and slowly stumbled back to my apartment. Climbing the one set of stairs to my apartment was exhausting. The attack had taken a toll.

Once inside, I went to the medicine cabinet, popped four Motrin tablets, grabbed my jacket, and headed down to my car. A game plan had formed in my mind as I stumbled home. I was tired of getting my ass kicked. I needed an additional set of eyes on me at all times, at least for a while. I was going to tap my retirement savings and make an offer.

But first I needed to take care of my damaged rib, or ribs. I couldn't tell how bad it was. I climbed into my car, pulled out of the parking garage, and made a left turn in the direction of the closest emergency room. As I drove, I kept an eye on my rearview to make sure I wasn't being followed. A well-earned paranoia had taken over. The possibility that someone could be following me no longer seemed far-fetched. Not spotting anyone or anything unusual, I drove directly to my destination. I checked in at the emergency room desk. The attendant said it would not be long because it was a quiet night so far. After sitting only a few minutes, I heard my name called out from the entry doorway. I stood up carefully and followed a tall, thin Asian male nurse back to a room. I told him what was wrong. He wrote down some notes, took my blood pressure, had me stand on a scale for my weight, then left, telling me the doctor would be in momentarily. As I waited, I caught a reflection of myself in a mirror in the corner of the room. A damaged version of Jon Fixx stared back at me. I hadn't realized I'd sustained damage to my face. The black eye from earlier in the week was yellow, on its way to healing. But, now, the socket around my left eye was swelling and bruising, my right cheek was scraped, red and swelling, and my lower lip was cracked and bleeding. I looked a wreck. The doctor's entry interrupted my self-analysis. She was in her early forties with cropped hair, thin cheeks, and swift, all business moves. She took one look at me, taking it all in, grabbing my chart as she did so and glancing at the nurse's notes.

"I hope the other guy doesn't look worse."

I shook my head. "Surprise attack. I didn't get any punches in."

She considered my answer as she inspected my face. "Too bad. Looks like he did a number on you. Please take your shirt off."

I did as she asked. She softly probed my ribs. When her fingers touched my right side just below my chest, I involuntarily winced, inhaling quickly, pain sensors shooting off signals to my brain. She stayed there with her hands, feeling all around my rib cage. When she was done, she grabbed my chart and wrote a few notes. "Are you having trouble breathing?"

"I feel a slight wheezing on my exhale."

"We'll need to take x-rays."

Without another word, she disappeared into the hallway. Moments later, the nurse was back, asking me to follow him. I did as he said, and ten minutes later was sitting in the same seat, waiting for the doctor. A few minutes later, she walked in. I noted the efficiency of this hospital.

"Nothing's broken, just bruised. Looks like your left side took the brunt of it, three ribs affected. We're going to wrap you up nice and tight. That's all we can do. I'm going to prescribe no more fighting for a few months." She stared at me pointedly. "Understand?"

"Yes, doctor."

"Do you want to file a police report?"

"What?"

"We usually report this kind of activity to the police. Shall I do that?"

"No, that won't be necessary."

Her pointed stare made me squirm in my seat. She looked down at her chart, pulling out a prescription sheet and filling it out. "Here. This will help with the pain. Those ribs are going to hurt for a couple of weeks."

I took the prescription and she turned to hang the chart back on its hook. Then she was gone. After a few minutes, the nurse returned with gauze and medical tape. He instructed me to sit up straight while he taped me up. Efficient and with a steady hand, he wrapped my torso tight in white gauze. The snug feeling around my rib cage decreased the pain a bit. When he was finished, he tended to my face, cleaning off the dried blood. Handing me a replacement set of gauze and bandages, he gave me instructions on how best to take the bandages on and off and how to shower. As it dawned on me that my normal day-to-day maintenance was going to be impeded, a fresh wave of anger for the Nickels clan washed over me. For the first time, I felt I wanted to take action against them. Enough was enough. I hadn't liked Candy or Edward from the day I met them. They were vapid, spoiled, self-indulgent people. If they called off the wedding, they surely couldn't blame that on me. Maybe Edward had smartened up, and the pull of the Nickels' money wasn't enough to keep him locked in after all. Maybe he saw the weird way Candy's brother looked at her. Whatever it was, they couldn't pin it all on me. What I owed them for the terrible job I did on their story I'd now paid back in spades. Next time Nick Jr. came around I'd be prepared.

I finished the paperwork at the front desk of the emergency room, grabbed my bandage paraphernalia up in my arms, and walked back to my Regal. I unlocked the car and tossed the medical supplies onto the passenger seat. A voice spun me around in a defensive crouch. I was on my toes, hands up, fists clenched.

"Hey, I come in peace." Williams stood a few feet off, hands up in mock surrender.

I needed to get better about spotting a tail. "What do you want?"

"For a writer, you sure talk tough. I have to say, you impressed me last time we met. You never lost your cool. But it looks like you had a rough night."

I turned my back on Williams, climbed into my car, and pulled the door shut. I could think of no reason why I needed to listen to this asshole, and I was too tired to be polite. Plus, if he had witnessed my beating in the alley and done nothing, all the more reason to ignore him. "Unless you have official FBI business to discuss with me, which I'm sure you don't, leave me alone." I stuck my keys in the ignition. "I will not bother Sara and Michelle anymore."

"It's Michel."

"Not to me." I turned the key in the ignition, revving the engine as it turned over.

"Fine. You want official business, Jon? Then let's talk about Tony Vespucci."

My hands froze on the wheel. I definitely hadn't seen this coming. Without turning my head, I asked, "What about him?"

"I'm just trying to understand your connection to him."

My experiences of the evening had made me careless and loose, my answer to him curt. "That's none of your business."

"Oh, I disagree, Jon. It's very much my business. In case you were not aware, he's what we affectionately call 'Familia.' Some colleagues and I have a great deal of interest in

Tony Vespucci, and we've discovered that you seem to have an open invitation to his home."

"Wherever you're going with this, I really don't care." I found myself wanting to defend Vespucci. If it ever came down to a choice of giving moral support to the FBI and Ted Williams or the Mafia and Tony Vespucci, there was no question in my mind where my loyalties lie. Williams could kiss my ass.

"As far as I'm concerned, Tony Vespucci is a legitimate businessman. He hired me to write the story—"

"We know. For the impending marriage of his daughter Maggie and Marco Balducci. You know the Balduccis are no lightweights themselves. Marco's father Giancarlo came up with Tony."

I'd heard enough. Discovering that the FBI knew what I was doing with the Italians in New York brought that feeling of panic back to my gut. I gripped my steering wheel. "Are you finished?"

Williams stepped toward the car, leaning down into my face. "Just be careful, Jon. If I were you, I wouldn't mention any of this to Tony. I doubt he'd like knowing you're intimately involved with an FBI agent."

I looked sideways at Williams with a grim look, holding his stare. He thought I was about to respond. Instead, I gunned the Regal, slamming the gas pedal and the brake to the floor. Over the years, I'd kept the car in tip-top shape. I took it back to Stan and Maribel's on a regular basis for service. One thing Stan's touch ensured was both the power and response time of the components. Even the slightest tap on the pedal made the car jump. My tires started spinning at breakneck speed. Williams involuntarily stepped back. I dropped my foot off of the brake, the Buick's tires grabbing the cement and taking flight as they did so. I left Williams standing in a cloud of stinking, burning, rubber smoke. In my rearview mirror, I could see him raising his forearm to block his nose. I reached out the window with my free arm and gave him the finger.

I drove to the closest freeway entrance, hopping onto the 101 South. While Nickels Jr. was beating on my body, I'd had an epiphany and wanted to put it into play as soon as possible. The unexpected visit from Williams helped to reinforce my decision. When the 101 hit the I-10 connector, I steered the car onto the eastbound side of the 10. I was returning to my favorite Howard Johnson's. As I drove, the tightness around my chest reminded me how crazy my life had become. I didn't place much belief in luck, good or bad. Rather, I believed people brought on their own destiny. Our actions day in and day out create the life to be, putting into play what happens around us and to us as our life unfolds. Everything happening to me now was a result of a choice or an action, or even inaction, on my part. I met Tony Vespucci because of the story I'd written for Judith and Cranston. The big kid at the funeral beat me up because I'd scared his girlfriend. Williams initially paid me a visit because I wouldn't leave my ex-girlfriend alone. Nick Nickels Jr. was harassing me because I'd handed his sister and her fiancé the story I really believed to be the truth. So my plan on the third trip to New York was to get some control over my future.

Tonight's events made it clear to me that I needed to protect myself. I could defend myself in a fair fight thanks to Luci, but I was getting blindsided. As I sped east on the I-10, the second visit from Williams began to sink in, the dots gaining connection inside my dulled brain. How could he know I was working with Tony Vespucci? I guess Sara could have told him, but I doubted she even remembered who I'd gone to New York to see. September had been a month filled with silence between us. She seemed uninterested in my work, to such a point that each time I went to New York I told her I was working on a new story for clients who were on a rushed time frame. As far as I could gather, Williams had only learned of my existence about a week ago when Michel asked him to pay me a visit. Before that, I didn't exist as far as Williams' world was concerned. Maybe Joey's recent visit after the memorial service sparked Williams' interest in my current job. But that meant he was following me. Why?

In August, I was just a guy who claimed to be a writer trying to salvage my relationship with the love of my life. A couple months later I was working for one of the biggest Mafia bosses in the United States. I had the California attorney general and his son looking for a quiet way to take me out. And a renegade FBI agent, whose cousin was sleeping with the ex-love-of-my life, had decided to take me on as his pet project.

As my mind kept rolling over the different pieces of this troublesome puzzle into which I'd gotten myself, the Los Angeles sprawl sped by. I found myself checking the rearview to make sure I wasn't being followed. I couldn't spot any particular car hanging back, but then again I was on the I-10, and it was crammed with cars speeding along, so I doubt I could have spotted a car that was tailing me. In time, the Howard Johnson rest stop appeared before me. I pulled off at the exit, slowly rolling into the parking lot. I didn't spot a tail. I drove the car close to the entrance, bringing it to a stop near the curb. Was he working? Was I crazy to ask? What would this guy say? Had I misjudged him? Maybe he had the night off. Visitors entered and exited, that look of travel on their faces, many of them on their way to, or on their way back, from Las Vegas, I was sure. Out of the corner of my eye, I spotted a large, black man walking across the parking lot, coming from the gas pumps. When he reached the entrance to the restaurant rest stop, I climbed out of the Regal. Spotting me, he stopped, turning in my direction.

"Jon Fixx."

He remembered my name. That was a good sign.

"You back to make another phone call?"

I shook my head. "I'm here to see you."

"Me?"

I crossed the distance between us quickly. "Can you take a break? I have a business proposition for you."

He stared down at me, curiosity reflected in his eyes. "Okay. Let me go punch out."

Five minutes later, we were sitting in a booth in the corner of the restaurant. I had just finished my pitch. Donovan was staring at me, trying to figure out if I was serious or crazy. "First, why me? You don't know me at all."

I pointed to the Special Forces tattoo visible on his forearm. I'd noted it the night he had helped me. "You were in the army, right?" Donovan nodded. "So I'm assuming you can handle yourself in a fight?" After a moment, Donovan nodded again. "And you're what, six feet two, about two hundred and thirty pounds, right." I didn't wait for an answer. "I'm assuming your size alone ends most fights before they get started." He shrugged. "That's the insurance I need."

Donovan stared at me, silent. I was sure my instincts were right this time. I saw intelligence reflected in his dark brown eyes. I wasn't sure why he was working this dead-end job, but I was sure he had his reasons. He seemed lonely to me. He was considering my proposal because I could see the wheels turning. I noticed the wedding band on his left finger, realizing maybe he couldn't make the decision without his wife's approval. "If you need to discuss this with your wife, I understand."

He stared down at his ring. "No need. She's been with the Almighty these last five years." The tone in his voice said more than anything I could have learned in a full interview. "Cancer."

He was lonely.

I stared down at the table, not sure how to respond. Looking back up at him, I said, "I'm sorry."

"That's all you need to say." He studied my face. "So, how

much trouble are you in, Jon?"

I gathered my thoughts, not sure how to be honest without making it seem too bad. Finally, I figured honesty would be the best approach. "I've been hired by one of the top Mafia bosses in New York to write his daughter's love story. The FBI has taken a great deal of interest in my activity, though I'm not sure why yet. And I've pissed off the attorney general of our state, whose entire family has vowed vengeance."

"You must have special powers to anger that many powerful people at once," he said. "Do you plan on doing anything illegal?"

"No."

His eyes inspected each damaged spot on my face, and then dropped down to my chest to the bandages peeking out just above the last button of my shirt. He nudged his chin toward my body. "That one of the reasons you're talking to me?"

"Surprise attack. If someone had been watching my back, this wouldn't have happened. Don't get me wrong, Donovan. I'm not afraid. I can handle myself in a fight. Generally speaking, my life is very boring. I'm a writer by profession and a loner by nature. Normally, I don't get much excitement of any kind, but for some reason the last couple of months have presented a good number of firsts in my life." I leaned forward, in earnest. "I want to put the odds more in my favor in case there's another first."

Donovan sat back. "So, you want twenty-four seven protection for the next two months and you'll pay me ten thousand cash?"

"Exactly."

"I'm the first person you thought of?"

"Yes."

"Based on this." Donovan looked down at the Special Forces tattoo on his forearm, then back up at me. "And my size. That's it?"

"Donovan, I make a living studying people, ignoring their words and listening to their eyes, their movements, their character, what they're thinking regardless of what they're saying. I'm a very good judge of character. I know I picked the right man."

Donovan sat back, his dark eyes sussing me out. He wasn't convinced.

I pushed my case. "I know I'm asking a lot." I sat back, wondering if I'd misjudged him. Maybe his soul wasn't as restless as I'd thought. When he'd mentioned his deceased wife, I was sure I'd read him right. After she passed, I guessed he started wandering, not sure what to do. Maybe he'd taken this guard job as a temporary gig until he figured it out. I was hoping my offer would shake him loose. His silence was discouraging. I waited a few more moments for him to speak, but he stayed silent. Finally, I decided to go, hoping if he thought about it, he'd change his mind. I reached into my pocket, pulled out my business card, and slid it across the table.

"Here's my information. I'm leaving for New York in a couple of days, so if you change your mind before that, call me. The offer stands." I turned to go, finally saying what had been hanging in my mind since we'd started talking. "I bet your wife was a special lady. What was her name, if I may ask?"

"Elenor."

"I'll bet she was beautiful."

"Like the sun."

I stood at the table out of respect while his wife's memory hung there between us, and then I walked away. I stepped out into the night air, looked over the car before unlocking it to make sure it hadn't been tampered with. I was definitely becoming paranoid. About to climb into the car, a deep bass holler spun me around. Donovan was standing at the entryway, calling my name.

I almost ran the distance between us.

"Is there a possibility I'll have to crack some heads?"

"With the way things have been going lately, I'd say there'd be a good possibility of that."

The answer seemed to satisfy him. He nodded. "Good. I've been here for too long. It's time I get moving. After you left, I only had to ask myself one question: Would Elenor approve of you? A moment later I saw her beautiful smile. So you must be a good soul, Jon Fixx." The long scar running over his eye across his forehead glowed with a red intensity. A large black hand reached out toward me and I grabbed it in a firm handshake.

I had a bodyguard.

My drive home was far more relaxing than the drive out. I now knew that no one would sneak up on me again, at least not for the next couple of months. I could reassess then and see where I was at, but for now I was covered. Donovan's size alone would be a deterrent for anyone considering to do me ill, but I had watched the way he moved on his feet, and he was dexterous for a man his size. If push came to shove, I was sure Donovan could manhandle the best of them. I was tapping my emergency savings-retirement fund to pay him, but up 'til now, I'd never had an emergency, and retirement was far, far away. Now seemed as good a time as any to utilize the funds. At the moment, my whole life was one big emergency. Donovan wasn't only protection against surprise attacks from Nick Nickels Jr.; he would also run interference with Williams and any of his colleagues should that come about. But even more than that, I wanted him with me in New York. Williams' second visit tonight had raised the warning signal from yellow to a blinking red. Vespucci was on the FBI's radar. And now, so was I. At least, according to Williams. But was he approaching me on a personal level or on official business? I realized it didn't matter. Williams worked for the FBI and knew I was working for Vespucci. That was enough. I was in way over my head. My sixth sense told me there was something much bigger going on here, and if I discovered what it was, there would be undeniable consequences for making the discovery.

I got back to my apartment without incident. I only had to get through the night, and then come morning, Donovan would be at my door. He wanted to go home and tie up some loose ends so that he wouldn't have to worry about his house while he was gone. I turned my laptop on, pulling up my almost-final draft of "The Coffee Shop Lovers." I needed to tweak it a bit, but I didn't feel it needed any major changes. I was wired and knew sleep was far off, so I decided to go back through the draft and finish it. Luci would be over first thing in the morning with his final mock-up for the book, so I could feel good before leaving for New York that at least one big obligation was completed. Sometime during the night, I passed out, head on the desk in front of my computer. A loud knock at the door roused me. I stumbled up out of my chair, tripping as I did so, falling on my face, a sharp pain shooting up from my ribs as I hit the ground. I heard Luci's voice from the other side of the door.

"Jon, you okay? What are you doing? I've been knocking on the door for a few minutes."

"I'm fine," I croaked. Slowly, I climbed to my hands and knees, crawled over to the door, unlocked it, and let Luci in. I held my hand out to him to help me up. As I stood clearing my head, I stepped into the kitchen to pour a glass of orange juice.

"Late for you to be sleeping, Jon."

I turned to him as I tilted the glass of orange juice down my throat. From the reaction on Luci's face, all of the previous night's actions came back to me in a flash. Without a word, I moved to the bathroom to get a look at my face. The bruises had settled in and darkened. The socket around my right eye was swollen, black with some red tinges around it. The dark color seeped up to the right side of my forehead and over to my cheekbone. In an attempt to give my face some semblance of balance, my left cheek was scratched and bruised as well.

"Jesus, Jon!" Luci exclaimed, as he examined the damage. "What happened? Did you go to another funeral?"

Laconically, I answered, "Our 'Internet Love Affair' family of psychos."

He stared at me for several moments to make sure I was serious. Finally, he said, "Are you kidding?"

"It appears the father has given the son permission to take care of things. They've made it their goal in life to get revenge."

Luci stared at me, taking it in. He set the mock-up on the table beside the computer. "Did you call the police?"

"Why? My attackers—"

"There was more than one?"

"—two of them. I don't know who number two was, but I'm sure Nick Jr. was the attack dog. I couldn't make a positive ID though. They had on ski masks. But I heard his voice. I'm sure it was him."

"Jon, this can't keep happening."

I finished off the orange juice. "I agree. And I've taken steps to deal with it."

"What steps?"

A knock at the door interrupted us. I pointed to the door in answer to Luci's question. I pulled it open to reveal Donovan towering in the doorway, carrying a small, military duffel bag over his shoulder. No one spoke. Donovan glanced around my humble abode, he and Luci exchanging a polite nod to one another as he did so. His gaze settled on me as he waited at the threshold.

"Come on in, Donovan," I said.

Donovan stepped inside, giving the tiny apartment a once-over. "Should I collect my money up front?"

I smiled. "Don't worry. These are temporary digs. I'll be moving out of them in time. They've served a purpose for me. Donovan, this is my best friend, Luci."

Donovan shook Luci's hand. Luci returned the handshake with a friendly but quizzical look. They made an imposing pair, both well over six feet, one white and lanky, the other black and bulky.

"Luci, this is Donovan. He's my new bodyguard."

Luci looked from Donovan to me and then back to Donovan. The quizzical look didn't completely disappear.

"How do you two know each other?" Luci asked.

A quick summary of my excursion to Howard Johnson's gave Luci all the information he needed. Without looking down at Donovan's arm, Luci said, "Special Forces. How long?"

"Spent twenty years in the service. Persian Gulf, I and II. A few non-publicized excursions. Not newsworthy 'cause of the political ramifications, if you know what I'm saying."

Luci nodded in appreciation. "A lot of action."

"Too much. Saw more than I needed to."

They stared at one another, sizing each other up.

"You'll be able to look after Jon?"

"With my life."

"Great pleasure to meet you, Donovan.'

"Same."

"Now that we've made acquaintances, I want to give you both a rundown of the craziness going on in my life so you have a clear idea of what could be possible in New York," I said.

Luci crossed to my living room, dropping down on his heels, his back against the wall, settling in to listen. He often took that position when we were working out the specifics on a project. Donovan crossed to the only chair in the room, making it disappear as he settled down on top of it. I ran through the last few months chronologically. Much of it Luci was aware of, though I was filling in gaps he wasn't privy to. I told them about the slow slide between Sara and me, how the distance between us and Sara's cold nature had begun to impact my writing. That because of it, I was unable to finish the love story for Candy Nickels, and since then her father and brother had decided they needed to punish me in every way possible. Nick Nickels Jr. had taken the route I would expect, crude schoolyard violence. Thus, the current damage on my face. However, moving forward, I was more concerned about Nickels Sr. He had far more pull and power, and his plan of execution would be more sophisticated and debilitating to me. As I said this aloud, I noted to myself there might be little Luci and Donovan could do for me if Nickels Sr. decided to come after me in a nonviolent manner. I pushed the disturbing thought aside and moved on to the breakup with Sara and the dramatic effect it had on my overall nature, explaining the move out, and the month-long hiatus from doing anything other than feeling extremely depressed and sorry for myself and burying myself in this cave of an apartment, that is—I noted with some embarrassment—except for the forays I took to make calls to Sara's house from untraceable pay phones and the nightly stalking sessions I spent down the block from her apartment to discover who had replaced me. Enter Williams with his threatening visit the morning after my last phone call to Sara from the rest stop off the I-10. I looked at Donovan as I recounted this part of the story, acknowledging our initial introduction.

I saved the Vespuccis for last, because even though Williams and Nick Nickels Jr. had given me ample reason to hire Donovan, deep down I knew I wanted both Donovan and Luci with me in New York for my final interviews with the Vespucci-Balducci clan. Though Vespucci seemed to like me, it didn't change the fact that he was a dangerous man and a wild card. I couldn't say with certainty where he stood. I explained to Luci and Donovan that my gut told me I was being used as a pawn in a bigger game, but I had no idea how or why or what for. I was sure Tony didn't like his soon-to-be son-in-law, and the feeling was mutual, so this was my greatest concern. I didn't like Marco Balducci at all and I couldn't understand what, other than his good looks, Maggie saw in him. I finished my rundown of the Vespucci's and what my shortened timeline was for the project. I went on to describe Jim Mosconi and what role the reporter had played so far, explaining that he seemed to be the only member of the media who had any current, in-depth understanding of what was going on inside La Cosa Nostra. I left out the eavesdropping episode between Marco and Vespucci and that Mosconi was on their radar. I wasn't ready to address it, or the implications it represented. I ended my story with the warning I'd received from Mosconi at the end of my last trip, but that I hadn't heard from him since, though it wasn't like I'd been trying to reach him.

Luci asked, "What do you think he meant?"

"I don't know. He's a jumpy guy. Strikes me as a bit of a conspiracy theorist, one of those guys who believes everyone is out to get him and finds intrigue in everything, whether it belongs or not. So I'm not sure what to think of him." Suddenly, I realized I'd left out one key piece of information. I told them about my second visit from Williams and his interest in my work for Tony Vespucci.

Donovan raised his hand. "Wait. I just want to make sure I've got a handle on this whole thing before I fly back east with you. You're working for a Mafia boss, but you're not doing anything illegal for him. By chance, you're ex-girlfriend's new boyfriend's cousin works for the FBI, and first he asked you to stop bugging your ex-girlfriend, and now he's talking to you about your work for this mob guy?"

I nodded at each correct point Donovan made.

"Sounds a little too out there to be coincidence."

"I know. It all sounds a bit far-fetched, but I can assure you, I'm living it."

Luci chimed in, "You forgot to mention one thing, Jon."

I turned toward Luci.

"You didn't mention how your feelings for the bride-to-be plays into all this."

At first I didn't answer, not sure what to say.

"Am I wrong?"

I was silent, considering how to answer that question. Finally, I responded, "I've never fallen for one of my clients, and I'm not going to start now. Is that enough for you?"

Donovan and Luci exchanged a glance.

"Okay."

"Sure."

I didn't know what else to say. Luci reached for the stack of material he'd brought for "The Coffee Shop Lovers" story and handed it to me. "This is ready for your approval. If you can give me the final draft, I can FedEx this to the binder. We'll have it done in time for the wedding."

"I just need to go back through it to make sure I'm good with it. We'll be able to send it off before we get on the plane."

"Sounds good." Luci looked at Donovan. "You can take care of our boy for the day? Make sure he doesn't get any more bruises?"

Donovan responded with a slight nod.

"Good. I'll be back tonight with a bag for our trip to New York." Luci began to open the door but turned back to Donovan and me before leaving. I looked up from the computer screen. I knew that look. He was worried. "Jon, do you really think there's something going on with Vespucci? Something that's putting you in danger when we go back there?"

I stared at Luci and then looked at Donovan. I shrugged, indicating Yeah, maybe. Luci accepted my answer with his usual aplomb. He glanced at Donovan. "I'll flip with you for who gets to take the first bullet for our boy."

Donovan deadpanned, "He's paying me, so I feel obligated. You'll have to get in line."

"Deal."

"Not funny, either of you."

Although they were making light of the situation, I knew Luci had been in some rough spots over the years, and he took this seriously. Donovan I didn't know yet, but he didn't seem like a guy who breezed through life. If I was in danger, my friends were as well. If they were hurt, it would be my fault. I wanted to convince myself that I was being overly dramatic, but the bruises on my face proved that violence could come from any corner. Flashes of my second trip to New York pulsed through my brain, reminding me of what I had seen, what I had discovered. I was not wrong. There was trouble there, trouble I didn't understand because I couldn't see the whole picture, but I knew enough to know I didn't want any of it. I pushed my thoughts aside, focusing on Luci and Donovan.

"Maybe I'm just being paranoid," I said.

"One thing about Jon, here," Luci said, directing his comment to Donovan. "When it comes to his personal relationships, the guy has the worst judgment ever. He falls in love with all the wrong women for all the wrong reasons. If it involves his own feelings, he makes the worst decisions. Sorry, Jon, it's true," he said, looking directly at me. "But when it comes to reading other people, interpreting their thoughts, figuring out what makes them tick, he's always right on target. If he thinks there's trouble brewing under the surface back in New York, I'd put my money Jon's onto something." He paused for emphasis before continuing. "That FBI agent didn't bring up Tony Vespucci to you to make idle chatter. There's more there than what you can see. But that's not your problem, Jon. You were hired to write a love story. We'll go with you to make sure you stay safe so you can do that. All you have to do is get enough information to write your story, then come back here and do what you were hired to do. You'll be free of them by the end of December. Right?"

I shrugged. "I hope."

Luci knew that meant I wasn't sure where we'd be at the

end of December. "Fine. Just so I know what I'm signing up for. I'll see you both tonight." The door closed on Luci's back.

"Your friend studied martial arts?" Donovan asked.

"He's master in a form of kung fu, among other things. How did you know?"

"The way he carries himself. Not a guy I'd want to cross. With him, what do you need me for?"

"Insurance."

The answer seemed to satisfy Donovan. "I'm figuring you got work to do, so I'm just gonna make myself comfortable by the door here."

Donovan walked over to the door, settling down in front of it, his duffle bag shoved up against the wood, his frame laid out perpendicular to the door itself, head resting on the duffle. His eyes closed almost immediately.

I watched him, considering his easy, relaxed nature.

"Don't worry, I'm a light sleeper. Anybody tries to come through that door, I'll be on 'em in a flash." His eyes remained closed.

"I'm not worried. For the first time in a long time."

I turned my back to Donovan to attend to my nearly finished project. Over the next four hours, into the early afternoon, I read and tweaked and finished "The Coffee Shop Lovers." It wasn't my best work, or my most inspired, but it was sufficient, and I knew my product well enough to know that my clients would be happy with it. I saved the final copy and emailed it to Luci, giving him last-minute directions on a few changes I wanted him to make to the final layout. I then spent the next hour poring over the material Luci had left for me to review for the couple: pictures, love letters, little knickknacks the couple held dear. Luci had done a fine job assembling it. After looking it over, I felt a sense of completion. I could put this project to rest.

I sat back a moment, reflecting on this mini-milestone. Not even two weeks before, I'd been at the bottom of full-on depression, wallowing in a valley of self-pity. I was so caught up in my breakup with Sara that I had barely given any thought to the bigger picture of my life. I spent no time evaluating what would have happened had I stayed in that terrible, dark, emotional place. The most telling sign of my complete and total disregard for my health and safety was my unwillingness to give any consideration whatsoever to the Vespuccis and the job I'd been hired to do for them. Throughout October, any time Maggie or Marco or Tony Vespucci crossed my mind, I dismissed it with a fatalistic attitude of what is supposed to be will be. I reached up and felt the tender spots on my face. If the Nickels family could do this to me for stiffing them, what would Vespucci do to me if I angered him? I shuddered at the possibilities. Looking back over the last week, I realized that Williams had done me a favor by paying me that initial visit. It had forced me out of my black hole of self-pity. I glanced over at Donovan silently resting against the door. Clearly, I'd turned a corner.

I stood up from my computer, stretching my arms. I walked over to the one window in the apartment and looked out at the blue sky. I reached into my pocket and pulled out the stunning ring I'd bought for Sara. Ever since I'd returned from New York and Sara had dumped me, I had been carrying it around in my pocket to remind myself of my foolishness. Even now, in the fading light of the day, the ring glowed. That day of the breakup came back to my memory in full force. I'd been on the ground in Los Angeles from New York for just over twenty-four hours when Sara walked into her condominium, the home we'd shared for almost two years, and told me it was over. I never did show her the ring. I kept it hidden in my jacket pocket, where it had been since I'd bought it. Our final lovemaking session before I left on my second trip had tricked me into believing we were on our way back, that there was hope, that Sara had turned a corner, our relations would improve.

I'd bought the ring, thinking it would solve any remaining problems between us, but when Sara uttered those fatal words, "breakup" and "another lover," I'd realized the ring represented nothing more than my own pathetic one-sided desire to be in love. Even now, I wasn't sure what I was going to do with the ring. I'd considered taking it back to Mrs. Goldschmidt on my final trip to New York, to see if she would take it back and return at least some of my money, but every time I had the thought, a hollow feeling took over, so for now I was content keeping it in my pocket until I could figure out what would be the right thing to do.

"That must of cost a couple points."

I started, not realizing Donovan was awake. "It did."

"Telephone girl?"

"A mistake," I said, resigned.

"Yeah, well, we all have one of those at some point. Part of the learning curve."

"Expensive learning curve."

"We don't get to choose our teachers. Or their cost. If you're gonna sell it, I know a guy."

"Not until I've learned my lesson."

"Maybe you did already."

I was about to respond, but he'd already gone back to dozing. As my gaze returned to the ring, a certain calm came over me, a calm I could attribute in no small part to the fact that I was to be accompanied by Donovan and Luci to New York. If there was any trouble, I wouldn't have to face it alone. I palmed the ring and placed it back inside my pocket, for some reason unable just yet to let go of what it was supposed to mean, unwilling to leave it in Los Angeles where it belonged. I wanted it with me. I heard Donovan's voice from behind me.

"She did you a favor, Jon. Time is truth. It tells us everything we're supposed to know."

I looked at Donovan but his eyes were still closed. "Thanks, Donovan."

I returned to my computer, pulling up my copious notes on the Vespucci-Balducci union. I clicked through the interviews I'd transcribed, realizing as I pored over them that I didn't need to go back to New York to finish this story. I was missing my key interview with Vespucci, but otherwise, I had enough information to write an adequate story, one that would probably satisfy Maggie and Marco. So why was I going back? I could do the interview with Vespucci over the phone, or on Skype.

Deep down, I knew why. I wanted to stir the pot. I felt there was something off about Marco Balducci, about his relationship with Maggie. This had been bothering me from the get-go, but only in the last few days when my mind started percolating again did I pin it down. If Marco wasn't in love with Maggie, he still had a lot to gain by marrying the Godfather's daughter, so it was very possible that Marco was motivated by more than his feelings for her. This didn't sit well with me. I'd been hired to write a love story and that's what I was going to do—as long as they were in love. This last trip would ensure the authenticity of what I wrote. It was going to be an interesting trip. Thank God I wasn't going alone.

10
Early November
New York 3rd Trip

Luci and I sat in the airport, waiting for Donovan's flight to land. I'd been unable to get a seat for him on our plane, so I bought a ticket on a different airline leaving the same time as our flight but with a connector in Atlanta that would delay him an hour. Luci and I spent our time talking about the Vespuccis. He had done research of his own on the Mafia, the Vespuccis in particular, through the law enforcement connections he had made over the years with his martial arts training.

"So, where does that put Tony Vespucci, according to your guys?" I asked Luci. Through the glass of the Delta terminal, I watched a 747 take off from the runway, its front wheels slowly lifting off the ground.

"There's no question from anyone in the know that Tony is somewhere near the top of the food chain," Luci answered. "In fact, a couple of my sources agree with Mosconi that Vespucci has become the de facto leading don of the Five Families in New York. He's a smart businessman and has several large, successful, and legitimate operations running. As far as the law is concerned, he's as clean as a whistle on the books. Never been caught doing anything. At least not yet."

"Giancarlo Balducci?"

"His underboss."

"That's what I figured. They grew up together, best friends. I figured they'd be close."

"Did you know Vespucci is heavily invested in Balducci's foundry business in Italy? Provided the start-up money."

"Really?"

"My source thinks they wanted to put business on the ground over in Italy, Sicily in particular, to connect the New World with the Old, work at building a bridge between the two. Create an Italian-American Mafia bond that would be unbreakable. The Prime Minister has been criticized for being soft on the Mafia, even accused of being connected up."

"Marco mentioned knowing him personally. How much can you trust your source, that what he's telling you is accurate?"

"He's one of my oldest students, been training him for years. He's retired CIA. We can trust him."

"Did he tell you anything about Balducci's son, Marco?"

Luci nodded, exhaling. "Yeah, that he's a mean one."

"That all?"

"Word is there's some friction between Vespucci and Balducci about Marco's position in the hierarchy. Balducci wants to bring him up a little faster than the Boss is comfortable with."

Before I could ask any more questions, I spotted Donovan over Luci's shoulder, carrying his compact military duffle and making his way down the terminal toward us. Luci and I stood up at the same time, grabbed our overnight bags, and stepped out to the walkway, waiting for Donovan to reach us.

"How was your flight?'

Donovan shrugged. "Got me here in one piece."

The three of us hitched our bags over our shoulders and headed for the exit. Walking shoulder to shoulder with me in the middle, Luci and Donovan towered over me, lean and muscled on one side, thick and powerful on the other side. I eyed people inadvertently stepping out of the way to give us room as we passed. No one tried to break our ranks, choosing to go around us rather than shoulder their way between us. A few minutes later, we found ourselves standing on the curb in the hustle and bustle of JFK. I glanced sideways at the faces of my companions, considering what we were doing here. I felt a risk with this trip that didn't seem part of the normal day-to-day business. By traveling with me, my companions had opened themselves up to this risk. Out of the corner of my eye, I spotted Maggie's compact Mini Cooper pull up to the curb.

I flagged her down with a wave of my hand. Luci and Donovan spotted the Mini Cooper at the same time.

Donovan spoke first. "We're getting in that?"

Luci added, "Are we going to do two trips?"

I chuckled, "Don't worry, I'll sit in the back."

"And that'll make a difference?"

Maggie climbed out of her car to greet us, a question on her face as she realized the two giants standing beside me were, in fact, with me.

Luci leaned toward me and quietly asked, "That's Maggie?"

I nodded.

Maggie stepped around the car to greet us. I met her at the curb, reaching out my hand to say hello. She brushed my hand away and gave me a tight hug. For a moment, my mind went blank, unable to think. Maggie stepped back to introduce herself to my friends when she noticed the bruises on my face. She reached up to touch my eye. I had completely forgotten about my appearance.

"What happened to your face, Jon?" she asked.

"Just a slight misunderstanding." I didn't want to explain the whole Nickels fiasco.

"How many times did they misunderstand you?"

I heard a guffaw and chuckles from behind. I looked over my shoulder. "Maggie, I'd like to introduce you to my finishing crew."

The confusion reflected in Maggie's eyes made me realize what that sounded like, given their size and Maggie's family background. "Let me clarify," I said. I pointed to Luci. "Meet Luci. He handles the visual aspects of the final product, the artwork, lay out, what photographs are used. Stuff like that."

"Nice to meet you, Luci," Maggie smiled.

"You as well, Maggie."

"And this is Donovan. He handles my security."

"Hi, Donovan." Maggie gave him a smile as well, but then turned to me. "You didn't have security on the previous trips."

"Let's just say the misunderstanders don't seem to want to understand. So."

"What did you do, for God's sake?"

I looked at Luci and Donovan for help, but they remained mute. I turned back to Maggie. I was tired from the flight, I hadn't slept much, and I couldn't think of a good enough lie. "I wrote the truth on my last job."

A look of disbelief crossed Maggie's face. "One of your clients did this to your face?"

Helplessly embarrassed, I nodded.

"So you hired a bodyguard?"

"Let's just say I didn't want any interference while I finish up your story."

"I could speak to my father—"

"No, no! Please. Don't tell your father. I feel unprofessional telling you. Can we keep this between us?"

Maggie studied my face, trying to decipher my reasons for being so adamant about her silence. Finally, she seemed to make a decision and moved on without another word, turning her attention to my friends.

"Gentlemen, sorry my car is so small. Jon didn't give me

any warning," she said, playfully admonishing me. "I would have brought a bigger car."

Luci responded, "Don't worry about us. We shrink on demand."

We threw our luggage in the back and I climbed in first, followed by Luci, cramming ourselves into the back seat. Donovan commandeered the front passenger seat. Maggie hopped into the driver's seat, taking a moment to look at the three of us in turn. "Cozy?" she asked with a grin.

She pulled away from the airport, hitting the I-678 toward Brooklyn. There was a chill in the air, November in New York, winter clearly on the way. I glanced forward, catching Maggie watching me in the rearview mirror.

"How did it go?"

For a moment, I didn't understand what she was asking.

"Did you do it yet?"

I noticed Donovan turn away from Maggie, apparently looking out the window, the motion jogging my memory. The ring. Mrs. Goldschmidt.

"Did you propose?"

I could feel Luci's eyes on me. This was news to him. I'm sure he was also wondering how much of my personal life I had shared with this client, something I never did.

Sheepishly, I responded, "We broke up."

"Oh, Jon, I'm so sorry," she said. "How long has it been?"

"The day I got back from my last trip."

Maggie considered that for a moment. "That's terrible. So that's where you've been."

I nodded, not sure what else to say.

"You must be so sad. I was wondering why we hadn't heard from you for so long. Now I understand. Does she even know about the ring?"

I shook my head. I glanced at Luci, his eyes telling me everything I needed to know. He was piecing it all together now, gaining further understanding of why the last several weeks had been so hard for me. But true to Luci's nature, he kept silent. I knew the time would come when he would want me to fill it all in for him. Embarrassed, I met Maggie's sympathetic eyes in the rearview.

"What did you do with the ring?"

Reaching inside my pocket, I pulled the ring out for all to view. "The ring in question." Sheepishly, I turned to Luci. "I bought it on my last trip. Maggie helped me pick it out."

"I'm really sorry, Jon," Maggie said.

"It's fine. Everything happens for a reason. She met someone else."

"She left you for another guy?"

"Yeah," I muttered.

"How do you know?" Maggie asked.

Luci finally spoke. "Yeah, Jon, how do you know?"

I turned my head to Luci, exasperated at his egging me on.

"She told me when she broke up with me."

"She doesn't sound very nice"

"She's not," Luci responded.

With an encouraging smile, Maggie said, "Don't worry, Jon. It just means there is someone much better for you out there."

Luci and Donovan nodded in consensus.

"I'm glad you're back," Maggie added. "My father was getting a little anxious, but I told him not to bother you. That you would get everything handled in your own way."

Apparently, Vespucci had not told her he'd needed to jump-start me with a threatening videoconference. I shoved the ring back in my pocket, vowing to keep it there until I could figure out what to do with it.

"If you want to take the ring back, Jon, I could talk with Mrs. Goldschmidt. I'm sure she'd work something out for you."

"Thanks, Maggie. I'm not sure what I'm going to do with it yet. I may keep it as a reminder of my foolishness, keep me from doing something like this again."

I could feel Luci watching me, his look quiet and thoughtful. Then he directed his attention to Maggie. "Maggie, you should know that in my years working with Jon in his unique profession, I've never known him to share his personal life with a client. You are the first."

"Really?" Maggie said, surprised. "Is that true, Jon Fixx?"

I didn't realize I was blushing until I saw my reflection in Maggie's rearview. "Luci's exaggerating. But that's basically true."

"Does that mean you'll give Marco and me extra attention when you write our love story?"

Marco. Oh yeah. I felt my stomach clench. "Yes, it does."

The car went silent for several moments. Finally Luci asked, "So, Maggie, are you excited for the wedding? Is all the planning done?"

"Ugh, the planning," Maggie replied. "I've hated it! I'm not that woman. I have friends who have loved it more than anything. I let my mom and my sister-in-law make most of the decisions. It'll be more pink than blue, and I hate pink!" Maggie laughed. "And I'd have to say I'm more nervous than excited. But that's normal, right? I mean you guys do this all the time."

"Completely normal," Luci said.

"Jon told me you handle the visual look of the book? How did you end up doing that?" Maggie asked.

"He begged me to do it," Luci answered and reached over and patted me on my shoulder in camaraderie. "As his unique business started to grow, Jon realized he was missing something, so he started talking to me about it and said he needed to add a visual element to the novella. That's where I came in. The rest is history."

"Is Jon the only author you do this for?"

"I don't know anyone else doing what Jon does. He's one of a kind, our Jon Fixx," Luci said. "Other than that, I have my own projects."

"He's also a kung fu master," I chimed in.

Maggie seemed genuinely impressed. She gave an appraising look around the car at each of us. "I have to say, you three make quite a trio." To Donovan she asked, "How long have you known Jon?"

Donovan glanced over his shoulder at me, looking for some guidance. I shrugged, indicating he should tell the truth. "I just met him last week."

"Oh." For the first time, Maggie was at a loss. "And you're his bodyguard?"

"Yup."

By now, Maggie had jumped off the highway, choosing surface streets to continue our journey. I assumed we were on the outskirts of Brooklyn by this point.

We spent the rest of the time in idle chatter, soon arriving at the hotel where I had booked reservations, only a ten-minute drive from the Vespucci's. Maggie unloaded us in front of the hotel and said she would call if things changed but that Vespucci was expecting me for dinner. She would let him know that Luci and Donovan were coming as well. Then she was off, leaving the three of us standing on the curb watching her pull away.

As the Mini Cooper disappeared into traffic, Luci looked at me. "You're in way over your head."

Donovan nodded.

I asked with more edge than I intended, "What do you mean?"

"If you don't know what I mean, you're in way, way over your head. Donovan?"

"Buried," Donovan added.

I looked from one to the other of them, choosing not to engage further. I just wanted to get up to our room. I was already thinking about what I would say to Vespucci to placate him. We picked up our travel bags, turned for the hotel in step, and disappeared inside. I reserved one room to keep the cost down and asked for an extra bed. We settled in for a few hours of rest. I didn't have anything on the agenda until the early afternoon, and none of us had slept much on the flight, so a nap was the first order of business. I put my head on the pillow with thoughts of what I expected our trip to look like.

Before falling into a troubled dreamland, Jim Mosconi's face appeared in front of me. I realized there was no way I could come to New York without seeing him to find out what he'd meant by his cryptic warning text at the end of September. Curiosity made me want to know what he'd uncovered in Italy. Did he have information specifically related to my subject? I had sent him a couple of emails over the last few days; all went unanswered. As I dozed off, I realized Mosconi was the key, but I wasn't sure what he had unlocked.

I hadn't been asleep long before I woke up to a scuffling noise, pulling me awake faster than I would have liked. Angry words were being tossed around the room, and then I heard someone pleading not to be harmed. I sat bolt upright, shaking my head to clear it of the sleep dulling my senses. As the room took shape before me, I saw a stranger of medium height and light weight strung over the back of a hotel chair on his stomach, his left arm bent at an excruciating angle behind his back, his toes barely touching the ground, his other arm pinned against the side of the chair. The back of the chair was sticking squarely into his guts, apparently impeding his breathing. Donovan had the stranger pinned in this uncomfortable manner. Luci was on his feet, going through the guy's pockets.

"What's going on?"

Luci and Donovan were too intent on their current task to respond. Luci took a step back with all of the stranger's pocket possessions in his hands. In one he was holding a wallet and two small electronic devices no larger than earplugs. In the other he held a small handgun. He emptied the bullets from the gun, including the one in the chamber. Donovan looked at Luci. Luci gave him an almost imperceptible nod.

Donovan leaned over, next to the intruder's ear. "I'm less than an inch away from ripping your arm out of its socket. Do you know how painful that is?"

From the squeezed, screwed-up look on the intruder's face, he was already in a lot of pain. Donovan leaned forward, putting more pressure on the intruder's arm, which, in turn, made our interloper begin to scream. Donovan backed off ever so slightly. The screams became whimpers.

Luci stepped in front of the chair. Donovan lifted the man's torso so he could look at Luci's face. Calmly, Luci began to question him. The intruder looked at me, the whites of his eyes revealing his fear. He didn't cut much of an imposing figure, though I'm sure I would have felt differently if he had been holding the gun. The guy looked to be of Latino descent.

Luci asked, "What are you doing here?"

"I was hired to plant those." He nodded his chin toward the electronic devices.

"What are they?"

"Transmitters."

Luci raised his brows in a question mark.

"Bugs, *cabrón.* Listening devices."

"What were you supposed to do with them?

The guy looked at Luci like he was dense. Luci remained calm.

"Well?"

Donovan gave him a quick nudge on his arm to motivate him to answer.

"I was hired to bug Sleeping Beauty over there."

This was definitely a new twist.

"Hired by whom?"

"I don't know the guy's name."

I raised my hand, stopping Luci from asking the next question. "How did you know I was here?"

The intruder looked over at me. "The guy told me your

room number."

The three of us exchanged looks. Luci and Donovan were asking me what they should do with him. I shrugged. Donovan looked to Luci. Finally, Luci motioned to Donovan that he should let him go. The intruder stood up, shaking his arms loose, trying to gain back some respect while also staying on guard.

I said, "You're free to go."

Surprised, the man checked Donovan's face to make sure he wasn't being tricked. Donovan stepped aside, giving the man enough space to reach the hotel room door. He glanced at Luci and asked for his gun. Luci handed the empty gun over to him. The man moved toward the door, trying to push his way past Donovan.

Donovan leaned forward, crowding the intruder up against the wall. Donovan towered over him, staring down. "If I see you again anywhere near my friend here, I'll break your arms and tie them around your neck."

The intruder squeezed past Donovan, disappearing into the silence of the hallway, the door closing behind him. Luci set the bullets down on the hotel dresser. Donovan stared at the door, then turned back to me. "You sure you're just a writer? You're not a government spy or something?"

I shook my head.

"Why'd you let him go? We should have called the police."

"I'm not sure how Tony Vespucci would feel about me having a visit from the police." My words hung in the air, sinking in.

Considering what I said, Luci added, "Whoever hired that guy has serious intentions." He held the listening devices up to the light. "These are government grade."

"Not a spy, right?" Donovan asked again, only half joking.

To Luci I responded, "You think Ted Williams? FBI?"

"I doubt it. Wrong M.O. Plus, that guy was clueless. He didn't even check to make sure we weren't here. I don't think he's doing this for a living. But whoever sent him has access to good technology, technology they've acquired on the black market."

Taking a seat on the chair he'd used for his impromptu interrogation, Donovan said, "That guy was low-street level. Why would someone send him in here to bug you?"

"Even more than that, who would be interested in what Jon has to say?" Luci added.

"Before I left Los Angeles, Williams intimated that his colleagues in the FBI are aware of my involvement with Tony Vespucci," I reminded them.

"So? You were hired to write his daughter's story about her marriage. They should know they're not going to discover anything useful here," Luci added.

I considered that a moment. "But his daughter is marrying into another reputed Mafioso family. Maybe they think I'm deeper in than I am."

I couldn't read the faces of either of my companions. I wasn't sure what they were thinking. What had just occurred raised the stakes substantially for both Luci and Donovan as long as they were around me. I wondered how they felt about it. I pushed these thoughts aside.

"Maybe they're hoping to hear something useful in my discussions with Vespucci?" I asked.

Luci responded, "Doesn't seem all that plausible."

Donovan added, "That guy was clueless. You really think any federal agent would hire that guy to do their dirty work? He's working for somebody else."

"Maggie was the only person who knew my plans. I emailed her the change in the itinerary before we left so she would know I was going to stay in a hotel."

"You didn't mention us?" Luci asked.

"No."

We sat quietly, considering our plight. Finally, Donovan said, "Who else would want to track you?"

"There are two possibilities. Nick Nickels Sr. is one."

Luci interrupted me. "Why would that guy go to the trouble of planting a bug on you?"

I pointed to my face. "Did you think his family would go to the trouble they've gone to so far?" After a moment, I added, "The only other person I can think of is Marco Balducci."

Donovan asked, "Maggie's fiancé? Why would he want to listen in on you?"

"I don't know."

"If you're considering that guy, why not consider the big guy?" Donovan countered.

"Vespucci?" I hadn't considered that. It scared me more than I wanted to admit.

"Why would Vespucci bug him? He hired him to write this story," Luci said.

Donovan looked at me. "You said you don't think he likes his daughter's fiancé, right?"

"But I don't have anything solid to base that on. Only instinct."

"Your instincts are generally pretty good, Jon," Luci added.

"Maybe he wants to hear everything you have to say about the Balduccis. Plus, if Vespucci is who you say he is, he'd have the connections to get government stock."

I sat on the hotel bed, considering the possibility. "I don't know, guys. Be a bit weird for Vespucci to bug me. Doesn't feel right."

Luci, always the clear thinker, summed it all up. "The bottom line, gentlemen, is that we don't have enough information yet to figure out who did this. However, someone carrying a gun did just try to break into your room and bug you. We need to be extra cautious now. Agreed? Jon doesn't go anywhere by himself. Either Donovan or I will accompany you everywhere," he said, looking at me, "including all your interviews. Understood?"

I nodded.

"Good. So what's on the agenda today?" Luci asked.

"I'm expected at the Vespuccis for dinner. But before that, I'd like to pay a visit to Jim Mosconi. See what he has to say."

"He's the reporter?" Donovan asked.

"He's a key."

"Key to what?"

"I don't know yet. That's why I want to talk to him."

Luci looked at me curiously. "Jon, as far as your story is concerned, Tony Vespucci's Mafia life doesn't really have anything to do with the story you need to write. I mean, there's never going to be a mention of the Mafia or what Vespucci does for a living in your story, right?"

"That's true."

"So why is it so important for you to talk to Jim Mosconi? He's not going to tell you anything about Maggie, or her relationship with Marco, is he?"

"I doubt it."

"Then talking to him only puts you in more danger, because he's a reporter. How would Vespucci feel if you told him you were asking a reporter questions?"

I already knew Vespucci wouldn't like my talking to Mosconi from the conversation I'd overheard on my last trip between Marco and him. But that wasn't enough to deter me. I felt a pang of guilt for not telling Luci and Donovan about my eavesdropping when I had given them a rundown of everything before we left Los Angeles. "I think it's important. I can't give you a better reason than that. Can you trust me for now?"

Luci and Donovan stared at me, each nodding in turn after a moment's consideration.

That marked an end to the discussion. Donovan returned to his nap. Luci took the gun and bullets and stuck them in the drawer of the nightstand beside his bed. I lay back down, knowing I was too ramped up from what had just happened to fall back to sleep. I stared at the ceiling, falling into a shifty, restless, afternoon doze.

At the tail end of the day, we piled into a taxi headed for Manhattan, Sixth St., officially named Avenue of the Americas—a sure way to let the locals know you were not one of them if you referred to the street as such. The offices for the *New York Post* were our destination. The morning adventures had taken their toll on the three of us, and in conjunction with our early morning flight, we all seemed drained. I knew I was not operating at full potential. The taxi pulled up to the high-rise housing the *Post.* We tumbled out of the taxi, our muscles protesting against any fast movement. A guard held us up at the front desk. The guard was heavyset, in his early twenties, not all that imposing, with a curly light-colored fro. When I told him I needed to see Jim Mosconi, he changed his demeanor.

"Do you have an appointment?"

"Uh, no."

"Sorry, I can't let you see him unless you have an appointment."

"Could you call up to his offices, at least?"

"No, against building protocol. What's your name?"

"Why do you need my name if you're not going to call him?"

He seemed nonplussed by my retort. "Well, if I see him come out, I'll tell him you were looking for him."

"So, he's upstairs?"

"I didn't say that." The guard suddenly seemed jumpy.

Luci nudged me, "Let's go."

I turned to leave, Luci and Donovan on either side. As I walked away, I said over my shoulder, "If you see him, tell him Jon Fixx was looking for him."

Back on the street, we exchanged puzzled looks.

"That guy got weird when you mentioned Mosconi's name," Donovan said.

"I know. I wonder what that means. If Mosconi—" Then, I was interrupted by my PDA ringing. I answered.

On the other end, I heard a low voice, "Why are you looking for me?"

"Jim?"

"Answer the question."

I looked at Luci and Donovan, pointing to the phone, indicating Mosconi was on the line. "I just had a few questions for you about our last conversation."

"There's a coffee shop a few blocks from where you're standing." He gave me the address. "You have it?"

"Yes," I said, as I mouthed the address to my friends.

"I'll see you in ten minutes." He hung up.

I hung up. "He wants us to meet him at that address in ten minutes."

"What's with all the cloak and dagger stuff?" Luci asked.

"I have no idea." Mosconi's nature had definitely piqued my interest. I was sure his caution had something to do with the warning text he'd sent me at the end of September. After several minutes at a fast clip, we came to a nondescript coffee shop situated on the corner of two small streets, set a block back from the main thoroughfare. There wasn't much foot traffic and only an occasional car passed on the street. We stepped inside. A young man was working behind the counter, and a couple of people sitting at opposite ends of the shop were working on their computers. I didn't spot Mosconi.

We ordered coffee and took a seat at a table near the wall so I could watch the door. As the server placed the coffee cups on our table, Donovan excused himself to go the restroom. When he disappeared down the hallway, I caught Mosconi's frame in the front door. He stood there, staring at Luci and me at the back of the coffee shop. Instantly, he pulled his PDA out and appeared to type on it. My PDA buzzed. I pulled my phone out to see what message had arrived. A text from Mosconi: "Who's the guy beside you?"

I texted back, "He's my best friend and business partner. Harmless."

Mosconi responded, "Why's he here?"

I looked at Mosconi only forty feet away, thinking his actions bordered on absurd. He was clearly paranoid about something. "He helps me on all my projects. This is standard protocol for me to have him with me on my final trip."

Mosconi didn't text back. He stared at us. From the corner of my eye, I could see Luci watching Mosconi and me communicating forty feet apart.

Luci whispered, "He's scared."

Finally, Mosconi took one step and then another, closing the gap between us in a few seconds. I didn't stand up. "Jim, good to see you."

He didn't respond, staring at Luci.

"This is my best friend, Luci Gardner," I said.

"Good to meet you, Jim."

Mosconi nodded but didn't sit down. "Are you sure you weren't followed?"

"Followed by whom?"

Donovan appeared around the corner. Mosconi's head swung in Donovan's direction, alarm registering on his face. Donovan was only a few feet away from our table as Mosconi reached behind his back. I watched Donovan acknowledging both the look on Mosconi's face and the motion of his arm, his steps speeding up exponentially.

Trying to keep my voice low so as not to alarm anyone in the establishment, I said, "Jim, no!"

Luci was out of his chair, jumping around the table to stop Mosconi from pulling his gun, but Donovan got to the reporter first. He wrapped Mosconi up in a bear hug, pinning his arms to his sides, the gun hanging limply in Mosconi's right hand. A split second later, Luci had taken the small gun and hidden it away before anyone in the shop could see it. Donovan looked at me, wanting to know what he was supposed to do.

I stood up, stepping close to Mosconi. "Jim, I don't know what your deal is, but you're overreacting. This is my other friend, Donovan. He's with me, too. None of us means you any harm. We're just here to get information. Okay?"

Mosconi stared at me, his eyes bulging. I could smell his fear. I indicated to Donovan to let Mosconi go. Slowly, we sat down around the square table. Mosconi was the last to take a seat. He kept glancing at the front door. Mosconi's eyes settled on Luci. "Can I have my gun back?"

"When we're leaving, you can have your gun back."

Mosconi didn't like the answer, but he didn't push the issue.

"Why is a reporter carrying around a gun?" Luci asked.

Donovan added, "And is so willing to pull it out in a public place at the slightest provocation?"

If my friends hadn't asked these questions, I would have. Clearly not ready to talk, Mosconi stared at each of us in turn. I got the sense he still wasn't sure about Donovan and Luci. "Jim, these are my friends. Anything you'd say to me in private, I'd run it by them later anyway, so speak freely. Why all the cloak and dagger stuff?"

Mosconi turned his intense brown eyes on me. "You really have no idea, do you?"

I shook my head, confused.

"I told you I've been following the Mafia in New York for a long time. The last few years I've been especially focused on your clients."

"Vespucci?"

"He and the Balduccis and several other guys who run in their vortex."

"Why?" I asked.

Mosconi leaned toward me for emphasis, "Because they're the guys running what I call Cosa Nostra 2.0. The old Mafia went down in the '80s and '90s with the RICO laws. Now the revived leadership is looking to avoid their predecessors' mistakes, and just like the rest of the world, they believe the best way is to consolidate the power base by forming trade groups."

"Trade groups?" Luci asked

Mosconi turned toward Luci. "Believe it or not, the biggest problem the Italians have had in getting back to the level of their old power base is not because of the government. It's because of the rise of other major competing groups, mostly out of Central America and the old Eastern European Soviet Bloc countries. So, in order to consolidate their power base, our American Italians are forging ironclad trade ties, legal on the surface to cover their illicit trade, with their Italian counterparts. The current Italian prime minister was the perfect candidate to help this happen. Much of his political funding has come from the Mafia, allegedly."

Marco had mentioned the Italian prime minister more than once. "And you've witnessed all this?"

"I started focusing on the Balduccis several years back, tracking the business they were running in Italy," Mosconi said. "I followed a hunch. I can't prove it all yet, but when I can, it will put the Mafia back on the front page."

"Jim, none of this explains why you sent me that text on my last trip to be careful. What was that about?"

Mosconi hesitated, clearly not sure now how to proceed.

"Look, Jim. I was hired by Vespucci to do what I do, write a love story. But when I write my stories, I like to know who I'm working for and be clear on what I'm writing about. I like to know the truth, whether I write it or not. What you tell us won't go beyond this table."

Mosconi glanced at each of us in turn, then he looked out the window, I assumed, to see if anyone was lurking there, though who, specifically, I wasn't sure. He leaned forward, dropping his voice a notch.

"I'm not worried about it going beyond this table because once I tell you this, you'll be in danger too. Are you sure you want me to continue?"

There was no doubting the look on Mosconi's face. He was serious. I glanced first to Luci, then Donovan, looking for input. Each silently nodded in turn. I turned back to Mosconi. "Go ahead."

"Giancarlo Balducci. His son, Marco, is marrying Vespucci's daughter, right?"

I nodded.

"What's your impression of Marco?" Mosconi asked.

"Not a nice guy. He's a bully. Doesn't like me much, either."

"Haven't you ever considered it strange that Vespucci hired you in the first place? I mean, why would a Mafia guy—especially one who's overly cautious about privacy, both personal and business—voluntarily want someone around asking questions about his family? Seems odd and risky, don't you think?"

"I've considered that. But after seeing him with his daughter, I understand why he'd want to give her as great a wedding gift as possible."

Mosconi ignored my reasoning. "I think he hired you to stir things up. I think he has reservations about his soon-to-be son-in-law. Marco was in Italy for close to ten years. He rarely made any trips back to the States." Suddenly, Jim stopped, apparently not sure how to continue. He looked out the window, again. Satisfied he didn't see anything, he continued. "When I discovered the Balducci business several years ago, that was what got me studying the links between the Italian mob and the American mob. I started taking trips to Italy to see what I could find out. Over the last year, I stumbled across information about Marco Balducci that was shocking on several levels. That's why I'm carrying a gun."

I had to press him to continue. "Go on."

"Because I think you're in a far more dangerous situation than you realize, I'll give this to you on two conditions. One, you do nothing with it until after I publish my story, which, by the way, is going to cause an international scandal. Two, if something happens to me before I can publish, make sure the right people know about it."

"Are you insinuating someone might kill you over what you're about to tell us?"

"I'm not insinuating. I'm telling you straight out." He paused to let that sink in. "About three years ago, not long before he ended up back in the States, Marco Balducci got involved with a local village girl outside Palermo, supposedly a real beauty. The only problem was that she was fifteen. Now, over here, that's a considerably worse offense than over there, at least in the public eye. They had sex. I don't know much more than that, if it was consensual, rape, if they had a relationship, whatever. She got pregnant."

That got my attention. My companions were no less alert.

Mosconi continued. "The girl's father didn't take lightly to the news when he found out. He confronted Marco at his factory. Marco, it appears, doesn't like anyone telling him what to do, even if it's the father of a fifteen-year-old girl he got pregnant, so things got out of hand and Marco allegedly beat the guy to death. Family wasn't rich or powerful by any standards, but murder is still murder."

"Did he get arrested?" I asked.

"No. Case never made the press. He was never arrested. It's like it never happened."

"Then how do you know about it? Where's your verification?"

"I got wind of something weird last year when I was in Palermo researching the bigger story. So I spent some time digging around. I didn't make much headway on that trip, but when I went back this fall, I got much further along. I'm sure it's true. Soon as I track down the girl and her daughter, I'm going to publish."

"So, you're telling me Marco Balducci has a kid running around somewhere over in Italy, allegedly?" I asked, dumbfounded.

Mosconi nodded.

The implications of what Mosconi was telling us were

beyond my comprehension. So many different thoughts crossed my mind at the same time that I had trouble separating them. I figured Marco to be a violent guy, but I hadn't considered how that violence could manifest itself. Beating a man to death was something I couldn't imagine. More than that, the implications of the entire incident—of Marco being a father, a teenage girl with a baby kept secret somewhere in Italy, a murder that should have landed Marco in an Italian jail—all swirled around in my head. Was Maggie aware of the child? Did Vespucci know of the murder? Luci's voice interrupted my thoughts.

"Jim, what you're saying has tremendous implications about who we're dealing with, and the information you just provided puts us all in danger. If it's true."

"I warned you."

Luci and I exchanged a look, acknowledging the magnitude of what we were hearing. I looked at Donovan to get his take, but his eyes were focused on something in the distance. I followed his gaze out the window, noticing a man standing on the sidewalk looking in. For a second, I could have sworn Williams was standing on the street. I blinked and looked more closely, but the man had moved out of my vision. Mosconi's story was making me jumpy, and I figured I was seeing things. I turned my attention back to Mosconi, who had missed the exchange.

Mosconi proceeded with his story. "In Italy, only two institutions could keep the entire story quiet and make the girl and the baby disappear: the Mafia or the government. If it's the Mafia, that would explain why I couldn't get anyone to talk to me. Either way, Marco Balducci is beholden to someone in a very big way, and I'm sure he'll have to pay up one day."

I'd heard enough. I felt overloaded and enervated, as if I'd just worked out. I hadn't expected any of what Mosconi had just passed on, and the weight of the implications was more than I could process in the time it took him to tell us.

Abruptly, Mosconi stood up. "I've got to get back to the press room. What I just told you cannot leave this table. Marco Balducci is dangerous. This is just a guess, but I'd bet none of the Vespucci clan has the slightest clue about any of this. If I were you, Jon, I would finish what you were hired to do without asking any more questions and go home to California as soon as you can."

"Our conversation will not go beyond this table. You have my word as a fellow writer."

With that, Mosconi turned and disappeared onto the New York streets.

My companions sat silently at the table. Our coffee cups slowly drained as we each sat lost in our thoughts. I was the first to speak. "He said there were only two entities that could handle a cover-up. One was the Mafia. But if the Mafia took care of keeping him out of jail, and paid off the girl's family to stay quiet, don't you think that Tony Vespucci would know about it?"

Luci spoke first. "Maybe. Maybe not. Could be a faction in Italy that finds it beneficial to hold this over Marco's head."

"For the moment, though, let's assume Vespucci does know. Let's assume Marco's Mafia connections took care of everything. If you're Tony Vespucci, do you let your daughter marry this guy? Do you tell your daughter about the incident, about the kid?" I turned to Donovan, "What do you think?"

"I think we're being followed."

The tired feeling was instantly gone. Luci sat up, alert.

"How do you know?" Luci asked.

"Been watching a guy out there on the street who I'm pretty sure has been watching us."

Luci said, "Let's get out of here. Donovan, why don't you go first, see if you can spot your guy. When you give me the signal, I'll bring Jon out, and we can get a taxi back to the hotel."

Donovan nodded, stood up, and walked to the exit. I watched him go, my heart pounding, worried that something might happen. Donovan exited the door, looking left, then right, then left again. He took a few steps toward the street, did another one-eighty survey, and then turned toward us, giving us the all-clear signal. Luci and I stood up at the same time. I left a ten on the table to cover the coffee and followed Luci out the door. A taxi was waiting at the curb by the time we got to the street. We climbed inside, instructing the driver to take us back to the hotel in Brooklyn. During the drive, Donovan sat in front, keeping an eye on the rearview mirror. The whole thing would have felt silly to me if the circumstances had been different, but only hours before, a guy carrying a gun had broken into our hotel room, and I had just discovered that one of my principals was an alleged murderer. So Donovan's precautions seemed appropriate. I hadn't expected Mosconi to tell us what he had uncovered about Marco.

Now that Mosconi had shared his secret with us, I wished I could give it back to him because I was now responsible for what I did with it. Which was what? Tell Maggie? Tell her father? Check with Marco to make sure it was accurate? None of these scenarios was appealing. On top of it all, what if Mosconi was wrong? If I started passing around unfounded rumors about Marco Balducci, I was sure there would be hell to pay from all parties involved. On the other hand, if Mosconi's story checked out, I figured it was safe to assume Marco would do just about anything to keep his secret tightly under wraps. Unless Vespucci already knew. Maybe Marco had told his fiancée, but I doubted that. I couldn't believe anyone in Maggie's family had any idea. I highly doubted that if Tony knew the truth—that Marco had an illegitimate child in Italy—he would allow the wedding to go forward. We were due for dinner at the Vespuccis in a few hours. I was not looking forward to it. As we pulled up to our Brooklyn hotel, we climbed out of the car, one at a time. I paid the driver and watched the taxi pull away. I turned to Donovan.

"Anybody follow us?"

Donovan shook his head. He looked to Luci for affirmation.

Luci returned the look with a shake of his head as well. "If we had a tail, I didn't spot them." He was silent a moment. "Not that it matters. Someone already knows where we're staying, so if they're following us, they want to know more than where we're staying. Or we're talking about two different parties."

Luci's words hung in the air as we considered the implications. Silently, we entered the hotel, crossed the lobby, and took the elevator up to the fourth floor. As the elevator doors opened, I stared down the hallway toward our room. "Paper-rock-scissors for who goes in first?"

Luci looked at Donovan. "I say we send Jon ahead of us and use him as a shield."

Donovan turned to me. "Don't duck. Your head will protect my chest."

We exited the elevator into the hallway. Donovan and Luci were suddenly all business. Donovan stepped down the hallway, Luci behind him. As they reached the door, they went to either side. Donovan looked at me, putting his finger to his lips. Luci held his hand up, palm out toward me. Then, as quietly as possible, Luci slid the room card into its slot, looking for the haze light. A slight clicking noise offered itself up from the unlocking mechanism. Donovan and Luci traded looks, Donovan nodded, and Luci pushed the door open, quickly and silently. Luci went in low followed immediately by Donovan. I stood in the hallway, feeling a bit useless.

Seconds later, Donovan popped his head out the door. "All clear."

I followed inside the room, not seeing anything out of place. I reflected on our situation, finding it hard to believe it had come to this. But it had. And it wasn't over.

For the next two hours, we didn't talk much about what we had discovered or where we were going for dinner. Donovan lay down for a nap. Luci excused himself, saying he needed to go to the gym and get a quick workout. I planted myself in front of my computer to work on the outline for Maggie and Marco's story. Until I knew otherwise, I would have to complete this project soon, so I figured I'd follow my normal pattern. I had the broad strokes and could see the story easily enough: a childhood love spark cut short in youth, only to be reignited years later in adulthood; fate would bring the two lovers together on their old stomping grounds and they would begin a wonderful life with each other; their families couldn't be happier; the fathers had grown up best friends on the streets of New York, and now their children were going to tie the families together.

I had the makings of a fairytale love story. But was it true? Did I need to add a footnote that the groom-to-be had a toddler running around somewhere in Italy? I sat back from my computer screen, considering this new information. Marco would go to any length to keep it quiet. There was nothing I could do about it right now, so why not make my time productive rather than sit and worry? I put thoughts of Marco aside and spent the remaining hours until dinner organizing the interviews of the other family members and friends I'd completed on my previous visits, pulling out important facts, anecdotal stories, and interesting tidbits about Maggie and Marco.

While I was working, Luci returned to the room, sweaty and relaxed. He took the first turn in the shower to get ready, followed by Donovan, then me. None of us had brought anything formal, so we all dressed casually. I had called Mrs. Vespucci to ask her if Luci and Donovan were invited. She was as friendly as always, saying she had more than enough food for everyone. When we were ready to go, Donovan hung back, setting a tell at the top of the door to let us know if it was opened while we were gone. Out front, we climbed into a taxi. Each of us, for our own reasons, was vigilant. Luci and Donovan appeared ready for anything, their eyes alert but their faces masked in a calm repose.

After a ten-minute ride, we arrived in front of the Vespucci compound, the ivy-covered green walls keeping the grounds in total privacy. We climbed out of the taxi, fanning out across the front of the house as we did so, exchanging looks but no words, staring at the wealth. From the opposite direction, a new Continental Bentley convertible came speeding toward us, slowing at the last second to cut a right turn with the nose facing the large iron gate. From our vantage point, I could see Marco's scowling face at the wheel of the sports car. As the gate began to open, he looked over at us. His eyes were more interested in my companions than in me. I could see him sizing up Luci, then Donovan, his gaze finally falling on me.

A smile crossed his face as he spoke, but I didn't see the smile reflected in his eyes. "Jon, welcome back. Maggie told me you had to do one final assessment of our relationship before putting it all on paper."

I tried to match his friendly tone as I responded, but for the first time my aversion for Marco bubbled to the surface. I did not like this guy. I got my lips working. "You guys didn't hire me to assess you. My job is to celebrate your love and marriage on paper and illustrate how unique and wonderful it is."

Marco took a moment to respond, then nodded to my buddies. "Maggie said you brought bodyguards with you. Had some trouble back in Los Angeles that might follow you to New York?"

I shook my head. I pointed at Luci. "Luci is my artistic director." I indicated Donovan. "Donovan here just wanted to come along for the ride. He loves New York."

Marco stared at each in turn. "Good to have friends here. The streets can be rough. From the look of your face, I'd say you need bodyguards more than you need friends." Noticing the gate was beginning to close, he nudged his car forward to activate the gate stopper, then pulled the car out of our sight. We watched his Bentley disappear behind the gate, tightening our ranks as the gate closed.

"He's charming," Luci said.

"I'd say that was a veiled threat," Donovan added.

I responded, "I really don't like that guy."

Our powwow was interrupted by a tiny face peeking from inside the front door in the center of the wall. Five-year-old Sabrina stared at us.

"Hi, Jon Fixx. Auntie Maggie told me to come let you in." She opened the door wider and stood in the doorway. She stared at my companions, not sure how to react to them.

"Hi, Sabrina. These are my friends. This is Luci, and this guy here is Donovan."

"Hi, Luci. Hi, Donovan."

Luci responded, smiling, "Hi there, Sabrina."

Donovan added gently, "Hi, little one. Are you the gatekeeper?"

"What do you mean?" Sabrina asked, a curious look on her face.

"You guard the door and decide who gets to come inside and who doesn't."

The thought of controlling who could enter and exit pleased Sabrina. "That's right. I'm the gatekeeper."

"Well, in that case, is it okay if we come inside?" Donovan asked.

"Of course!" Sabrina answered enthusiastically.

Donovan moved aside to let me pass. Luci followed and Donovan brought up the rear. Sabrina leaned out the door to make sure there was nobody else, then pushed the gate hard, making sure it was locked.

"Thank you, Sabrina," I said.

Sabrina was staring at Donovan. "Are you a genie?"

"A what?"

"You look like a genie. I have this book, and the genie looks like you. He has big muscles and he's your color."

I looked away so Sabrina wouldn't see me laughing. Luci did the same.

Donovan leaned over, his face close to Sabrina's. "But if I'm a genie, where's my bottle?"

That gave Sabrina pause. We could see her trying to figure out the riddle. She was sure Donovan was a genie and, not ready to let it go, she walked around him. We heard Maggie's voice coming from the front of the house.

"Sabrina, did you let our guests in?" Maggie asked as she appeared on the path. "Hi, guys," she said, waving to us. Sabrina turned on her heel and ran to her aunt.

"I'm the gatekeeper," Sabrina said, her face proudly turned up to her aunt. Sabrina pointed at Donovan. "He's a genie, but he won't admit it. He's hiding his bottle." Sabrina looked back at Donovan, winking at him as if they shared a secret, then disappeared into the house.

Maggie watched her niece run inside. "I hope Sabrina didn't say anything to offend you."

Donovan answered, "Quite the opposite, she's very charming." I'd never thought to ask Donovan if he had any children, but he was clearly comfortable with them.

Maggie led us into the house, taking us straight to her father's study. "My father told me he'd like to see you as soon as you arrive."

My nerves were so shot from all the action of the last week my guts tightened up. I figured her father's needing to see me was a bad sign. Maggie led us down the hallway, past the paneled walls to the library. In single file, we entered the cavernous library. Once again, I was hit by the effect of the floor-to-ceiling shelves of books covering every wall. My love of books momentarily made me forget my underlying fear of Tony Vespucci and what he might have in mind for me. Maggie stepped to one side, presenting my friends and me. Across the room, her father sat at his large oak desk, staring at some documents before him, reading glasses perched on his nose. Off to my left, close to the desk, Joey was relaxing in a comfortable armchair. Marco sat in a chair opposite Joey.

"Papa, Jon's here."

Vespucci looked up from his work, taking his glasses off, the shade of a smile crossing his face. "Jon, I hear you've been getting yourself into some trouble."

I could feel Donovan and Luci tensing up behind me. I wasn't sure where this was going. Joey remained seated in his chair. I wasn't picking up any energy from him, but I sensed a scowl from Marco's direction.

Vespucci gave Luci and Donovan a visual once-over, then said, "Gentlemen, welcome to my home. Jon, please, will you introduce us."

"This is Luci , my artistic director. He handles the visual look of my stories. And this man here," pointing to Donovan, "is Donovan."

"Please make yourselves at home. I believe you've met my daughter's fiancé, Marco." Marco acknowledged us with a stare. A dark look passed over Vespucci's face as he noted Marco's not-so-friendly reaction. He turned his head the other way. "This is Joey." Joey acknowledged us with a slight nod. "Jon, come closer, let me get a look at that face."

"I'm going to help Mom finish dinner," Maggie said. "Make your selves comfortable." Then she exited Vespucci's office.

I turned in time to see my friends seat themselves and catch Maggie's admonishing look at Marco, I assumed, for his icy reception toward us. The negative energy in the room was palpable. I was hit with a strong urge to spill everything we'd been told by Mosconi and see what came of it, but one glance in Marco's direction immediately put a stop to that line of thought. His scowl had deepened. If Mosconi's allegations about Marco weren't true and I carelessly accused him in front of Vespucci, a man who would soon be both his boss and his father-in-law, I was sure I would regret my actions.

Vespucci's voice broke my train of thought. "I hope you gave as good as you got."

"Surprise attack. I got mugged in an alley."

"They definitely meant business. Have the police caught them?"

"Uh, no."

Vespucci studied my face. "Did you call the police?"

I shook my head.

"Why not?"

"I couldn't give a positive identification. They were wearing ski masks. I'd rather deal with it on my own."

"You just contradicted yourself, Jon."

I was feeling flushed. Vespucci's questions were beginning to feel like an interrogation. I didn't respond.

Vespucci leaned forward in his chair. "If you'd rather deal with it on your own, then you must have a good idea who did this to you. And why."

With the slightest hesitation, I nodded. "I have a fairly good idea who it was. And I do know why. And, yes, I'd rather deal with it in my own way."

Vespucci studied me a moment, considering my answer, then nodded his head slightly. "I respect that. One last question and then we can move on. Will this situation have any impact on the job you're doing for us?"

"Only if they kill me." I was trying to make a joke, but it fell flat. I looked around the room, all stone-faced looks staring back at me, including those of my companions. I turned back to Vespucci. "That was a joke, Tony. They're not going to kill me, so, no, you don't have to worry about anything."

Figuring Vespucci had seen what he wanted to see on my face, I took a step back from his desk, sitting down in the nearest chair.

Vespucci glanced over my shoulder at my friends. "So,

Luci, you handle the visual aspect of Jon's novellas. I saw the Jefferson's sixtieth anniversary book. It was beautiful. You do nice work."

"Thank you," Luci responded.

Vespucci turned to Donovan. Donovan returned the look evenly, without challenge or fear. Even though he was a mercenary, I felt Donovan would step beyond the role of paid protector to make sure he kept me out of danger's grasp. "Donovan, right?" Donovan nodded his head. "You are here in what capacity?"

Donovan looked to me before answering. I gave him the slightest of shrugs, indicating he could answer as he wished. "I'm here to make sure Jon doesn't get mugged again."

Maggie popped her head in the doorway. "Time for dinner."

Vespucci said, "We're on our way. Gentlemen, after you."

Everyone stood and moved toward the doorway, Luci first and Donovan a step behind. I brought up the rear when Vespucci's voice stopped me. "Jon, do you mind staying behind? I'd like to speak with you."

Luci and Donovan turned back, looking to me for direction. Joey hadn't moved from his seat. Donovan began to retrace his steps. Marco also turned around, not ready to leave the room if there was more to be discussed.

I returned to my seat, Donovan close on my heels. Marco stood in the center of the room halfway to the door, Luci just behind him.

Vespucci spoke again, his words meant for all of us but his look directed at his future son-in-law. "Was I unclear? I'd like to speak to Jon. Alone."

Marco didn't look happy about being reprimanded in front of us. "Of course, Tony." Reluctantly, he moved toward the door.

Staring at Joey, Donovan said, "I don't leave Jon's side unless he tells me to."

"Jon, your friends take their jobs very seriously." Vespucci motioned to Joey to leave. With a relaxed manner, Joey headed for the doorway. I nodded to Donovan, giving him the permission he was looking for. Moments later, Vespucci and I sat alone.

"Jon, I've been looking forward to your trip since you last left."

"Me too, Tony."

"But this is my home. Please explain to me why you show up at my house with two bodyguards in tow."

For a split second, I considered telling him the truth. I weighed the pros and cons, realizing as I sat there that no matter what, Vespucci was a client. Telling him about the Nickels would not reflect positively on me, either as a professional or as a writer. I opted for partial truth.

"Luci always joins me on my final trip. That's standard protocol for us. Donovan, well, I hired him in Los Angeles to watch my back. I felt it was necessary that he travel with me." I stopped, not sure what else to add. Vespucci sat silent, staring at me, waiting. "Let's just say that over the last several months, I've developed a couple of negative relationships with some people who feel it is their job to remind me on a regular basis that I am not their favorite person."

Vespucci didn't say a word. I couldn't read him at all. I decided to throw a little caution to the wind and see how Vespucci reacted.

"In fact, I'm glad I brought him with me, because he's already saved me once. A guy tried to break into our hotel room today. We're not sure what he was doing there, but he was looking for me. Donovan neutralized the guy."

For the first time, I saw a slight reaction cross Vespucci's face. Surprise, if I wasn't mistaken. "What was he doing there?"

"We don't know. He had some type of listening device on him."

Vespucci became very still. "Are you sure?"

I nodded. Vespucci stood up, crossing around to the front of his desk, sitting down on the edge of it, quietly studying me. "Jon, do you know what I do? For a living?"

Was that a trick question? I couldn't hold Vespucci's stare any longer, so I looked away a moment to gather my thoughts. I turned back to him, nodding my head once in the affirmative.

"I figured as much. However, I want to remind you that I have brought you into my family in an intimate manner, and as far as I'm concerned that means anything and everything you discover stays within the family. Do we understand each other?"

"Yes."

"Good. I should have been more upfront when I hired you, but I needed to get to know you first. My daughter is getting married very soon, and I want to be able to give her this gift. Moving forward, if you come across any information you feel I should be aware of, I expect you to tell me immediately. Got it?"

Information? Like your future son-in-law got a teenage girl pregnant in Italy and murdered her father? You mean like that? I nodded in assent, not ready to divulge anything I couldn't verify because I was sure that the information Jim Mosconi passed on to me, if it was true, could get me killed.

"This guy who came your way today, what did you do with him?"

"We let him go."

"You didn't call the police?"

"I'm not a big fan of the police."

"Have you told anyone about this?"

"No."

"What about your friends?"

"They both understand discretion. I'm sure they haven't said anything to anyone."

"Good." Vespucci looked off into the distance. "Have you been approached by anyone asking you questions about your relationship with my family and me?"

I stared at Vespucci as Williams' face floated in the air between us, the words of his warning to be wary of Tony Vespucci running through my mind. But he had paid me a visit as a favor for his cousin. His warning about Tony Vespucci had only come as a friendly aside, so I had no reason to mention it to Vespucci.

"No. Why?" I answered. I did my best to look innocent, not moving or breaking Vespucci's stare.

"Jon, I'd like you to keep quiet about this intruder. Don't tell anyone, okay? I'm going to look into this."

"Okay."

He returned to his seat. "How's Marco responding to your interviews?"

I hesitated. "He's been fine. I've been able to get enough information from him to make the story work."

"He didn't much like the idea when I sprung it on Maggie and him. He and I don't always see eye to eye. How's their story coming?"

"I'm almost done. I should have enough by the end of the trip to finish everything up." I considered asking Vespucci about what had happened between Marco and Maggie and him when she was sixteen. I wanted to find out if that was the reason Marco went to Italy, but I wasn't sure how he would take the question. Maggie's voice saved me from getting myself into deeper trouble. "Everyone is waiting. The food is going to get cold."

We stood and followed Maggie to the dining room. Marco was seated near the head of the table, across from where Maggie indicated I should sit. Michael and his wife Caroline sat to Marco's left, their children Mikey and Sabrina beside them. Donovan was seated closest to Sabrina. He was entertaining her and her older brother with sleight-of-hand magic tricks. I watched him make a quarter disappear from his hands, only to reappear as a fifty-cent piece from behind Sabrina's left ear. She squealed with delight. Even Mikey

Jr. seemed fascinated. My estimation of Donovan, already high, grew at that moment. Maggie's Grandma Jean sat at the end of the table. Luci, Barbara, Maggie, and I sat in a line on the other side. Vespucci took his seat at the head of the table to my right. With Maggie to my left, Marco seated directly across from me, and Vespucci on the other side, I felt surrounded.

The table was covered with two kinds of pasta, one with a red arrabbiata sauce, the other with a green pesto sauce, a huge bowl of antipasto, and several types of grilled vegetables. Two large meat dishes had been placed near Vespucci at the head of the table. As he sat down, he eyed the meat dishes with a smile and a wink at his wife.

"Gentlemen, my wife pulled out all the stops. Before you, we have *Bracioline Ripiene alla Siciliana* and *La Cotoletta alla Milanese,*" Vespucci announced.

I asked, "What's the English version?"

Barbara responded, "The *Bracioline* are stuffed veal cutlets, my mother's recipe, and the *Cotoletta* are breaded veal cutlets."

"Sounds delicious!"

Vespucci said grace. Then the table erupted with chatter and food passed around. Caroline was the first to ask what Luci and Donovan did for a living. When I finished explaining, Caroline responded, "Maggie showed me your website, Luci, and the books displayed there look absolutely gorgeous."

Luci smiled. "Thank you."

"What else do you do?"

"I paint, sculpt. Some of it I sell, some not."

As the table talk wavered for a moment, Marco picked up the cue, looking down the table at Donovan. "What's your part in all this?" There was an underlying challenge in Marco's voice.

Donovan glanced up to see all eyes on him. In a serious tone he responded, "I'm here to protect Jon from the bridesmaids. They can be a little rough when they all get together. "

The table erupted in laughter. Marco didn't join in, passing me a dark look while everyone else was focused on Donovan.

Placing her hand on my shoulder, Maggie added, "I have some very attractive bridesmaids, and a few of them are very single."

"I went down that path once. I don't think I'll do it again," I responded, as lightly as I could.

Caroline asked, "Don't you have a girlfriend?"

"We broke up. She was a bridesmaid. I've learned my lesson."

Maggie leaned over to me with an affectionate tone. "Don't worry, Jon Fixx. I'm sure there's somebody much better out there for you."

I gave Maggie an appreciative nod, while praying that someone would change the subject immediately.

"Why do you always call him Jon Fixx?" Marco asked, unable to hide the irritation in his voice.

Maggie gave her fiancé a cross look. "I like it. I think it has a nice ring to it."

Caroline added, "Me too."

Sensing the tension between her daughter and Marco, Barbara moved the discussion to another topic, asking the three of us how we liked living in Los Angeles. I was glad to have the conversation moved away from me. The rest of the meal was uneventful, the discussion shifting from one topic to another, always in the end coming back to the fact that the wedding was little more than a month away, and there was still a lot to do.

Vespucci said almost nothing the entire dinner, concentrating on the food before him. To me, he seemed distracted. Dinner slowly came to an end as the women cleared the plates and took them to the kitchen. Only the men were left at the table. Vespucci cut the silence.

"What's your next order of business?" he asked me.

"I'll need to set a time to do one more interview with Maggie and Marco together. Before I leave, I'd like to meet with the family all together," I replied. "And I have to interview you, of course. Other than that, I'll spend the rest of my trip visiting the places Maggie and Marco spent together while they were dating. I'm planning on visiting the old neighborhood where you used to live, where they grew up together. By that point, I should be all set."

Vespucci glanced at Marco as he directed his words at me. "If you need anything, ask Marco and he'll get it for you. Right, Marco?" Marco responded with a reluctant nod. Vespucci continued. "If you need something from me, you know where to call."

Michael jumped in. "Jon, you better prepare yourself to come back here sooner rather than later."

"Why's that?"

"In case you couldn't tell, my wife is fascinated by what you do. I think I'll be hiring you for our tenth wedding anniversary, which is coming up soon. So be prepared."

"I'd love the opportunity," I said with my most winning smile, though I didn't feel it. The thought of continual involvement with the Vespucci family filled me with a sense of impending doom. I figured by then Maggie would be pregnant, not something I had any interest in seeing.

Barbara cut the discussion short when she entered the dining room with a large chocolate soufflé and ice cream. As the dessert was passed around the table, I looked to my friends to see how they were holding up. Catching Donovan's eye, his return stare told me he was doing fine. I glanced across the table at Luci. I could see questions and concern in his eyes. He was worried, though it didn't show on the rest of his features. In a room full of people, he had the amazing ability to read people's emotional state like it was on a visible heat scale. He knew who was stressed, who was angry, who content. He was always an asset on my trips, but on this one he was essential. He'd give me a full rundown when we were alone.

After everyone finished dessert, the women began to clear the table. Though Vespucci knew I had to set a meeting time with him, he didn't provide an opportunity to do so. When we were ready to leave, there were lots of kisses on the cheeks and hugs all around. Grandma Jean had taken a special liking to Luci, more than once conspicuously squeezing his biceps while commenting on his "Herculean" build. I'd seen Luci blush only a few times as long as I'd known him, so I found it amusing to see a woman in her eighties bring redness to Luci's cheeks. Both daughter and granddaughter found Luci's reaction endearing. Vespucci waylaid me as we exited the front door.

Walking down the path toward the front gate, he held me back, taking my arm in his, his voice lowered. "Jon, I know you're almost done with this thing, and you're doing what I hired you to do. But I want to make it clear that we are a very private family. We keep our business inside the family. Do you understand what I'm saying?"

I most definitely did. "I do."

"Good. If anyone approaches you asking questions, I want to know immediately."

"Okay," I said, as I thought about Williams and Mosconi. Was he testing me? What did he know?

"Good. Call me tomorrow and we'll set a time for you to interview me." He turned, about to walk back to the house when I stopped him.

"Tony, can I ask you something?" I called back to him.

Now seemed like as good a time as any to ask Vespucci about what happened before Marco left for Italy. "When Maggie was sixteen, I know you caught her and Marco together." I stopped, watching for Vespucci's reaction to decide whether I should continue. His face remained neutral. I pressed on. "What happened afterward?" Vespucci didn't respond. After several uncomfortable moments, I considered his silence to be his response.

I was about to apologize for asking and say goodbye when Vespucci's voice came at me in the darkness. "The boy needed to learn respect," he said quietly. "I had certain ground rules when it came to my daughter. Marco disrespected both my daughter and me."

"Is that why he ended up in Italy?"

"Yes, it is. His father and I decided rather than punish him here that he'd go to Italy to help Giancarlo open the first foundry."

"And you've forgiven him for that?"

"Let's just say the marriage is what my daughter wants, and I have no good reason to oppose it." With that, Vespucci turned and walked back toward his home.

I exited the compound through the main door and joined Donovan and Luci on the street. Donovan suggested that we walk rather than take a taxi because it would be much easier to spot a tail. The walk was only a few miles, an hour at most, and would give us time to talk. Luci and Donovan gave their impressions of the personalities around the table, especially of Vespucci and Marco. I filled them in on everything I discussed with Vespucci, both in his study and on the front path.

"You still think there's something else going on?" Luci asked.

"Vespucci doesn't like Marco. That much I'm sure of."

"It's strange that a guy so high in the mob hierarchy would intentionally bring someone around his family whose job it is to ask questions."

"That's what my sixth sense has been telling me all along," I said.

"Maybe you're his mole," Donovan said.

"What do you mean?"

"This guy hired you to write his daughter's love story, but what if that's just a cover. What if he wants to know about Marco from a different angle? Vespucci figures people tell you things, things they might consider innocent, but you may see them in a different light. He can't go snooping around because of who he is. But you can. Maybe he figures you'll uncover something."

What Donovan suggested made sense, and it jived with what I had been thinking since my first meeting with Vespucci. He wanted more than just a love story for his daughter. He wanted dirt on his daughter's fiancé. And that's what I had found. If Mosconi was right, I now knew that Marco had bred a bastard child and killed a grandfather over it. Unless Vespucci already knew about that. "Do you think Vespucci knows about the illegitimate kid in Italy?"

Luci shrugged.

"Hard to say," Donovan added.

I considered who Vespucci was. "Regardless of whether he knows or not, Vespucci is not only the head of his family, he's the head of the Family. If he doesn't like Marco marrying his daughter, why doesn't he just say 'No,' he won't allow it?"

"Imagine the ruckus that would cause. Not only would he be going against his daughter's own wishes, he'd be speaking out against the son of his best friend and a made member of the organization," Luci said.

Donovan added, "Better to let his daughter marry the guy than stir up that hornet's nest."

"Enter Jon Fixx," Luci quipped.

"But if Vespucci doesn't want Maggie to marry Marco, hiring me to find compromising information seems like such a long shot."

"Not looking like such a long shot now," Luci retorted.

"Mosconi's information is not verified. Imagine what Marco or Maggie, or even Vespucci, would do to me if it wasn't true. And what if Maggie, or her father, already knows about what happened in Italy. Then I would just look like a troublemaker. I mean, how do you bring that up in conversation? 'Oh, by the way, did you know your fiancé got a fifteen-year-old girl pregnant in Italy, then beat her father to death, and has an illegitimate child over there? I wasn't sure if you knew, but just wanted to check.' I don't think that would go over too well with anyone."

"Jon, put yourself in Marco's shoes for a moment," Donovan said. "Let's assume what Mosconi told us is true and that Maggie and her father have no idea. If you're Marco, you wouldn't want them, or anyone else, to find out." Luci nodded in agreement. Donovan continued. "That's the kind of information you would do just about anything to keep under wraps."

"That would explain why Mosconi's so jumpy," Luci added.

I looked at them both, realizing the implications. "And Marco knows I've met with Mosconi, so . . . " My words trailed off.

"Exactly."

"Yep."

"I need to speak to Mosconi again. Find out who his source is," I said, feeling this piece of knowledge was urgent.

"I'll call my guy, see if he can give us anything," Luci said. He knew quite a few people at the C.I.A.

We walked down the sidewalk past the chic Brooklyn homes, the apparent danger we were in weighing down on me. Over the years, I'd discovered indiscretions on both sides—some occurring within a week of the wedding—that I knew would have ended the wedding festivities. But I had always believed that my job had nothing to do with the infidelities of the couple. I was hired to write a love story. Any information I uncovered that went counter to the overall goal was solely for my notebook. It bothered me to keep the damaging information secret but, in the end, I believed it was their karma to work out, not mine. They'd chosen each other for a reason and, therefore, they had to deal with the other person's issues, good and bad. My dilemma with the

Vespuccis, however, presented a unique situation for me. I was sure Tony would not take it well if I withheld pertinent information about his future son-in-law that could harm his daughter's happiness. I noticed we weren't far from the hotel. The buzz of my PDA grabbed my attention. I pulled it out, a New York exchange number on the display screen.

I put the phone to my ear. "Jon here."

Mosconi's voice came at me in a ramble. He was drunk. "Fixx, you need to keep what we talked about today quiet, just between us. Do you understand?"

"Jim?"

"Who else? Listen. Soon, I'm gonna have enough to break this whole story wide open. I've got a source in Italy who's going to give me the story of a lifetime. Crime connections between Italy and the United States, Mafia, politicians, business ties. Oh, it's gonna be my biggest story ever. And your boy Marco is only a small piece of the big puzzle." There was a pause. I could tell he was taking a swig of something. From the slur in his words, I figured it was something strong. "I'm going to bring them all down. You wait and see. But you need to keep your mouth shut! Until I've gathered all my evidence. Do you understand?"

"I do understand. What we discussed today will not be repeated to anybody," I assured him.

"Because this is going to be my Watergate."

"Can I ask you something?"

I heard another gulp. "Sure."

"What you told me today, do you have proof?"

"I will soon enough. But you're just gonna have to wait like everybody else."

"Could we meet again?"

"Maybe. I'll call you. I've got work to do." Hiccup. "I gotta go, Fixx. Time to write."

Then, silence. I thought maybe he'd passed out.

"Jim, I'll call you tomorrow." Silence. "Talk to you later."

I was about to hang up the phone when I heard Mosconi's

voice, speaking so quietly I could barely make it out. "Be careful out there. The world's dangerous, so just—" followed by the sound of snores.

I hung up.

"That was Jim Mosconi."

"What'd he want?" Luci asked.

"I'm not sure. Sounded like he was well into a bottle of Jack Daniels. He was reiterating his request for us to keep silent about today. I'd say he was scared, but he was too drunk to be sure."

"He say anything about his proof?"

"No. But he said he'd soon have everything he needed to break the story wide open."

We were standing in front of the hotel. Luci reached the entryway first, holding the door for Donovan to enter, followed by me. We crossed the lobby to the elevator, Donovan stutter stepping so he could fall in beside Luci. A silent exchange passed between them, and then we were inside the elevator going up.

I looked from one to the other. They had the same look on their face, prompting me to ask, "What?"

Donovan answered, "Guy sitting in the lobby. Did you see him?" I shook my head. I'd been lost in my own thoughts. "Cop, enforcement officer, something."

I looked to Luci to see if he concurred. He nodded. We were silent the rest of the way up, considering the implications. The elevator doors opened on our floor, the three of us on guard. Silently, we walked down the hallway in single file, Donovan taking the lead. He held his hand up, stopping us just before the hotel door. He put his finger to his lips. Luci and I stood still. Donovan pointed at the door, indicating his mark had been moved. Luci stepped around me to Donovan's side, the two of them straddling the door. As quietly as he could, Luci inserted his plastic card into the lock. The lock light lit up green, making a slight noise as it did so. Donovan motioned for Luci to step back, Donovan doing the same. They were in sync. I stood off to the side, feeling hyperalert and helpless. Seconds ticked by, first ten, then twenty, then thirty. Luci and Donovan exchanged a glance. Donovan reached down to the door handle when the sound of someone grasping the other end signaled him to stop. Donovan quickly pulled his hand back, preparing himself, standing aside to remain out of view as the door slowly opened. Donovan spun on his toes, shoving the door inward, pushing his way inside. Luci followed closely on his heels and they disappeared from view. I rushed to the doorway opening, hoping to be of some assistance, if necessary, but Luci and Donovan had it handled.

A man's legs spread across the floor were keeping the door ajar, with Luci straddling the guy, his knees pinning the man's arms. Donovan was quickly looking around the room, making sure we had only one visitor. Satisfied, he returned to our uninvited guest. Luci backed off the guy's arms, pulling him up off the ground in a full nelson, keeping his arms locked up. Donovan patted the guy down and pulled out a gun from a shoulder holster. Deciding it would not be good if a passerby saw what was happening, I stepped in and let the door close behind me. Up to this point, our visitor was silent. As I crossed through the narrow hallway, following Luci into the larger bedroom area, I got a look at our visitor's face. Too much had happened for me to be surprised.

Williams spoke first. "Hey, Jon, is this how you treat a guest?"

"An uninvited guest. Gentlemen, meet Ted Williams."

Luci asked, "FBI Ted?"

Williams answered, "The one and only."

Luci reluctantly let loose of Williams' arms.

"Can I have my gun back?" Williams reached out toward Donovan, expecting to have it summarily returned to his possession.

Donovan, however, was not so accommodating. He shook

his head, placing the gun in his waistband. "You get it back when you leave."

Williams groaned. He turned to me. "Can we talk?"

I took a seat in a chair near the bed. "You're a long way from California. Don't you guys have like a local jurisdiction or something? Aren't you in the wrong air space?"

"You read too much fiction, Jon. Listen, I'm on your side here, and I'm here to help." He could see from the looks on the three faces before him that none of us believed him. "Could I speak with you privately? This information is somewhat sensitive."

"No. My friends understand discretion."

Williams stared at each of us in turn, before speaking again. "That's good, because it might be your life we're talking about." He gave me the serious, advisory FBI look. "Jon, listen, the first time we met was not official business. I was doing a favor for my cousin."

"Michelle?"

A look of annoyance crossed Williams' face, but he let my comment pass. "That's not why I'm here. This is far more serious. I've been reassigned to the task force dealing with organized crime in New York. And your name keeps popping up linked with Tony Vespucci."

Luci asked, "You know as well as we do that Jon is not doing anything even remotely illegal in relation to Tony Vespucci. How has Jon's name come up?"

"I can't disclose that information. But we would like your help."

His words fell like a heavy stone in the room that no one wanted to pick up. After several moments of silence, I asked, "What kind of help?"

"For starters, we'd like you to wrap up whatever it is you're doing with Vespucci, stop any further research and interviews, and get out of here." Williams was met with a wall of silence. "Or, to be honest, we'd like to strap a wire on you for the remainder of your visits until you get us something incriminating on tape."

I blanched at the thought. Alarm registered on my friends' faces.

After a pregnant pause, Williams laughed. "Just kidding. I love using that one."

Donovan frowned. "Not funny."

"Geez, tough crowd." Williams looked at me. "In all seriousness, I was brought in because of my unusual connection to you, Jon."

"Through Michelle?"

Irritation flitted across Williams' face. He was losing patience, what little of it he had. "There's something much bigger going on here that has far more significance than the little job you've been hired to do, and we need you to get it finished up and move on."

Williams' jokes at my expense had both angered me and cleared my head. As he spoke, I started imagining scenarios for why the FBI would send him to visit me. Only one thing could have caused such a ruckus, at least as far I could see. I decided to throw a name at Williams.

"Is this about Jim Mosconi?"

I saw recognition in the FBI agent's eyes. I'd hit a bullseye. Williams was silent a moment. When he finally spoke, there was an edge to his voice. Any humor he'd brought with him was gone.

"Jon, counter to what you might think, I like you. You're not a bad guy. But you've been warned. Stay away from this. You have absolutely no idea what you're involved in, and if you're smart, you'll make sure you finish up your job before you ever find out."

"Are you done?"

Williams didn't answer me. He looked at Donovan. "Can I have my government-issued Glock back?"

Familiar with the gun, Donovan popped the magazine out from the handle of the Glock and handed a harmless gun back to Williams without saying a word.

"Oh, c'mon, is that necessary?"

Donovan stuck the magazine in his pocket. Reluctantly, Williams took the castrated weapon back, but before sticking it into the shoulder holster, he pulled a spare magazine from inside his jacket pocket and reloaded the weapon. Luci stepped aside to give him room to pass. Just as Williams reached the door, a thought occurred to me. "Ted, why did you guys send someone in here to plant a bug?"

He turned around, having trouble hiding his surprise. "If we did, you wouldn't be asking the question. And I wouldn't be paying you a friendly visit." Then he turned to go, but before allowing the door to close on his uninvited presence, he said over his shoulder, "Jon, stop digging. Go home."

The door closed on his back. We exchanged glances, the concern on my face registered on those of my companions.

Luci spoke first. "What the hell was that all about?"

"I think you've stepped on a pressure release IED," Donovan said.

Luci and I both stared at Donovan.

"Improvised explosive device, with a twist. The Germans used them in World War II. Viet Cong in Vietnam. They've had a resurgence in Iraq and Afghanistan. Bomb's buried in the ground and the pressure of your weight only starts the process. The actuating device for the bomb is a release of the pressure switch, so as soon as you remove your weight, take the pressure off, you're blown all to hell."

Luci asked, "He should keep the pressure on?"

"I'm saying it could be much worse if he takes the pressure off."

I looked at each of them, trying to keep the panic out of my voice. "Could you please tell me who I'm pressuring?"

No one answered.

"Why would the FBI want me to stop doing what I'm doing, when all I'm doing is writing a love story for Maggie Vespucci's wedding?"

Donovan added, "Why would someone try to bug our room?"

Luci returned the query with another, "Why would Mosconi call you and warn you to be careful?"

"And why is he scared? I could hear it in his voice. More importantly, who is he scared of?" But all three of us knew the answer almost before I was finished speaking. Given the information we had, Mosconi had only one person to be afraid of. The thoughts began to gel in my brain, and the beginnings of a plan started to form.

Off the look on my face, Luci asked, "What?"

"Nothing, nothing. Let's table this for tonight. I'm not sure yet. Let me sleep on it, and we can talk in the morning."

With that, we decided to call it a night. The day had been exhausting. Donovan blocked the door with his body, and within minutes we were all asleep. I was so tired, I didn't dream, which was good, because I knew I was going to need my rest for what was coming.

11
Early November New York 3rd Trip

I slept like a log that night. I was exhausted from all the excitement of the day, and with Donovan and Luci in the room, I wasn't worried that anything would happen. But when I woke up, my mind was flooded with questions from the previous day's happenings. Was what Mosconi told us about Marco Balducci true? Did Maggie or her father know Marco had a kid in Italy? Did Vespucci have an ulterior motive when he hired me? Were Maggie and Marco in love? Did any of this really matter for the job I was hired to do? Were my feelings for Maggie interfering with my ability to be objective? My Voice chose to answer the last question loud and clear.

Of course, your personal feelings are interfering with everything!

I looked around to see if Luci or Donovan was watching me. For a moment, I was sure I'd spoken out loud. Luci's bed was vacant. No sign of Luci. I could hear Donovan's even breathing coming from the cot near the door. I lay back down.

C'mon, Jon, your inability to see yourself for who you truly are is gargantuan. Let's start with the main problem: Maggie. How do you feel about her?

I stared at the ceiling considering the question. How did

I feel about Maggie? Well, she was beautiful, and intelligent, definitely sexy, unique and—

Jesus, Jon, what is this, a dating game? Get to the point. I don't have all the time in the world, and neither do you. If you got your head out of your ass, you'd see that.

I raised my head off my pillow and shook it hard to try to silence my Voice, but to no avail.

Are you really this dense?

Fine, you're right, I have feelings for Maggie. So what?

So what! So what are you going to do about it?

What can I do about it?

Exactly! That's my point. What can you do about it? Nothing, Jon. She's getting married in a month. And that's not all. Let's add some color to this picture. Her father is one of the biggest players in the Mafia, and her soon-to-be husband is not far behind. Sounds like two guys I wouldn't fuck with.

I stared at the wall and saw images of Tony Vespucci in a tux, walking Maggie down the aisle, of Marco standing at the head of the church beside the smiling priest, of Marco and Maggie exiting the church and the guests throwing wedding rice on them, of Marco standing over a body holding a pistol and putting three quick successive bullets into the body underneath him! I blinked and the images were gone.

These guys are the real deal. So guess what? Maggie is off limits. Period. Even if she wasn't off limits, she'd be off limits. So this bullshit idea you have deep, deep down in your subconscious that maybe, just maybe, you and Maggie might, what, might end up together? Forget it. Okay, that's the first thing. Second, Jon, is whether you think Maggie and Marco are in love, because, let's be fair, you have a legitimate beef if you're asked to write a love story about two people who aren't in love. So, could you please outline for me the reasons you don't think they're in love? And remember, I have the added benefit of knowing your deepest, darkest secrets, because I own your subconscious, so don't lie to me.

My Voice was so damn irritating. I tried to list the reasons

I'd uncovered for why I thought Maggie and Marco were a less than perfect match, but I quickly realized I didn't have much of a list. Nothing in my interviews with either of the principals or, in fact, anyone in the extended group of family and friends gave me any solid evidence that my instincts were correct.

Did you hear that, Jon? You're basing all this on your instincts, nothing more. Therefore, big boy, time to stop all this nonsense, get the job done, and move on.

But—

You're so damn stubborn!

Why is Tony asking me to keep him informed about Marco?

In the past, how many fathers have you met who had reservations when it came to giving their daughter away to another man? They all did, Jon!

Good point. I rarely met a father who entered the unfamiliar position of father-in-law without some degree of concern and hesitancy toward his son-in-law. That could easily explain Vespucci's reasons for asking me to give him any unusual information I discovered about Marco. Marco. Wait. What about what Jim Mosconi told me?

What about it?

Well, if it's true, then—

What does that have to do with him marrying Maggie, huh, Jon? If Marco has a kid, let Maggie and Marco sort that out. That's no business of yours! Anyway, what gives you the right to be judge?

I stared at the wall trying to gauge the overall picture with an objective eye. So far, I'd done nothing to damage Maggie and Marco's relationship, but my Voice was paranoid, fearful I was on a self-destructive path that would create an irreversible flow of events that could only end in my, and his, demise. Over the years, there'd been quite a few grooms I didn't much care for, but I was sure that not one of them, with the exception of Edward Bronfman of Internet Love

Affair fame, had even the slightest clue how I felt. In this case, if I let Marco know my personal feelings toward him, it would not only be unprofessional it would also be suicide. If I was reading Vespucci wrong as well, and he liked Marco more than I thought, I'd be in even deeper trouble.

I lay back, focused on the blank canvas of the ceiling, wondering how I'd gotten myself into this mess. As I stared at the ceiling, the image of a man throwing fists hard and fast took shape before me. A second man fell, the attacker kicking him furiously without pause. The kicks came in a rush with no concern for where they landed. Blood was flowing from cracks in the downed man's head. A baby's cry filled my ears. I spotted a tiny pink bundle floating in the air behind the two men. The attacker's foot lifted high in the air and came crashing down on the second man's skull. The attacker slowly looked up from the body to stare at me with contempt, Marco's dark scowl now focused on me. I was next. I shook my head to rid myself of the image, my heart pounding. This was the man marrying Maggie. Did she know? My Voice cut into the flow of my thoughts.

Jesus, Jon! First and foremost, what Marco did before he and Maggie got together has nothing to do with the present or future, and it most definitely has nothing to do with your current assignment. You weren't hired to write about all the bad things your principals have done. So stop thinking about it, get on track, and finish this up. Then get the hell out of here before something bad happens, do you hear me? I don't care if you like Marco or not, and I surely don't care if you have some misplaced, rebound-induced feelings for his fiancée. Keep your eye on the ball and get this over with. Need I remind you what happened with Candy and Edward? Oh, that's right, I don't need to remind you, because all you have to do is look in the mirror! Most of all, Jon Fixx, your judgment of Marco is based on nothing more than your gut instinct and the word of a drunk, disaffected reporter who would have done far better if he'd been writing in 1968 than now. So would you just do your final interviews this week so we can go home!

I hated when my Voice made sense. Everything he said was right. Maybe I needed to get the job done as quickly as possible and move on.

Maybe? Jon, c'mon.

I know. Just finish it up and—wait! There was one piece of the puzzle that didn't make sense. Where did the FBI fit into all this? Why did Williams have such a hard-on for me to leave?

Silence. No response. There it was. That was the key. I'd shut my arrogant Voice up, because neither my conscious nor subconscious had any idea why Williams was working so hard to warn me off the Vespuccis. In fact, I would expect the FBI to want to recruit me since I had such open access to Vespucci's home. Williams knew I had nothing to do with the Vespucci's or the Balducci's illegal activities. Why did he, and the FBI, want me out of the picture so badly?

The sound of a knock on the door roused me from my mental gymnastics. I heard Donovan shifting his weight, getting up from the cot. From my angle, I could see him looking through the peephole, then moving his cot out of the way and opening the door for our third musketeer. Luci entered the room, his hair and face wet with sweat from training in the hotel gym, I guessed correctly. He stepped from the hallway into the main room, followed a step behind by Donovan.

"What are we doing today, Jon?" Luci asked.

"I don't know yet."

Donovan crossed the room to the window, lifted the curtain, and looked out. He asked, "Neither of you is involved in any illegal shit, right?"

"No."

"Not that I'm aware of," Luci answered.

"Right. So explain to me what it is, Jon, you're doing that has the FBI on your ass?"

"I've been wondering that myself."

Donovan turned away from the window, the sunlight

glancing off the scar above his eye. "I've been thinking about that all night. You know what I think? The FBI must have something to lose."

I could not think of a single thing I was doing that the FBI would be interested in. I glanced at Luci to see if he had anything. He stared back.

"Jim Mosconi is the key," I stated. "We need to pay him a visit. Quietly."

"Agreed," Luci and Donovan said in unison.

I got up and stepped into the bathroom to take a shower and get ready for the day. Looking in the mirror at the yellowed bruises on my face, I noticed that the swelling had gone down. For less than a second, I considered packing up and heading back to Los Angeles, knowing as soon as the thought crossed my mind that it wasn't an option. A quitter I was not. I was going to see this through. I vowed the Nickels project would be a category of one, leaving them the only dissatisfied client I'd had in my eight years of business.

My official schedule didn't begin until early evening. I had a dinner meeting lined up with Marco and Maggie to tie up any loose ends about their story. That left us the entire day to pay a visit to Mosconi. By midmorning, we were up and out. I'd left a message on Mosconi's mobile that I had some information that might be useful to him and could we meet. I wasn't sure exactly what information I had, but I figured I'd dangle it out there to motivate him to get back to me right away. We found our way down to the street and hailed a taxi to take us into the city. While we waited for Mosconi to get back to me, I decided a visit to Cranston Jefferson might be wise, hoping he could shed some light on the Vespucci clan and the FBI. I called his office to see if he was available. Cranston was the only person in New York I knew I could trust to be both honest with me as well as discreet.

We didn't talk much on the ride into the city. Luci and Donovan were both alert, keeping an eye on our surroundings and on the traffic around us, making sure we weren't being followed. After about twenty minutes, the taxi started passing the high-rises of Manhattan. As directed, our driver dropped us a block away from the office building where the headquarters for the Jefferson's large clothing empire resided. Before going in, we made sure we had not been followed. After a few minutes, we felt safe entering the glass doors to the lobby.

We stepped inside the elevator and I pushed the button that said PH. The doors closed and the elevator sped up the shaft, the upward pull so fast it made my stomach lurch. The elevator slowed and stopped as quickly as it had started. The doors opened to a wide foyer. Across the open space, floor-to-ceiling windows presented Manhattan in all its glory. We stepped off the elevator, staring at the intimidatingly magnificent skyline.

The secretary's voice interrupted my thoughts. "Jon, Mr. Jefferson is expecting you." She was in her mid-twenties, a natural blond beauty, petite, unflashy, with a warm, friendly smile. She'd been new to the job when I was working with Cranston and Judith. She remembered who I was and what I'd done for the Jefferson's.

As we passed the desk, she said, "I loved the story you wrote for Mr. and Mrs. Jefferson. It was so romantic."

"Uh, thank you," I replied.

"Maybe if I get lucky, someday you'll be able to do the same for me."

"I would love to." I gave her a small wave as we passed through the doors into Cranston's inner sanctum and closed them behind us.

Cranston sat behind his desk, staring at his computer screen. In frustration, he tapped his keyboard hard. "Damn computers! I thought they were supposed to make our lives easier." At the sound of the doors closing, Cranston looked up. "Jon! I didn't think I'd see you again so soon. What a pleasant surprise." He stopped talking, appraising my friends. He came out from behind his desk, his slow shuffle betraying his age. His gaze fell first on Luci, then on Donovan, then back to Luci. Cranston put his arms out and gave me a strong hug. Releasing me, he stepped back, his hands on my shoulders, "How are you, son?"

"I'm good, sir."

He studied my face, looking over the yellow bruises, then at my friends. "And who are these fellows? They look like bodyguards. Did you suddenly become famous on me?"

"Something like that."

"What happened to you?"

"Nothing worth discussing." I brushed off his concern, knowing I had more important issues to talk about. "Cranston, I'm sure you remember Luci. He's the man—"

"I know, the man responsible for the image and look of our novella. We met only that one time." Cranston's eyes sparkled, taking Luci in. "Good to see you again. The novella gives my wife so much joy. I have to tell you two that she looks through that thing every week. I'll come home and catch her flipping through it in the dining room, a smile on her face. You did something special with that book. I'll always be indebted to you both."

"You don't owe us anything, Cranston. We were just doing our job," I said.

"I've been in business long enough to know that when someone puts their entire heart and soul into their work for you, you become indebted to them. Employers often forget that." He paused a moment, his weathered, wrinkled face looking us over, his eyes settling on Donovan. "Come here, son."

Donovan crossed the short distance between them. Cranston reached out, his wizened hands taking hold of Donovan's arm, his eyes staring down at the tattoo on Donovan's forearm, then back up to Donovan's face. "How long?"

"Twenty years. Retired."

"You saw some things. Did some things."

Donovan didn't respond, staring into the old man's eyes. An understanding seemed to pass between them.

"World War II. It was a bit different in my time. The military was a hard place for a black man to be a professional." He let go of Donovan's arm. "How did you get linked up with Jon here?"

"He needed someone to watch his back. I needed something to do," Donovan answered.

Cranston turned to me. "Is he because of the Vespucci's?"

"Funny you should ask that."

Cranston slowly stepped back around his desk, sitting down in his chair. Donovan returned to his spot beside Luci. "I hope those bruises aren't related to the Vespuccis?"

"No, no. This happened before we came to New York."

Cranston raised his hand, palm out. "Stop. Go back. I need to know everything, Jon. Obviously, there's a lot going on here if you feel it's necessary to have a bodyguard or two with you."

"Well, let's just say my life has gotten a little strange. Ever since my relationship with Sara started to fall apart . . ."

"You broke up with that girl?"

I nodded.

"Only good can come from that."

I was about to start telling Cranston everything when suddenly I heard Vespucci's words echo through my head. He clearly did not want me talking to anyone about his business. I imagined what Vespucci might do to me if I ignored his order. For several moments, I couldn't find my voice.

"Jon, are you okay?" The concern on Cranston's old, wrinkled face was evident.

I nodded, still not sure what to say. I was scared. The reality of our predicament hit me like a wave. "Cranston, what I'm about to say is completely confidential."

"Nothing leaves this room. You have my word."

With his promise of discretion, I recounted everything

that had occurred. I told him about the breakup and how it had affected my writing, both pre- and post. I told him about the Nickels clan, and my comeuppance in the alley, and their constant harassment. I recounted my multiple visits from Williams and how, at first, they had only seemed related to my indiscretions regarding Sara but recently had taken on new color. I told him about the break in at our hotel room. After talking for almost thirty minutes without interruption, I paused to let Cranston process what I had told him. He sat quietly, considering all I had said. I held back when it came to Mosconi and what I'd learned from him. I wasn't ready to talk about that yet.

"What does Vespucci know about any of this?"

"Only a little. But I can't be sure about how much."

"Are you done with all your interviews for Maggie and Marco?"

"Just about. I have my final meeting with them tonight."

"You don't know who sent that guy to your room?"

I shook my head.

"And you are in direct contact with the FBI?"

"Well, not exactly. They're in direct contact with me. I didn't search them out."

Cranston sat in his chair, his wrinkled brow furrowed in thought. Finally, he said, "Tony Vespucci would definitely not like that. What's this FBI guy want? He's not asking you to do anything, is he?"

"No. He seems to be warning me off."

"What do you mean?"

"He wants me to leave. Literally. But why that could be, I have no idea."

Cranston sat back in his chair, considering everything I'd told him. Finally, he said, "Tony found you through me, so I feel responsible here, and responsible if something happened to you." He looked at my friends. "That goes for you two as well. I wouldn't forgive myself. Therefore, I feel compelled to tell you more than I would under different circumstances. But like Jon said, this doesn't leave the room, gentlemen. Understood?"

The three of us nodded in unison.

"My history with Vespucci, and his predecessor, goes almost as far back as my life here in New York. As long as we've been in the clothing business, we've had to deal with the Familia, if you know what I mean. Unavoidable, far as I'm concerned. The benefits far outweigh the moral dilemma. And over the years, I'd say I've grown fond of Tony Vespucci and his family. They're good people, and he's always done right by me. My connections keep me in the know and help me keep a healthy distance from any kind of trouble. Lately, I've been hearing chatter that the FBI has renewed its efforts to bring down the Mafia in New York. 9/11 created a vacuum of economic opportunity and the Mob has used it to their advantage, regaining an incredible amount of power and wealth. Word on the street is that Tony is behind a lot of this and he's close to running all of the East Coast. The FBI wants to take him out before he gets there."

We sat in silence. It had been one thing to know that I was working for *a* mob guy. To know for certain that I was working for *the* mob guy was frightening. I had feelings for a mob guy's daughter. The FBI was paying me visits. What would Vespucci think of that? I was sure I didn't want to find out. I looked up to three sets of eyes on me.

"Can you give me any insight into the relationship between Tony and Marco Balducci?"

"The official position is that Tony's very happy about connecting the families. Giancarlo and Tony go all the way back to childhood. And Tony wants to make his daughter happy. Off the record, I don't think Tony likes Marco much. I know I don't like him. He doesn't have manners. I'm not sure what Maggie sees in him. He's a thug." Cranston paused a moment, then said, "But let's keep this all in perspective, Jon. Tony is a very careful man, and thorough. I doubt there's anything you've come across in your interviews about Maggie and Marco that would pose any threat to him. Can you think of anything you've heard that Tony would consider, how shall I put it, compromising?"

Yeah, Marco got a fifteen-year-old girl pregnant in Italy and then beat her father to death. Without blinking, or looking away, I said, "Not that I can think of." Without verifying Mosconi's claims, I wasn't about to pass the story on.

"But the FBI is something different. I think it would be better if Tony hears about their visits from you before he hears from anyone else. Do you want me to come with you?"

I sat in silence, considering Cranston's offer. This job had moved far outside my normal scope of practice, and I didn't have any previous experience to guide me. "Thank you for the sage advice. I think you're right. But you don't need to come with us. I can handle this."

Cranston sat up in his seat. "Just be careful, all three of you. A simple misunderstanding could have irreversible effects."

"We know," I replied. A few minutes later, we said our goodbyes. In the lobby, as we passed the front desk, the secretary smiled at me. "Will you be coming back to visit?"

"If we can, just depends on our schedule," I said.

"Nice to see you, again." She locked eyes with me as we filed onto the elevator. I caught a wave from her just as the elevator doors shut.

Luci said, "You should have asked for her number."

"She's just being nice because I'm close to her boss."

Donovan turned to Luci. "Is he always this clueless?"

Luci nodded.

When we hit the street, each of us took in our surroundings, the noise of the city hammering our ears.

Luci asked, "Now what?"

"Jim Mosconi."

Luci stepped to the curb and hailed a cab. Moments later, we climbed into a yellow Toyota Prius—a first for all of us—and told the driver to take us to the *New York Post* offices. The interior of the car was quiet, our driver, unlike some of my previous experiences with the city's cabbies, appeared to like his anonymity and remained as unobtrusive as possible. The nametag on his dash indicated he went by Julio Hernandez. The radio was on a classical station, playing low. Donovan sat in the front, his large frame taking up much of the passenger seat. He stared forward out the window, the reflection of his face coming at me from the side view mirror. I looked to my left, checking on Luci, who was also lost in thought.

Our meeting with Cranston had not been encouraging. If anything, it was clear to all of us we were in a situation that could become considerably more dangerous than it already was. My thoughts locked on Marco. He was at the center of all my concerns. From the very beginning, if Marco had been friendly and forthcoming, I wouldn't have had any misgivings about him—or this project. If I thought Vespucci liked his future son-in-law, I wouldn't have started digging so deep. Maybe Marco hired the guy who tried to break into our room. Marco had the most to lose here, if what Mosconi said was true. But I decided as we drove toward the *Post* that if Mosconi couldn't give me any further information about Marco Balducci, or substantiate his current claims with some kind of facts, I was going to bring my research to an end and finish this project as quickly as I could. I would then go back to Los Angeles, try to forget about Maggie Vespucci, and move on. If Mosconi were willing and able to back up his claims, however, that would be different. The thought gave me the chills. I wasn't sure what I would do then.

We pulled up to the office building housing the *Post* and climbed out of the taxi. Luci and Donovan stood like sentinels on the sidewalk, one on either side of me, as I paid the cabbie. Each of them was scanning the street, keeping an eye on what was around us. I stepped between them and crossed the sidewalk, sidestepping the pedestrians moving in both directions. My bodyguards turned on their heels and followed me through the building doors. We crossed the lobby, in luck because the guard was dealing with what appeared to be a bungled shipment and an irate delivery person and we were able to slip by him. Quickly, we reached the elevators, stepping inside the first one to open before us. Donovan pushed the button and we ascended to the *Post's* main floor.

I decided that, rather than draw attention to the three of us, I'd track Mosconi down myself. I told Luci and Donovan to stay near the elevator lobby and walked into the maze of desks and chairs and people running around. The space was huge. I knew I'd never find Mosconi without asking someone, so I stopped at one desk with a man hunched over his keyboard typing, asking for directions to Mosconi's desk. He stopped what he was doing and looked up at me with a strange look. After a moment, he pointed to the back corner of the room. I thanked him and then moved in that direction.

I passed several cubbyholes, arriving at what I realized was the last one and figured it was Mosconi's space. As I rounded the divider blocking my view, I spotted Mosconi's nameplate. Hearing movement behind the partition, I took one last step, expecting to see Mosconi's high-strung face. Instead, I saw a woman going through his desk. She was law enforcement, a badge hanging on a cord around her neck indicating she was an undercover detective. I stopped in my tracks, but not fast enough to avoid her eyes. In one glance, I could see she was in her mid-forties, wiry and slim, a severe look on her face. Her voice flew at me as I turned on my heels. It had an authoritative quality that I couldn't ignore.

"Excuse me, can I help you?"

I turned back, a slight smile on my face planted to pretend confused innocence. I decided that a police officer going through Mosconi's things couldn't be a good sign.

Who knew what kind of illegal shit he was into, and I had enough trouble as it was. "Uh, yeah, I'm looking for the restroom."

She didn't like my answer. I could tell by the way her brow furrowed. She sat up. Now I was on her radar. I figured I might as well jump in with both feet.

"Well, I was kind of looking for Jim Mosconi. Hoping I could find him around here."

"What is your interest in Mr. Mosconi?"

Huh. She was all business. I couldn't fathom what Mosconi had done to bring on the ire of the NYPD undercover.

"If you don't mind, who's asking?"

Her left eyebrow hitched up slightly in response. "I'm Detective Hunt of the NYPD." She waved her badge in front of me, just like in the movies. "And you?"

"I'm Jon Fixx."

"And what's your business with Jim Mosconi?"

"I've been corresponding with him regarding some articles he wrote."

"Was he expecting you?"

I shook my head. Suddenly, I had a very bad feeling. It dawned on me why Detective Hunt was here. "Is Jim okay?"

She stared at me, her mind working over her answer. After a dramatic pause, she said matter-of-factly, "He's dead."

I blurted out, "What! How?"

She didn't respond immediately, her eyes on me, studying my reaction. Her gaze made me think maybe I had something to do with it. She clearly saw guilt written all over my face. I figured she used that look often to get a confession.

"Hanged himself. Apparent suicide."

"Suicide?" He hadn't seemed suicidal when we met with him at the coffee shop. I suddenly realized Detective Hunt didn't think he'd committed suicide. Why go through his things like this if she did? She'd used the word "apparent."

Whatever happened, the police were still doing an investigation.

"Jon Fixx." I didn't like the way those words came out of her mouth, like she was recalling a bad memory. "You met with Mosconi yesterday. Had it on his schedule."

I nodded, not liking where this was going. It was bad enough that I'd just found out Mosconi was dead. I didn't want to be tied up in the investigation as well.

Detective Hunt interrupted my panicked train of thoughts. She'd softened slightly, probably seeing the fight or flight look on my face—mostly flight. "Can we go talk somewhere a little more private? I'd like to ask you a few questions."

I nodded, turning as she stood up. We walked through the maze of desks and chairs, and I saw a few heads turn our way as we wound our way back toward the elevator. As I approached my friends, I saw them both looking past me at Detective Hunt. I stepped between Luci and Donovan, turning around to face Detective Hunt. She stopped in her tracks, taken aback by the sudden wall of six-foot muscle before her, reassessing her situation.

"Detective Hunt, meet Donovan and Luci. My friends. They were also at my appointment with Jim Mosconi yesterday."

The detective took a second to lock eyes with Donovan and then did the same with Luci. No one spoke. An elevator door opened instantly and the four of us piled into the elevator. Luci pressed the lobby button, the initial descent adding to my upset stomach.

To bring Luci and Donovan up to speed, I said, "Mosconi's dead. Apparently, he committed suicide." I had to give my friends credit. Whatever reaction they had to the news didn't show on their faces. "Detective Hunt here was going through his personal belongings."

Luci asked, "How did he do it?"

Detective Hunt returned Luci's stare a moment before

answering. I decided maybe it was an effective interrogation tool she'd learned over the years: Always pause before speaking, so the interrogated feel their answers are under constant scrutiny. "Apparently hanged himself."

"Apparently?" Donovan spoke quietly, but his voice still filled the elevator. "You have reason to think otherwise?"

Detective Hunt suddenly seemed to deflate ever so slightly before the questions of my large friends. "I didn't say that. What I'm doing is standard procedure. We have a guy who died in his apartment with no witnesses. We just want to be sure what we think happened is actually what happened."

The elevator doors opened, interrupting further discussion. We walked as one through the lobby, the guard at the desk registering a surprised look when we passed his desk. As we stepped into the chilly New York afternoon, Detective Hunt took the lead, moving us quickly down the street to a nondescript coffee shop near the corner. Inside, we spread out around a table near the entrance.

"Coffee?" Detective Hunt asked.

We all declined.

"Can't get enough of it, day or night. I'll drink coffee anytime." She headed to the register counter, ordered, and brought a cup of dark coffee back a few moments later. "Black, that's how I like it. Strong." She sat and got straight to the point. "Tell me why you met yesterday."

"With Jim Mosconi?" I asked.

In response, Hunt stared at me like I was an idiot, finally nodding once in response to my question. A small pad and paper appeared in her hand. Luci caught my eye, tacitly warning me to be careful.

Luci asked, "What reason do you have to think that Mosconi didn't commit suicide?"

Detective Hunt turned on Luci, her eyes boring into him. "Who's asking the questions here?" Luci, not one to ruffle easy, matched her look calmly, waiting for an answer.

From across the table, Donovan responded, "We should be because we haven't done anything. Sitting here talking with you is more of a favor on our part than out of any legal requirement. So if there was a quid pro quo, the outcome could be much more successful for both of us."

I had trouble not smiling. Luci and Donovan were tag teaming the detective. Hunt slowly peeled her eyes off Luci and pinned them on Donovan. He met her gaze with the same implacable demeanor as Luci's, not leaving much room for Detective Hunt to maneuver. She could either get angry or play ball. She sat back in her chair, assessing the situation, her eyes slowly moving from Donovan to me to Luci and back to Donovan. Finally, she settled on me.

"Okay, Jon Fixx. You're the one whose name came up more than once in Mosconi's daily journal. The guy was a strange bird, didn't have a lot of friends. He'd been notified that he was becoming a bit of an anachronism at the paper, so his job was on the line. We think he was working on a big story, but we're not sure what. He clearly had a drinking problem." She paused. "Okay. Quid pro quo, Fixx."

I glanced at Luci and Donovan to see if they had any objection to my speaking, but they had both sat back in their chairs, quiet. I turned back to Detective Hunt, trying to match her stare as my friends had, but I kept blinking, ruining my chance of seeming tough and unruffled. In addition, the combination of feminine and masculine qualities inherent in the detective's persona threw me for a loop. Upon first meeting her, I had found her looks too severe, too tough, the angles of her face and chin too masculine to find her attractive. But her face had softened a bit, and her ability to sit with three men, two of whom would make any normal person nervous, made her seem sexy. I'd caught Donovan giving her a head-to-toe once-over before we entered the coffee shop, so he had noticed the feminine side of Detective Hunt before I did. Realizing I was getting lost in my writer's head, I quickly refocused, getting my mind back on task. "I met with Mosconi because I've been researching a book about the history of the Mafia in the United States. He'd written a few articles of interest about the Mafia's current state of affairs, and I wanted to see if he had any unpublished information that would help me with the book. Didn't really get very far. I was hoping to meet with him again, but . . . " I trailed off. "Quid pro quo, why do you doubt he committed suicide?"

She responded, "The alcohol level in his body was over point four. We're not sure he could even function enough to follow through with the act."

"That's it?"

A twitch started at the right corner of her mouth, quickly moving up Detective Hunt's face across her cheek to her eyelid and then her forehead. "And he left his door unlocked."

"Doesn't seem like much to turn a suicide into foul play," Luci said.

Detective Hunt accepted Luci's words without a response. "Fixx, what else can you tell me?"

I decided there wasn't much else I wanted to tell her. The panicked feeling was returning. I'd begun to calm down since initially discovering Mosconi was dead, but now the whole picture was beginning to settle in. I was gaining clarity, and I didn't like my position in the overall scheme of things. If Mosconi was murdered, where did that leave me? Would I be next?

I wanted to extricate myself from this whole New York world as quickly as possible. Telling this detective as little as I knew about Jim Mosconi would be a start. "There's not much else I can tell you. Yesterday was only the second time I met with him, so I didn't really know him."

"Then, what were you doing at the *Post* today?"

"I had hoped to talk to him more about his research."

Detective Hunt searched my face for clues, trying to decide if I was holding back on her. I couldn't tell what she'd decided when she said, "Fine. I need all your contact information in case I have more questions."

I gave her my cell phone number and the address of the hotel where we were staying. Donovan and Luci followed suit. She wrote the information in her notepad, slapping it shut when she was done and standing up from her chair. "Gentlemen, it's been a pleasure. I may be in touch." She patted Donovan on the shoulder as she passed him, making Donovan look over his shoulder at her as she did so. It was a power gesture on her part, letting us know she was not in any way intimidated by us. All eyes were on her backside until she disappeared through the front doors.

When she was gone, Donovan said, "She's tough. I like her."

Luci responded, "I wouldn't want to be her husband. With that interrogating look on her face, I'd always feel guilty about something, like I should confess every day."

Luci's comment lightened the mood. We all laughed. After a moment, though, our laughter dissipated, the reality of our situation settling in around us.

"This is not good."

"You think he was murdered?" Donovan asked.

Luci said, "Possible."

I added, "She didn't tell us everything, but she told us enough. You met Mosconi yesterday. Did he seem like a guy about to commit suicide?'

"No," my friends responded together.

Luci said, "The unlocked door indicates he could have let someone in who left in a hurry. If Mosconi was really drunk, like she says, hanging yourself takes some work. It's not as easy as they make it look on TV."

"Do you think he could have been killed because of the story he was working on?" I looked back and forth between the two faces staring at me. Luci nodded. Donovan followed suit. Uncomfortably, I laughed. "C'mon. Seriously, now we're talking about murder."

I took a deep breath. "I'm interviewing Maggie and Marco tonight for the final couple interview. Maybe I'll just throw that in the interview and see if we can get this all settled. 'Marco, by the way, while you were in Italy, did you get a fifteen-year-old girl pregnant, kill her father when he confronted you, covered it all up, and then killed Jim Mosconi because somehow he found out the truth?' For some reason, I don't think that would go over too well." I stopped, considering what I'd just said. "It can't be what we think. Maybe he did just commit suicide."

Donovan responded, "Jon, I'd agree with you, except you've got the FBI warning you off, and some guy tried to break into our room to plant a listening device. Now this reporter is dead. You gonna tell me there's not something going on?"

I shook my head in frustration. The realization that Mosconi was dead hit me full force, and the understanding that he had possibly been murdered was too much for me to handle. I looked up at my two friends, both willing to go all the way with me, putting themselves at risk on my behalf. "After my interview tonight, I'll have enough information to finish this project. We could just leave tomorrow, go back to L.A., and I'll finish it up back there. If I'm missing anything, I can get the information by phone and email."

Neither of my friends responded.

"Okay. I'll see how tonight goes and we'll figure out what we're going to do after that."

As one, we stood up from the coffee table and walked outside. The sun was gone, a dark mass of clouds covering the sky. The smell in the air threatened snow. We decided to walk back to the hotel. No one spoke the entire way. Mosconi and Detective Hunt, Maggie and Marco, Williams and Tony Vespucci—their images kept crossing my mind. I felt the buzz of my mobile in my pocket. I pulled it out and stopped in my tracks. A knee-jerk thrill shot through my body as I recognized Sara's picture on the screen. Luci and

Donovan were a step ahead and turned around to see what had stopped me. Slowly, I hit the answer button and put the phone to my ear.

"Hello."

"Jon. It's Sara."

"I know."

Silence. I waited, an overwhelming feeling of nervous excitement making me tingle, though a part of me could not decide if I liked her calling me after everything that had happened between us.

"How are you?"

"Fine. I'm fine. How are you?"

"I'm okay."

The post-break-up phone calls were like talking to a familiar stranger.

"Where are you?"

"I'm in New York. Working."

She was quiet a moment, then, "That's why I'm calling."

"What do you mean?"

"I'm worried about you."

I liked, and didn't like, what I was hearing. Liked because the thought that Sara was worrying about me created an unhealthy, addict-like feeling of warmth in my stomach. Didn't like because what could suddenly have given her reason to worry about me. "Worried about me. That's silly. Why?"

"It's Michel's cousin, Ted."

Hearing Michel's name sent a spasm of jealously through my system. Williams' name set off alarm bells, making my head ring. My eyes caught those of my friends, my concern reflected in their inquiring looks.

"What about him?"

"I was talking with Michel this morning, and he was going on about his cousin Ted and the FBI and how they've got a big case going and somehow you're involved. What are you doing back there?"

I was processing her information, trying to figure out what she was talking about. Nothing she'd said indicated danger for me, but 'Ted Williams' and 'big case' registered. So he was working on a big case. "What does that have to do with me? Why do you think I'm in danger?" Upon hearing the word danger, Luci and Donovan both took a step toward me, getting in a little closer.

"Ted told Michel you were in way over your head, that you were interfering with their case. That if you weren't careful, you might end up being disappeared by the very people they're going after."

I was silent, my mind quickly considering the implications.

"Jon, I don't want anything to happen to you. I know we're broken up and a lot of things have gone down between us, but I still care about you."

Another time, Sara's words may have had greater impact, but at the moment I was more concerned about my own survival, so I had trouble focusing on what she was saying.

"When you come back to Los Angeles, can I see you? I'd like to talk about what happened between us. I'm not saying I want to get back together, but I think we should see each other. What do you think?"

What did I think? Was she insane? Before I could say anything I knew I'd regret later, I said, "Thanks for the information. Don't worry about me. I'm safe. I have to go." I hung up. It seemed like the only thing to do.

My head felt like it was about to explode. I wasn't sure what was going on with my ex-girlfriend, but I'd gotten far enough along in the break-up period to allow my mental capacities to override any positive physical reaction my body was having to Sara's voice. She did give me a warning, though, so I'd have to thank her for that some day.

Luci interrupted my panicked thoughts. "That was Sara."

"Yep."

Donovan asked, "Phone-booth Sara?"

"Uh huh."

"What did she say?" asked Luci.

"She said I'm in danger."

"How does she know that?"

"Michel. Seems Williams was blabbing and told Michel I was interfering with a big case. If I wasn't careful I might just disappear."

Donovan asked, "And Michel is who?"

"The guy banging my ex, Williams' French cousin." I mulled over everything Sara had said. "Why would Williams be blabbing to his cousin about a big case he was working?" I looked at my friends. "Luci, you've trained a lot of these FBI and CIA guys over the years. Doesn't that seem a little strange to you?"

Donovan looked at Luci. "You train FBI and CIA?"

"Martial arts. Kung fu. Years ago, I took on a guy who was high up in the company, and it sort of snowballed from there."

"He even met George Tenet once."

Donovan turned to me. "What am I doing here, then?"

Luci responded, "Our dear friend here needs all the help he can get." He patted me on the back in a supportive gesture. "But back to what you were saying. I highly doubt Williams was just inadvertently talking about this case. He must have had some intention behind it."

"You think he's trying to scare me, figured Michel would tell Sara and Sara would call me?"

"Sounds like a desperate roundabout way to get something done, but it's possible."

"Why, though? The only damning information I have is alleged and unproven, and it would only damage Marco's standing with Vespucci and Maggie." I stopped, realizing what I had just said, piecing it together. "And the man who gave me that information is now dead." If what Marco had done in Italy was true, and no one knew about it, the revelation would almost guarantee no wedding and no Marco in any future with Maggie or the Vespucci family, either personally or professionally. Suddenly, I was hit with an epiphany and it all gelled. The fog cleared and the pieces came together in a rush. I remembered what Donovan had said about the FBI that morning. "Marco is the only person who will lose anything if I, or Mosconi, make public what I know. And he's the one person who would have important information for the FBI."

Luci understood where I was going. "You think he's an informant?"

The words hung out there while we stared at each other, considering the implications.

"That's how you're interfering with their case," Donovan said.

"It would explain why the FBI wants you out of the picture," Luci added.

I looked over my shoulder, glancing around to make sure no one was around us within earshot. Donovan and Luci did the same. If we were right, the FBI was trying to build a case by placing a mole high up in the Vespucci organization. Who better to do it than the son of Tony Vespucci's best friend and business associate? Better yet, as Vespucci's son-in-law, Marco would remain above suspicion while having some of the best access to Vespucci's inner circle. Looking at the scope of the sting, the FBI must have put a lot of time into it. If I had left Mosconi alone, the FBI would probably have done the same to me. But if what I uncovered ruined the relationship between Marco and Maggie, then Marco could lose his access to Tony Vespucci and the FBI would no longer have an informant.

As for Marco, I presented a direct threat. He had more to lose than the FBI did if Vespucci discovered he was a rat. Not only did he have to hide the murder of his child's father, he also had to hide the fact he was informing on his own people. Taking it one step further, if we were right, I wondered when the FBI had gotten to Marco. Before or after he was involved with Maggie? If it was before, that could mean even their relationship was a setup. The implications of it were staggering. The bottom line for my companions and me, though, was that the FBI and Marco Balducci would be happy if we just disappeared.

I turned to Luci. "Your guy in Europe, think you can reach him?"

"Only one way to find out."

"Can you have him look into Mosconi's story about Marco and the girl? See if he can verify it." Luci nodded.

"What are you going to do?"

"I'm going to set the stage. I've got my final interview with Maggie and Marco tonight. I'm going to see what Marco's made of. It's time to put up or shut up. I'm going to find out once and for all if what we think is true is actually true."

With the dark November evening settling in, I met the eyes of my friends, and full commitment was mirrored there. We hailed a taxi and climbed inside. I couldn't stop thinking about Maggie. If we were right—if Marco was an informant, if the wedding was a setup—it would end badly, regardless of my actions. One way or another, Maggie was going to be heartbroken. So if that was the inevitable outcome, the sooner it happened, the sooner Maggie could pick up the pieces and move on with her life. Thoughts of what I planned on doing that evening began to crowd out my thoughts about Maggie. Did I really think I was going to call Marco out, expose him as a snitch? If I did that, what would Maggie do? Leave him? Realize I was the right guy for her? Fall in love with me, simple as that?

And then what?

The more I thought about it, the more absurd it all seemed. The closer our car got to Brooklyn, the greater my doubts about my seemingly well-laid plan to expose Marco. Then I started considering what would happen if I was unable to prove my accusations, or worse, if my accusations were unfounded. Marco seemed unlikely to be the forgiving type. If I went down this path, and I was unable to see it all the way through, Marco's wrath would be far more damaging than anything Nick Nickels Jr. had sent my way. As the thoughts and scenarios and possible outcomes swirled around in my mind, doubts settled in like a cold blanket. I looked out the window of the taxi, staring at the buildings as they passed by, my mind muddled. Did I owe Maggie the truth? What if Maggie already knew everything that happened in Italy, and we were wrong about Marco being an FBI informant?

Within blocks of the hotel, I tried to shut down my brain for a little while to give it a break. I decided I would play it by ear when I arrived at the Vespucci's house and do what felt right at the time. That was my decision of non-decision. I had no idea how it was going to play out. All I could do was show up and find out.

12
Early November
New York 3rd Trip

The taxi came to a stop in front of the Vespucci compound. I stared at the wall, not sure about stepping inside its protective boundaries because those I needed protection from were already inside. Before leaving the hotel, I'd spent an hour and a half going over everything I knew, running every scenario I could think of, considering where the holes in my logic were—because I knew there were holes. One thought nagged at me the whole time. What if I was wrong? What if Tony Vespucci already knew everything? Where would that leave me? I didn't have enough information to accuse Marco of being an informant—it was a hunch at best—but I was beginning to convince myself, even without the facts, that it was true.

I climbed out of the car, Donovan following me. Luci had stayed back at the hotel to work on his CIA contact in Europe, planning on meeting us as soon as he'd made his calls. We rang the buzzer at the iron gate and waited. The gate opened quickly. Sabrina ran out to greet us. From inside the doorframe, she was staring up at Donovan with a big grin on her face.

"Hi, Donovan."

Donovan smiled back. "Hi, gatekeeper."

"It would appear you have an admirer," I said.

Donovan squatted down. "Have you been practicing the magic tricks I showed you?" Sabrina nodded. "Will you show me inside?"

"Okay!" Sabrina turned and ran ahead of us.

Maggie greeted us at the front door, her dark hair pulled back over her shoulders. She was wearing a long-sleeved, formfitting black t-shirt wrapped over another t-shirt peeking out from the neckline, a pair of workout tights covering her trim legs. For a brief moment, I thought maybe she was worth risking my life for if it meant I would have a shot with her. I felt such a strong attraction I looked away for fear she'd notice me gawking.

"Hi, guys."

"Hi, Maggie."

She gave me an affectionate hug. It lasted maybe a second, but it was more than long enough to create a longing on my part for much, much more. Out of the corner of my eye, I could see Donovan watching the exchange with more than mild interest. Maggie let me go, taking Donovan by surprise and giving him a quick hug as well. "You had quite an impact on my niece," she said. "Sabrina can't stop talking about you and your magic tricks."

"Just a few things I learned in my travels. Kids usually find the tricks neat," Donovan responded.

Maggie added, "Not just kids. I find the tricks neat. I might have you teach them to me. Come in. I'm still waiting for Marco to get here."

We followed her through the entryway, down the hallway, to the dining room. We took a seat at the dining room table, while Maggie filled two glasses of water for us and set them on the table. Sabrina ran into the room holding a big silver dollar in her hand, looking up at Donovan.

"Can we practice now?"

"Show me what you got."

Sabrina started doing sleight-of-hand imitations, trying

to hide the coin in her palm, even though she couldn't close her hand fully around the silver dollar. With mock seriousness, Donovan gently took Sabrina's hands, trying to reposition them to show her how to correctly make the coin disappear. I turned to Maggie.

"Where is everybody?"

"Caroline is running errands. Mama and Grandma Jean are at the grocery store. Papa should be home soon. How's our story coming along? It's not going to be boring is it?"

"Of course, it won't be boring. Everyone loves stories about long-lost, unrequited love reignited years later by fate," I said.

"Oh, that's good, Jon Fixx! Are you sure you're not going to make stuff up? I just can't see my love life being all that interesting to anyone."

Boy, Maggie, you do not have a clue. "Don't worry, you're story is going to sizzle."

"If you say so. But it's going to be because of your writing, not our story," Maggie said, not insincerely.

"I've interviewed a lot of couples over the years and, trust me, I have written about some boring romances. Yours is not one of them. How are you and Marco holding up with the run-up to the wedding, all the planning and prep and tension that goes along with it? This is about the time when the stress starts to show."

"We're hanging in there. I'm afraid it's going to be anticlimactic."

I sensed something amiss in her tone, but given what I was about to do, or not do, when Marco arrived, I knew I could be reading her wrong. "What do you mean?"

"There's all this planning and hard work, and it's so emotionally draining. Then everything happens in an hour and we'll be married. I'm afraid it'll go so fast I won't be able to enjoy it," she said, frowning.

"Don't worry, it won't be like that. You're Catholic. It's going to be at least two hours," I said with a straight face.

Maggie lightly punched my arm in reproach. "Jon, you're terrible."

I decided to take advantage of this unexpected opportunity alone with Maggie before Marco arrived. "Can I ask you something?"

"Haven't you been doing that since we met? You almost know more about me now than my fiancé does."

You have no idea. I paused, gathering my thoughts. Where was I going with this? I wasn't sure. The point of no return would be coming soon, and I knew it was either now or never. Was I actually going to unmask Marco to Maggie and Vespucci? Accuse him of doing things I could not prove? Call him out as the father of a bastard, a murderer, and an informer? Was I crazy? My decision hinged in no small degree on whether I believed him to be in love with Maggie. Had he manufactured this relationship, or was he truly in love with her? I wanted to know how serious Maggie and Marco had been as teenagers. If it had been more than just a fling then, there was a good chance it was real now. If so, I would need to re-evaluate my suppositions about Marco's current intentions. I knew I was grasping at straws.

"I doubt that's true," I said. I took a breath. "I want to open the story in your teen years, when you and Marco first got involved. Treat it like Romeo and Juliet minus the family drama. That you and Marco were first loves. You fell madly for each other, but unforeseen life circumstances pulled you apart. Then fate brought you back together years later and the first love spark was reignited."

"I'd rather you start the story later when we met as adults." Something I'd said clearly bothered her.

"But it will make for such a great hook. That you knew Marco since you were a baby, and then one day you woke up and realized you were madly in love with him."

"But, Jon, you know how that first time ended. I'm not so sure my father would like to see that in print."

"Don't misunderstand me, Maggie. I would never write

anything about what happened that night between Marco and your father. But stressing that you were teenage first loves will make for a great story."

"But I'm not sure it's even accurate, Jon. Remember, Marco is almost five years older than me. I'm not sure I was his first love," Maggie said.

"You don't think he was in love with you back then?"

"I don't know. Why don't you ask him?" Maggie snapped. Her tone pushed me back into my chair. I was most definitely onto something, though I wasn't sure if Maggie's reaction was more how she felt or how she thought Marco felt. Her tone softened. "Sorry, Jon. Like I said, it's been stressful around here. Marco has been preoccupied lately."

I'll bet he has. "I'm sure it's just the stress of the wedding. We don't need to talk about this anymore. We can wait until Marco gets here." And then I'll sign my own death warrant.

"Your questions just brought up a lot of emotion for me. I'm not sure why," she added, laughing uncomfortably. "Marco worked for my father by that time, so I was more like the boss's daughter than a family friend. Maybe the idea that he was moving into a forbidden zone was mixed in there. I don't know. We didn't date that long. Maybe a month, maybe a little longer. Marco had wanted to keep it quiet because he didn't think Papa would approve. He was sure right about that part."

Something occurred to me at that moment. "Has Marco ever forgiven your father?"

"What do you mean? For what happened that night? Oh, I'm sure he has. My father reacted the way I think any father would."

"I don't mean for that. I mean for making him relocate to Italy?"

A look of surprise and consternation crossed Maggie's face. She had clearly never considered that possibility. She was thinking about it now, though, and it wasn't sitting well with her. Before she could respond, I was startled by a voice from behind me, making me almost jump out of my chair.

"Maybe you should be asking me that."

Marco stepped into the kitchen. From the corner of my eye, I could see Donovan across the room, still in his chair but his feet planted, ready to move in a split second if necessary. With a slight movement of my hand, I told him to hold. Marco crossed the few steps from the doorway to my chair, resting his hand on my shoulder. I inadvertently shuddered at his touch.

"Hey, Jon, are we a little jumpy today? Had too much coffee?" Marco crossed in front of me to get to Maggie, kissing her on the cheek. "What are we talking about?"

Maggie was unfazed by her fiancé's kiss, her attention still fixated on this new revelation I had apparently sprung on her. She turned to Marco. "Is that true, Marco? Did Papa and your father send you to Italy because of what happened between us when we were kids?"

Like a flash of lightning, I realized I hadn't thought this all the way through. The last thing I needed was Maggie getting angry at her father for a years-long secret I had uncovered.

"They felt that things would settle down if I went to Italy to learn how to run the family business overseas," Marco said matter-of-factly.

"Is that a yes?"

"I'd say there were multiple factors, and that was one of them." He looked at me. "Jon, are you digging a hole for yourself?"

His eyes flashed a red warning at me. Was he talking about the topic at hand, or was he referring to something more sinister, like Jim Mosconi? Having Donovan close by gave me strength.

But before I could respond, Maggie jumped in. "Jon was laying out for me how he wants to write our story, so he was checking on the facts of our childhood to make sure it would work. That's why we're talking about this. I never put two and two together."

I knew I would have to tread carefully if I was going to uncover Marco's secrets. But I had no idea how to proceed, or how far to push. Who was I to think I could draw this guy out? If everything I uncovered about Marco was true, that meant he was able to work day in and day out with a Mafioso Boss, sleep with the Boss' daughter, even ask for her hand in marriage, all the while snitching to the FBI. The absurdity and improbability of it hit me so hard that it almost knocked the wind out of me. To cover my panicked reaction, I started coughing but, to my chagrin, I was unable to stop. With a concerned look on her face, Maggie handed me my glass of water. As the coughing jag finally faded, I took my time drinking the water to gather my thoughts.

I recognized that if Marco was an FBI informant, then his nerves were made of something stronger than steel, which begged the question, "How was anything I did going to draw him out?" Amused at my self-delusional belief in my capabilities, I was suddenly overcome with a second attack of self-deprecating laughter. No one realized I was laughing, however, because I choked on the water going down my throat, forcing the liquid back up through my nose and throat, spewing water out both orifices of my face. Maggie grabbed a towel for me to wipe myself off. Marco stood off to one side, a disgusted look on his face. Donovan crossed the room to pat me on the back. I kept coughing to remove the remaining remnants of water from my windpipe, finally settling back in my chair. Sheepishly, I looked around at everyone. "Sorry about that. Something got stuck in my throat."

Maggie leaned forward. "Are you okay, Jon?"

I nodded. From out of nowhere, Sabrina appeared at my side. "Can I show you my trick?"

The last vestiges of my coughing fit were just finishing up with a tear running down my right cheek. She looked so cute, standing before me with an earnest look on her face, that all I could do was nod.

Maggie stepped over to her niece, putting her hands on Sabrina's shoulders and said, "Sabrina, darling, I'm not sure if right now—"

"No, it's okay, Maggie. Sabrina, let's see the trick."

She glanced back over her shoulder at Donovan for encouragement.

Donovan responded, "Do it just like you did for me."

Excited, she said, "Okay." She pulled the silver dollar out of her pocket and held it out for all to see. "Here I have this coin in my hand." We played along. Out of the corner of my eye, I stole a glance at Marco. His jaw was clenched, his right hand balled up. I was on dangerous ground.

Sabrina took her left hand and passed it before her right, doing a good job imitating a magician, even though the coin was too large for her hand. She moved the coin from one hand to the other, her right hand staying up, her left hand dropping low. "See, no more coin. Now, look!" She moved her hands around again, and said, "Everyone watch Jon." All eyes turned to me as Sabrina's right hand touched my ear, crossed behind it, and then reappeared for all to see. "And, voila! I just pulled it from behind Jon's ear," she exclaimed.

We all clapped. Maggie leaned over, kissing her niece on the top of her head. Sabrina stood in the kitchen, beaming, accepting our accolades. She turned to Donovan. "Can you show me another trick?"

Donovan answered, "I don't know if I can do it right now."

Sabrina's beaming smile suddenly became a frown.

I quickly responded, "Go ahead, Donovan. We'll be in the study."

I could tell from Donovan's reaction that he didn't think it wise for me to go into the study without him. But during my coughing-laughing-water episode, I decided to see this thing all the way through and I needed to be alone with them. I would do what I had planned, and if I was wrong about Marco, it would all come out in the end. Looking over his shoulder at me, Donovan let Sabrina drag him back to the table, her excitement making her oblivious to anything else around her.

Doing my best not to let Donovan's concern affect me, I turned to Maggie and Marco. "Shall we?"

"Our last official interview," Maggie said, taking Marco's hand and giving him an affectionate kiss on the cheek as she pulled him toward her.

I brought up the rear, following them as they walked hand in hand down the hallway into Vespucci's high-ceilinged study. Marco and Maggie sat down on a love seat on the far side of the room. I sat on a plush reading chair set at an angle to the love seat—adjusting it so I could face my couple—and pulled out my handheld tape recorder and set it on an end table near the sofa. I was about to ask my first question when my mind went blank. I didn't know where to start, wondering if I was really foolhardy enough to ask questions of Marco that might make him want to kill me on the spot. I realized Maggie and Marco were staring at me, waiting for me to begin. I started with something innocuous.

"Are you both ready for the big day?" I asked.

Marco tilted his head in a nonchalant, tough guy gesture I interpreted as indifference. I didn't understand what Maggie saw in this guy.

Maggie responded, "We still have a lot of work to do. All the setup is done, so now we're putting it all together. Mama is helping with everything, taking a lot of the stress off."

"Are you sure you want to spend every day for the rest of your lives together?" I ventured.

Maggie gave me a searching look, clearly taken aback by my question. With a scowl on his face, Marco growled, "What kind of a question is that?"

I had to agree. I still wasn't sure what direction I wanted to take, but my question had started me on a path. Trying to gather my thoughts, I scrambled. "I ask this of every couple in my final interview. It's more rhetorical than anything, kind of a reminder of the beautiful commitment you're making to each other every day for the rest of your lives."

My answer didn't satisfy Marco. I couldn't read Maggie's expression. She was staring hard at me.

I just pushed through. "Let me give you a rundown on how I'd like to write the novella. I'll open with your childhood, that you grew up in the same neighborhood and your families were very close, that you spent a great deal of time together. Because of the age difference, though, nothing much happened between you early on. But when Maggie started blossoming into a beautiful, young woman, things between you changed. At this point, our older Romeo found it impossible not to notice our Juliet and started coming around the house more, finding reasons to stop by and talk to her, even outside the family gatherings. A budding romance started, but the innocent lovers kept it quiet from the parents because they weren't sure how it would be taken. Suddenly, the budding romance is cut short by Romeo leaving for Italy to learn the ropes in the family business."

Maggie sat up, and turning toward Marco, said, "Why didn't you tell me that Papa had you sent away?"

Irritated, Marco responded, "I already explained what happened. We can discuss this in private later if you want."

"Jon already knows everything and he's not going to put any of it in the story."

"That's true," I said, my heart rate increasing.

Uncomfortable, Marco shot a fiery look at me before responding. He paused a moment, his tone of voice calmer than his eyes. "Like I said, I think that was one small factor in the overall decision-making process between my father and yours. It doesn't matter now."

"Of course it does. I want to know what my father did."

If Maggie confronted her father about his role in Marco's exile, this could backfire on me. Rather than make Marco look bad, it could strengthen the bond between Maggie and Marco while putting a strain on Maggie's relationship with her father. Vespucci would not be happy about that and would have only one person to blame. I immediately shifted gears, deciding to come at Marco from a different angle.

Cutting Maggie off before she could respond to Marco, I said, "Let me tell you the rest." Maggie shifted uncomfortably in her seat, not ready to let it go. She turned back to me without interrupting.

"For the next ten years or so, Maggie grows up into an intelligent, beautiful young woman, doing extremely well with her academic studies, transitioning smoothly from high school to undergraduate school at NYU, finding her direction in life." I could tell Maggie was only half listening. Marco was glaring at me. I pressed on. "She discovers a love for anthropology and decides to go to graduate school to get her Ph.D. However, something's missing. The men she meets never measure up. No one she dates has that something special. Over the years, there are a few boyfriends of some significance, but no one who comes close to being marriage material. It's all about her studies and her family. But she knows that one day she definitely wants children."

The word "children" got Maggie's attention. Unlike many of my brides-to-be who often brought up their desire for children, Maggie had been silent on the subject. Maggie laughed uncomfortably. "I've never mentioned children."

I produced my most winning smile. "That's called poetic license. But I am right, aren't I? You do want kids." I was heading toward the point of no return. Was I really going to do this? Before Maggie could respond, I pushed on. "And, then, we have Marco. The next ten years of his life begin with an abrupt change in lifestyle, a move to Italy to learn the ropes of the family business and eventually run the foundry. As time passes, Marco finds himself in the same predicament Maggie found herself in. He can't seem to meet anyone he really connects with. He has a fling here or there but nothing serious. Within a few years, the factory is extremely profitable, much of the success a credit to the man running it. The Balduccis, Marco specifically, become favorites of the Italian administration and begin to make friends in powerful positions. Marco is living the good life. But with all this success, he feels something is missing. He is feeling the desire to settle down, to begin a family."

I paused, not sure where to go from here. Do I jump off the cliff? My lips were moving before I could silently answer my own question. "Marco, I do need to verify one thing. You don't have any children either, right?"

Marco's eyes narrowed on me, a malevolent shadow darkening his face. I didn't need verification from Luci's connection in Europe. Everything Mosconi had told me was true. I could see it in Marco's reaction. The question now was how far to push. At that moment I still had a job, and if I backed off, I could wrap this interview up, fly back to Los Angeles, write the story, have Luci put the visual touch on it, and send it back to New York for the wedding. My eyes slid from Marco's dark look to Maggie's open confusion. She clearly had no idea. I could see she wondered why I was asking the question. Her look of ignorance coupled with my complete and total dislike for Marco recklessly egged me on.

"I came across one discrepancy in my research. I wanted to ask you about it, just to make sure when I write the story it's as accurate as possible. Now, you're sure you don't have any children or, more specifically, a child in Italy?"

Things happened very fast. Maggie was no longer smiling. Marco was moving. With the speed and agility of a man in top form, Marco was on me in less than a second. He grabbed the front of my shirt, pulling me out of my chair. "You piece of shit! I haven't liked you from the first day.

How dare you try to embarrass me in front of my fiancée!"

I could see the shock on Maggie's face over Marco's shoulder. "Marco, what are you doing?"

"What I should have done back in September."

"Is it true?"

"Is what true?"

Marco's words were directed at Maggie, but I could feel his breath on my face. I hung limp, not wanting to fight back, at least not yet.

"Do you have a child in Italy?" Maggie asked with dismay.

Marco spit the words at me. "Of course not. Don't you see it, Maggie? This writer fuck has a crush on you. He's had it from day one. I can't believe you don't see it."

I could see recognition in Maggie's eyes, finally piecing it all together, at least in relation to me. "Jon, is that true?"

I shrugged my shoulders as best I could with Marco's hands on my chest. I now knew the truth, but I had no way to prove it. I suddenly felt weak, knowing I had nowhere to go from here.

"Marco, let him go," Maggie demanded.

Marco reluctantly released my shirt. We stood chest to chest, though he had a good two inches on me. Standing a few feet behind Marco, Maggie looked sad and disappointed. "Jon, why would you try to put a wedge between Marco and me? You're supposed to be writing our love story." Her eyes bored into mine.

Even though I was sure Marco's reaction proved his guilt, I began to doubt my actions. Maybe Marco and Maggie were right for each other. She was the daughter of a mob boss, and Marco was a key player in the organization. Maybe it would be best if they got married and had little mobster children.

I turned away from Maggie, unable to meet the look of pain and betrayal registered on her face. But as my eyes met Marco's evil stare, my resolve quickly returned. The hatred in his eyes fueled my conviction. Marco was a cruel individual, so much the opposite of the woman he was soon to marry, I was sure of that. Over time, his terrible nature would break Maggie down.

"Marco, are you sure you don't have a daughter in—"

I never did get the remaining words out. Marco pummeled me, taking me over the top of the chair I'd been sitting on. I landed square on my back, his full weight on top of me, knocking the wind out of me. In that instant, I was trying to figure out why I hadn't asked Donovan to stay with me. It was a foolish oversight on my part. Gasping for air, I took a left to my right cheek and felt a right cross connect with the left side of my jaw. I saw stars flying all around Marco's head. In a jumble, I heard a scream I assumed to be Maggie's followed by a voice I knew would give me at least a temporary reprieve.

"Marco." Vespucci's voice echoed throughout the room.

Marco's left arm was hooked ready for another blow. He froze at Vespucci's voice. I caught my breath. I could feel my face throbbing all over. Maggie stood behind us, horror on her face. Joey and Donovan stood several feet inside the entrance, Joey's hand on Donovan's chest. Vespucci stood in the doorway, his anger palpable.

"Marco, get up."

Marco stared down at me, making it clear we weren't done. Slowly, he climbed off of me, taking a step back toward his fiancée. Donovan pushed his way past Joey, helping me off the floor.

"Are you okay?" Donovan's face reflected his concern. "I should have been in here."

I took a breath, wincing, feeling the damage in my ribs again. "My fault completely," I said. Looking around, I realized all eyes were on me. I glanced at Maggie, disappointment, pain, and disenchantment wrapped up in her stare. Vespucci's voice grabbed my attention.

"Jon, are you okay?"

I eked out a "Yes," but barely.

"Maggie, could you leave the room. I need to speak with Jon and Marco alone."

Maggie turned to her father. She looked like an orphan surrounded by men. "Papa, I have to ask you something."

Marco leaned over and whispered in her ear, "Now is not the time, Maggie."

Impervious to her fiancé's warning, Maggie pushed forward. "Did you make Giancarlo send Marco to Italy when we were kids?"

Vespucci was clearly taken off guard by his daughter's question. "Did Marco tell you that?"

Marco pointed at me. "You can thank this piece of shit for that accusation."

Vespucci was silent for a moment, considering what he'd just heard and turned to his daughter. "Maggie, I need to speak with Jon and your fiancé privately," Vespucci said, his voice firm.

Maggie looked around at the men. I was sure this was not the first time she'd been asked by her father to leave a room so he could discuss business. Maggie stared at her father, finally deciding not to pursue the battle with him at the moment. She turned to her husband-to-be, clearly wanting answers from him. "Marco, please explain to me what that was about?" She gestured to me, indicating my face.

"I'm sorry. I don't like this guy. As far as I'm concerned, he's been wanting to get his hands on you since the moment he showed up."

"Don't be so crass," Maggie admonished him.

"I know it as well as you do. The loser's on the rebound, and he set his sights on you. You said it yourself."

Marco was airing private conversations between them, and for a brief second Maggie appeared ruffled and embarrassed. Maggie looked at me. "Jon, I'm sorry this happened."

"Don't apologize to this loser!" Marco barked as he stepped

toward me. Donovan quickly blocked Marco's path.

My mind was racing, trying to figure out how best to gain advantage here. My plan had failed. I had not gotten Marco to admit to anything. Now I needed to figure out how to get Donovan and me safely out of Vespucci's compound. "No apology necessary, Maggie. There's some truth in what Marco said. The moment I met you, I knew you were special."

Maggie's face reflected pained interest in what I was saying. Marco clearly wanted to inflict lasting damage on me.

"And Marco's right. I am on the rebound and I think these feelings may have colored my views of Marco in a less than flattering light. I've been completely unprofessional. What I can do now is promise that I will forget everything that happened tonight and will get your novella done to everyone's satisfaction. I'll consider tonight nothing more than a misunderstanding."

Before Maggie or Marco had a chance to respond, Vespucci said, "Maggie, I'm not going to ask you again."

Without as much as a glance my way, Maggie gave Marco one last searching look, then turned and left the room.

Vespucci walked toward his desk, setting the room in motion. Marco immediately crossed the room away from me, a hateful stare directed at me. Donovan positioned himself between us to block Marco's path. Joey hung back, shadowing Donovan.

Vespucci settled into his chair. "What the hell was that?"

Neither Marco nor I proffered an explanation. I wasn't about to go into any detail about Marco without proof I could hand Vespucci.

"Fine, neither of you wants to talk. Then sit down."

I hadn't heard this tone of voice from Vespucci before. He was in Boss mode. I took a seat in the chair I'd sat in previously, angling it toward Vespucci's desk. Marco sat opposite me, on the love seat where he and Maggie had been sitting while I interviewed them. Donovan and Joey stood in the back, ready to move in an instant.

"Jon, I'm extremely disappointed. I hired you to write a love story for my daughter, and instead I come home and you're fighting with my future son-in-law. How should I take this?"

At the moment I didn't have a good response, so I remained silent.

"If you were in my position, what would you do? Is Marco right? Have you developed feelings for my daughter? Are you trying to cause trouble between her and Marco?"

I had already said as much. I saw no purpose in adding to it, so I responded with a nod. I could feel the blood throbbing in the areas of my face where Marco's fist had connected. I wondered if I should ask for ice to keep the swelling down.

Vespucci turned his attention to Marco. "Marco, I don't appreciate you bringing violence into my house. Under my own roof, you attacked a man I hired." Marco accepted the verbal slap in silence, though he was seething. "Jon, I don't appreciate you stirring up the past, encouraging my daughter to ask questions about things she'll never understand. She only needs to know what I decide she should know."

Vespucci's eyes traveled over my head and settled on Donovan. "I want to remind you both where you are." As if on cue, Joey reached inside his jacket and pulled out his .357 Magnum. The sight of the gun created an immediate, overwhelming sense of fear in my belly. I felt Donovan tense up behind me. Sure we understood the threat, Joey put the gun back. A self-satisfied smirk crossed Marco's face.

"Jon, I hired you on Cranston's recommendation, believing that the product you provided would be a unique, wonderful gift for my daughter. And to be honest, upon meeting you, I just liked you, which is something that doesn't happen with many people. But over the last couple of months, I'm afraid you have broken the trust I must have for anyone I let into my home. I expect those I invite into my home to use the utmost discretion. I don't believe you have information that would be of any great assistance to someone trying to do harm to me, or my family, but I consider it a direct offense if you pass on to anyone even one ounce of information you have obtained about my family." Vespucci paused. "Do you understand what I am referring to?"

I was wracking my brain for what he could consider my breach of ethics but could not come up with any good reason why he would think that. I shook my head.

"Well, it started with your attendance at my godmother's funeral, Carol Zefarelli. Ever since then, I've wondered what you were doing there."

"But that was a total coincidence, Tony, like I said. Nothing more."

"That is what you said. But given everything since, I have to reconsider your words." He picked up a picture from his desk, tossing it toward me. "Do you know who this is?"

I stood up, dizzy from moving too quickly. I grabbed the chair, Donovan coming from behind to steady me. I got my balance and then crossed the few steps to the desk, picking the picture up. I felt sick looking at the image of Williams coming out the front door of our hotel. Watching my face, Vespucci saw the recognition. He picked up several more pictures, slowly flicking them one at a time in my direction. More pictures of Williams. Someone must have gotten on a rooftop in a building across from the hotel, because several of the pictures had been taken through our hotel window and showed Williams standing in the room with Donovan and Luci and me. The last picture was of the three of us sitting in the coffee shop with Detective Hunt.

"Why are you talking to these people?"

"Tony, I can explain. None of this is what you think."

Vespucci put his hand up. "No explanations needed. We're too late in the game for that. I'd say speaking to the FBI and the police are most definitely not necessary for you to complete your assignment for my daughter's love story. Wouldn't you agree?"

I needed to understand why this was happening. "If you hired me to write this story, why would you follow me?"

"He didn't. I did." Marco's voice came at me from the side. "I haven't trusted you from day one. I knew you were a weasel. I was the one who put guys on you. I knew I'd find something sooner or later."

Marco's words hit me like bullets. In that moment, I hated him with a passion I couldn't recall ever feeling so strongly toward anyone, not even the Professor or the Frenchman. Overcome with red-hot anger, I lunged at Marco, a right hook shooting at his head as hard as I could muster. My fist connected with his left temple, knocking him completely out of his chair, toppling him to the ground. Luck had thrown me on top of him this time, giving me the advantage. If I was going down, I wasn't going down without a fight, or at least not without feeling like I'd gotten in a few good shots. I was through being everybody's punching bag. Marco writhed beneath me, trying to get some leverage with his hips and legs against the ground. My left connected with his cheekbone when I suddenly felt large hands gripping my arms, yanking me off. As Donovan wrapped his arms around me to hold me back, the initial rush of adrenaline disappeared and I felt empty and spent. I didn't have anything left. Marco scrambled to his feet taking a step toward me, but Donovan immediately put himself between us. Marco reached inside his jacket, unsheathing his revolver, pointing it at us.

"Put it away." Vespucci's voice brooked no argument.

A red welt lit the skin above Marco's left eye. Seething, he held the gun for several seconds. My eyes focused on the gun barrel. It looked much bigger pointed at me. I took two quick steps, placing myself between Donovan and Marco's gun. As scared as I was, I wasn't about to let Donovan take a bullet because of my actions. From the corner of my eye, I could see Joey's .357 aimed at Marco. Doubt crept into Marco's eyes. He glanced at Joey's .357, then at Vespucci.

Marco slowly replaced his gun into his shoulder holster. Joey did the same.

"Jon," Vespucci said quietly.

I looked toward Vespucci, trying to catch my breath. My chest was still heaving.

"You will go home without saying goodbye to anyone. Tomorrow, you will call my daughter and tell her that you have to go back to Los Angeles and cannot complete the project for personal reasons. You will never contact my family again."

I thought my life had been in the toilet before Vespucci hired me, and now it was even worse. I had trouble focusing on Vespucci's words. His voice sounded like an echo.

"You do not want to know what will happen if you don't follow my instructions. Do you understand?"

I felt crushed. Everything had ended. I nodded, in defeat. I turned on my heel toward the door, my feet heavy as lead. Donovan tracked with me, placing his hand on my shoulder in a sign of solidarity, following one step behind. As I passed Joey, I nodded, trying to let him know that I appreciated the help he'd given me over the last few months. Joey didn't respond. I stopped steps from the door, turning around to Vespucci. "I'm sorry." I turned to leave when I heard Marco explode behind me.

"That's it? You're going to let him leave?"

I ducked and turned back as I heard steps coming my way, Marco moving in our direction. Joey crossed between us blocking Marco's path, shoving his palm into Marco's chest.

"Enough!" Vespucci bellowed.

It was the first time I'd heard him raise his voice. Marco immediately stepped back away from us. I stared at Vespucci, locking eyes with him. He returned my look, showing his anger, but there was also something else. Pain? I wasn't sure.

"Joey, please see Jon and Donovan out."

Joey left Marco standing in the middle of the room, staring at our backs as we left the library and turned down the hallway. Faintly, I could make out Maggie's voice coming from the kitchen, entertaining Sabrina, though I could not hear what she was saying. I didn't want to leave without saying goodbye and not giving her an explanation, but Joey's square frame kept us moving toward the front door. Before I could think of anything else, Donovan and I were in the front yard, following the path leading to the outer gate. Not a word was said. I reached the gate first and opened it onto the street, followed only a step behind by Donovan. Standing at the gate about to close it and, in effect, end the Vespucci chapter of my life, Joey glanced at my face, seeing something there that gave him pause. "Watch your back." With a respectful nod toward Donovan, Joey closed the gate.

Donovan and I stood there for several moments. Finally, I asked, "Taxi or walk?"

"Walk. Easier to see if anyone is following us."

We turned in the direction of the hotel, neither one of us speaking the first couple of blocks, processing everything we'd just been through. I called Luci, getting his voicemail. I left a message telling him we were on our way back to the hotel but nothing more. He'd find out soon enough what had happened.

Finally, Donovan broke the silence. "Thanks."

"For what?"

"You know what."

I tried to play it down. "Marco's fight was with me. I knew he wouldn't fire his gun in Vespucci's house."

"No, you didn't."

He was right, I didn't.

Neither of us talking, the traffic of Brooklyn filling our ears, we walked slowly, staring at the low-rise homes, the neighborhood shifting from bourgeois, upper middle class to middle class to working class, the distance between the houses diminishing as they became more narrow, less detailed, and needing more care and attention. Apartment buildings began to replace the blocks of houses, small businesses appearing on the corners. Lost in my thoughts, I sensed Donovan was diligently watching our surroundings, eyeing every passing car, checking out the sparse number of pedestrians crossing our path as we moved toward the hotel.

I went over the events of the evening. I now realized Marco had wanted me out of the picture from the start. I recalled my first meeting with him at the factory and his threatening nature even in the early stages of the interview process. Given what I'd discovered tonight, I wondered when Marco had decided to put a tail on me. I was sure now he had hired the guy to have my room bugged. I was also convinced that everything Mosconi told me about Marco was true. After what had happened tonight, I would never be able to tell Maggie or Vespucci the truth. The opportunity was gone. Maggie was going to marry Marco. We would fly back to Los Angeles. The end.

But not really and there was this: I knew Marco's secret. And now he knew that I knew. How long was he going to let me live with his secret? Not long, I was sure.

As we closed in on the hotel, I wondered what my next move should be. I was sure if Maggie discovered Marco had a child in Europe by a fifteen-year-old girl, she'd have second thoughts about going through with the wedding. I was even more confident that Vespucci would do much more than just stop the wedding if he discovered Marco was an informant for the FBI. But was Marco an informant for the FBI? The baby I was now sure of, but the FBI charge was more complicated. I had no proof. Everything was circumstantial.

Donovan and I passed through the doors into the hotel. I was suddenly hit with the silly thought that I might have to find another way to make a living. Until recently, I had successfully finished every story I'd ever been hired to write. But now I had two failed projects back to back. Maybe the writing was on the wall. Then I figured it might not matter because Marco could end my writing career for good.

A familiar voice broke my thoughts.

"Jon Fixx."

I turned in the direction of Luci's voice, spotting him walking out of the restaurant and bar toward us. As he approached he said, "I hope you're night has been as productive as mine. You'll both like what I found—" He stopped in midsentence when he got close enough to see the new bruises on my face. Alarmed, he asked, "What happened?"

"Long story. I'm starving. Donovan?"

"Me too. Guns make me hungry."

"Guns? What guns?" Luci asked sharply.

"Let's eat and I'll explain," I said.

Luci did a one-eighty and followed us back into the restaurant. We walked the length of the bar and took our seats at a white square table in the corner easily out of earshot of anyone in the restaurant.

"What happened?"

"Marco," I said.

Luci stared at us both, waiting for more.

I did a recap for Luci of the evening's events, starting with our arrival at Vespucci's house and my initial discussion with Maggie. How I ended up in the study alone with Marco and Maggie while Donovan was entertaining Sabrina. How I pushed Marco over the edge.

Luci pointed at my face. "That's when he did that?"

I nodded. "I'm sure what Mosconi told us is all true. Marco's reactions were those of a guilty man trying to hide something. Maggie has no idea. I don't think Vespucci knows either."

"We'll come back to that. Tell me about the guns."

I resumed my story, telling him what happened when Vespucci entered the picture. I told him Marco had pictures of us with Williams and Detective Hunt and had told Vespucci that we were working with the authorities.

"And Vespucci still let you two walk out of there?" Luci asked.

Donovan added, "I've been thinking about that myself."

"Vespucci fired me. He wants me out of the city tomorrow."

"You're lucky all he did was fire you," Luci said.

"I'm not sure what to do here. Vespucci's instructions left no room for interpretation. He wants me to leave, and I don't want to anger him further. But what about Maggie?"

Donovan and Luci remained silent, giving me room to answer my own question. Suddenly I was overcome with the desire to lay my head down on the table and go to sleep. I sighed. "She's not my problem, right? So." I submitted to my exhaustion, dropping my head on the table, taking a long breath and exhaling.

"Want to call it quits?" Luci asked quietly.

With my forehead resting against the table, I nodded my head, forcing the tablecloth to scrunch up under my skin.

"What if I told you I got confirmation that Mosconi's story is true?"

I raised my head slightly off the table, looking up at Luci, my chin inches from the tabletop. "What?"

"My guy did some more checking for me. About three years ago, Marco Balducci was arrested in Palermo for murdering a man. But almost as quickly, he was let go. No charges were ever filed."

I was now sitting up straight in my chair, renewed energy coursing through my body.

"According to my source, the dead man's wife and teenage daughter disappeared within days of the murder. The girl was pregnant." He paused for dramatic effect.

"With Marco's kid?" I asked, almost breathless.

Luci nodded.

"Did Marco kill them too?"

"No. This is where it gets good. The Italian government took them under protection."

Whatever I had expected Luci to say, this wasn't it. I sat back in my chair, exhaling. "Wait. Are you saying Marco's working for the Italian government?"

"Not exactly."

Donovan and I sat rapt.

"It's what we thought, sort of. For years, the FBI has been trying to figure out how to get information on Tony Vespucci's organization. They've had next to no luck getting their hands on anything incriminating. Vespucci has done a better job than any recent don keeping his soldiers in line, and silent. When Marco got his teenage housekeeper pregnant, it started a chain of events that made him vulnerable. When the girl's father found out what happened, he went to Marco, demanding he marry his daughter. A fight ensued and Marco beat the guy to death. The Italian authorities moved in, arresting him almost immediately." Luci paused for a moment, then continued. "But according to my source, the FBI was behind the arrest, and that's why he was let go. They made a deal with Marco. Spend his life in an Italian jail for murder, or come back to the States and help them gather enough information to bring down Vespucci and his Mafia chain of command."

My mind was working overdrive. "That's why Williams wanted me out of the way. He didn't want me interfering with the investigation."

"Exactly. Williams wasn't involved with the original investigation, but when he started snooping around, tracking you for his cousin, he got wind of who you were working for and got himself reassigned to the investigation in New York. Higher command must have put him in charge of getting you out of the way."

Suddenly, a realization hit me like a lightning bolt. I slapped my hands down on the table. "That means Marco's entire affair with Maggie was a setup to get him close to

Vespucci! The marriage is a sham. Marco doesn't love her."

Luci nodded almost imperceptibly, as if to say, that could only truly be answered by Marco himself, but given all the facts, yeah, probably.

"But you do, don't you?" Donovan asked, his voice quiet.

I felt my companions' eyes on me. I nodded. Yes, I do.

We sat there quietly, considering the implications of everything we'd just pieced together.

"Still want to go home tomorrow?" Luci asked.

I recognized that every moment we stayed in New York beyond the morning placed us in harm's way. Vespucci had given me a direct order to leave the city. The FBI wanted me gone. Marco wanted me dead. If I was in danger, then so were Luci and Donovan. Donovan must have read my mind.

"Don't worry about me. There ain't nothing waiting for me back in L.A. I'm all in."

"Me too, Jon."

I could see the commitment and loyalty reflected in their eyes, strength as well. "Then, we're staying. I'm going to finish this story if it's the last thing I do."

As I said those words, I realized I very well might get my wish.

13
Early November
New York 3rd Trip

Having collectively decided to ignore Vespucci's direct order to leave New York, we settled into the hotel restaurant for dinner and planning. After ordering our food, we huddled around the table, laying out everything we knew, what pieces of the puzzle were facts, what was inference, and what was guesswork.

"We know for certain Marco Balducci got a teenage girl pregnant and killed her father. My guy verified what Mosconi told us," Luci said.

"Two sources providing matching information. Safe to assume it's fact. But did your guy give you anything to prove Marco is working for the FBI?" I asked.

"No."

Donovan raised his hand, as if we were in a classroom. "I know I'm the new guy here, so I don't want to step on your toes, but you don't have a government clearance for classified information, do you?" Luci shook his head. "So why is this guy so helpful? How can you trust his information?"

"He's been studying kung fu with me for over eight years. I met him in Philly back when my wife was in medical school. I was teaching at a local dojo, and his ten-year-old daughter was in my youth class. At the time, I'd never trained any of the government agency guys—FBI, CIA, NSA. He asked me to train him privately. I worked with him for over two years before I actually knew what he did for a living. By the time I started to piece it together, he'd already introduced me to a couple of his colleagues. Soon after, I found myself instructing for the CIA and the FBI on a regular basis. The pay is good, and I find most of the trainees are well disciplined, though some of them are a little too John Wayne for my taste." Luci paused for emphasis. "I trust this man with my life. Any information he's passing on to me is accurate, at least to the best of his knowledge."

When Luci finished speaking, Donovan turned to me. "Please explain again why you need me here? Luci seems more than qualified to do my job."

"I wasn't sure Luci could provide twenty-four seven security. And it just felt right to me."

Luci added, "You definitely look more intimidating than me. Just putting the sign up in the yard often stops most burglaries."

"Don't get me wrong, fellas, I'm glad to be here. It's just that when Jon offered me the job, I didn't realize I'd become part of a plot straight out of a Jason Bourne movie."

"You're very much one of the team, Donovan," I said sincerely. I looked at Luci. "Can you get the name of the girl in Italy?"

"Already on it. I should have it by morning."

"Good. I'll need that."

"But you need to know he cautioned me, and this guy is not prone to exaggeration," Luci advised. "If we're correct about Marco, the FBI has a mole near the top of one of the largest Mafia organizations in the U.S., and it's taken years of work and planning. If the FBI has even the slightest concern that we could screw that up, they'll take us out in the blink of an eye. Then there's Marco Balducci to consider. Think what will happen to him if he's exposed. Marco will go to any length to protect his secret. Finally, we've got Tony Vespucci to deal with. He's a wild card. Given the way he behaved tonight, he's not a safe bet. We better have ironclad proof to hand him. Marco Balducci is engaged to his daughter. If we do this, and we're wrong, we won't be leaving New York."

The table fell silent, all of us considering Luci's words. He was right, and we all knew it. Our internal musings were interrupted by the arrival of our dinner. The server quickly circled the table, setting down a plate in front of each of us. Far hungrier than I had anticipated, I dug into my pasta without another word, using my fork to twirl up a large swirl of noodles and stuff them into my mouth. Luci and Donovan followed suit, a large steak before Donovan, salmon in front of Luci. For the next few minutes, none of us spoke while we ate. After my initial bout of hunger was satiated, I sat back, taking a sip of my water. I set my fork down on the table. "If Luci's source is correct, the FBI will go to any length to protect Marco, right? And Marco will do anything to protect his own life, right? So all we need to do is make him implicate himself."

"Just like that?" Luci asked pragmatically. "Do you have a plan for this simple task?"

"I'm not sure, but I'm working on it."

"Is that supposed to be reassuring?"

Donovan added, "Let's not forget Jon put Marco on notice tonight. My guess'd be that Jon's demise is at the top of Marco's "To Do" list right now."

"That's why we to need act immediately."

We skipped dessert, paid the bill, and left the restaurant. Entering the lobby of the hotel, we were on high alert, all three of us scanning our surroundings for anything suspicious. Every moment we spent in New York was dangerous now. But even if we left in the morning for Los Angeles, I knew I'd always be looking over my shoulder for Marco's payback. That's why I wanted to put my plan in motion as soon as possible. The only problem was that I didn't have a plan yet. We piled into the elevator, climbed to our floor, and exited cautiously. Donovan wouldn't let me leave the elevator until he made sure the hallway was clear. Moving quickly, Donovan stopped before our door, checking his tell to make sure no one had been inside. Not seeing anything out of place, he unlocked the door and we disappeared into the safety of our room.

We immediately sprawled out. Donovan dropped into his cot near the door, and Luci slid into the lounge chair by the window so he could check out the view. I fell onto the bed closest to the door, nervous and exhausted. After only a moment in that position, I turned my head toward Luci, watching him gaze out the window, suddenly remembering the pictures Vespucci had shoved in my face. I quickly stood up, crossing to the window and stared at the buildings across from us as if I might be able to spot the perpetrators of the damning pictures. Unable to see anything incriminating, I stepped back from the window and closed the shades from any prying eyes.

Luci got up out of his chair and rolled onto the second bed. Within minutes, the sound of even breathing came at me from both sides of the room, my friends both falling into an easy sleep. If either of them was worried about our currently tenuous position, neither showed any sign of it. Unlike my relaxed co-conspirators, I couldn't settle down. Pushing my tiredness aside, accepting that it was going to be a long night, I got to work. I grabbed my computer and powered it up. From the moment Vespucci had asked me to leave his house and not return, my thoughts of Maggie and her predicament weighed on me. I now had proof that Marco was a father. If Luci's guy came through in the morning, I'd even have a name for the mother. The urge to expose him to Maggie was overpowering.

I began reading the rough outline of Maggie and Marco's love story. A thought occurred to me. My fingers began to trip across the keyboard, the germs of an idea taking shape. I decided even if my patron had fired me, I was going to finish the project whether the key players wanted to read it or not, and I was going to write the truth. But this time, unlike in the case of the Nickels clan, I was fully aware of what the consequences could be. The clock ticked away, the regular breathing of Donovan and Luci keeping me company as I typed. I jumped back and forth between my notes and the rough draft, inspired as I wrote. As I lost track of the time—a good indication I was in the flow—Maggie and Marco's love story took shape on the screen. I glanced at the clock in the corner of the computer screen. It was well past midnight, but I still had a long way to go. I began writing the section covering Marco's long hiatus outside the States. I'd had trouble with this section previously because I had a dearth of information about Marco's time in Italy, so I used poetic license to fill in the gaps and make the story flow. Marco became a young, savvy entrepreneur on Italian soil, taking the family business to a new level of economic success while developing connections with powerful politicians. Women came and went. But after several years in country, he was getting bored. He needed excitement, thrills, something more. So maybe it was boredom, maybe he'd found his first true connection since leaving the States, maybe it was just an undeniable urge that made him want to sleep with a fifteen-year-old girl.

As I focused on Marco, my cheek started to throb, feeling Marco's fist connect with it over and over. I heard Vespucci's voice telling me to get out as Marco began laughing hysterically, a hyena-like sound that hurt my ears. After a few moments, I raised my hands to my ears, the sound of his laughter getting louder. I knew I was imagining it, but the sound in my head was real. The touch of my palms to my ears shut the laughter off, and Marco's face disappeared from view.

"Jon, you okay?"

It was Donovan's voice. I had been working in the dark,

the glow of my screen the only light in the room, so it was hard for me to see him. I turned on the small nightstand beside my bed. Donovan was up on one elbow, shadows riding across his face. Sensing movement from the other direction, I turned to see Luci's eyes open as well.

"Yeah. Why?"

"You yelled 'Stop it.'"

"Marco was laughing at me." As soon as the words came out of my mouth, I realized I sounded foolish, maybe even a little bit crazy.

"Marco?" Luci asked.

Sitting up, Donovan asked, "You sure you're okay?"

"Yeah, yeah. Forget it," I answered. "I'm sorry for waking you guys up. When I'm writing, sometimes I get lost in my thoughts and I talk to myself. It's nothing."

Donovan and Luci stared at me for several seconds, trying to decide whether they should take my word at face value. Finally, they exchanged looks, both deciding it was safe to go back to bed. Their heads returned to their respective sleeping positions, and soon I was surrounded by the sounds of regular breathing again. I returned to my keyboard, my fingers tapping the keys, knowing exactly what I wanted to write. I spent the remainder of the night finishing up the story, laying it all out with an inspired hand, leaving certain questions unanswered, but with a subtle finger pointing in the right direction. By 4 a.m., I had put the finishing touches on the "Love Story of Marco and Maggie." It was all there, everything I had learned, as well as my own suppositions as to what I believed to be the truth.

My eyes felt heavy. During my nightlong jag of writing, only once did I question my motives. What if I was wrong? What if Maggie and Marco were truly in love? What then? For her part, I was sure she was in love with him. If my plan went without a hitch, Maggie was in for a rude awakening. I even considered the possibility that she would hate me for being the one who uncovered Marco as a fraud. Knowing I would be causing Maggie pain, even if for the right reasons, didn't sit well with me. The one question I had no answer for was whether Marco was in love with Maggie. Had he come back to the States and searched her out as part of his plan to get closer to Vespucci? Or had he run into Maggie by accident, and his involvement with her just happened alongside his private scheme to eventually rat out Vespucci? I'd been writing these stories for too many years not to feel guilty that my goal here was to do the opposite of what I was always hired to do. I was trying to break a couple up, not bring them closer together. After a moment of reflection, I pushed the thought aside and went back to the keyboard to finish up.

During the night, my plan of action had crystallized, though I still wasn't sure about the execution. I would need Donovan and Luci to agree because it would be dangerous. My fingers came to a halt. I'd typed the final sentence. Surprisingly, I felt at peace for the first time in a long time. I had completed the job Vespucci hired me to do back in September. He'd wanted me to write their love story by December, and I had done it with time to spare. I'm not sure "Love Story" was the accurate terminology any longer, because I had turned their story into a confessional device, a biographical exposé of the life and times of Marco Balducci. For a moment, a smile of satisfaction crossed my face, the sense of accomplishment too good to ignore.

My self-satisfaction didn't last long, though, as I began to think about what else needed to be done. Was I ready to expose Marco to Vespucci and Maggie? Would Vespucci believe me? Would he cooperate with my plan? What would the FBI do when they got wind of what I was doing? How would Marco react? What was I missing? What would the unintended consequences be? How could we stay out of harm's way? With these questions chipping away at that brief moment of peace I'd felt, I fell asleep staring at my computer screen, Maggie's name glowing in print before my eyes.

I woke with a cramp in my neck, my head hanging half off the pillow, my right arm underneath my body at a weird angle. I slowly extracted my arm, which had fallen asleep. I rubbed my eyes, feeling like I'd been drugged. My computer rested on the bed beside my head, the screen saver unabashedly promoting Apple computers as the Apple icon danced around the screen. I reached over, hitting the keyboard to disable the screensaver. My writing jumped out at me. In the lower right corner, the clock read 8:15 a.m. I'd slept for a little over four hours. That explained my drugged feeling. The final words I'd written before passing out were, "The End. . . . Maybe."

I didn't remember writing that. During the late night, the brief halcyon feeling of completing the story must have made me a little heady, allowing me to write something so pat. Whatever positive feelings I had during the night had been replaced with feelings of foreboding. "Execute" was the word of the day, the double entendre not lost on me. According to *The American Heritage Dictionary*, "execute" had several definitions: 1) to put into effect, carry out; 2) to perform, do; 3) to create in accordance with a prescribed design; 4) to make valid, as by signing; 5) to perform or carry out what is required by; 6) to put to death, especially by carrying out a lawful sentence; 7) to run. In my mind, definitions 1 and 6 were the most apropos to my situation because if I didn't handle 1 properly, then 6 might be the result, minus the "lawful" part. What I planned on doing would heavily impact several lives, including my friends and me, so I needed to seriously consider my actions.

I hit save and pulled the thumb drive out of the computer and stuck it in my pocket. I looked around the room, still dark with the curtain shut. Noises emanated from the bathroom, the sound of the shower pattering against the tub. I climbed out of the bed, crossing to the window and pulling the shade slightly to peek outside. The brightness blinded me momentarily. I let my eyes adjust and scoped the street and the buildings across from us, as if I might see a person holding a camera staring at our room, a big red arrow hanging in the air showing me where to look. But I saw nothing. I dropped the curtain and turned around, no longer hearing the shower. The room was quiet. As I stood there, I realized that if anyone was watching, we needed to look like we were leaving. I crossed back to the window and opened the curtains. I grabbed my small travel pack and threw it on the bed to begin packing. Luci's voice interrupted my actions.

"What are you doing? Don't you think we should keep that window closed, just in case?"

"Whoever's watching us should know we're packing to leave. Right? That's what we're supposed to be doing."

Luci considered that.

"Where's Donovan?"

"He went to see an old friend of his from his military days. Guy lives in Queens. Donovan was out of here at 6:00 a.m. sharp."

Donovan had made it clear he wouldn't leave my side, and up until now, he hadn't done so. This was not the time to set a new precedent. "He's on a social visit?" I asked. "Don't you think it's a little dangerous for any of us to be going out alone?"

I was met with raised eyebrows. "You think Donovan can't handle himself? He'll do a better job taking care of himself than I could. He made me assure him I wouldn't let you leave until he got back. And he's not on a social visit."

"What do you mean?"

"He felt we were riding a bit light in the protection department, so he made a couple of calls to remedy that."

It took me a moment to understand what Luci was talking about, and then suddenly it dawned on me what "riding light" referred to. "You mean?" With my right hand, I imitated shooting a pistol.

Luci nodded. I'd never even touched a gun before, not once in my life. I was hoping I wouldn't have to today.

"Then I guess that means you guys have made up your minds?"

"Minds for what?"

"To stay. To do this."

"Jon, for me, you don't need to ask. You know that. As for Donovan, honestly, I don't think he'd leave even if you told him you couldn't pay him anymore. I think he's having fun."

I sat down on the edge of the bed. "If we stay today, it could get bad."

"Do you have any other option?"

"Sure," I said, not convincingly.

"You made your choice yesterday when you showed Marco you know about his kid. Even if you go back to Los Angeles, do you think that will be enough for him? You're a liability, regardless. If you don't neutralize Marco now, you'll never be safe. And if he's waiting for you in a dark alley, his method will be far more definitive than Nick Nickels Jr.'s."

I knew Luci spoke the truth. I'd already considered everything he was saying, but it just sounded worse when he said it aloud. "What about Izzy?"

"If I call her, she'll definitely come out and help."

I glanced up just in time to catch Luci's grin.

"Seriously, Luci, how would she feel about this?"

"She'd never forgive me if she thought I left you hanging."

A single knock at the door interrupted us. Several seconds passed, followed by two more knocks in quick succession, our agreed upon secret code.

Luci crossed to the door, looked through the peephole, and opened it. Donovan hurried in, carrying a double-lined paper grocery bag cleanly folded three times at the top.

"Hey, Jon, good to see you awake." Donovan set the package down on the dresser across from the beds.

"How did it go?" Luci asked.

"Mission accomplished. Take a look."

Donovan unfurled the top of the grocery bag. Luci whistled at what he saw. I jumped up, crossed the few extra steps, leaning in to get a view of two, shiny, black Beretta pistols and several boxes of ammunition at the bottom of the bag. I took a step back, the contents repelling me momentarily, a sick feeling in my stomach. The sight of the guns brought home the reality of our situation. The whole thing felt surreal.

"I guess we're doing this."

Donovan and Luci both nodded.

"What's the plan?"

"You do have a plan. Right?" Luci asked.

I nodded, glancing at the open window. "We should check out of the hotel and head to the airport." Their surprised looks forced me to add, "We're supposed to be leaving, so let's leave. Once we're out of here, I'll tell you what I'm thinking."

Without further discussion, Luci and Donovan packed up. We didn't know if we were being watched, and if we were, I wasn't sure who it might be, whether it was Vespucci's people, someone working for Marco, or the FBI who had taken the pictures. Regardless, we didn't want to take any chances. If anyone was watching, I wanted him to think we were leaving. Once we were in the hallway, I started my plan in motion. I called Cranston and gave him a short explanation of what I needed. Cranston said he'd take care of my request immediately. I hung up, having executed the first step. Carrying our bags to the front desk, I checked us out and we walked into the chilly November morning. A taxi was standing at the curb. The driver climbed out, waving to us, asking if we needed a ride. I waved the guy off. I wanted to outline my plan to Luci and Donovan on the way to the airport, and though I felt I was becoming paranoid, I didn't want to take any chances. We stood on the curb for thirty minutes before a limo pulled up. A smartly dressed, trim older woman climbed out of the driver's door.

"Jon Fixx?" she asked, a raspy smoker's voice directed our way.

I nodded.

"I'm Cheryl, your driver, at your service. JFK coming right up." As she spoke, she hustled around the car to open the door for us. The three of us froze momentarily as Cheryl stood at the ready with the back door to the limo ajar. Letting a woman open the car door was a first, I was sure, for all of us. I felt the urge to replace Cheryl at the door and ask her to get in. Hesitantly, I climbed into the back seat, unable to shake the feeling that what I was doing was slightly wrong. Luci and Donovan followed suit, the strange look on their faces indicating they were feeling the same way. The door closed behind us, followed moments later by Cheryl climbing into the front seat and driving the limo away from the curb. With Cheryl at my back, I sat across from Donovan and Luci, who were staring at me, waiting expectantly.

Before I could speak, Donovan patted the grocery bag beside him, and said, "Just a guess, but I don't think I'll get very far with my luggage at the airport."

"I know. Let me tell you my plan, and then you guys can tell me whether you think I'm crazy or not."

Luci smiled. "We already know you're crazy. The right question is whether you are deluded. Tell us your plan and then we'll decide. But," Luci leaned forward as he spoke, dropping his voice to a whisper, "how do you know we're safe talking here?"

I looked over my shoulder at Cheryl, who appeared completely oblivious to our existence. "Cheryl works for Cranston. I told him I needed a favor and would explain it later. He was happy to accommodate."

Luci relaxed, leaning back. "All right, let's hear it."

I took a breath and began to explain what I had outlined during the night. I described what I'd written and how I planned to utilize it. Up until the time Vespucci asked me to leave, I had harbored a belief that underneath it all Vespucci hired me to do exactly what I'd done: uncover dirt about Marco. But Vespucci's reaction the night before, and his willingness to believe Marco, forced me to reconsider this theory. It also made it harder for me to implement my plan. If I had Vespucci's trust, I could go to him privately to discuss what I'd discovered. As things stood, that was not an option. So I was going to improvise. "Somehow, I'm going to corner Marco and get him to tell the truth," I said.

Donovan blinked, not saying a word. Luci glanced at Donovan, then back at me. "Did I miss something? I didn't hear a plan."

"I'm not there yet."

Donovan asked, "Do you think Maggie knows anything about the child in Italy?"

"I'm betting my career that she doesn't. And neither does Vespucci."

Luci said, "We're all in agreement about that. But what's this plan you're willing to bet your career on?"

Hearing an edge in his voice brought home to me how real the danger was. I took a deep breath, getting it straight in my head. For the remainder of our trip to the airport, I outlined my plan, explaining who all the key players were, what the timeline would be, and how best to execute it. We were minutes from the airport when I finally stopped talking. Luci and Donovan were staring at me, the look on their faces a combination of respect and utter disbelief.

Luci asked Donovan, "What do you think?"

"I think you were right. He's crazy and delusional." Donovan paused a moment, then added, "It's gonna take some doing. And it's dangerous, mostly for you, Jon."

"I know. But do I have a choice?"

"How do you know Vespucci will bite?" Luci asked.

"Once I tell him what I'm going to tell him, will he have a choice? If you were Vespucci and Marco worked for you and was going to marry your daughter, what would you do?"

For a moment we were silent, considering Vespucci's position.

"Are you sure you'll be able to draw Marco out?" asked Donovan.

"I think that'll be the easy part. When he finds out I haven't left, he'll hunt me down, unless I tell him where I am, and then he'll come willingly."

"The FBI. They're the fly in the ointment," Luci said.

I agreed. Luci was right. The FBI and Williams were the unpredictable element in my plan, and I wasn't sure how to deal with them. I needed to keep them at bay, away from the action. They could ruin everything, and if they showed up too soon, I'd never be able to prove to Vespucci that it wasn't my doing that the FBI was watching me, or him. The car suddenly came to a stop. I hadn't noticed we were at the airport I was so focused on our planning.

Cheryl lowered the window separation between the driver and the passengers. "We're here, Mr. Fixx. What are your instructions?"

"Were we followed?"

"Yep. Six cars back, Lincoln Town Car."

Luci and Donovan scrambled to turn around in their seats to see the car she was referring to. "That's FBI," Luci said.

"Yep."

"Agreed," Donovan added.

"Cheryl, we're going to get out here. Can you lose the guy when you leave and meet us back at Terminal 6 in thirty minutes?" I asked.

"Not a problem," she answered, her voice so raspy I imagined a cigarette permanently hanging out of her mouth.

We climbed out of the car, our bags in tow. Donovan paused as he stepped out, leaving the grocery bag lying on the back seat. He looked at me, as if to ask what he should do with it. I motioned with my hand for him to leave it.

With an uneasy look on his face, he climbed from the back seat and closed the door behind him. We walked across the wide airport sidewalk through the sliding glass doors into JFK. Crossing the space of the intake area, we headed in the direction of departures. I watched the Lincoln from the corner of my eye. Cheryl's limo had pulled away from the curb as soon as we disappeared through the airport doors. As we walked farther into the bowels of the structure, the Lincoln finally pulled away from the curb, mixing in with the other airport traffic and disappearing from my angle of view. I stopped in my tracks, Donovan and Luci following my lead.

Luci said, "If the FBI is getting their information from Marco, as we think it is, it's going to be tough to get to him without them nearby."

I nodded. "I know. I've considered that."

"And?" Donovan asked.

"I think we can use it to our advantage."

"Oh, really?" Luci said, with a hint of sarcasm.

"Does my service include bonus pay if I have to serve jail time?"

I looked sharply at Donovan.

"Just kidding."

"Donovan brings up a good point. There's no room for error here."

We stood in the airport, our travel bags on our shoulders, travelers of all ages, shapes, and sizes moving around us. I turned in the direction of Terminal 6 and started walking. It took us almost fifteen minutes to get to our destination. The three of us spread out as we walked, keeping an eye on our surroundings, tracking for anyone suspicious. Just as we stepped outside of Terminal 6, the limo pulled up to the curb. Cheryl hustled out of the limo around to the passenger side.

"Any problems?" I asked.

"Nope. This was my second pass. I didn't want to stop at

the curb and draw attention."

As we climbed in, Luci asked, "Are you sure you weren't followed?"

Disdain in her voice, Cheryl responded, "Is the sun out now?"

Donovan and I chuckled at her response. We climbed into the car one after the other.

Cheryl settled into the driver's seat, looking in her rear-view. "Where to, Mr. Fixx?"

"Cranston's office."

Cheryl nodded, pulling quickly away from the curb. The limo slid in and out of traffic, Cheryl driving it more like a sports car than the tank it was. I spent the trip going over my game plan again with Donovan and Luci, discussing any possible problems, trying to see all of the angles. I was now past the point of no return. A big part of me wanted to do this to save face, to save my reputation, to show Vespucci that if I was anything, one thing I wasn't was a snitch. I had to clear my name with him. Then there was Maggie. For the time being, I didn't want to think about her. My motivations became muddled as soon as I threw Maggie into the mix.

After close to an hour in the limo, we were back in Manhattan. Cheryl pulled into an alley and drove up to the rear of a tall office building. She rolled down the glass partition. "Mr. Fixx, this is the back entrance to Mr. Jefferson's office. He said you should enter here."

"Thank you, Cheryl."

"Mr. Jefferson asked me to wait here for you. He said I'm to be at your disposal all day." As soon as she finished speaking, she jumped out of the limo and opened the door for us. We climbed out and headed for the utility entrance, waving our thanks to Cheryl as we disappeared inside. Entering a hallway covered in drab gray paint, we passed doors leading to the working bowels of the building, some locked, some open, revealing dusty machinery. Then, like magic, we reached a small unmarked doorway that opened into the large, presentable lobby we had entered only days before. Taking a quick look around to make sure no one was lurking in the shadows, we crossed to the elevators and Luci pushed the call button. It lit up with a servile green glow. Moments later, the ding of arrival sounded in our ears. Luci, Donovan, and I piled in. Without a sound, the doors closed and the elevator seamlessly moved upward into the sky.

I glanced at Donovan, noticing a concerned look on his face. Luci saw it at the same time.

"What?"

Donovan shook his head. "Don't know. Something doesn't feel right."

"What do you mean?" I asked, panic spreading up my spine.

"Just a feeling. My gut. Used to happen to me sometimes before we went on a mission."

Before Luci or I could respond, the elevator doors opened. Trying to keep a lid on my rising panic, I looked from Luci to Donovan and back, both staring out of the elevator focused on the same thing. I looked out and my eyes locked onto Joey's unsmiling face, standing directly in front of the elevator. Donovan moved to block me from stepping out. Luci reached for the panel of buttons, pushing the button to close the elevator doors. Nothing happened. Luci went into action immediately. He relaxed his body, glancing at Donovan as he stepped forward. Donovan read his actions, one step behind. I remained frozen, realizing that Cranston may have betrayed us. Luci's shoulders were slumped, as if he were surrendering. As soon as he cleared the elevator doorframe, he jumped at Joey, catching Joey mid-stomach. As Joey flew backwards, he reached into his coat pocket to grab his gun. At the same time, Donovan cleared the doorway on his way to help Luci when another man slid right up to him, a gun pointed at his temple.

"Stop!" I yelled. I jumped out of the elevator into the

commotion, not wanting it to go any further. Luci had Joey pinned to the ground. An unidentified thug had Donovan frozen with a small pistol to his temple. From the corner of my eye, I saw Vespucci standing several feet away, Cranston only steps behind him.

"Jerry." It was all Vespucci said.

Donovan's handler slowly lowered his gun.

Vespucci turned to me. "Jon, I want to talk with you."

I stared at Cranston, his tall frame hunched over slightly. I couldn't believe the man I trusted with my life would betray me. Luci looked over his shoulder towards me, waiting for a signal. I shrugged my shoulders. He looked down at Joey, then jumping off him in one fluid move, offered his hand to help him up. Joey accepted the gesture. Cranston and Vespucci turned away from us at the same time, moving back in the direction of Cranston's inner offices. I followed their steps, Donovan and Luci a few feet behind me, Joey bringing up the rear. We passed from the main lobby into the office lobby, empty except for the secretary at the front desk.

As Cranston walked past her desk, he said, without looking up, "Shelley, no interruptions please."

"Yes, Mr. Jefferson."

Shelley watched the parade of men pass into Cranston's inner sanctum, the testosterone in the air around us palpable. I lost sight of her as I walked through the double doors and saw New York spread out before us like a 3D floor-to-ceiling canvas. Cranston moved toward the large office chair behind his desk, as Vespucci settled on the edge of it. I looked over my shoulder, Luci and Donovan two steps behind me, with Joey guarding the door. Jerry, Vespucci's other thug, was apparently on the other side of the door, making sure no one came in. I turned back to the power players in the room, waiting. From the moment we'd exited the elevators, I'd been running scenarios in my head, trying to figure out how we ended up here, and the only one I could come up with that made any sense involved Cranston ratting us out, setting us up, breaking my confidence. I hated thinking it, but I could not figure out any other way this would happen. Vespucci interrupted my thoughts.

"Jon, first I want to apologize for last night at my house. For more reasons than I can outline here, it had to be done. Cranston warned me you'd be unpredictable."

Funny, that's what I think about you. "How did you know we were coming here?" Vespucci tilted his head in Cranston's direction.

Picking up the cue, Cranston responded, "It's not what you think, Jon. I feel responsible for what's happening now. When you called me this morning, I needed to bring Tony in on this."

"Cranston, I called you in confidence," I said, unable to hide the hurt and dismay in my voice. I glanced over my shoulder at Joey, who was guarding the door. I didn't appreciate feeling like a prisoner, realizing maybe my friends and I actually were prisoners. Turning back to Vespucci and Cranston, I said, "Whatever you're planning on doing, Tony, this has nothing to do with my friends here, so I'd like you to let Donovan and Luci leave, and we can talk about this alone."

Luci said, "I'm not leaving."

Donovan added, "Me neither."

From my vantage point, I saw Vespucci's face tighten up. Cranston suddenly sat up in his seat. I looked over my shoulder to see what had made them react that way. Somehow, Donovan had slid the few feet across the floor, a Beretta in his hand pointed at Joey's head. I didn't realize he'd grabbed one from the bag. If Joey was scared, it didn't show on his face.

"Donovan, no."

Luci had moved in tandem with Donovan and was beside Joey, disarming him. Joey didn't put up a fight, looking to Vespucci for guidance.

Cranston's voice flowed out over us as my friends' actions unfolded. I looked back at him. He was half raised out of his chair, his hands planted firmly on his desk to help keep him upright. "Gentlemen, stop! You misunderstand what we're doing here. Tony does not mean you any harm."

Luci and Donovan had each stepped away from Joey in opposite directions, so they were out of his immediate reach.

"Tony, please explain to them what's going on before these young upstarts shoot up my office," the last part of the sentence coming out as Cranston lowered himself back into his chair.

Vespucci motioned to Joey to move over near him. Joey did as he was asked, walking across the room and taking a seat in the corner of the office behind Vespucci. He appeared relaxed, unruffled, and unaffected. Luci and Donovan closed ranks beside me.

As the room settled, Vespucci said, "Gentlemen, what I am about to discuss requires the highest discretion and cannot leave this room. Ever. Is that understood?"

I nodded, looking to Luci and Donovan who each silently agreed.

"Good. Let me start from the beginning. Jon, I didn't ask you to do this job with completely innocent intentions. I love my daughter beyond words. I would do anything for her. But when she fell in love with Marco Balducci, it put me in a very tough position. As you know, his father and I go all the way back to childhood. We came up together. He's not just a business associate. He's also one of my closest friends. So, when Maggie started dating his son, I had to keep my mouth shut, hoping she would eventually lose interest in him. I've never liked Marco, and my daughter is aware of that. But that didn't stop her from falling in love with the guy." Vespucci paused at the thought of his daughter ending up with Marco. He continued. "Then one day, Maggie comes home and tells me they're engaged. Everyone's ecstatic. The Balduccis and the Vespuccis will be linked forever. So, I have had to suffer this in silence, seeking my own counsel on how best to handle the situation."

Everything he said verified what I believed to be true. My sixth sense had been right on target, but by this point I was beginning to have trouble believing him. He was Tony Vespucci, purportedly one of the most powerful organized crime figures in the United States. How was I supposed to believe he couldn't take care of this problem with a phone call? "You expect me to believe that you couldn't just take care of this problem yourself?" I asked.

Vespucci started chuckling, trading looks with Cranston. He looked back at me. "Simple as that, Jon? Just tell my daughter she can't marry the guy, or else? Maybe someday you'll have a daughter and you'll understand."

"Well, I didn't mean . . ." My words tapered off, knowing I meant exactly that.

"My daughter is in love with this man. She won't believe anything I tell her. She thinks I'm biased against Marco because of what happened when she was a teenager."

"Italy."

Vespucci nodded. "It was the compromise Giancarlo and I made back then. I thought that would be the end of my problem. But then, when Marco got back to the States last year, Maggie ran into him one day, and they started dating quietly. She didn't tell me for months. By the time I found out, it was too late. As far as the rest of my family is concerned, Marco's a great guy—"

I interrupted Vespucci. "Your mother-in-law doesn't like him much."

"Really?"

"She thinks he's a bully."

Vespucci glanced down at Cranston.

Cranston looked up at Vespucci. "I told you. He's good at getting people to talk."

Vespucci turned back to me. "Jon, that's why I brought

you on board. I needed someone to show her what he's really like. Late in August, I was confiding in Cranston, telling him about my dilemma, and that's when he suggested you. He said that if there was anything to be discovered about my soon-to-be son-in-law, you would find out. I figured I had nothing to lose. That's how you ended up here. Last night, though, I needed Marco to think you were out of the picture. Otherwise, I was afraid for your safety. He doesn't like you much. Or your friends."

"I'm aware of that. If last night was a ploy, to what end?"

"I want Marco to feel safe."

I nodded, still not completely understanding. I wondered what Vespucci did, and didn't know, about Maggie's fiancé. "But what about the pictures of the FBI that Marco gave you?

"We'll get to those in a minute. First, I need to know a few things."

"Such as?"

"I need to know the truth about Marco."

"What do you think the truth is?"

"For starters, what can you tell me about Marco's legacy in Italy?"

I started, realizing Vespucci knew more than he let on. "What do you know?"

"Rumors only. A baby. A nosy reporter named Mosconi. But that's about it. Nothing more."

I glanced over at Luci. Responding to my look, he said, "By the end of the day."

To Vespucci, I said, "I'll have a name for you tonight."

"Name for whom?" Vespucci asked.

"The name of the mother of Marco's baby."

"So, it's true." Vespucci took a deep breath. "Tell me."

In short order, I outlined everything I'd found out from Mosconi, along with the verification from Luci's source.

"What else does this reporter know?" Vespucci asked.

"I don't think it matters what else he knows. He's dead."

The room fell silent. Cranston sat back in his chair. Vespucci looked at his lieutenant, getting a shrug and shake of the head from Joey. He looked back at me. "Marco?"

"It was made to look like a suicide, but we saw the guy the day he died. He didn't seem suicidal to me."

"You can prove this?" Vespucci asked.

"The murder, no. Everything else. Yes," I replied. "But you need to know it doesn't end with the baby. There's more. The mother of the baby was only fifteen at the time. When her father discovered she was pregnant, he went to Marco demanding that Marco marry her. Marco beat him to death."

For several moments, no one spoke. Quietly, Vespucci asked, "You're sure of this?"

"I'd stake my career on it."

Vespucci sat silent for several moments, thoughts clearly racing through his mind. Finally, he looked over at his lieutenant. "Where's Marco?"

"He had some business at the factory."

Vespucci said, almost to himself, "He's having dinner with Maggie tonight at your place, Cranston."

Cranston barely looked up at the mention of his name. He seemed lost in thought.

Vespucci focused back on me. "Last night, you indicated you have feelings for my daughter. Is that true?"

I looked down at the floor, not expecting the question, not wanting to discuss feelings of the heart in the current situation. I returned my gaze to Vespucci, answering with a nod.

"Are those feelings interfering with your judgment?"

"Absolutely not, Tony. When this is all over, your daughter is going to be heartbroken because of me. The thought of that doesn't bring me any pleasure. But I don't think I have a choice. Their relationship has been a setup from the start."

"Setup for what?"

"To get to you."

As if coming out of a stupor, Cranston spoke up. "Jon, in Italy, how did Marco avoid arrest? Hiding a dead body is hard enough. But hiding a pregnant teenage girl is something else altogether. Fifteen is still fifteen. Even in Italy, that's statutory rape."

"Marco didn't hide her. The government did."

That got Vespucci's attention. "What are you talking about?"

As I spoke, I realized I was missing one piece of information that now seemed of great importance. "Tony, I'm assuming you control the movement of your, um, people, right?"

Vespucci didn't answer. I took that for a "yes."

"Did you sanction Marco's return to the States?"

"Giancarlo asked me for it. I thought enough time had passed."

Giancarlo's desire to bring his son home didn't implicate him. I had to assume Marco was the one pushing his father to request the return. Marco had set the whole thing up: his return, the romance, all of it. I was sure. Now I needed to prove it to Vespucci.

"You hired me to write the love story for Marco and your daughter. Well, last night I finished what you hired me to do." I crossed the room as I spoke. "Cranston, can I use your computer?"

He nodded.

"Does it have a printer?"

Cranston pointed across the room to an industrial-sized copier and printer. I pulled the thumb drive out of my pocket and stuck it into the USB port. In a few seconds, I opened the file and sent it to print. No one spoke while I waited for the story to finish printing. When it was done, I crossed the office, pulled the indictment from the exit tray, and turned back to Vespucci.

"Here you go, Tony. This is what you hired me to do." I

walked over to him, placing the stack of papers in his hands.

Two hours later Vespucci placed the last page on Cranston's desk. The rest of us were sprawled out around the room. Cranston had called his restaurant and ordered pizza, which gave me a food coma and knocked me back into my chair for a light snooze. Donovan and Luci were sitting quietly, looking as if they could be meditating. Joey was standing in the back eating. Cranston was almost asleep in his cushioned office chair, reclining it back to get more comfortable.

Vespucci was looking down into his lap at his hands. Instinctively, my eyes opened, feeling a shift in energy. From across the room, I could see the dark scowl on his face as he looked up to meet my gaze. "You're sure? You have proof?" he asked.

In seconds, I'd wiped the sleep out of my eyes. "Italy I can prove," I said, "and everything else stems from that. I don't have proof I can hand you, but nothing else makes sense. My feelings for your daughter aside, I did not seek the story out. The story found me." I caught my breath before I proceeded. "Tony, I would like nothing more than for it to be total fiction, because then my life, and the life of my friends, wouldn't be in danger. Your future son-in-law would like nothing better than to disappear me from the face of the earth. I'm sure it was Marco who tried to plant the listening device in our hotel room. I'm sure he killed Mosconi. I'm sure Marco got involved with your daughter to get close to you."

"And the FBI?"

I paused a moment, considering the implications of the FBI's part in all this. "I'm sure."

Vespucci turned toward the New York skyline and stared out the window into the distance. Silence filled the room. We sat like that for several minutes, no one speaking. Finally, Vespucci pulled his eyes away from the November afternoon sun, pinning down my gaze. "Jon, I have to be sure."

I nodded. I realized I could still put the plan I'd outlined for Luci and Donovan into action with only a slight modification. "If Marco admits it to you, will that be enough?"

"How are you going to do that?" Vespucci asked.

I outlined my plan to him. Cranston was awake now, listening with interest. Vespucci's eyes glowed with intensity, not missing a word. When I came to the end of my summation, my last words hung in the air, surrounded by the electric silence in the room. Vespucci didn't take his eyes from mine. I held his stare, feeling it important that he see I spoke the truth.

Cranston was the first to speak. "I told you he was no dummy."

Vespucci accepted Cranston's words without comment, looking in the opposite direction at his lieutenant. Joey returned Vespucci's gaze, locking eyes with him. Silent understanding passed between them.

Vespucci turned back to me. "Do it."

Once Vespucci gave his assent, everything started happening quickly. He and Joey left Cranston's office immediately after I'd given them clear instructions for the evening. In the overall plan, Vespucci had very little to do except wait. Taking advantage of Cranston's office, I put my plan into motion. I printed up a second copy of the "Love Story of Marco and Maggie," packaging them both, sticking a note on the cover specifically for its intended receiver, then calling a same day messenger delivery service for pickup. When the messenger showed up twenty minutes later, I pulled him aside. I handed him a one-hundred dollar bill, telling him he would need to deliver the packages to different addresses than what I had logged with the dispatcher and he would need to use discretion. A twenty-something face stared back at me with a grin. I asked him if he understood. He nodded. I asked him if he had any questions. He shook his head. Something struck me as odd about the way he responded, prompting me to ask him if he could answer by saying yes. He raised his hands, hitting me with a flurry of hand movements. I blinked, confused for a moment.

"You're deaf?"

He nodded matter-of-factly.

"Oh." I felt stupid. But then I wondered how he understood my directions. "Wait, how do you know what—"

He interrupted me with his hands again, but kept it simple for my own thickheaded edification, pointing first to his eye, then to his lips.

"You read lips?" I asked.

Again, the matter-of-fact nod of the head. I smiled, embarrassed for giving him a difficult time.

"Great. Then on your way. Godspeed."

I don't know why I said "Godspeed," but something about this whole experience made me feel like every action carried a level of heightened importance. With the grin still planted on his face, my twenty-something deaf delivery boy grabbed the packages under his arm, turned his back on me, and hustled out the door. As I turned towards the elevator, Donovan was standing a few feet behind, a bemused look on his face.

"What?"

He just shook his head and smiled. In the War Room, my new nickname for Cranston's office, I called Cranston's restaurant, making reservations for two. By this time, it was late afternoon and the sun was fading in the sky, slowly layering the office in shadow. I stepped up to the window, staring out at the darkening sky. Luci moved up beside me.

"Looks like we have snow coming."

Donovan joined us at the window. "I think you're right."

Shoulder to shoulder, we stared out at the Manhattan sky, the buildings breaking the lower half of our vision, an uneven multitude of shapes zigzagging horizontally across the horizon with a large mass of dark clouds forming a roof of power above, preparing to unleash its white fury upon the unsuspecting structures below. In the distance, I caught the glimpse of a plane climbing into the sky, centered between the tops of the buildings below and the dark mass of clouds above. I watched the plane gain altitude, inexorably climbing toward visual extinction within the cloud mass. I blinked and the plane was gone. The vision created an eerie feeling in my gut. I turned away from the window, surveying Cranston's office. Paintings of famous black figures covered the walls. A large, elongated, deeply colored picture of the French Alps took up another wall. Except for Luci, Donovan, and me, the office was empty. Cranston had left to check on Judith, who had not been feeling well the last few days.

I glanced at the old school clock ticking above the double doors. Fifteen minutes had passed since my deaf messenger had left with the packages. Unless I was completely remiss, I would receive a phone call within the hour that would put my plan into play. But first, I needed to make a few calls to get the ball rolling. I pulled a business card out of my wallet, dialing a number I never thought I'd be using. After several rings, a voice picked up on the other end.

"Ted Williams" came the voice.

I had put my phone on speaker so Luci and Donovan could hear.

"This is Jon Fixx." My response was met with silence. "We need to talk."

Williams thought I was on a plane. "Where are you?"

"Not in Los Angeles."

"Jon, you're swimming in deep waters here."

"Then it's good I brought two tanks down with me. I'll have enough oxygen to stay under for awhile."

"You should be careful. I've gone diving quite a bit. Those tanks have a way of malfunctioning."

"I'll take my chances."

"What do you want to talk about?" he said, a nonchalance slipping into his voice. He'd regained his composure.

"This 'n that. About why you've been following me around

since I got to New York. About Tony Vespucci. About Marco Balducci. About Italy."

There was a long sigh on the other end. I pegged Williams for one of those slow-to-anger sadistic types. Rather than expressing his anger through a modicum of yelling and screaming, he went inward, becoming calm, thoughtful. He probably relished interrogation, torture.

"Jon Fixx. May I remind you that you are nothing more than a hack writer whose ex-girlfriend was sleeping with my cousin long before you two split? And there were others before him. I tell you this only to remind you of your place in life. So I ask you, what are you doing here, Jon? This isn't Little League. You are severely lacking the talent to play in the majors. You can't even keep your girlfriend in line, what makes you think you can handle this?"

I closed my eyes, taking a deep breath, trying not to rise to the bait. For a moment, I saw Sara's image. Were there others, I wondered? I could feel the heat rising to my cheeks. I opened my eyes and took another deep breath, pushing all thoughts of Sara aside. "I guess it's good she's with your cousin now, then. I've heard French men have a penchant for loose women. You're French too, right, Ted?"

That was met with silence. Donovan tapped his index finger on his wrist, indicating I shouldn't keep the call going too long.

"Look, Ted, I'd love to talk with you about your sexual predilections, but I've never paid for sex so I can't speak from experience. We need to meet tonight."

"For what purpose?"

"There's a package waiting for you at your office. Read it. I'll call you in two hours with instructions." I hung up, trading glances with Donovan, then Luci. "Think he'll go for it?"

"We'll find out soon enough," Luci answered.

My phone started to buzz, the sound making me jump. I didn't realize until that moment how tense I was. I checked the number on my PDA. It was a Brooklyn exchange. Marco Balducci's number. I let it ring two more times before answering.

"Hello."

"You have no proof of any of this," Marco hissed across the phone line.

"I've got more proof than you know."

"What do you want?"

"Tonight, 7 p.m. Fanelli's. Come alone. And I mean alone, Marco. No eavesdroppers. No thugs. Just me and you, see if we can come to an understanding."

"What have you told Maggie?"

"Nothing yet. I wanted to talk to you first."

"You have no idea who you're fuckin' with!"

"That's where you're wrong, Marco. I have a very clear idea of who I'm fucking with."

"You have no proof of any of the shit you've written here."

"Think Tony Vespucci will see it that way? 7 p.m. Come alone. Don't be late." I hung up the phone before he could respond and swear at me some more. "Think he'll show?"

Donovan responded, "Does he have a choice?"

I pondered the question, trying to put myself in Marco's shoes, wondering what he would consider to be his options. Killing me would be one option. I hoped he didn't choose that one right out of the gate. I guessed he would feel out Vespucci to see what he knew, then would base his plan of attack on that. I decided it didn't matter what Marco considered his options to be as long as he showed up.

I took a deep breath, exhaled, and prepared for the last call I needed to make before the evening. I had to tell Maggie I was leaving and that I wouldn't be finishing the project, and do it without giving her any hint that the next few hours would define the direction of her life. I picked up the phone, dialed her number, and listened as the phone rang on the other end, once, twice, three times. I hoped it would go to voicemail, though I wasn't sure how much I should say in the message, when suddenly I heard her voice on the other end.

"Hello." Her voice was missing some of its usual warmth.

"Hi, Maggie."

There was a brief pause. Maggie was still reeling from the night before, probably confused and unsure what it all meant. That put me on unsafe ground with her.

"Jon, what happened last night? I've been unable to reach Marco or my father today, and I want someone to explain to me what the hell that was all about."

"Me too, Maggie." I paused, not sure how to continue. I needed Maggie to think I was out of the picture. I didn't want her anywhere near that restaurant tonight. I pushed forward. "I'm sorry it happened. I'm more sorry I can't finish the project for you."

"Because of last night?"

Well, let me see, shall I name the reasons? One, your fiancé is an asshole. Two, he's a killer. In fact, three, I'm sure he would fall into the definition of a sociopath. How's that for reasons, Maggie? I said, "Given the exchange between Marco and me last night, I don't think it's feasible for me to continue working with you both."

I was met with silence. I glanced out the windows of Cranston's office, realizing that daylight had receded, the dark of night settling over the Manhattan skyline. Snow began to fall. It had been many years since I'd seen the first snow of the season. Maggie's voice suddenly brought me back to the present.

"Jon, what happened between you and Marco? What are you not telling me?"

For a split second, I debated telling her the truth about her monster of a fiancé, but just as quickly dismissed the idea. For now, she needed to be kept in the dark. I needed to catch Marco unawares, and I needed leverage. As far as he was concerned, no one else knew his secret and he would do whatever he needed to keep it that way. "Maggie,

I'm really sorry."

"Is this because of what Marco said about you last night? Your feelings for me?"

Oh, geez, I should have known this would not be easy. What should I say to that? Yeah, Maggie, I'm in love with you, and that's why I can't write this story. Fuck it, why not? "To be honest, Maggie, that's the one thing Marco and I can agree on. He wasn't wrong."

"Oh."

That was it. I knew what that meant. Oh, well, that's too bad you feel that way, Jon, because in case you didn't notice, I'm in love with another man, and even after you are instrumental in trying to destroy his life in a few hours, thereby breaking my heart when I discover the truth, I'll never fall in love with you because you're not in my league.

"Have you spoken with my father about this?" Maggie asked.

"Yes. It was his idea I go home."

She didn't respond. I had no idea what she was thinking, but I knew I needed to get off the phone before I started blabbering about what was really going on.

"Maggie, I have to go." I struggled with how to finish the conversation without being too abrupt. "I'm sorry."

"I am too."

I hung up, staring at the phone in my hand. Finally, I looked up. Donovan and Luci were watching me from the window.

"How'd she take it?"

"I'm not sure."

"Put her out of your head for the rest of the night, Jon. You can't have any distractions. Don't take this lightly. You've laid the trap, but for Marco it's all about survival. He's going to do whatever he feels is necessary to protect himself." Donovan's eyes bored into mine. "Do you understand what I'm saying?"

"You're saying I better be prepared for anything?"

"You know what they say about battle? The advantage always goes to the side that can adapt to and incorporate the unpredictable changes that occur during the conflict. Pre-battle plans become secondary to the unforeseen changes that occur while the forces engage."

"Okay."

Luci crossed over to me. "Don't worry. If it goes sideways, we'll be right there." He patted me on the back reassuringly.

I looked up at the clock on the wall. It was 5:22 p.m. I had ninety-eight minutes left before the official showdown. I looked at each of my companions in turn. I saw calm and strength in their gazes. I tried to take comfort from their looks, from knowing they would be nearby, but a solid, quiet fear was creeping up my legs into my belly. There would be no room for that when Marco showed up. I stuck my phone in my pocket and zipped up my coat, indicating it was time to go. I grabbed my computer, shoving it inside my jacket.

"All right, let's go."

One at a time, we exited Cranston's office and headed for the elevator. We found our way down to the lobby and retraced our steps through the building and back to the alley. Upon our exit, the driver's door quickly opened and Cheryl hopped out of the car. She hustled to the passenger's side back door, opening it for us to climb in.

"All is well, I hope?" she asked.

"So far. Thanks, Cheryl," I said as I climbed into the roomy back seat. Donovan and Luci followed, each mumbling a thank you, all of us still having trouble letting a woman open the door for us.

Cheryl climbed back into the driver's seat, looking in the rearview. "Mr. Jefferson said I'm at your disposal for the evening? Where to?"

I told her and she nodded. A moment later we were moving.

Luci turned to me. "What do you think Williams will do?"

"I don't know," I said. "I've given that a lot of thought. They have to tread lightly, because if they make their presence known around Marco, they run the risk of blowing his cover, so I think they're in a corner. They can't do much."

So many thoughts were crisscrossing my mind I did my best to slow it all down. What if Marco didn't show up? What if the FBI moved in before I could get the truth out? What contingencies had I overlooked?

The sound of Luci's phone interrupted my thoughts. He flipped his phone open, putting it to his ear. "Go." Without speaking, he listened intently for close to a minute. "Thanks. I owe you. Next time you're in L.A. Okay." He hung up, satisfaction on his face. "Her name is Louisa Adduci."

I nodded, a tight smile on my face. The pieces were falling into place. As we drove through rush hour traffic, I wondered what I was missing. What was I not thinking about? Finally, I decided there was no point in thinking about it anymore. I'd laid the trap. As Donovan said, if something went wrong, I'd have to adapt. I started wondering how adaptable I was.

Guess I was about to find out.

14
Early November
New York 3rd Trip

Fanelli's was packed, not an empty table to be found anywhere. The bar was overflowing too, every stool taken with more people standing shoulder to shoulder, vying for space anywhere they could find it. I was strategically seated in the back corner with a clear angle of the front door. Off to my left, the bar ran the length of the restaurant, ending near the kitchen doors just out of my visual range.

My eyes were glued on the front door, waiting for Marco's arrival. I hadn't expected it to be so busy, and I couldn't decide if that was good or bad for my plan. With so many people, it would be easier for one of Marco's cronies to blend in with the crowd unnoticed. I glanced away from the front door momentarily to scan the people at the bar, but it was far too crowded for me to see every face. I decided this was a positive because I hoped Marco wouldn't try anything stupid with so many witnesses. Then again, maybe he'd shoot me with a silencer, lay my head down on the table, and leave before anyone even noticed I was dead.

I was hyperaware and extremely tense. I had no idea how Marco would react or what he would do, and time was moving at an excruciatingly slow pace. I glanced down at my laptop on the table before me, the screen open to Marco and Maggie's story, the cursor blinking at an even pace, patiently waiting for my next command. This computer had been the key to my plan from the start. Prior to Marco's arrival, I would connect with Vespucci on Skype to ensure that he could hear and see what Marco said and did. Then all I had to do was get Marco to admit to everything. Simple as that. But a plan was only as effective as its execution. And the best-laid plans could unravel in the blink of an eye.

I felt my palms sweating. I was scared. I didn't like admitting that to myself, but it was true. If I was successful, it would bring Marco's world crashing down around him. The marriage would be called off. His current business relationships, legal and illicit, would be severed. The FBI would no longer have any use for him. The Italian government would probably file formal charges. Considering what Marco had to lose, I started to question my sanity. Marco was cornered, no question, but did I really believe he was going to fall for this? There was no way he was going to let me walk out of this meeting alive. If I couldn't get him to admit his guilt, I would not get another chance. Then it would be my world that came crashing down.

Sitting in the back corner, I felt some comfort that I had a wall behind me. At least Marco or one of his goons couldn't sneak up on me. From my angle, I could watch the activity in the entire restaurant. As I waited, I thought back over the last ninety minutes as my plan had fallen nicely into place.

After we left Cranston's office, my phone buzzed again. Williams' calm sounded almost apoplectic. He had received my package. "Jon, are you aware you are interfering with a federal case?"

"So, Marco Balducci is working for you guys?"

"I didn't say that."

"You didn't have to. I wrote it, remember? I wonder what Tony Vespucci would say if I showed it to him."

The eruption from the phone displayed the temper I

knew was beneath Williams' calm exterior. "You fucking little shit! When I find you, I'm going to strangle you with my bare hands."

I didn't respond. The phone went silent. Finally, I said, "Ted, are you listening?"

A pause, and then, "Yeah."

"I'm the one with all the cards here, in case you haven't noticed. I'm innocent in all this. I was dragged into it by circumstances beyond my control, so I decided it was time to push back and get a little somethin' for Jon-Jon."

Luci glanced at me, silently mouthing, "Jon-Jon?"

I shrugged in response, as if to say, I'm just making it up as I go. Back to the phone, I added, "I've got the name of the girl in Italy and her dead father's. I know about the baby. I know about the deal with the Italian government. I can guess the rest."

"You've been talking to Jim Mosconi too much."

"You mean the same Jim Mosconi Marco killed?"

"He committed suicide."

"Right. And I'm black." It was Donovan's turn to throw a questioning glance my way. "How about this, Ted? Louisa Adduci. The name ring any bells?"

Silence. I could hear Williams' breathing. Several moments passed, then Williams asked, "What do you want?"

"I want to make sure I don't end up like Mosconi. I want to meet."

"Where?"

"The Brooklyn Bridge. Center. 7:00." I hung up.

With a chuckle, Donovan said, "Jon-Jon. Nice touch."

"Where'd all that come from," Luci said, more statement than question.

"Stream of consciousness. I was just going with the flow." My friends continued to chuckle.

Minutes later, we arrived at the restaurant. We unloaded quickly from the limo, sending Cheryl off on a long leisurely drive through Manhattan back toward the Brooklyn

Bridge. I tossed my mobile phone in the back seat before climbing out, hoping that would throw the FBI off track, at least for a while, if they were tracking it. We gave Cheryl Luci's cell number so she could call us if she had any problems. Donovan handed his phone over to me so I wouldn't be without one.

I had trouble sitting still. I needed to stay focused. I leaned forward to see if I could spot Luci at the end of the bar near the kitchen doors. As planned, he was calmly sitting on the last bar stool, an untouched drink in front of him. He was doing his best to blend in, chatting with a young woman sitting next to him. If he saw me look over, he gave no sign. I glanced away from Luci toward the opposite front corner of the restaurant farthest from the door, spotting Donovan's large frame looking more than a little uncomfortable in the two-seater table he'd been shown to. We were both sitting along the same wall at opposite ends of the restaurant. When we'd put the plan together, the three of us had decided these positions would provide us with the best vantage points.

I looked at the clock on my computer screen. 6:47 p.m. Almost show time. I felt my stomach tighten. All around me, I heard multiple conversations, the ring of silverware on plates, occasional laughter. Servers hustled in between the tables. I'd ordered a plate of linguini to blend in but hadn't taken a bite, getting more nervous as each minute passed. I glanced around the restaurant again, looking for thugs, unable to believe that Marco would actually show up by himself.

6:55.

I pulled my computer closer, checking to make sure everything was set up. I opened Skype, going full screen. I clicked the dial button, watching the dialing icon blink. After four rings, I saw Joey's face pop up on the screen. I looked down at the lower left corner to see what the computer's camera was focused on, spotting my yellowed, bruised, slowly healing face staring back at me. Quietly, I asked him, "Can you hear me?"

He gave a thumbs up. The camera panned slightly, and Vespucci's face came into view. I nodded to him, acknowledging his presence. I then hit the mute button on my computer and reduced the Skype screen to a minimum, leaving only my desktop visible. Now, all I needed to do was get Marco to admit to his transgressions and I was home free.

6:58.

A guy walked through the front door, an Italian thug without question. With shoulders as wide as Donovan's but on a five-feet-eight-inch frame, he reminded me of a fire hydrant with legs and a potbelly. His eyes found mine and he froze at the door. He stared at me a moment, then walked over to the edge of the bar. It took every ounce of my self-will not to look at Donovan or Luci for fear of giving up their positions to Marco's crony, but I wanted to be sure they saw what I saw. Seconds later, Marco sauntered through the front door. The restaurant seemed to get darker. If he was nervous or scared, he didn't look it. I figured I was feeling enough of both for the two of us. At my side, Donovan's cell phone started buzzing. I almost jumped out of my seat at the sound. I quickly pulled it out of my pants pocket.

"Yeah?"

"FBI pulled Cheryl over a few minutes ago. Hurry up." Then Luci hung up.

I put the phone back in my pocket. The maître d' had just walked up to Marco as he spotted me. Even with the distance between us, I could see the hate in his eyes. Marco dismissed the maître d' with a wave of his hand and headed in my direction. As he got closer, I could see a slight smile on his face. I figured he was thinking of how he was going to dispose of my body after he killed me. The complete absurdity of my situation made me start to laugh.

What was I doing sitting in an Italian restaurant in New

York attempting to pin down a hard-hitting Mafioso who was allegedly double-crossing his boss? The whole thing seemed hysterical to me at the moment. As Marco closed in on my table, my laughter had become an uncontrollable cackle. I knew I looked and sounded crazy. I was losing it. I could see the people around me shifting uncomfortably in their seats, taking sideways glances at me. From across the restaurant, Donovan's concerned look was visible above the other heads. I could only imagine what Vespucci and Joey were thinking.

Marco stepped up to the table, the sociopathic-like grin gone from his face. My own crazy-sounding laughter must have thrown him. Quietly, he said, "What the fuck is wrong with you?"

The sound of his voice triggered a switch inside me and suddenly, just as quickly as it had come, the urge to laugh was gone. All business, I stared up at him with a straight face. I gathered my wits together, doing my best to ignore the feeling of dread and fear I felt throughout my body. "Join me for dinner?"

As I spoke, I pushed my computer off to the side, apparently out of Marco's way, but angling the computer screen slightly toward him. I doubted Vespucci could see him, but he would definitely be able to hear him.

"This is not a social call, asshole." Marco sat down. A server closed in on the table but Marco dismissed him with a shake of his head. The server turned away.

"I asked you to come alone," I said, indicating with a look at Marco's goon standing at the edge of the bar.

Marco's head swiveled in the same direction. "Gino? Don't worry about him. He's just here to watch the door." Marco's gaze settled on my computer.

I panicked, thinking he was already onto my plan.

Instead, he asked, "Is it on there?"

I realized he was focused on the story I sent him. "No, it's here." I pulled the thumb drive out of my pocket, holding it up for him to see.

"What do you want?" he said, his voice a low growl.

"The truth."

Marco stared at me, clearly assessing his options.

"I'm going to finish what Jim Mosconi started." Mosconi's name elicited no response from him. "When reporters are about to break big stories, they will often visit the subject of the story the night before they publish to provide their subject an opportunity to respond to the allegations. In case you haven't figured it out yet, that's what we're doing here."

Marco hissed, "You have no proof. That story you wrote is bullshit! If you pass it on to Vespucci, or Maggie, or anyone else, I'll kill you."

I returned his stare, considering his threat, doing my best not to blink, not to show any fear. Funny enough, I'd been more afraid when thinking about the confrontation than I was feeling now in the confrontation. Watching Marco, I sensed the combination of panic and desperation under the surface. I figured the longer I remained calm the greater my chances of drawing him out.

"I don't think that would be a good idea because I really don't want to die yet. There are so many things I still want to do with my life. I haven't seen the Grand Canyon. I haven't been to Europe. I feel the need to put my genetic stamp on the world, so I want to have at least one child. I'd like to learn calligraphy—"

"Get to the fucking point!"

"I am. You can't kill me." I paused, gathering my thoughts. Then, "From a logical standpoint, Marco, I'm at a bit of a loss. On the one hand, you're telling me the story I wrote about you and Maggie is all bullshit, but your actions belie your words. If there's no truth in what I wrote, why are you threatening me? What are you doing here?" I stopped, waiting, a small smile forming on my face. The smile had a greater effect than the words. I glanced down at Marco's hands gripping the table, his knuckles white. I was definitely getting to him, but I needed him to say the words. "Just tell me one thing, do you even love her?"

A wolfish grin spread across Marco's face. "Oh, of course, so that's what this is all about. You're in love with my fiancée. Let me be the first to tell you she wouldn't give you a second glance. Look at you! Look at what you do for a living. You call that a job?" He paused a moment, sitting back in his seat. "Let me tell you one thing, Jon. She's amazing in the sack. That part's been a lot of fun."

I had my answer. Any man truly in love with a woman doesn't talk about his private sexual life to other men. I saw an opening. "What about Louisa Adduci? What was she like in bed?"

I hit the bullseye. Marco's bravado was instantly replaced with a look of fear. "How did you get her name?"

"I do my homework. I want to make sure that if I'm going to extort somebody, I have all my facts to make sure I'll get what I want."

"Is that what this is about? You want money?"

I nodded.

"How much?"

"I was thinking somewhere in the range of one hundred thousand." I could see his mind working. I was now on ground Marco felt comfortable with, discussing something he understood.

"You want me to pay you to keep a story you wrote based on a bunch of hunches and lies under wraps?"

"Hunches and lies? I know about Louisa. I know about your daughter. I know you beat her father to death. I'm pretty sure you killed Jim Mosconi when he started getting close to breaking that story."

Then I paused, about to throw Marco for a big loop. In the copy I'd sent to him, I had removed the pages that covered his alleged position as an informer. I wanted to spring it on him at the restaurant, hoping the surprise would throw him off balance. I knew if I didn't break him with this revelation, I would fail at my task. I took a deep breath and jumped. "But what I don't understand, and maybe you can help me with this, is why the Italian government arrested you, then suddenly released you. Can you shed any light on that for me?"

As I spoke, Marco's face darkened, an evil scowl spreading across his face. I was sure that if we'd been alone, Marco would have reached across the table and snapped my neck with his bare hands.

"Want to hear what I think? Well, let me tell you anyway. I think you made a deal with the FBI to turn informer on Tony Vespucci so the Italian government would dismiss the charges. I think you came back here and saw an opportunity with Maggie. Or maybe you even planned the whole thing ahead of time, and your relationship with her was all a setup. How better to get in tight with the father than to marry his daughter. But that's been a problem, hasn't it? I mean, ever since Vespucci sent you away all those years ago when you almost did to Maggie what you did to Louisa Adduci, you've had a lot of trouble getting back into his good graces, haven't you?"

Marco reached under the table, his hand slowly reappearing with a Beretta outfitted with a silencer on the end of it pointed in my direction. He was going to kill me with a silencer! I was a mind reader. He placed it on the table, still in his hand, using his other hand to cover it up with a large, white napkin.

"Smart boy, aren't you, Jon Fixx? So smart, you're going to get yourself killed. I'll tell you what you want to know, because when I'm done, you're going to leave here with me and I'm going to kill you."

I felt unclear about what to do next. I wasn't sure what he would, or wouldn't do. The gun on the table was real. All he had to do was point and shoot, which I knew he could do instantly. I inadvertently glanced around the restaurant trying to gather my thoughts.

"Don't get any ideas. I pull the trigger, the first bullet will tear your liver apart."

I took a breath, steeling my nerves. There was no going back, so I figured all I could do was forge ahead and hope for the best. "Before you kill me, just answer my question. Do you love her?"

Marco chuckled. "Are you kidding? Seriously, talk about high maintenance. Tony spoiled that girl. She's been such a pain in the ass since we got engaged. She called me a little while ago, so upset that you're going back to Los Angeles. She wanted to know what our fight was about, why you were asking if I had a kid in Italy. I told her you were making shit up to cause trouble so you could have a shot at her."

My blood started to heat up, Marco's incendiary dialogue having the intended effect, but I kept my mouth shut. From the corner of my eye, I was suddenly distracted by something off to my left. I glanced away from Marco toward the distraction, almost bounding out of my seat at the sight of Nick Nickels Jr. and a skinny blond being seated by the maître d' only a few tables away. He was positioned such that he'd have to turn his head no more than forty-five degrees to see me. I froze in my seat. My eyes darted back to Marco.

"The poor girl is wrapped around my finger. She'll do whatever I tell her. Even when her father goes down, she'll be dependent on me."

"So you are working for the FBI."

"I'm not working for anybody. I'm working for myself."

"I don't think you'll be very popular when everyone finds out what you've been up to."

"When the FBI takes Vespucci down, I've got everything lined up to handle business. My exit strategy is in place."

A commotion at the front door drew my attention away from Marco. At first, my brain couldn't process what I was seeing, but as she crossed from the front door into the restaurant, making a beeline for our table, the fog cleared, putting Maggie's name to her face. I glanced back at Marco to see if he had noticed my abrupt change in demeanor, but he was still talking, clearly relishing the fact that he could tell me everything because soon he'd be killing me. My eyes jumped away from Marco over to Nickels' table. He appeared to be happily lost in a glass of wine and his date.

"—Vespucci thinks he's so smart. I can't wait to see him go down."

I sat back in my seat as Maggie closed in on us. From my left, I could see Luci leaning forward, beginning to stand up, doubt on his face. He wasn't sure if this was part of the plan. From across the restaurant, Donovan was sitting up straight in his seat. Maggie strode up behind Marco. Over Marco's shoulder, I saw Joey run in through the front door, stopping at the entrance and frantically scanning the restaurant. I started preparing my body for action. Maggie stepped up to Marco's side, her face flushed, mascara smudges under her eyes, tears on her cheeks. At the sight of his fiancée, Marco froze. Maggie stared back, not saying anything for several seconds, and then everything in the room erupted into chaos.

"You son-of-a-bitch!"

Her hand flew through the air, palm connecting squarely on Marco's cheek and jaw. Putting some hip into the swing, Maggie almost knocked him out of his seat. Marco crouched down to avoid a second swing. Over his head, I spotted Gino moving quickly down the bar aisle toward us. Donovan appeared beside him, throwing a right foot hard at Gino's left knee. The fire hydrant faltered, swaying back and forth, trying to keep his balance while turning on his aggressor. A right cross came down on his jaw, dropping Gino to the ground.

Maggie's voice brought me back to what was happening in front of me. She was crying again. "How could you? I was in love with you."

Recovering from his initial shock, Marco's glance darted

from Maggie to me, then down to my computer, quickly putting it together. "You set me up."

Before I could respond, another voice joined the increasing maelstrom.

"Jon Fixx."

Nickels was standing on the other side of Marco opposite Maggie, an impetuous, coyote-like look on his face. Ducking away from Maggie, Marco looked over his left shoulder to see who was standing so close to him. Nickels seemed to have tunnel vision, though, unable to notice anything but me.

I heard Maggie's voice. "Answer me, you piece of shit."

I glanced up at Nickels. "This is not a good time, Nick."

"Do you know where my sister is now? She's in a mental hospital. She tried to kill herself. All because of you."

As Nickels spoke, I quickly looked down at the table to see what Marco was doing with the pistol. It hadn't moved. I looked back at Nickels. I'd had enough of everyone. I was beyond feeling responsible for any of these people. "Maybe she tried to kill herself because she's tired of having a brother who wants to sleep with her? Or did you two already do that and she couldn't handle the guilt?"

Nickels reacted the way I expected him to. His face contorted into a mask of rage, his body instantly in motion. Nickels dove over the table, knocking me backward to the floor. We rolled around, each trying to gain an advantage. I wanted to use Nickels as a shield in case Marco became reckless and decided to put an end to me. Our roll came to a stop, my feet tangled up in the cloth hanging down from the table. Nickels looked triumphant above me, gloating with his advantage. He had pinned my arms to the ground with his knees, rearing back with both arms to let fly on my face. Gazing up at him, I saw a crazed man. I wondered how he had made it this long in life without ending up in a mental institution himself. As his left fist came toward my face, I closed my eyes preparing for an impact that didn't come. I felt a whoosh of air, opening my eyes just in time to see Luci flying across me, Nickels wrapped up in his arms, piling into the next dining table, already vacated by the terrified patrons. Resting on my elbows, I sat up trying to grasp what was happening. Glancing up, I saw Marco's frame standing over me, his gun pointed directly at my head.

"Are you getting what you wanted? Couldn't leave it alone, could you?"

Only a few feet away, Maggie said, "Marco, no!" She rushed at him, but he shoved her down with his free hand, knocking her to her knees. Her eyes locked with mine.

"Put it down, Marco!" I heard Joey yell. I spotted him halfway across the restaurant, his hand reaching into his jacket.

A second voice rang out from the opposite direction. "NYPD! Put down the weapon!"

I looked over my right shoulder, spotting Detective Hunt with another man beside her. What the hell were they doing here? They both had guns out, badges hanging from their necks. Marco looked around wildly, hesitating. I could see Donovan restraining Gino in a full nelson. To my right, between the NYPD and me, Luci had Nickels pinned to the ground. Marco's eyes found their way back to me. I stared up at him, preparing for the bullet I knew was coming my way. Marco relaxed, making a slight indication of dropping his right hand and lowering his pistol. Then in one swift motion, he spun toward Detective Hunt, dropping to a knee, his right hand swinging up and pulling the trigger in quick succession, the sound of his gun not much more than a whisper. I heard a thud as Detective Hunt took a bullet, slamming backward into the wall. Cool and in full possession of his senses, her partner aimed his gun at Marco, pulling the trigger three times in quick succession, the sound loud and harsh, each bullet finding its target, dropping Marco to the ground. His body crumpled before me, his right arm arranged at a weird angle at his side. I could see blood forming a stain on the front of his shirt. I quickly crawled the few feet over to him, pulling his gun out of his hand and then sitting back on my haunches, evaluating his condition. With blood now visibly seeping out from his backside, I looked down into his eyes. For the first time in my life, I saw someone dying.

Marco whispered, "I curse you," his voice rough and faraway. A moment later, he died. There was complete silence, no one sure what to do.

Then all hell broke loose at the front door.

"Everybody freeze! FBI! Don't move!" Williams and five FBI agents, three men and two women, fanned out from the door, guns drawn, federal badges visible on their vests. I could see Williams surveying the scene, trying to figure out what had just happened.

From the opposite corner of the room, I heard Detective Hunt yell out, her voice strident and clear, "NYPD. We're on the scene. Everything is under control."

She was on her feet. I realized then she was wearing a bulletproof vest. Detective Hunt's partner appeared over my right shoulder, gently pulling the gun out of my hand. I let go without hesitation and heard a sharp intake of breath. Over my opposite shoulder, I saw a mixture of fear and pain and anguish on Maggie's face. I shook my head to let her know he was gone. She put her hands to her face and started to cry. I stood up to comfort her, but she shrugged off my touch.

Everything seemed to be happening in slow motion. I tried to get my bearings. Off to the side, I spotted Luci. He was keeping Nickels under control, his lips moving close to Nickels' ear. Nickels looked scared, his eyes darting my way and then veering away as if he wasn't supposed to be looking at me. I spotted Donovan near the bar, Gino standing beside him. I was sure the sight of the NYPD, coupled with the entrance of the FBI, had made Gino think twice about throwing his support behind his now dead capo. Donovan appeared calm and relaxed. More NYPD police streamed in through the front door. Most of the dining and bar patrons had bunched together toward the front of the restaurant, wanting to be as far away from the dead body as possible. I gave the restaurant a once-over, and then looked around a second time. Joey was gone. I turned to where Maggie was standing to see if she was ready to talk, realizing too late she was also gone.

"How you doing?" I heard Luci's voice in my ear before I realized he was standing beside me.

The panic rising, I said, "Where did Maggie go? Where's Joey?"

Luci put a reassuring hand on my shoulder to calm me down. "They're gone. I saw Joey take her through the kitchen doors."

Donovan found his way over to us. He was staring at Nick Nickels Jr., who was sitting quietly in his chair, his date trying to comfort him. They both appeared to be in shock.

"Who's that guy?" Donovan asked.

"He's the main reason I hired you."

"Nick Nickels Jr.? He followed you across the country?"

Luci said, "Not according to him. Pure coincidence. This is his favorite restaurant when he's in New York."

Nickels glanced away from the concerned attentions of his date and our eyes met. He was unable to hold my gaze for even a moment, immediately looking away. All I saw there was fear.

"What did you say to him, Luci?"

"Just cleared the air. I don't think you'll need to worry about him anymore, Jon. Or his father for that matter."

"I want to know what she's doing here?" Donovan asked. "That wasn't a coincidence, I'm sure."

Luci and I both looked in the direction of Donovan's gaze, seeing Detective Hunt work the room.

At the moment, I didn't care why she was here. She'd saved my life. I would have to thank her. A sound from the front of the restaurant grabbed my attention. I spied Williams doing his best to take charge of the scene. Several police officers were asking people to take a seat.

"Jon Fixx!"

Williams came charging my way. Luci and Donovan immediately closed ranks in front of me. Marco's crumpled and lifeless body stopped Williams in his tracks. He stared down at the dead FBI informer for several moments, his body more tense the longer he stood there. When he finally looked up at me, the anger in his eyes was palpable. He quickly closed the distance between us, coming up short when he realized Luci and Donovan were not easily intimidated. I tapped them each on the shoulder, letting them know it was okay to move aside. I stepped in between them, going toe to toe with Williams. He had a good four inches on me so I had to crane my neck to look into his eyes.

He glowered at me. "You're in a lot of trouble."

"Hey, I didn't shoot him. Her partner did." I pointed at Detective Hunt who had hustled across the room to join the conversation.

Detective Hunt interjected, "You two know each other?"

I responded, "We go way back. His cousin is sleeping with my ex-girlfriend."

Pointing at Marco's body, Williams asked, "What happened to him?"

"He pulled a gun. Discharged it, in fact. I took a bullet in the gut. My partner shot him." Williams glanced down at Detective Hunt's stomach, as if he was wondering where the hole was. Hunt added, "The vest stopped it."

"What were you doing here in the first place?" Williams asked.

"The deceased is a suspect in a murder case. Just a hunch really, but now I guess maybe it was a good hunch," Detective Hunt answered.

Mosconi! Somehow, she'd connected Marco to Mosconi's death. I wondered what she knew.

Detective Hunt gave him an unflinching look. "May I ask what you and your federales are doing invading my crime scene?"

Williams stared at her doing everything he could to control his temper. Unable to keep my mouth shut, I added, "Yeah, Agent Ted, why don't you tell her what you're doing here?"

Without hesitating, Williams threw a right cross straight at my chin, but I had figured he might react that way so I was ready for it. Using the years of training Luci had given to me, I tilted my head back and to the left just enough to watch the fist swish past my chin by millimeters. As my body swayed, I allowed the power to gather in my fist, bringing it up hard and fast, shoving my feet toward the ground and shifting my hips to give the punch added force. My fist connected with Williams' jaw, a solid force of bone on bone. The power of my punch lifted him off his feet and sent him onto his back with a loud thud.

Recovering from the initial blow, Williams scrambled to his feet, seething. He lunged at me, only to be met by Donovan and Luci quickly closing ranks again to protect me. They both shook their heads in warning as Williams pulled up short.

Detective Hunt took a step toward my FBI nemesis. "Agent Williams, if you can't control yourself, I'm going to have to ask you to leave my crime scene."

Williams made no further move, though his anger only appeared to increase. From the corner of my eye, I spotted Marco's shoes, covered in the blood still seeping from his body. The sight sobered me up. Someone had just been killed. Suddenly, in the time it would take me to snap my fingers, I dropped to my knees and threw up.

Over the next two hours, the police interviewed every patron present in the restaurant. As an associate of Marco's, Gino was taken in for questioning related to the murder of Jim Mosconi. Detective Hunt turned out to be an ally, while Williams and his FBI agents became a nuisance to the NYPD. Later in the evening, I had settled in a corner with Luci and Donovan, waiting for Detective Hunt to release us. Williams stomped over to me, two agents in tow demanding I leave with him for questioning.

"I can't leave," I said. "The NYPD has asked me to remain here for questioning."

"Look, Fixx, I need to ask you questions about Marco Balducci."

Detective Hunt stepped in. "What is your interest in the deceased, and why do you need to question Mr. Fixx?" she asked. "You still haven't explained to me, Agent Williams, what you're doing at my crime scene."

He turned on her, irritated. "Look, Detective, as I've already explained, we're investigating a federal case that I cannot discuss with you, but Jon Fixx may have information about the case that could be useful to us."

"Does this information have anything to do with the deceased Marco Balducci?"

Williams responded with a frustrated silence.

"Well, then, Mr. Fixx stays here. I'm not through with him."

"I need to take him in for questioning."

"Are you charging him with anything?"

Williams said nothing, staring at his interlocutor.

"If not, I'm going to ask you as friendly as I can to please get the hell out of here. I've had enough. You know as well as I do that if you're not charging him with anything specific, you don't have a legal right to take him in. In addition, if you continue to harass my witness, I will consider you to be interfering in a murder investigation."

"Murder? Your partner shot him," Williams spat out.

Detective Hunt's irritation grew. "I'm referring to Jim Mosconi. As I said before, Marco Balducci is a prime suspect in that case."

Williams responded, "That was ruled a suicide."

Williams' answer gave Detective Hunt pause. She studied his face a moment. "You're familiar with the case, I see. Maybe you can shed some light on it, Agent Williams."

Williams knew he'd said more than he should have. "I can only tell you what I read in the papers."

Detective Hunt nodded her head. They stared at each other in a standoff. Finally, with a disparaging look my way, Williams turned around and left, his lackeys in tow. I figured I hadn't seen the last of him, but I was glad that for now I wouldn't have to deal with Ted Williams any longer.

Detective Hunt turned to us, saying in a conspiratorial whisper, "FBI agents are such egomaniacs." She chuckled at her own joke and then went off to confer with a police officer requiring her attention.

Luci, Donovan, and I sat back and waited our turn. When Detective Hunt finally got to us, about half the restaurant patrons had already been questioned and released. She interviewed Luci and Donovan in turn, quickly moving through her questions with them. Other than what they had witnessed, they had little to say.

Cranston's arrival interrupted my Q&A.

Detective Hunt introduced herself to Cranston as the officer in charge. He seemed to take it all in stride, because, I assumed, Vespucci had already given him a shortened version of events. When she discovered Cranston and I knew each other, she wanted to know how, which gave me the perfect segue into what I did for a living, and why I was in New York writing Marco and Maggie's love story. My story sounded plausible, especially because it was the truth. Eventually, Cranston excused himself, explaining that his wife would get worried if he was gone too long. He made his way over to my friends, letting them know, I learned later, that Cheryl was at our disposal for the remainder of the evening.

I provided Detective Hunt with the sanitized version of my involvement with Marco and Maggie, giving no indication that I had any idea of Marco or Vespucci's involvement in the shadier side of life. When she asked me about my interest in Jim Mosconi, I apologized for not telling her the truth when we first met, explaining that Mosconi's seemingly paranoid nature had encouraged me to be careful about explaining my connection to him. I now told her that I only contacted him as a source to get some background history on the New York Underworld to provide some general color for my story. From the look on her face, I knew she wasn't buying it, but she let it pass and didn't ask any further questions on the subject. I was grateful for her discretion. She did want to know what I was doing with Marco alone that evening, and I told her the truth, sort of. I was discussing his life before he got engaged.

When she finished questioning me, I asked, "Can I ask you something?"

"Sure."

"Why was Marco Balducci a prime suspect in Jim Mosconi's murder?" I was fishing to see how much she knew.

"I was hoping you could help me with that. Almost all Mosconi's notebooks were gone. We couldn't find anything useful. So we're not really sure."

"If you didn't find any information in Mosconi's notes, how did you get onto Marco's trail?" I was confused. If Detective Hunt was telling the truth, she didn't know what Mosconi had discovered about Marco but was following him anyway.

Her eyes bore into mine, searching for the truth hidden behind my blank stare. I could tell she was weighing the pros and cons of what to disclose to me, and how much.

"Mosconi sent a letter to his attorney with instructions that it be forwarded to the authorities if he were to die unexpectedly. The letter said that it would most likely be at the hands of one of the people he listed. Marco Balducci was at the top of the list."

Mosconi was smarter than I gave him credit for. "Did he

give any reason why these people wanted to kill him?"

A smile crept across Detective Hunt's face, as if she were reading my mind. "You know why Balducci wanted to kill Mosconi." There was no doubt in her voice.

"Why do you say that?"

"Just a hunch. In fact, you're the only connection I have between Jim Mosconi and Marco Balducci at the moment."

I didn't know what to say. I was not about to tell her everything I knew.

Detective Hunt read the concern on my face. "Don't worry, Jon, I don't think you and your friends are guilty of anything. In fact, as far as I'm concerned, this case is closed. My partner and I were having dinner here. A suspect in a murder case happened to be here as well, and he started waving a gun around and got shot. Case closed."

I breathed a sigh of relief. Soon after questioning me, she released us. Luci and I found our way out to the street. Donovan indicated he needed to speak with Detective Hunt privately. When he emerged from the restaurant a few minutes later, Luci and I both turned to him, waiting for an explanation. With a sheepish grin, he held up a business card, flipping it over to indicate handwriting on the back.

"I got her cell number."

Luci asked, "Think she carries her gun everywhere?"

"I'd like to find out," Donovan said.

A moment later, Cheryl pulled up to the curb. The three of us rushed the back door before Cheryl had a chance to exit the driver's seat to hold it open for us. As we drove out of Manhattan, Cheryl explained what had happened with the FBI. They'd pulled her over at about 6:40 p.m. When they realized she was alone, they got angry, wanting to know where she'd dropped me, but she said she never answered questions for authorities without her attorney present. Unless they were going to charge her with a crime, they needed to let her go on her way. I would have loved to see Williams' reaction. Once they ran the plates on the limousine, however, they discovered who she worked for and put it all together. They left her at the side of the road. After that, she called Luci to warn us and then called Cranston, who advised her to return to the restaurant. I thanked her profusely for her discretion, wondering to myself what would have happened if we hadn't led the FBI on a wild goose chase. If they'd shown up a few minutes earlier at the restaurant, the outcome might have been very different. I may have been the one in a body bag.

Cheryl dropped us at Vespucci's house, where Joey was waiting in the courtyard. He led us into Vespucci's study where he was sitting behind his desk, the creases in his forehead appearing deeper, the stress of the evening's outcome clearly written across his face.

"How's Maggie?" I asked

"She's asleep in her room. Her mother is with her."

For several moments, we didn't say anything. Finally, Vespucci said, "Jon, I guess your job is done here, but I have to ask you for a favor."

I waited, not sure what else he could want of me.

"I need you to destroy the story you've written. I know Maggie will want it destroyed. There is no need to tarnish the Balducci name. After tonight, what has happened will never be discussed again." His look traveled from me to my companions and back.

"We understand."

Luci and Donovan nodded in agreement.

I reached into my pocket and pulled out the thumb drive with "The Love Story of Marco and Maggie" on it. I crossed to Vespucci's desk and set it down. "This is the only copy I have." Returning to my chair, I asked, "Can I ask you something?"

I took Vespucci's silence as a yes.

"How did Maggie end up in the restaurant?"

"I knew she wouldn't believe me if I told her the truth. She would want proof. So I let her read the story you wrote, which of course upset her, to say the least. I decided to bring her along in the car so she could see for herself how Marco had betrayed her. She jumped out of the car before we could stop her."

"Is she going to be okay?"

"She'll recover much faster from this than if she'd married that man."

"What about the girl in Italy?"

"I'll let Giancarlo know about her. He'll make sure she's taken care of." Responding to the worried look on my face, Vespucci raised his right hand, rubbing his thumb and forefinger together indicating money. "I mean this, Jon."

I relaxed. "Of course. I knew that's what you meant."

Vespucci stood up, crossing from behind his desk, holding a check in his hand. I stared at it, not sure if I should accept it. The madness of the last twenty-four hours was too fresh to completely process, but accepting money after what had happened made me feel more like a mercenary than an author. I wasn't sure I'd actually done the job I was hired to do. The groom was dead. The bride was in her room, mourning more than just the death of her future husband. Not the usual outcome for my novellas.

"I'm not sure I can accept that, Tony, given everything that's happened."

"Jon, you found out the truth. That's what I hired you to do. You earned this."

Reluctantly, I took the check. "Thanks."

Vespucci shook the hands of each of my companions. As he crossed the room to leave, he turned to us one last time. "Gentlemen, if you don't mind, I'm going to bed. It's been a tough day. Since I know you don't have a hotel booked, we took care of that. Joey is going to escort you to the Waldorf Astoria in Manhattan, so you can get a good night's sleep before you head back to Los Angeles. I owe you a debt of gratitude, all three of you. If there's ever anything I can do, don't hesitate to call." Then, he disappeared into the dim light of the hallway.

The remainder of our time in New York went by quickly. As promised, Joey drove us to the Waldorf Astoria, and the three of us spent the night in the posh comfort of the ultra-exclusive hotel. Upon Joey's insistence that Vespucci wanted us to enjoy ourselves on his dime, we indulged in the bourgeois hotel services, including excessive room service, a room-tendered masseuse who gave an enviable Swedish-styled massage, and a huge breakfast in the morning. By midday we were on a direct flight back to Los Angeles, the amazing, scary events of the last few days now a memory. I didn't hear from Maggie before I left. I was afraid to call her. For all I knew, she wanted to stuff the entire affair away into a distant corner of her mind, and any interaction with me would do nothing more than be a reminder of what had happened.

On the flight home, I reflected on how my interview with Marco devolved into the unplanned mess it became, even though the night's overall events turned out more boon than bane. For Marco, of course, the night was all bane, literally. For his family, and Maggie specifically, the outcome was a combination of both good and bad. For the Balduccis, they'd lost they're prodigal son, the man who was being groomed to take the reins from his father, and hopefully, one day take the coveted position of Don currently bestowed upon Tony Vespucci. However, if and when Marco's truth was revealed, his turn as a snitch would have disgraced the family name, reducing the Balducci moniker to the level of vermin. In that respect, Marco's death was a boon of which the Balducci family would never be aware. As it stood, they were left mourning the loss of their son.

For Maggie, it was more complicated, both logistically and emotionally. In the short run, Maggie had a jumble of competing feelings to deal with, anger and pain, shame and regret, lost love. To complicate matters, she had to put her feelings aside over the course of the next week and present a good front to deal with the funeral of her supposed beloved. In the long run, Marco's death was a boon, saving Maggie from a wedding that would have caused her a lifetime of grief and anguish when she discovered Marco's true feelings for her, of his motivations, of his ultimate betrayal. That future would have been far worse than the one Maggie would soon begin to build anew. I hoped one day Maggie would realize that I did what I did because I cared for her.

After a six-hour bumpy ride, we touched down at LAX, back home in the City of Angels. Lost in our own thoughts, Luci, Donovan, and I walked quickly through the airport without a word, stepping outside into a balmy November afternoon, the sun shining down on our heads. We grabbed a shuttle to long-term parking and my Buick. Piling into the car, we rolled down the windows, exited the lot onto Century Boulevard, and headed north on the 405. Veering off on the I-10 east, I figured I'd take Luci home first. With the windows down, the warm California air blowing through our hair, the radio turned up loud enough to be heard over the whistling sound of the wind, for a few moments I felt normal, forgetting about everything that had happened over the last days and weeks and months. With a sideways glance at Luci in the front passenger seat and a quick glance in the rearview mirror at Donovan, I could tell they felt the same way, both staring off at the L.A. landscape as it whizzed by us, happy to be home.

Pulling up before Luci's Craftsman in the heart of Silver Lake, I popped the trunk for him to grab his luggage. Before climbing out, he turned in his seat, looking at me.

"Jon, it's been fun. Let's do this again sometime, minus the guns and the Mafia and the FBI."

"I agree."

Luci reached his hand over the front seat to Donovan's hulking frame tucked into the back, grasping his hand in a firm shake. "Couldn't have had a better man watching my back."

Donovan returned the compliment. "Feel the same, Luci." Donovan glanced over at the house. "Is your training dojo in the back?" Luci nodded. "Show me some moves sometime?"

Grinning, Luci said, "I'd be honored. We could use Jon here as our sparring partner." They both looked at me.

"No way!" I blurted out. "I wouldn't want to embarrass either one of you."

Luci and Donovan laughed. Izzy stepped onto the front porch, as striking as ever. Luci waved to her and climbed out of the car, grabbing his bag and crossing the lawn. He held Izzy in a tight embrace, pulling her feet off the porch. Arms wrapped around Luci's waist, Izzy yelled over to the car, "Thanks for bringing him home safe, Jon."

I leaned across the passenger seat for a better vantage point. "I owe Luci all the thanks."

Izzy turned to Luci with a questioning look on her face, waiting for an explanation. Donovan climbed out of the back seat and took Luci's place in front. After a few words from Luci, Izzy turned back to us. "Sounds like you had an exciting week. This weekend. Dinner over here. Okay?

"Donovan, that means you too," Luci added.

We both nodded and waved as I pulled away from the curb. Donovan directed me toward Glassell Park, where he said he'd been living for many years. I avoided the freeway, winding our way through the narrow streets of Silver Lake, traveling up and down over the hills, through Mount Washington, then Eagle Rock, finally finding our way into the perimeter of Glassell Park. Donovan indicated his house was coming up, pointing me down a small side street into a cul-de-sac that abutted the lower hill holding up the 134-freeway system high above. Driving to the end of the cul-de-sac, I pulled up beside a tidy, compact home resembling a hunting lodge. The yard was neatly trimmed, smartly dressed rose bushes lining the path leading to the front door. I pulled the car up to the dirt driveway. We sat quietly, staring at the house.

I broke the silence. "Beautiful rosebushes, Donovan. Must take a lot of work."

"They're my wife's. The rose was her favorite flower. After she passed, I kept them going."

I stared at the roses, wondering what Donovan's wife had been like. Suddenly, I realized I still had to pay Donovan. I reached over the front seat, grabbing my small travel bag and taking out my checkbook. I wrote a check covering the remaining money I owed him. I tore the check out of the book, handing it to him. He finally turned away from the roses, looking first at the check and then me. I could see he was having an internal debate as to whether he should take it, probably feeling the same way I felt when Vespucci handed me a check. "A deal's a deal. You agreed to work for me. I owe you far more than this money, believe me."

After hesitating, Donovan accepted the check. "Next time, it's on me."

I laughed. "Hopefully, there isn't a next time."

As he opened his door, he said, "Don't be surprised, Jon, if you wake up one day missing all this action and the adrenaline rush that comes with it. I took the security job because I was trying to avoid that truth in myself."

I couldn't imagine I would ever wake up wishing I had even one ounce of the strain of the past days. "Think you'll be heading back to New York any time soon?" I asked.

Donovan considered his response. "Who knows? Nothing better than Times Square at Christmas. Gotta see which way the wind is blowing. See if Detective Hunt wants a visitor." He climbed out of the car, grabbed his bag from the trunk, and came back to the passenger window, looking down at me.

"If you go, I might join you. I've got some loose ends there as well," I said.

"I know you do."

With that, he turned his back on me and took the few

steps off the street onto his humble, well-dressed property. Stopping at the first set of bushes, he gently leaned down to a red rose, holding it in his right hand and bending over to push his nose deep into the center of the red petals. A breeze blew across the flowers in my direction, carrying the scent of roses and a rush of memories of family picnics from childhood.

Donovan took his nose out of the flower, standing up straight. "Don't be a stranger, Jon Fixx."

I smiled, and then kicked the car into gear. Minutes later, I was on the 134, heading back to my Cave. I wasn't excited to return to that place but was glad, all the same, to be going home. I decided I'd start looking for a new apartment, one with more light and space. As the 134 West merged into the 101 North, Sara's face popped into my mind's eye, but there was no feeling attached. I was over her. I closed in on my exit, wondering how Maggie was handling everything. I figured I'd give it a few days, then check in with her father. I wondered if the FBI was going to pursue the Vespucci case without the star witness. I wondered if I'd ever see Ted Williams again.

My apartment building appeared up ahead across the intersection of Woodman and Moorpark. I turned right on Moorpark, making an immediate left into the first floor parking garage. Pulling into my parking space, I shut the car off, leaning back against the driver's seat, exhaling with a sigh of relief. I was home. Safe. I rolled the window up, climbed out of the car, grabbed my bag, and climbed the steps to my first floor single. A note on the front door stopped me in my tracks. My key in my hand, I stared dumbfounded at the note. It was from my neighbor upstairs, who I'd never met.

It read, "Sorry for the trouble, but I had a slight leak in my kitchen while I was gone for the night, and I think it may have gone into your apartment. Please call the manager if you have any problems. Brandii."

My phone began to ring. I grabbed my phone, answering as I fumbled for the keys in my pocket. "Hello."

"Jon?"

My heart skipped a beat.

"Hi, it's Maggie." Her voice was soft and subdued. "I didn't get to see you before you left."

I blurted out, "I'm really sorry for everything. I didn't mean for it to turn out this way."

"I know. I don't doubt that. I just wanted to call to thank you."

Thank me! Thank me for what? Exposing your fiancé for a snitch and getting him killed? I'm not sure "thank you" was the proper response. I didn't know what to say to that.

"Having the father I have, I've learned over the years that some things are what they are. The best way to deal with reality is to accept it, process it, and move on. That's what I'm going to do."

"That's brave of you, Maggie." I didn't know what else to say.

"I don't have much choice, Jon. Otherwise, I'd just curl up into a ball and hide in the corner." There was a brief pause. "You think you'll be coming back to New York any time soon?"

I smiled in spite of myself. "In fact, I was thinking of coming back at Christmas."

"Well, my father wanted me to tell you that next time you're here, we absolutely want you over for dinner."

"Okay, I'd like that."

"So you'll let us know?"

"I will. Definitely."

"Good. Then we'll see you soon."

"Yes, you will."

"Okay, bye."

"Bye."

Maybe my luck was turning around. I hung up the phone, staring at it, my right hand still searching in my pocket for my door key. But instead of pulling out my key, I pulled the infamous engagement ring out. I had completely forgotten about it. Staring at the huge diamond, I wondered what I should do with it. Almost instantly, without further thought, I realized exactly what I would do with it. Someday. I stuck it back in my pocket, a smile on my face. I grabbed the key, turning the lock and opening the door in one move. The door swung open to a total mess. The note had said a "slight" leak! Her kitchen must have flooded. There was an inch of standing water in my living room, water still dripping down from the ceiling. The walls had water streaks rolling down toward the floor. The one set of curtains covering my only windows were dripping. I figured God was trying to tell me something. The decision to move sooner than later was made for me.

I took a step back from the doorway, pulling my phone back out of my pocket. After a couple of rings, I heard Donovan's baritone barrel down through the earpiece.

"Everything okay, Jon?"

"Oh yeah, everything's fine. Just one question. You have a spare room I could crash in tonight?"

The end. For now. . . .

Acknowledgements

There are many people in my life to whom I owe thanks, so this is just the short list. I am eternally grateful to my mother for encouraging me ever since I first put pen to paper in 2nd grade, and then without complaint, tirelessly reading and editing everything I've written since.

Special thanks to both my mother and father for providing me with an endless number of books year in and year out since that very first series I fell in love with by Walter Farley.

Thank you to my sister for providing her skill and expertise and endless time to this project and allowing me to focus on my writing while she focused on actually getting this book into print.

Lou, your first pass before anyone on the outside had read this helped me believe maybe I actually had something. Donna Walker, thank you for your early and continued support of both bookscover2cover and Jon Fixx, you helped Jon become a reality.

Many thanks to my wife Miriam for providing the time, space, support, and belief in me to get the project done, and a very special thank you to Zion, whose birth lit the fire under me and made me get movin'.

Author

Jason Squire Fluck was raised in Pennsylvania, and spent most of his childhood with his nose in a book. He currently resides in North Hollywood with his wife, Miriam, and son, Zion.

Jon Fixx is his first novel.